EXTREME RISK

X-TREME LOVE SERIES
BOOK 1

KAY MANIS

Extreme Risk was originally published under the title, *Skater Boy*, X-Treme Boys Series, in September 2013.

ISBN: 978-0-6926772-3-0

To my beautiful daughter, Kimberly.
With four small words, you changed the course of my life forever.
"Just write it, Mom."
Thanks for always believing in me.

CHAPTER 1

HINDLEY

I FUMBLED with the straps on my high heels as I tried to catch up with the other girls. Given my history, you'd think I'd be able to slap on these stripper shoes in record time. But no, of course tonight I was all thumbs.

"All right, ladies, let's make our way over to the center pole," a woman said.

I glanced up and watched the other girls follow the lady. I couldn't help but wonder, not for the first time—who in the hell had a bachelorette party at a pole dancing studio?

My dimwitted stepsister, Geneva Barton, that's who.

She'd probably read that pole dancing parties were the latest trend in *Brides* magazine. Right under the article about how to reach multiple orgasms with your fiancé in three easy steps. Like that really happens without batteries.

Fastening the last hook on my shoes, I yanked on the straps. A shoe slipping off mid-performance was dangerous. I didn't need that kind of attention tonight.

"Is everyone here?" the instructor asked.

I stood and glanced around the group.

Geneva glared at me, arms crossed over her ample breasts that were probably fake. "Come on, Hindley. Everyone's waiting on you."

"I knew she'd ruin this for you," her friend, Wendy, said. The girl had the voice of a hyena and the brains of one too.

I clenched my teeth to keep from saying anything I might regret. It was no secret that I didn't want to be here any more than Geneva did. But my mother said we were family, and when Geneva's father begged me to come, I couldn't say no.

My stepfather was the only reason I was here tonight, and right now, Paul Barton was slowly working his way up my shit list.

I reminded myself that none of these girls knew about my past. I couldn't look as confident as I actually was in this setting. To these shallow twits, I was still Geneva's nerdy stepsister from high school. Forget that I had a bachelor's *and* law degree hanging above my desk at work.

Well, tonight, I would personify that geeky older sister even if it killed me. I gave my ponytail one last tug to tighten the holder as I trudged across the hardwood floor.

"Uh," Geneva groaned, rolling her eyes, "finally. Can we start now?"

"Be my guest." I motioned to the instructor.

"Hi, ladies." The instructor smiled. "Welcome to Miss Understood Dance Studio."

I snorted. *Miss Understood*? The name was fitting, especially for me.

"My name is Sadie Sunnydale." The chick swung her long, scarlet-colored hair over one shoulder like she was Cher.

"Wow," Wendy sighed, "what a name."

Sadie laughed. "It's my stripper name."

"You're a stripper?" Geneva gasped.

Sadie's face puckered like she'd bitten into a lemon. "Oh, no, honey." She shook her head. "I'm a *real* dancer."

Real dancer? What the hell did that mean? Like a stripper wasn't?

"Oh, thank God," Geneva sighed as if her credit card hadn't been declined.

What judgmental assholes.

"You'll each come up with your own stripper name," Sadie said.

Geneva waggled her brows. "Oh, this is going to be so much fun."

"Wait." Sadie held up a red-tipped finger, stopping the girls. "There's a special way you come up with your name."

"How?" Wendy asked, practically bouncing on her toes.

Everyone leaned forward and stared at Sadie like they were watching a freaking Nicholas Sparks' movie.

"First," Sadie said, "we'll begin by selecting the name of your very first pet."

A low buzz filled the small room as the girls discussed pet names and other irrelevant nonsense.

I thought back over the years to the only two pets I'd ever had.

Harold was a hamster I had when I was five. My mom left him in the garage over Christmas break and he ended up as a New Year's Eve popsicle. I didn't think Harold, or the story, made a good stripper name.

Thinking of my second pet brought tears to my eyes. He was a stray dog I'd found a few months after Harold died. I'd named him Rocky, since I loved that movie, and because his front paws were black and looked like boxing gloves.

Two weeks after I found him, the landlord knocked on our door and told my mom if she wanted to keep the dog, she'd have to fork over another five hundred bucks for a pet deposit. The ride to the animal shelter was the longest of my life. There was no way my stripper name would be Rocky.

Sadie's soft voice cut through my thoughts. "Your last name will be the name of the street you grew up on."

This assignment was growing more difficult by the minute. Having moved way too many times as a child, I decided that wouldn't help me. Instead, I chose the name my friends from law school had given me. It was perfect for me, and made me laugh every time I thought of it.

"Does everyone have their name yet?" Sadie asked. "There's a prize for the best one."

The girls shrieked with excitement. I covered my ears to drown out the noise. The prize was probably a two-headed purple dildo. Wait, maybe I should get serious about this name thing after all.

"Now," Sadie continued, "what I want you to do is take hold of the pole like this." She reached up and grabbed the pole high above her head. "Then kick your leg up and let it fall naturally as you swing around, like this."

I watched as Sadie kicked her right leg high in the air then let it fall, curling her foot behind her as she made a beautiful swan circle around the pole.

"My name is Sadie Sunnydale," she practically purred, her voice smooth and sexy as her body came to a gentle stop.

The girls jumped and clapped like spastic cheerleaders, their high-pitched squeals deafening.

I was going to kill my stepfather.

Each girl took their turn. I wasn't surprised that their stripper names were just as atrocious as their kick turns on the pole.

I'd said I would keep it low key tonight, but I couldn't help myself. Growing up, there was nothing I did better than Geneva Barton. This was one thing I knew I could beat her at. The fact that I had no student loans after three years of law school proved just how good I was.

"All right, let's see what you got," Sadie said, motioning toward me.

I rubbed my hands on my pants out of habit before blowing gently on my palms.

"Ooo," Wendy said.

I hadn't even started and I already had their attention. Good.

Grabbing the pole with one hand, I kicked my leg straight up in the air, completing a perfect aerial split. After holding the pose for several seconds, I let my leg fall, the momentum effortlessly swinging my body around the pole two full revolutions. I finally came to a stop, my back arched with one leg on the floor and the other wrapped around the pole.

"Hello, everyone," I said in the sexiest stripper voice I could muster. "I'm Krystal Shanda-Leer." The entire studio was silent except for one lone giggle. Mine.

CHAPTER 2

HINDLEY

"No way, no how, Paul," I yelled into my phone. I stood by my car, watching the other girls walk out of the studio. Glancing up at the marquee, I laughed to myself.

Miss Understood. No truer words.

"Please, Hin, for me, your old man," he said.

"No, not even for you, Paul." I loved my stepfather, but this time he'd gone too far.

"But, she's your sister."

I laughed. "Not technically," I reminded him.

"Come on, Hin. She needs you."

"She's never needed me, Paul, and you know it."

"Well, *I* need you," he said.

Oh, hell. Those three words, 'I need you,' gutted me.

Paul Barton didn't beg. He didn't have to. He had money, power, all the accolades life could offer—including my mother's love. And yet, here he was, begging me for my help. He needed me. How could I refuse him?

I couldn't.

"You're not playing fair, old man." I shook my head, holding back my amusement. "Why do you do this to me?"

"Because I know you love me. And you'll do anything for me, right?"

"Ugh." He was right. There was almost nothing I wouldn't do for my stepfather, even babysit his stupid daughter tonight. "Sometimes I hate you, you know that, right?"

"I know." He laughed, his baritone voice vibrating through the phone. "But most of the time you love your old man, don't you?"

I nodded in silent answer.

"And most of the time, I love you too," Paul said. "Well, actually, that's a lie."

My stomach tightened as old fears of abandonment flooded my mind.

"I love you *all* the time, Hinny Bin."

Hinny Bin. Uggh. I blew out a heavy sigh and smiled.

Hinny Bin was Paul's nickname for me. It was a term of endearment I'd hated at first. But the more I'd grown to love Paul, the more I accepted it. Although I would kick most people in the ass if they tried to use it.

My stepfather was an amazing man. He'd met my mother, Caroline, when I was in eighth grade and his daughter, Geneva, in seventh. She and I went to different schools, mine public and Geneva's private.

Our families were polar opposites, literally from opposite sides of the tracks. Paul was a rich, successful real estate broker who'd fallen head-over-heels in love with my mother the moment he'd laid eyes on her.

He'd been showing us a five-bedroom mansion he had for sale. My mother and I both knew she couldn't even afford the property taxes, but that wasn't going to stop my mother. Their meeting had been a set-up from the start. Paul had walked right into my mother's trap. Not that I would ever admit that to him.

My mom and I had been on our own since I was born. She'd become pregnant in high school and had always told me she didn't know who my father was. She said it could have been any number of guys, but I knew that wasn't the truth. My mom wasn't slutty. She knew exactly who my father was. She just wasn't going to admit that my birth father bailed on her when he found out she was pregnant.

Her parents tried to talk her into having an abortion, even threatening to cut her off financially if she kept me. But my mom refused to succumb to their pressures, fully believing that once I was born, they'd change their minds.

She was wrong.

To my mom's surprise, and mine now that I was a grown woman, my grandparents had stuck by their threat and kicked us both out of the house when I was only two months old. They said they were too old to raise another child. Their mindset baffled me. What kind of people do that to their only daughter and grand-daughter?

Assholes, that's who.

Wherever we went, men flocked to my mother like flies on honey. With emerald green eyes, long blonde hair, and an ass you could still bounce quarters off of, it was easy to see why. She was gorgeous. Women around the world paid thousands of dollars to look as beautiful as Caroline Hagen-Barton did naturally.

My mom knew how gorgeous she was, not in a conceited way. She often used her looks to get us through tough times. Caroline was resourceful to say the least.

Once, some guy hired her as a nurse at an old folks' home, even though she'd never finished high school. The manager was an old dude, just a few years shy of residing at the place himself. As most men, he'd fallen in love with my mom the instant he saw her. I couldn't blame him. There wasn't a man alive immune to my mother's good looks and southern charm.

I envied my mom. What I had to work years for came easily to her. Men were putty in her hands. Most guys in my life had done nothing but use me for their own gain. When they realized how hopeless and damaged I was, they quickly cast me aside.

The minute I met Paul, I knew he was different, in a good way. They'd had a whirlwind romance and married soon after they'd met. Since then, Paul had made it his life's mission to give my mother everything she ever wanted. Even if what she wanted wasn't good for her. And Paul was equally as devoted to me.

As easily as their relationship had bloomed, Paul's daughter and mine had not. I never liked to say I hated people. I always wanted to think there was room for everyone to redeem themselves. But Geneva Barton was the exception.

I hated my stepsister. And the feeling was mutual. There was nothing redeeming about her. I'd given up hope years ago, settling into the knowledge we'd never be friends.

Geneva was beautiful, like my mother, and their relationship grew effortlessly from the beginning. It was always hard for my mom to relate to me, given the fact I wasn't drop-dead gorgeous like she was. I was actually relieved when my mom found Geneva. She finally had someone to impart her golden nuggets of beauty and fashion wisdom.

Geneva had tons of friends, went to the best schools, had the trendiest clothes, and dated more boys than you could shake a stick at. One of the things that irked me the most about her was that Geneva was actually very smart. I would never admit that to her, or anyone else. Unfortunately, she'd never developed her intellect. Instead, she'd chosen to skate by on her good looks and sex appeal rather than apply herself.

The only reason I could think why Geneva hated me was because of my close relationship with her father. Paul Barton had pulled me out of a dark place and protected me, even when the law couldn't. He'd motivated me over the years, pushing me past my own limits. He'd even encouraged me to go to law school when my college grades had been sub-par.

Any good thing I accomplished in life, I always attributed to Paul. Yet I still kept him at arm's length, preparing myself for the day when he would inevitably leave me and my mom. Twelve years later, I was still waiting for that day.

Paul relied on me, asking my opinion on all kinds of issues. From the most mundane, like what tie to wear, to the more serious, like what piece of real estate to invest in next. Paul wanted to know what I thought. He truly valued my opinion, sometimes relying on it too much. I think Geneva resented that most of all.

Everyone who met Paul agreed he treated me as if I were his daughter by birth. I think that was another motivating factor for Geneva's hatred of me. There wasn't anything Paul wouldn't do for me. Looking back over the years, I had to admit that Paul was probably closer to me than to his own daughter, and something told me she knew it too.

"I can't believe I'm doing this for you," I groaned. "You know I hate clubbing."

"But tomorrow is her wedding, Hin," Paul said, "and I've shelled out a small fortune for it. Money I don't have right now, just to make her and your mother happy."

I rolled my eyes.

"I don't want her to show up at her own wedding hungover from her bachelorette party. It would kill your mother."

I felt bad, I truly did. Paul's company had taken a big hit when the real estate market tanked several years ago. That was one of the reasons I'd decided to put myself through law school, even though he assured me he could help. I was blown away by Geneva's selfishness. She knew Paul's financial situation was still rocky, and yet she'd asked for this big-ass wedding.

My mom and Geneva had been blissfully unaware of the financial pressure Paul had been under the last few years. Either that, or they'd chosen to ignore it. Asking for such an elaborate and costly wedding during Paul's financial struggles only proved how much of a selfish bitch Geneva was. And I was disappointed with my mother's demands on Paul as well.

"I know, Paul," I said, sighing. "I'm sorry you're spending so much money on this stupid wedding."

The entire event was pointless anyway. Hell, the ink on the marriage license probably wouldn't even be dry before Geneva filed divorce papers.

"Don't be sorry," he said. "It's my fault. I just can't seem to say no to my girls."

"Well, I don't have a problem telling Geneva no."

"I know, Hindley. You're much stronger and smarter than I am. You're often my only voice of reason. I don't know what I'd do without you."

I swallowed down the lump in my throat. I don't know what I'd do without you either, I wanted to say, but the words got stuck in my throat.

Even though Paul was asking me to do something he knew I hated, his words weren't being offered up as bribery. Paul was nothing if not honest. He was a man of integrity and truth, admired by everyone who knew him.

I thanked God every day that my mother had fallen in love with his photo in that real estate magazine twelve years ago. Without Paul Barton, my life would have been tragically different. He had saved me from myself.

Everything good in my life I owed to him.

I switched the phone to my other ear and released a disgruntled sigh. "Fine. What exactly do you want me to do?"

"Just go out to the clubs with them," he said. "Make sure Geneva doesn't drink too much or get in to trouble."

I stifled a laugh. Trouble pretty much followed Geneva Barton. She was a bitch, especially when she was drunk. "She'll never listen to me, Paul. Hell, she doesn't even want me there."

"She listens to you, Hindley, more than you know."

Paul may have thought his words were true, but I knew differently. Geneva couldn't care less what I thought. She considered me a complete idiot on most of life's subjects.

"Fine." I blew out an exasperated sigh. "But only for you, because I don't want you and Mom embarrassed tomorrow."

"Oh, thank you, Hinny Bin."

I could hear the smile in his voice and it brought one to my lips as well. Pleasing Paul had always made me happy.

Balancing the phone between my ear and shoulder, I dug around in my trunk. "Crap."

"What's wrong?"

"I don't have any clubbing clothes," I said.

"Do you want my credit card?" Paul would have given me the world if I'd asked for it. Unlike his daughter, I never did.

"No, there's no time," I groaned. "The outrageously expensive Hummer limo you rented for this blessed event just drove up. I'll have to wear my yoga pants and sports top. Seriously, Paul, what were you thinking? A Hummer?"

"I love you, Hindley."

"Whatever. You *so* owe me, Paul Barton."

I ended the call and slammed down the trunk, shoving my phone in the inside pocket of my pants. I glanced at the limo parked a few feet away.

I couldn't believe Geneva had talked Paul into renting her a ridiculously over-priced limo to cart her and her dumbass friends around tonight. She was such a selfish bitch. At least she wouldn't be driving drunk though.

I leaned down and checked myself in the side mirror of my car. Stray hairs sprung free from my ponytail and my eyes were rimmed with smudged mascara. I looked like a hot mess, but there was nothing I could do about it now. Even dressed in my best clothes, I still paled in comparison to Geneva Barton.

I rubbed my finger under my eyes, wiping away the running makeup. I smoothed back my hair, as if that would magically make me presentable. Geneva would revel in my haggardness. Only one thing was for certain. This night was going to suck balls.

CHAPTER 3
HINDLEY

WE WERE at our third bar of the night. Despite what I'd told Paul, I was not keeping a watchful eye on Geneva. In fact, I myself was quite good and liquored up. I usually didn't drink, at all. But being around Geneva's friends had driven me to the edge of sanity.

"Do another one," Wendy shouted above the blaring music. She shoved a shot glass full of tequila into my hand.

If I didn't know better, I would have sworn they were all trying to get me completely smashed. I didn't care though. I was grateful. I'd do just about anything to drown out their constant jabbering about wedding crap.

Geneva had been planning this event for over a year, which was twice as long as she'd known her fiancé when he proposed. They'd met at one of my mother's numerous charity events.

Geneva's fiancé, Stanley Winston III, or 'Third' as I affectionately referred to him, came from money. That's all Geneva needed to hear when they were introduced eighteen months ago. In the last year since Third had proposed, Geneva had spent more time planning the wedding with her friends than she actually did with poor Third.

Third was a decent looking guy, but nothing compared to the

hunks Geneva usually dated. Her engagement to such a normal looking guy had surprised everyone, me included.

Geneva was more in love with Stan's money than with him. The reality of her shallowness didn't surprise me. I felt sorry for Third most of all. I mean, he had his moments of dorkiness, but for the most part, he was a decent guy.

Third, like most men, deserved a woman who adored him. Geneva Barton was not that woman. I'd tried to tell everyone, even Stan himself, but no one would listen. Instead, everyone buried their heads in the sand and pretended like Cinderella had met her Prince Charming. Who was I to question Walt Disney?

I slammed the shot glass down on the bar. "Give me another one!" I yelled, disgusted with the fact that I was actually going along with this charade of a wedding.

The bartender leaned over the bar, shouting in my ear. "I'm afraid you've had enough for this hour."

"What the hell? You're cutting me off?" I yelled. "This is bullshit."

Could they do that?

Geneva grabbed my arm and hauled me away from the bar. "Calm down, Hindley. You're making a scene."

"I thought you wanted me drunk."

Geneva glanced over her shoulder. "I do, but not belligerent."

She'd just admitted what I'd suspected all along. Geneva Barton wanted me plastered but I had no idea why. And right now, I couldn't care less. I just wanted another drink.

"Screw you, Geneva," I yelled, yanking out of her hold. "I'll say whatever the hell I want to say."

Well, at least those were the words I *tried* to get out of my mouth. I had no idea what I sounded like to others.

"Let's dance," Mirabelle shouted. She hooked her arm through mine and dragged me toward the dance floor.

I peered back over my shoulder as I clutched Mirabelle's arm, afraid I might topple over.

Geneva marched behind us. Her mass of friends followed like trained soldiers.

I turned my head again and my stomach lurched. Quick movements were not a good idea at this stage in my drinking. I was already three sheets to the wind. I stopped and balanced on Mirabelle's shoulder to gain my equilibrium.

Geneva pulled on my free arm. "Come on. The dancing will make you feel better." The smile on her face was in direct opposition to her words. She had no intentions of trying to make me feel better, but I was too drunk to stop her.

Our group of girls commandeered the dance floor, parting the other dancers like Moses did the Red Sea. The vibrations of the music beat through my body as I twirled around on the dance floor, hands in the air. I stared up, mesmerized by the flashing, multicolored lights. I had to admit, I was having fun.

I'd never done most of the things kids my age did—drinking, dancing, partying, having random sex with random guys—all the things that Geneva did. Instead, I'd been too busy preparing for the future. Unlike me, Geneva had made the most of every single day, filling her senses to excess, at her father's expense.

I was jealous of Geneva's carefree attitude. Tonight, I made up my mind. I wasn't going to give two shits about anything, least of all Geneva Barton. I surrendered my body to the music, thankful I had one night to be young.

After what felt like hours on the dance floor, a slow song came on. I couldn't have been more thankful for the break.

My legs were already weak from the bachelorette pole dancing party. And jumping up and down like a spastic dog for the last thirty minutes on the dance floor hadn't helped any. Not to mention what the constant gyration had done to the alcohol in my stomach. Sweat rolled down my back and my body swayed as the room started to spin. I needed water, or a toilet.

I reached out to grab Geneva's hand but someone's arm wrapped around my waist and pulled me back.

"Geneva," I called out.

Geneva glanced over her shoulder, a devious smirk spreading across her beautiful face. "Have fun," she said, wiggling her fingers good-bye.

I knew she was being sarcastic. She didn't care whether I had fun or not.

Screw her. I hadn't felt the embrace of a man in a long time. I was too drunk to fight him anyway. That should have been my first sign to pull away. I never let myself lose control—ever—and for good reason.

I slowly turned and glanced up at the guy standing before me. He looked to be my age, maybe a little younger. He wore khaki slacks and a starched polo shirt. It was a weird outfit for a club, I thought in my hazy fog.

His eyes roamed over my body and I felt dirty. When his gaze finally met mine, I was surprised to see them dark with desire. I looked a mess, still dressed in my yoga pants and tank top. And I could only imagine what my face looked like, makeup smeared half off.

The man loomed over me, his eyes half-lidded. He was attractive, in a Gap commercial kind of way. But then he smiled, and something in my gut tightened. Not in a good way.

He leaned down, his fingers wrapping around my neck. "Come here often?" he whispered in my ear.

It was painfully obvious he was trying to be seductive, but his high-pitched voice came across as creepy and whiney. Only a guy with a voice like Johnny Cash could deliver such a cheesy line and have a girl swoon.

I rolled my eyes and that was my undoing. Whatever I'd been holding down in my stomach decided it wanted out. Now. I pushed past Gap Boy and ran straight for the bathroom, barely making it to the first stall before I vomited.

"Eww," a girl shrieked behind me. "That's disgusting."

I'd heard of people praying to the Porcelain Throne but had never quite understood the religious connotation. Until now. Real or imaginary, I was thanking this god of the toilet that my hair was already pulled back in a ponytail. I fell onto the floor, pledging my eternal allegiance to this unseen deity if he'd make this wretched heaving stop.

Suddenly, a hand was on my back.

"Are you all right, sweetheart?" someone asked with a deep southern drawl.

I nodded, not really sure if it was the truth.

"Here, doll." She handed me a wet paper towel

I leaned back on my rear and wiped my lips with the towel. My stomach rumbled and I prepared for round two.

"Let me help you up, sweetie." She extended a small hand.

I grasped her hand as she hoisted me off the dingy bathroom floor.

"Thank you," I whispered, leaning my head against her shoulder.

"You need some fresh air, hun," she said in a soothing voice. "Come on."

I followed her through the crowd but slowed when I saw Geneva sitting at the bar.

She was sandwiched between two gorgeous men, both of whom were either strippers, male models, or both. She batted her eyes, flirting even harder than usual. One of the guy's hands squeezed her bare thigh. His fingers worked their way higher, with no protest from Geneva.

"I'm going outside," I yelled to her above the music.

"Don't forget. Eleven o'clock tomorrow. At the restaurant. For my bridal luncheon." She punched out each phrase.

I nodded, not sure I'd remember her warning tomorrow.

"Don't be late, Hindley, or I'll kill you."

That, I would remember.

My mystery goddess laughed. "Wow, she's a sweetheart."

"You have no idea," I groaned.

We staggered to the exit of the club and my goddess pushed the door open. A gust of cool air hit my face and my stomach lurched again.

"Breathe, girl," she said gently.

I drew in a deep breath through my nose and exhaled from my mouth. I had to admit, I felt a tiny bit better.

She slowly released me.

I balanced on wobbly legs like a newborn deer, reaching out for her.

"You okay now, hun?"

I rubbed my head, my fingers pressing into my temple. "I think so."

"I've got her." A voice rumbled from behind me as long arms snaked around my waist.

I recognized the voice and froze. Gap Boy. From the dance floor.

My goddess looked from me to Gap Boy. "Is he with you?"

I remained silent, unable to form words.

"Yeah, she's with me," he said.

"Are you sure you're gonna be all right, sweetheart?" The woman asked.

Her eyes beseeched me for an answer, but I couldn't give her one. I was frozen with fear. I didn't even know where the hell I was, let alone who this guy was that was man-handling me.

She mistook my silence for affirmation. "Stay outside until you feel better, okay, sweetie?" She caressed my back.

I instantly felt the tension melt away.

"Take care of her," she told Gap Boy.

I stood in silence, watching as she slowly walked back inside the club. The echo of the door clicking closed behind her was a sobering reminder that I hadn't kept my promise to Paul to keep an eye on Geneva.

A sick feeling washed over me as I realized Geneva's safety was the least of my concerns.

Gap Boy stared down at me, his eyes darkening.

My body stiffened when I felt his hands roam freely over my body. A familiar pang of unease spread over me as I was gripped with fear. Suddenly, I realized, it wasn't Geneva I should be worried about, it was me.

CHAPTER 4

RORY

I STOOD outside the noisy club, leaning against the brick building. The music inside was giving me a headache.

Why the hell had I let my best friend, Leif Jennings, talk me into going out tonight? I needed to rest. I had a competition next weekend and I couldn't afford any setbacks.

I stared down at the cigarette in my hand and laughed. Smoking definitely wasn't good for my health. But it beat the hell out of drinking and drugging.

Suddenly, the club door swung open, hitting the brick wall with a bang.

Two chicks stumbled out. One woman had her arm wrapped around the other. She was obviously trying to balance her friend, who was pissing drunk.

I laughed. How many times had I been that wasted?

They stumbled toward the curb. "You okay, hun?" The smaller girl asked her friend.

The taller woman rubbed her head, mumbling something incoherent. God, she was toast.

I studied the drunk girl more closely. She wasn't dressed for the party scene, no mini-skirt and sky-high heels. Instead, this chick was wearing yoga pants, a fitted T-shirt, and tennis shoes.

I rolled my eyes.

Her outfit reeked of Pilates, or some other bullshit workout those rich white girls did. Her glazed over eyes and nearly comatose body made it painfully evident she didn't know how to handle her liquor.

I flicked my cigarette into the street and pushed off the wall. I needed to get back inside and say good-bye. I stopped when I heard another voice.

"I've got her." A male voice I hadn't heard earlier echoed behind me.

Curious, I glanced back over my shoulder.

Some tall, lanky dude had Drunk Girl wrapped in his arms. He clutched her to his body like she was a gold medal at the X Games. Where the fuck had this guy come from?

Drunk Girl stiffened in his arms. Their conversation was muted but her body language said it all. Drunk Girl was definitely *not* okay with this guy.

The hairs on my neck stood on end. Should I stay? Shit. Without another thought, my mind made the decision for me. I could hang out a while longer and smoke another cigarette, just in case.

I stood silently and studied Drunk Girl again. There was absolutely nothing special about her, at least not from where I was standing. Frat Boy sure as shit thought so, though. My jaw clenched and I found myself almost jealous of the way he was groping her.

The smaller woman studied Frat Boy with narrowed eyes. She must not know him. She leaned in to Drunk Girl and spoke but Drunk Girl only stood there, saying nothing. With one final nod, the woman turned and left the two standing on the sidewalk.

What the fuck? Why was she leaving her friend with this douche if she didn't know him?

The woman breezed by me, nodding her head toward the couple. "I gotta get back inside before my boyfriend starts freaking out. Keep an eye on him, will you? I don't trust him."

"You don't know her?" I asked.

She shook her head. "I don't know either one of them. Keep an eye on them, okay?"

Before I could ask any questions, like why the fuck should I care, the chick disappeared into the club.

Well, shit. Now I was stuck.

The little wench had involved me in a situation I had no desire to be a part of. If this scene went to shit, I'd be responsible. I didn't need that kind of publicity. Not now. Why hadn't I just stayed inside with all the other guys? Or better yet, stayed home. It seemed that tonight, cigarette smoking had become more hazardous to my health than I'd realized.

Stuffing my hands in my front pockets as a sign to Frat Boy that I didn't want any trouble, I slowly strolled toward them.

"You two know each other?" I asked.

He yanked Drunk Girl closer to him, his hands possessively running up and down her body.

My temper flared and I had no justifiable reason why.

Frat Boy leaned his head to one side and narrowed his eyes, glaring at me. "What's it to you?"

I cocked my head, my brows raised in disbelief at this asshole's comeback. I glared, warning him not to piss me off. I was a pretty big guy, well over six feet. There was no doubt in either one of our minds that I could, and would kick his ass if necessary.

I shrugged as if mildly interested. "It's not."

"Then why don't you mind your own business?"

Oh, fuck no. I moved to take a step forward, clenching my fists but thought better of it. Instead, I drew in a deep breath and counted backward from three like I'd learned. I needed to calm the fuck down before I punched this ass hat square in the face.

I glanced down at Drunk Girl whose head was lulling to the side. "Looks like she's pretty wasted, man."

His face lit up like the chick was a Christmas present delivered by Santa himself. "I know, right?"

My guard went up, my brain ringing with alarm bells. Was this dick face seriously going to take Drunk Girl home and fuck her comatose body?

"What's her name?" I asked, knowing I shouldn't get involved but unable to stop myself. Someone had to protect this girl.

"Fuck if I know." He laughed in amusement. "Drunk-as-a-Skunk is what I'm calling her tonight."

My fists flexed and my eyes burned with anger. I readied my feet, preparing to punch this fuckface square in the jaw. Before I could make a move, Drunk Girl startled to life.

"What the hell did you just call me?" she shouted. Drunk Girl twisted in his arms, pushing him away with such force, I was amazed the douche bag didn't fall on his ass.

I turned to the sound of brakes hissing to a stop next to me. A bright yellow car pulled up close to the curb.

A balding man leaned over the passenger seat and yelled out the window, "Somebody call a cab?"

"I'm sorry, sweetheart," Frat Boy said into Drunk Girl's ear. "Why don't we get in the cab and I'll take you home?"

Oh, hell no. I wasn't going to let that happen.

Drunk Girl rolled her eyes and suddenly her face washed ashen. Sweat beaded on her brows as she bent over, grasping her thighs for balance.

Oh, shit. She was going to hurl. I tried to jump back but it was too late.

Her body lurched, her head heaving forward as she puked all over the sidewalk. Vomit splattered over all of us.

"Shit," Frat Boy wailed. "You got vomit all over my new loafers, you stupid bitch."

Lunging toward Frat Boy, I tightened my fists, preparing to light his ass on fire. Instead, I nearly tripped over Drunk Girl. Gazing down, I noticed she'd fallen down onto the sidewalk on all fours, dry heaving. The scene was disgusting and heartbreaking all at the same time. I couldn't help but pity her.

As much as I wanted to walk away, as much as my mind

screamed to leave this chick alone, it just wasn't in my nature. Fuck.

I glanced behind me when I heard the club door clank shut. Frat Boy was nowhere in sight. Well, fuck me. Here I was, all alone with this vomiting, pathetic creature. That's it. I was giving up cigarettes for good.

I knelt down beside Drunk Girl. "Do you live around here?" I asked, tucking a wayward strand of blonde hair behind her ear.

She shook her head.

"Did you drive here?" I asked, sounding more patient than I felt.

She shook her head again.

"Are your friends inside? Maybe we could go back and get them."

"I don't have any friends inside." Her words were a whisper, but I caught the desperate, distraught tone in her declaration.

"You came to a club all alone with no car?" I asked, my words scolding like a mother's. "What's wrong with you? Why would you do that?"

"Spare me a lecture, asshole." She sat back on her heels and wiped her mouth with the back of her hand. "I'm sick as a dog here, as if you can't tell. I just want to go home."

Asshole? Seriously? I was the only asshole out here helping her.

I drew in a calming breath, again, debating what to do. Most of me wanted to walk away, but honestly, I was worried for Drunk Girl. What if this cab driver assaulted her while she was passed out? I'd grown up in the mean streets of Five Points in Denver. I knew what could happen to vulnerable chicks like Drunk Girl.

Nope. I couldn't take that chance. Not with her.

"Get up." I yanked Drunk Girl to her feet and walked her to the cab, opening the back door. "Get in."

She fought against me and I almost let her go.

"Get in," I repeated, ducking her head and shoving her inside. The last thing she should be doing tonight was roaming the streets of downtown Austin, drunk and alone.

"But wait," she said. "I don't have any money." Her huge brown eyes stared up at me like a lost puppy.

Fuck.

"Scoot over, I'll pay. You can thank me later." I pushed her across the seat and tucked my long legs inside the cramped space.

"Where to?" the driver asked.

I turned to Drunk Girl. "So where do you live?"

Tears filled her chocolate brown eyes.

Oh, hell.

"Why?" she asked. "So you can take me home and screw me like Gap Boy?"

"What the hell are you talking about?"

Her eyes slammed shut, one lone tear rolling down her cheek as she fell face first into my lap. She was passed out cold.

"Great, just great," I muttered, shaking my head. "Do you smoke?" I asked the cabbie.

"Yeah, but you can't light up in here." He pointed to a huge *no smoking* sign on the plexiglass.

"Don't worry," I said, reaching into my jeans. I pulled out my pack of cigarettes and tossed them into the front seat. "I never plan to smoke again. Ever."

CHAPTER 5

RORY

"What's the address, son?" The driver asked.

I gazed up and saw the him staring at me in the rearview mirror, brows raised.

"Um, give me a minute."

"One minute and I start the meter."

I shook Drunk Girl but she was unresponsive, out for the count. "Shit."

"Does she have a phone?" the driver asked.

"What?"

"Maybe you can find her address on her phone."

I dug around Drunk Girl's shoulder but didn't find a purse.

"Sometimes chicks stuff phones in their bra," he said.

I glanced up.

"No, seriously," the driver nodded, "chicks do that all the time. That's where my girlfriend stashes hers when she doesn't have pockets."

"I'll look for pockets first, thanks." I pushed Drunk Girl off my lap and examined her clothes. "She has on stretch pants."

The driver twisted over the front seat. "Look on the inside of her waistband. Sometimes they put a secret pocket inside workout pants."

"How do you know all this?"

"I've got a girlfriend, a mom, and six sisters." He laughed. "I know a lot about women."

I stared at his yellowed teeth and the over grown man-bushes he called eyebrows, pretty sure he didn't know *everything* about women. I had no choice but to trust him on this one though.

I slid my palm around Drunk Girl's waistband but felt nothing. Shit. I slowly moved my hand to her back and I sucked in a breath when my fingers grazed her bare skin. Heat raced up my arm and everything below my belt jerked to life. I cursed myself for being such a pig.

Just as I was about to pull away, I felt a bump in her waistband. I slid my fingers inside, careful not to touch anything else for fear I may combust.

"I found her phone," I yelled, holding it up in the air. "Now what?"

"What cell service does she use?"

"How the hell should I know that?"

"Go into her settings and find out who her network provider is." The driver rattled off instructions as if people did this shit all the time.

"I have no idea what you're talking about," I said.

"Here, give it to me." He reached over the seat, grabbing the phone. He scrolled through the screens and within a matter of minutes, produced her address.

What the fuck?

"How the hell did you do that?" I asked, dumbfounded, and more than a little worried.

"Sisters." He snorted, handing me the phone back.

"I don't even want to know, do I?"

He put the car in drive, shaking his head as he glanced over his shoulder. "Nope, probably not."

After a short drive, the cab rolled to a stop in front of a small house. The driver put the car in park, turning to look at me.

"We're here," he said. "Now what, Ace? How are you going to get inside?"

Shit. I hadn't thought that far ahead.

"Hey." I shook Drunk Girl's shoulders.

"Hmmm," she moaned.

Oh, thank God, she was alive.

"We're at your house. Where's your key?"

"What key?" she mumbled.

"The key to your house."

"Where's my car?"

"I have no idea." I bit back my frustration. "Look, we need to get you inside your house. You can worry about your car later."

She bolted up like I'd hit her with a taser, her eyes darting from the driver to me. "It's not locked," she said. Her eyes slammed shut and she fell into my lap, again, passed out cold.

"What the fuck was that?" I asked to no one in particular.

The driver shrugged his shoulders.

"What? Your sisters never got drunk?" I asked.

"We're Catholic. We stay drunk twenty-four seven." The driver laughed. "Why don't you look under the mat for a key? People do that shit all the time."

I knew that fact better than most.

"Or try the door," he said. "Maybe she really didn't lock it."

"No way. What woman doesn't lock her door?"

"Maybe she's dumber than she looks."

I gazed down and studied Drunk Girl more closely this time now that she was nearer.

Long, pale lashes fanned over her smooth skin. Her rosy lips stood in stark contrast to the pale skin of her flawless complexion. From this vantage point she didn't look dumb, not to me. Even though she'd done a stupid thing by getting trashed and putting herself in harm's way tonight, something told me she wasn't dumb, not like me anyway. Naive yes, but dumb? No.

I opened the car door and pushed it open. "Keep an eye on her. I'll be right back."

"Meter's still running, Ace."

I shut the door and jogged to the front of her house. Shit. There were two front doors. This was a duplex. How the hell was I supposed to know which one was hers? For all I knew, this might not even be her house.

I glanced at my watch. It was a quarter to midnight, way too late for visitors. The cab still sat idling next to the curb. As much as I wanted to walk away, my innate need to protect people propelled me forward.

Lights glowed from the duplex on the right so I stepped up onto the porch. I reminded myself that Texas was an open carry state. People probably shot first and asked questions later. I knocked cautiously on the door and took a huge step back.

Within seconds, the door swung open. A red-headed woman stood in the doorway, one hand on the knob and the other on her small hip. She looked young, maybe in her early twenties.

I glanced over her shoulder. A huge muscled man sat on the couch, glaring up at me as he nursed a beer.

Why the hell had he let his girlfriend answer the door? I could have been anyone, a serial rapist, for all he knew. These people obviously hadn't grown up in the same neighborhood I had.

Red cocked her head to the side. "Can I help you, sweetie?"

"Umm, I'm sorry to bother you so late."

Her gaze travelled the length of me.

Instead of desire, my body heated with embarrassment. What the hell was that about? Garnering a woman's attention was normally something I enjoyed, but not from this chick. Not with her muscle-headed boyfriend sitting ten feet away.

One side of Red's mouth crooked in a wicked smile. "Oh, no bother, sweetheart." Her eyes traveled down to her chest.

My gaze followed. Shit. Her boobs were practically busting out of her tiny halter top. My head snapped up, eyes trained on her face. The last thing I needed was a fight with her boneheaded boyfriend.

"I was wondering if you know the person who lives next door?"

"Who? Hindley?"

"I'm not sure."

"Why? What's going on?" Red stepped out onto the porch and scanned up and down the street. "Look, we paid our balance off last week. We've been on time for the last three months. I don't want no trouble."

"What?"

"You're not here collecting?"

"Collecting what?" I asked, shaking my head. Did she think I was a bounty hunter? I'd been accused of a lot of things.

"No?" she said.

"No, I'm not collecting anything. I found this woman drunk and passed out at a club downtown." I pointed toward the cab. "I'm just trying to bring her home. Her phone says this is her address."

"She in the cab?" Red nodded toward the curb.

"Yes."

She laughed. "I can guarantee you, if you've got a passed-out chick in *that* car, it sure as shit ain't Hindley."

Hindley? Was that Drunk Girl?

"Well, if you don't mind," I stepped off the porch, "would you mind taking a look at her? I just want to make sure she gets home safe."

She stared me up and down, crossing her arms under her ample breasts. "Well, aren't you Prince Charming."

I averted my gaze. Again. Shit, "Uh, anyway, would you be willing to help me?"

"Why not?" She turned toward gorilla man. "I'll be back in a minute, hun."

He grunted, the only indicator he gave a shit.

Red walked beside me toward the cab, popping her bubble gum. The sound irritated me, and whatever male lust I might have felt earlier completely dissolved.

I swung open the back door to the cab and lifted Drunk Girl's upper body so Red could get a good look.

"Holy shit," she exclaimed, "that *is* Hindley. I can't believe it. That chick never gets hammered. Where did you say you found her?"

"At a club downtown."

"Hindley was out clubbin'? Who knew she had it in her?" Red smiled with a look of adoration and surprise.

"She doesn't normally act like this?" I asked.

"Hell no. She's the most straight-laced, uptight chick I know. I wonder what happened to make her tie one on like this."

Drunk Girl's words from outside the club earlier rang through my mind.

I don't have any friends inside.

Had she been telling the truth? Obviously, she didn't have any friends that gave a shit about her.

"Do you have a spare key to her place?" I asked.

"Hindley never locks her door."

I cut my eyes to Red. "Are you serious?"

"As a heart attack."

"Why?"

She shrugged. "Beats the hell out of me."

"That's the dumbest thing I've ever heard," I muttered.

"I know, right? She locks it when she's home though."

"Well, I guess that's something." I shook my head in disbelief. The cabbie may have been right. Drunk Girl was dumber than she looked.

Reaching into the cab, I tugged Drunk Girl toward me. Her shirt rode up, revealing a patch of smooth, ivory skin. I pulled down the material but not before my fingers grazed against her bare abdomen. A sharp pain of desire shot straight to my mid-section.

God, I was a dick.

Unable to carry the dead weight of her body, I bent low and swept her over my shoulder in a fireman's hold. God, her legs were long and toned, but I tried to forget that part. I wrapped my arms around her hips, securing her to my shoulder. I took a few blessed moments to admire her tight, round ass. An ass just begging to be spanked. Maybe there was something to Pilates classes after all.

I turned to Red, forcing the images of Drunk Girl rolling around naked in my bed from my head. "Will you get the door for me?"

"Sure." Red ran ahead of us.

I held my breath. Surely—

"Here you go," Red said, pushing the door open.

Son of a bitch. I couldn't believe this chick really left her fucking door unlocked. What the hell? She really did need a good spanking.

I walked into the small living room and dropped Drunk Girl onto the first piece of furniture I could find—an oversized chair next to a nice leather couch. Studying the woman now spread out before me, I shook my head. How could she not be more concerned for her own safety?

I looked over at Red. "Will you keep an eye on her for a minute while I go pay the cab?"

"Just for a second. Robby doesn't like me hanging out with Hindley. He says she fills my head with too many dumb ideas."

"Who's Hindley?"

Red threw her thumb over her shoulder and motioned toward Drunk Girl. "You really don't know her?"

"Nope."

"That's funny."

"Why?" I asked.

"If you knew Hindley, you'd know why."

I dug out my wallet and jogged outside toward the cab, wondering what Red's comment meant? Obviously Drunk Girl's behavior tonight was out of character for her. What could have made her go to such extremes tonight?

I leaned through the passenger window and handed the driver a hundred. "Thanks for all your help, man."

He held up the one-hundred-dollar bill and smiled broadly, revealing missing teeth. "Anytime, my friend. Anytime. Good luck with her."

"Thanks," I nodded, "I think I'll need it."

"You're doing the right thing. If one of my sisters had gotten this drunk, I'd be glad a man like you found her." He rummaged through the glove box and pulled out a card, holding it out the window. "Hey, here's my number. When you're ready to go home tomorrow, give me a call. I'll drop you off anywhere you want. No charge."

"Tomorrow?" I laughed. "What makes you think I'm spending the night with her?"

"You're not quite the bad ass you think you are, Ace. I know a good guy when I see one."

"Good guy?" I laughed to myself. This dude obviously didn't recognize me. I was anything *but* good. "Not sure about that."

"We'll see, Casanova. Call me tomorrow when you're ready to go home."

I glanced down at Raul's card, debating which was worse— being a bad ass or a good guy. Neither seemed an appropriate title for me. Not anymore.

I walked back to the duplex, twirling Raul's card in my hand. Why the hell did I give two-shits about this girl anyway? Unable to come up with an answer, I stepped through Drunk Girl's front door.

Red had switched on a lamp, illuminating the living area.

I watched as her next-door neighbor wiped Drunk Girl's face with a wet rag. When she was finished, Red reached up and gently tugged her ponytail loose. Golden blonde hair tumbled across Drunk Girl's shoulders as her head lulled back onto the chair. Her smooth, ivory skin glowed in the light from the lamp beside her.

I sucked in a breath and bit back a grown, captivated by her natural beauty. I'd been wrong about this one. She was remarkable.

Red glanced up at me. "I think she's out cold. She looks awful. You staying?"

Shit, was I? I hadn't planned on any of this.

The shrill ring of my phone interrupted the silent debate in my mind.

"Hey, listen, I gotta go," Red said, stepping over Drunk Girl's long legs as she bolted toward the door.

"Wait. What did you say her name was?"

"Hindley," she said. "H-I-N-D-L-E-Y. Hindley Hagen."

What the hell kind of name was that?

"I know, right?" Red laughed, answering my silent question "Apparently, it's a character from some famous book. I don't read much."

"Me neither." I laughed wryly.

"Knock if ya need anything." Red nodded toward her side of the duplex. "Night, Lover Boy." She blew a kiss and waggled her fingers before quietly closing the front door.

And just like that, I was alone with Drunk Girl. Again.

Fuck. What the hell did I do now?

I stared at my phone. A missed call from Leif. He'd be worried if I didn't call back soon but I had no idea what to tell him.

Leif and his buddies would give me shit for leaving. Especially when they found out I wasn't even going to get laid.

I stared down at my damsel in distress.

Drunk Girl's body was sprawled across the huge chair, arms and legs dangling over the side. She didn't look very ladylike but she had a gracefulness about her even in her current state. I couldn't imagine letting anyone think I'd taken advantage of her. Especially if her drunken stupor truly was out of character for her.

Without thinking more, I quickly dialed Leif's number.

"Dude, where the hell are you?" Leif shouted above the blaring music pulsating in the background. "This place is crawling with hotties."

I had no choice. Raul had already threatened my reputation as a bad ass. I would have to sacrifice Drunk Girl. My man-card was on the line.

"This better be good, asshole," I said. "I've got a hot chick underneath me." Technically, it wasn't a lie. Drunk Girl was in the chair *below* me.

"I don't know how you do it, man." Leif chuckled. "Girls will do just about anything for you."

"What can I say? Chicks dig pro athletes." I winced at my shitty response. It was official. I was a complete jackass.

Leif laughed hysterically.

I hit the END button and groaned. Add 'lying sack of shit' to my growing list of offenses.

I turned my attention to Drunk Girl, my eyes roaming over her body. Obviously, I wasn't a total asshole like some people thought. I'd at least gotten her home safe. I had a few redeeming qualities, even if most people never saw them, or wrote about them.

Drunk Girl's body shifted and she fell to one side, her head flopping over the arm of the chair. She remained unconscious. If she stayed in that position all night, she wouldn't be able to walk for a week.

I scooped her up in my arms and walked down the hall. I pushed open the first door I came to, thankful it had a small bed in the center of the room. Standing above the mattress, I dropped Drunk Girl onto the white comforter with a thud.

Her lifeless body collapsed into a messy heap of limbs and hair, feet hanging off the side. That's when I noticed her shoes and pants were spattered with vomit.

Ah, shit. I couldn't let her sleep in her own puke. I was going to have to undress her.

Untying her shoes, I pulled them off, along with her socks. I laughed out loud when I saw her bright blue toenails. From what Red had told me earlier, Hindley seemed to be an uptight girl. Blue toenail polish was *not* a color choice for most neurotic, self-controlled women I knew.

Hindley had a playful side. The thought brought a genuine smile to my face as I thought about the possibilities.

There may be hope for you yet, Drunk Girl.

CHAPTER 6

HINDLEY

I ROLLED OVER WITH A GROAN, rubbing my throbbing head. My stomach lurched with the movement and I swallowed back the urge to puke. Prying my eyes open, I glanced around the room, unable to focus on anything. Where the hell was I?

A loud bang echoed through the room. It sounded like a door crashing into the wall.

"What the fuck is going on in here?" Someone yelled.

Oh, shit. I recognized that voice. Dana Di Grazio. My best friend, most days.

I wrapped my arms over my head for protection.

"Holy hell," she yelled, "you got laid."

I bolted upright. "What the hell are you talking about?" The room spun and I reached out to balance myself, jumping when I felt a hard, warm body next to me.

Startling images flashed through my mind—pole dancing, tequila shots, Gap Boy, vomiting—lots of vomiting. This wasn't a dream.

"I'm talking about that hottie next to you," Dana said.

My eyes focused on my pint-sized friend and I stared at her in disbelief.

"Look," she said, pointing to the other side of my bed.

Oh, shit, she wasn't kidding.

I slowly turned and gasped when I saw a man's body laying mere inches away from me. I wrapped the covers around my body, scurrying to the opposite side of my small bed, nearly falling off.

"Holy hell." Dana laughed. "You finally screwed some random dude from a bar."

"I did not," I said, mortified by her accusation.

Dana raced toward the bed, her hands grasping the comforter. "Do y'all have any clothes on under there?"

"Dana, stop!" I clutched the blanket tighter. Slowly lifting the covers, I peered underneath, afraid of what I might find. I'd never had a one-night stand before, and I didn't want to start now.

I blew out a sigh of relief and silently thanked God when I saw I was still wearing a tank top and undies.

Unconvinced, Dana grabbed the blanket and gave it one quick yank, jerking it from my grasp. Suddenly mystery man and I lay completely exposed.

"Dana!" I screamed.

Her lips curled into a devilish smile, revealing two trademark dimples on either side of her face. Her blue eyes shimmered with mischief. "Damn, girl. You held out for a fine one didn't you. I'm completely jealous, you skank."

"Dana, please give me the blanket."

She shook her head. "Uh, uh. I want to look at this hottie all day."

I glanced at the man next to me, making a quick sweep of his body. He was also wearing underwear, thank God. Maybe we hadn't had sex after all. Or maybe he just didn't like sleeping in the nude. Shit.

I continued to stare, unable to avert my gaze. His long, muscular body glowed like a bronzed god in the soft morning light. His skin stood in stark contrast to my pale white legs. He looked peaceful, like an innocent angel. Something about the small smirk he wore, even during sleep, warned me he was probably trouble though.

The throbbing in my head suddenly moved to other parts of my body. Trying to ignore the tingle spreading from my center, I continued my perusal of this mystery man lying next to me.

His light brown hair was cut short and streaked with gold. He laid on his stomach, one arm clutching a throw pillow like it was a life preserver. My heart ached with an overwhelming need to keep him safe.

Where the hell had that come from? I didn't even know this guy's name. Or did I?

His face looked familiar but for some reason I couldn't place it. Probably because I was still half drunk. Upon further inspection I could tell he really was handsome. His face could definitely grace the cover of any magazine. Dana was right, the guy was super-hot. Whatever we had or hadn't done last night, at least I'd picked a gorgeous man to share my bed.

I'd never had a one-night stand before so I didn't know whether to be ashamed or proud. It wasn't like I was a virgin or anything. According to Dana, I hadn't had nearly as many sexual conquests as a twenty-five-year-old should. I couldn't help it. I wasn't into cheap, meaningless sex. When I was intimate with a man, I wanted to at least know his name.

I laughed to myself at the absurdity. I had no idea what this guy's name was.

Suddenly the nameless man rolled over with a soft moan.

Oh, God, what if he was hard?

I jumped back, afraid he might touch me, secretly wishing he would.

He raised his arms over his head, stretching his lean body as he sprawled out on to his back.

Oh, my. Even more muscles appeared…everywhere. Holy crap, this guy was ripped.

I pushed further away as he scooted closer to me but it was impossible in my tiny bed.

The mystery man yawned loudly, displaying perfectly white teeth, before finally settling into the bed like he'd slept here for years.

"Holy shit," Dana said, "he looks even hotter on his back. And look at that massive ink on his side. That's awesome."

I leaned over and studied the man's torso, holding my breath.

The tattoo started at the top of his ribs on the right side and wrapped around to his back, down his hip, disappearing into his underwear. The artwork was a picture of a man skateboarding in some kind of park. The skater was in mid-air, skateboard glued to his feet. The bottom of the board ran diagonally across mystery man's ribs with the words 'SK8R BOY' painted on it.

Skater Boy.

For some strange reason, I could tell the name fit him.

I didn't have any tattoos of my own but I had to admit, this picture was true artistry.

"That ink is bad ass." Dana would know, her body was littered with more tattoos than most. Many weren't visible unless she was fully undressed, but that never stopped her from showing them off.

"And look at his chest." She drooled over sleeping beauty. "You could serve a five-course meal on those rock-hard abs." She flattened her hand, about to rub his bare chest.

I reached over and swatted her hand. "Stop it."

"Stop what?" a deep voice rumbled below us.

Oh, God. It was Skater Boy. And he'd totally busted me checking out his body.

My gaze swept up his broad chest until our eyes met. His were stunning, a mesmerizing mix of copper and blue that I'd never seen before.

My mystery man interlocked his fingers beneath his head and smiled like he owned the place.

Oh, swoon. Sexual awareness warmed every part of my body and I shivered. I'd never felt this way before just from a man's gaze.

His pose showcased new muscles and I bit back a moan.

Another wave of desire swept through my body like fire. I quietly beat myself up for not remembering being intimate with him the night before.

"Good morning, Drunk Girl," he said, his voice rough, and sexy as hell. "Enjoying the view?"

My face reddened, mortified he'd caught me staring at his naked body.

"Very much," Dana answered, her dimples deepening.

"Dana," I said, narrowing my eyes.

Dana and Skater Boy stared at me.

"What?" I asked.

They both remained silent.

Suddenly I was hyper aware of my own nakedness. And the fact I was wearing white cotton granny-panties. Why couldn't I be wearing something sexy? Because I don't have anything sexy, I thought.

I bolted out of the bed and grabbed the blanket from Dana's hand, wrapping the comforter around me.

Skater Boy propped up on one arm, obviously comfortable in his own skin—and in my bed. He could be a centerfold of any lady's magazine. His blue eyes held my gaze. I was trapped, truly captivated.

"Damn, dude, you're fine." Dana's voice broke the silence.

I turned to face my best friend, not surprised to find her molesting the guy with her eyes.

An unfamiliar pang of jealousy swept through my body. What the hell? It wasn't like this guy was mine. I didn't want him to be mine. Did I?

This man's entire being screamed trouble. He was a player. Anyone could tell by the casual way he laid in my bed, wearing a smirk and skimpy underwear.

I turned to find Skater Boy staring at me, completely unfazed by Dana's comment. His eyes roamed up and down my body as his lips curled into a devious grin.

Heat crawled up my spine and I swallowed hard. "Did we, um…" I pointed my finger between us.

"What? You don't remember the best night of your life?" He winked.

Oh, crap.

"Well," he shifted in the bed, waggling his brows, "that's what you said it was for you. Honestly, it was for me too." He smiled as if he woke up in a stranger's bed every day. Maybe he did.

My face flushed red. We *had* done the dirty deed, and I'd been too drunk to remember. I was ashamed of my blatant disregard for my own well-being. I, of all people, knew better.

"You screamed out my name in ecstasy, begging for more." He chuckled.

"Fuck yeah, she did," Dana cheered in approval.

Tears burned my eyes as sordid memories flashed through my mind. My heart thundered in my ears as I gasped for breath. Fear consumed me and I felt myself being pulled under. I needed to get out of here before I collapsed in a total panic attack.

"Hey, hey, wait. Don't get upset." The man grasped my arm, holding me down. "I'm just kidding. We didn't do anything. I swear."

I wanted to believe him, but something in his devilish smile told me to be wary. This man was trouble.

He kept one hand wrapped around my wrist as he crossed his heart with the other. "I promise. You were drunk as a skunk and passed out the entire night. I brought you home and put you to bed. I tried to sleep on that shitty couch of yours in there, but it killed my back. I can't afford any injuries right now so I decided to sleep in your bed."

I raised a brow.

"On top of the covers," he added.

Slowly, my heartbeat slowed and my breathing evened out.

"But, apparently, somewhere during the night, you let me under the blanket." Skater Boy smiled.

Heat crept up in my cheeks.

"That was your fault." He pointed at me and chuckled.

The vibrations of his laughter hit me square between the legs. I crossed my ankles, trying not to squirm.

"That's it," he said, holding up his hand in the air. "I swear, that's all that happened."

His blue eyes searched mine, and something told me he was telling the truth. He was trying to make me feel better, and strangely enough it was working.

"Well, shit," Dana said, plopping down on the bed.

"What?" I asked.

"You're not the slut I thought you were born to be. So much for random sex. But...," she held up a finger, waggling her brows, "there's always tonight, right?"

I laughed in spite of myself. The humor died quickly when I remembered Geneva's warning from last night. "Oh, no. Tonight," I said. "What time is it?"

"It's ten-forty," Dana said. "Why?"

"Crap." I flew up from the bed. "I have Geneva's bridal luncheon in twenty minutes. She's going to kill me if I'm late."

"Who gives a shit about that bitch?" Dana said.

"Lord knows I don't," I said, "but I promised Paul I'd keep an eye on her last night. I can't even remember what I did last night, let alone what Geneva did."

Skater Boy scowled at me. "Who's Paul?"

"Paul's her dad," Dana said.

"Stepdad," I corrected, staring at Skater Boy. "Paul's my stepfather."

Dana rolled her eyes. "Whatever, Hindley." She leaned closer to Skater Boy. "As far as you're concerned, he's her dad and he'll cut your dick off if he finds out about this little event." She waved her hand around the room. "Know what I mean, Skater Boy?"

I shook my head. It was futile to argue with Dana. Instead I walked to my closet, pushing back the doors. I searched for anything remotely appropriate to wear. "You coming?" I called over my shoulder.

"Who me?" Skater Boy asked.

I turned and watched with disappointment as he tugged on his jeans. "No, not you." I laughed. "Dana, are you coming?" When she didn't answer, I glanced over at her.

Dana's gaze was glued to Skater Boy, her eyes roaming over his body like he was a steak dinner. "It really should be a crime to cover up that body," she sighed, shaking her head and falling back on the bed.

She was right, but I couldn't say so, not out loud. "Dana!" I yelled.

"What?" She sat back up.

"Focus."

Her blue eyes met mine. "Oh, yeah, right. Boring ass bridal buffet with rich bitches? Uh, hell no."

I searched my room for clothes. "Well, I have to go. Where are my keys?" I stopped mid-motion, staring up at Skater Boy. "Oh my God. Please tell me I didn't drive drunk last night, did I?"

"No, we took a cab," he said.

Random memories of last night flashed through my mind. "We took that ridiculous Hummer to the club. Shit. My car's still at the pole dancing studio," I said to myself.

"The what?" Skater Boy laughed, pulling his shirt over his broad chest.

It was unbelievable how putting *on* clothes could be so sexy. Watching Skater Boy get dressed was one of the most erotic things I'd ever seen. God, I was pathetic. Dana was right, I needed more experience with men.

"Yeah," Dana said, "she went to a pole dancing class last night."

"You take pole dancing classes?" He tugged on his boots, tying the laces before glancing at me.

His blue eyes caught mine and I was lost. Again. God, he was gorgeous.

"That's kind of hot, Drunk Girl." He smirked with that trade-mark sideways grin.

My heart tripped in my chest. Parts of my body that had lain dormant for too long began to burn with desire.

"Actually, it's way hot," he added with a wink.

"Oh, you should see her," Dana said.

"Shut up, Dana."

"She doesn't need any lessons," Dana continued, unfazed by my warning. "Hell, Hindley could—"

"Dana! Enough!"

They both stared at me, eyes wide. I rarely shouted. I didn't care though. This guy was a stranger to me. He didn't need to know anything about me, especially since he was leaving soon.

"Sorry," I said, "I just…I need to go. Dana, can you give me a ride?"

"Uh, sure. What about you, Tat?" She glanced at Skater Boy. "You need a ride?"

"If you're going my way, sure, that would be great."

"Oh, I'll definitely go your way," Dana said, wiggling her brows.

Skater Boy stood, laughing as he smoothed over his clothes. "I think one missed opportunity last night is more than my delicate ego can handle today."

Dana snapped her fingers. "Damn. I was so close."

"Give me five minutes, Dana," I said. "I'll be right back."

"I'll go put some coffee on," she said as she left the room.

Skater Boy and I stood alone. The silence between us grew awkward.

I pulled a skirt over my bare legs. "Hey, I'm sorry about last night."

His eyes roamed my body but oddly enough I didn't mind. Actually, I kind of liked it.

I selected a top from my closet and reached to remove my tank top. A wave of self-consciousness washed over me and I stopped. I stared at Skater Boy, silently asking him to turn around.

"You're funny." He chuckled as he turned his back.

I tore off my tank top and wiggled into the blouse, tucking it into my skirt as if I were being timed for a game show. "Why am I funny?" I asked, walking over to the dresser. I refused to look at my reflection. Instead, I picked up a brush and tried to run it through my tangled hair. God, I was a mess.

"We slept together all night," Skater Boy said, "in our underwear. And now you want me to turn my back so I don't see you in your bra?"

"Well, technically, we didn't see each other in our underwear."

"Oh, I saw you."

I turned, mouth gaping.

He stared at me, totally serious. And hot as hell.

I swallowed hard then twirled on my heels so he wouldn't see me blush. "Yeah, about that," I said.

"What?" His warm breath caressed my neck.

I shivered. Shit. He was right behind me, literally breathing down my neck. And I liked it. I held my breath, wondering what he'd do next.

His fingertips slowly grazed the bare skin on my neck.

I startled. His touch sent a current of need surging through my body. What the hell was that?

Oh, God, did he want sex? Now? Maybe he was pissed I hadn't put out last night.

I swatted his hand away and turned to face him. "What are you doing?"

"Your tag." He reached around to tuck the label back into my shirt. "It was hanging out."

"You could have just told me," I said, fumbling nervously with the tag. This man stirred things inside me that were better left unmoved.

He remained silent.

I looked up, not surprised to see his smile had fallen, his blue eyes darker now. I'd offended him. That had never been my intent, I'd meant to protect myself.

He'd been nothing but nice to me this morning. Hell, he'd brought me home last night when I'd been too drunk to take care of myself. He'd obviously taken care of me when no one else would, staying with me all night to ensure my safety.

I was being a bitch.

I reached out and took his hands in mine, mindlessly rubbing my thumb over his knuckles. "I'm sorry," I whispered, squeezing his fingers.

He tugged me close to his body, wrapping one hand around my waist.

I was surprised at how natural it felt to be in his arms. We fit.

I melted into his embrace.

He gazed down at me, his blue eyes locked on mine, lost in thought.

"So, what, you two going to finally consummate this one-night stand?" Dana said.

Skater Boy released me and we both stepped back as if we'd been electrocuted.

"Come on, shake a leg, ho," Dana said. "We have ten minutes to get you to Bitchville, USA." Just as quickly as she'd entered, Dana disappeared.

We stood alone again, staring awkwardly at one another.

I drew in a breath to speak but Skater Boy broke our gaze and walked toward the door. I didn't want him to leave. Not yet. I had an overwhelming need to touch him. So I did. I grabbed his muscled arm. God, his skin felt good against mine.

He stared down at my hand.

"Hey," I whispered.

His eyes met mine, his pupils flared.

A sharp pang of desire burned in my chest. "I, I, just wanted to say thanks, for last night. I appreciate you taking care of me."

He tilted his head, his eyes narrowed, forehead creased. "Why do I feel like thanking me might have been one of the hardest things you've ever done?"

I stared at him with a dazed look. How had he read me so well? I prided myself on keeping my emotions hidden from strangers.

"Probably because it was," I said, pushing past him. In that moment, I felt more vulnerable fully dressed than I had lying next to him in my underwear.

I raced toward the bathroom, shutting the door to escape his scrutiny. He could see me, the real me, the parts of me I'd worked hard to keep hidden. I could never afford to be that vulnerable again. I knew in my heart I wouldn't survive, and so did the people closest to me.

CHAPTER 7

HINDLEY

"Everybody in?" Dana slammed the door of her fire-engine red BMW convertible.

"Nice car," Skater Boy said, folding his long, lean legs into the back.

"Thanks. It was a gift from my parents." Dana winked at me.

I rolled my eyes. This was no gift. It was an inheritance, one bequeathed to her too early.

Dana twisted in her seat and peered back at Skater Boy. "Got enough room back there, One-Nighter?"

"Here, I can switch with you," I offered, reaching for the door handle.

"No, forget it. I'm fine," Skater Boy said. He looked at Dana. "What did you just call me?"

"Oh, uh, sorry," Dana said. "I still don't know your name so I called you One-Nighter." She flicked her thumb in my direction. "You know, my girl's first one-night stand."

"Dana!" I hit her square in the arm with my fist.

Skater Boy laughed. "Well, I guess since we didn't actually have sex last night, you can call me Rory instead."

"Ah, man, no sex?" Dana pouted.

"Nope, not even a good feel." He laughed.

Dana dropped her head and let out a deep sigh. "Damn it."

"Call me old fashioned," Skater Boy said, "but I prefer my one-night stands alive and alert so we can both enjoy the evening."

My mouth fell open and I turned and stared in disbelief. Was he serious?

His full lips curled into a delicious smile as his blue eyes locked on mine.

My stomach fluttered. It actually fluttered.

"Might want to close that." He reached out and slipped his hand under my chin. His thumb caressed my cheek as he lifted my jaw, closing my mouth.

I swallowed, my eyes wide. He was good. I flipped around in my seat before I did something stupid, like crawl into the back and kiss him.

Dana pulled out onto the street. "I like you, Rory. And your real name is much sexier than One-Nighter."

"Rory," I whispered under my breath, letting his name roll off my tongue. I twisted off the cap to my water bottle and took a sip.

"Hey, Rory?" Dana said.

"Yes?"

She stared at him in the rearview mirror. "I'm alive and alert and I can promise to stay that way until tonight. Want to have a go?"

Rory bellowed with laughter, his amusement so infectious I snorted and choked on my water. He had a great laugh.

"Is she always this bad?" he asked me.

I wiped my mouth with my shoulder as I glanced back at him. "Worse sometimes I'm afraid."

"Wow."

"Yeah, you try being best friend sometime."

"You know you love me, Drunk Girl." Dana hit my arm with her elbow.

"I do. Lord only knows why, but I do."

We drove the short distance to the restaurant in comfortable silence. I needed quiet time to mentally prepare for the shit storm I was about to walk into.

Geneva and fifty of her "closest" friends were gathering for a bridal luncheon. As if she wasn't spending enough money on this mammoth wedding already, my mother had insisted Geneva have a pre-wedding party too. A luncheon for "just the girls," as she had explained to Paul. The problem was, I didn't know three-quarters of the girls attending. The small amount I did know, I couldn't stand.

"Hey, Skater Boy, what are you doing tonight?" Dana asked.

"Are you asking me to be *your* one-nighter?" Rory said, his deep voice resonating between my legs.

Holy shit.

"You wish." Dana winked at him in the rearview mirror. "Nah, I was going to tell you that you should come to this farce of a wedding tonight. As Hindley's date."

I glared at Dana.

As usual, she ignored me, keeping her gaze squarely on the road.

"You mean, Drunk Girl?" Rory said.

I turned in my seat to face him. "Why do you keep calling me Drunk Girl? I don't like it."

"Um...because you were drunk off your ass last night and I didn't know your name. I didn't think Shit Faced would be very appropriate."

Dana snorted.

My face flamed with embarrassment and I turned to stare out the front windshield.

"You seemed classier than that, *Drunk Girl*," he added.

I gritted my teeth.

Dana burst into laughter, jerking the car. "Classic, One-Nighter. I love it."

Oh, no, they were bonding. This wasn't good.

"Well, my name is Hindley," I said. "You can call me Hindley from now on."

"Jeez, what crawled up your ass all of a sudden?" Rory said.

I twisted in my seat. "What did you just say?"

"Your ass," he said. "What crawled up it?"

"Forgive her, One-Nighter," Dana said. "She's just pissy because this is going to be a shit day for her. That's why I thought you being there would make it easier for her. I mean, who wouldn't feel better looking at you all day."

I rolled my eyes. My stomach lurched and I swallowed down the bile climbing my throat. I couldn't tell if the rumbling in my gut was the tequila from last night or the fact that what Dana had said was true. Skater Boy was a dream to look at. Having him close may not be a good idea though.

"We're here, kids." Dana shouted.

Her voice twisted through my skull like a dull knife. My head fell back on the seat as I stared out of the passenger side window. Unlike Dana, I wasn't used to hangovers. I rarely drank to excess. I hated that out-of-control feeling.

I stared blankly at the restaurant in front of us. How the hell was I going to make it through the next twelve hours of my life? I'd never survive. Geneva had already made sure of it.

A few weeks ago, my mother had told me that Geneva's fiancé was friends with an old boyfriend of mine. My face had gone ashen at the mention of Chris Putman's name. I had no choice but to tell her the story of how he'd humiliated me in front of half the student body in college by calling out my virginity. He accused me of being a prick tease just because I wouldn't sleep with him.

The minute Geneva had discovered Chris was the guy who'd broken my heart, she decided he *had* to be in the wedding. She was just being a bitch, as usual, doing anything she could to make my life a living hell.

I'd tried not to think about my reunion with Chris for the past few weeks but now, sitting in front of the restaurant just hours before Geneva's wedding, I had no choice. Today was going to suck balls.

Someone's hand squeezed my shoulder.

"Is everything okay?" Skater Boy's voice called from the backseat.

I looked down and noticed Rory was squeezing my shoulder. I'd almost forgotten he was here.

Dana patted my thigh affectionately. "You'll be all right, sweetie. Deep breaths," she encouraged.

Rory released my shoulder. "What's wrong?"

"Nothing." I stared at Dana, pleading with her not to say anything about Chris.

Dana glanced over her shoulder at Rory. "There's a shit load of high maintenance bitches inside, waiting to eat her ass alive." Thankfully Dana didn't share more.

"When I know I'm going to be around a bunch of douche bags, and I get nervous, I always think of the time Timmy Dubowski pissed himself during recess and I always feel better," Rory said.

"What?" I laughed. Dana and I both turned to face him. "Okay, I *have* to hear this story."

"Me too," Dana said, clutching the seat back.

"Well," Rory said, smirking. He hadn't even started and I could already tell he was a talented storyteller. "You see, Timmy Dubowski was a douche bag. He was big, fat, and mean. He bullied everyone on the playground, stole their money, their dolls, you name it, he took it."

Dana giggled. "You had dolls?"

Rory crossed his arms over his broad chest. The muscles in his forearms flexed and his full lips curled into that trademark smirk.

Oh, my damn.

"I plead the fifth." Rory laughed.

I smiled, realizing Skater Boy had a playful side. Now I was more curious than ever. "So, what happened, to Tommy I mean?" I asked.

"It's Timmy," he corrected.

"Oh, sorry."

"You're forgiven." He smiled and his eyes danced with amusement. The sexual innuendo in his voice lit my body on fire. As if reading my thoughts, he winked. He. Winked. At me.

Who knew something as simple as a wink could turn me on so much? It wasn't really the wink, but the promise the expression made. Of what, I had no idea.

Rory cleared his throat. "So anyway," he started again, "Timmy was untouchable, or so we thought. One day after school, I overheard Timmy's mom talking to our teacher. She was yelling, telling the teacher that the school had to get an exterminator out there as soon as possible."

"Why?" I asked, surprised by the eagerness in my voice. Skater Boy's story captivated me.

"Timmy had been out of school for two days," Rory said. "The entire playground was so peaceful and calm without him around to terrorize us. Kids were playing and laughing. It was like heaven."

"Where was Timmy?" Dana asked.

"According to his mom, Timmy was deathly afraid of spiders. Apparently, he'd seen some in the classroom. He told his *mommy* he wouldn't go back to school until they got rid of them."

I laughed at his high-pitched tone.

"Well, right then and there," Rory said, "I devised a plan with my best pal, Jeremy."

I glanced over at Dana.

She leaned forward, her eyes wide. She was just as enthralled by Rory's story.

"So, what did you do?" I asked.

"After school that day, we went to the store and bought up a shit load of plastic spiders." Rory smiled deviously. "I wanted to dump them all in his desk, but Jeremy said that wouldn't be good enough. He wanted the entire school to see Timmy freak out. Jeremy convinced to put all the spiders on the playground so everyone could watch."

"So, what happened next?" Dana asked.

"When Timmy finally got back to school the next week, I snuck out of class a few minutes early before recess and covered the sand under the playscape with a ton of spiders. Hell, even *I* freaked out a little, they looked so real." Rory chuckled, obviously reliving the moment.

Dana and I giggled.

"I stood there waiting." Rory rubbed his hands, a gleam in his eyes. "And then Timmy came barreling through the doors with the other kids. He thumped a kid on the head and tripped another guy. God, he was such an asshole." Rory scowled, his voice thick with anger.

I realized in that moment that Rory was a protector. He'd taken care of me last night, kept me out of harm's way. And now, his childhood story confirmed that he'd been doing it most of his life.

I rarely let others take care of me. Even those close to me. It made me uncomfortable to rely on others. I couldn't help but wonder if there was anyone in Rory's life who protected him. I brushed the thought aside and focused on Rory. His bright blue eyes sparkled with amusement as he recounted the story.

"Then what happened?" I asked.

"I yelled at him, 'Hey asshole! Why don't you pick on someone your own size?' That douche bag stared at me like he couldn't believe I'd talked to him like that. No one ever dared speak to him like that. He looked ready to kick my ass."

Dana laughed. "I know a few assholes like that."

"Me too," I said. "So, did he, kick your ass that is?"

Rory grunted. "Please. As if. No, Timmy marched over like he was *going* to kick my ass. As soon as he got closer, I backed up so he would follow me under the playscape. All the kids circled around him to make sure he had no escape."

"Oh, Lord." Dana glanced at me. "This is going to be good."

"Yeah, it is." Rory nodded. "Finally, when Timmy had almost reached me, I looked down and shouted, 'Oh my God! Spiders!' I pointed down at the sand and started jumping around like I was on fire." Rory roared with laughter.

Dana and I joined in, snorting.

"I swear," Rory clutched his stomach, "it was like slow motion animation, watching Timmy look down at the sand before he let out the most god-awful, blood-curdling scream I'd ever heard. He couldn't move, he just stood there crying. Then that's when it happened."

"What happened?" I asked breathlessly.

"Timmy Dubowski peed all over himself." Rory laughed hysterically, rolling in the backseat.

Dana and I burst into a fit of uncontrolled giggles.

"Oh my God, it was so funny," Rory stuttered through his laughter, barely able to get the words out. "All the kids pointed at Timmy and laughed. I almost felt sorry for the dipshit. But then I saw the boy who Timmy had tripped earlier, blood running down his elbow. That's when I realized, it was all worth it. Once an asshole, always an asshole, I always say."

I wiped the tears from my eyes and tried to catch my breath. "That's a great story. I think it might help me if I picture Geneva peeing all over her wedding gown."

Dana roared with laughter. "That would be some funny shit."

"Well, if that doesn't help," Rory stuck his hand between the front seats, "you can have this."

I glanced down and saw a small plastic spider sitting in his palm. "You actually still have them?"

"Not all of them," he said. "I've lost a few and given some away. You never know when you're going to run into a Timmy Dubowski, right?"

I stared up into his eyes, a mesmerizing mix of azure blue and copper, rimmed with chocolate brown. The compassion I saw overwhelmed me and my heart ached from his act of kindness. Had any stranger ever cared about me this much? I reached out and took the spider in my hand, clutching it close to my chest. His gift was perhaps one of the nicest things anyone had ever given me.

I drew my gaze away from his, staring down at the spider in my hand. Suddenly I realized how symbolic this gesture was for him.

Rory was giving me a part of himself that he hoped would give me strength.

"Thank you," I whispered. I peeked at him through my lashes, not surprised to find him carefully studying me.

"No problem." He winked with a sideways smile.

A spark of desire shot from my core and ran all the way to my fingertips, burning me from the inside out.

"Everyone needs a little help now and then, right?" he asked in a husky voice.

We sat in silence, staring at each other for a long moment. We were survivors, Rory and me. In that moment I'd never wanted to kiss anyone more than I did this man. Skater Boy.

I jumped when a loud bang shook the car.

"What the fuck, Hindley? It's ten minutes after eleven."

I turned and saw Geneva standing outside the passenger door, glaring at me through my window.

"Here we go," I sighed, tugging on the door handle and pushing it open. I stepped out of the car, preparing myself for Geneva's wrath.

"I ask you for one thing, Hindley, one *fucking* thing." Geneva shoved her pointer finger in my face. "Not to be late today. And what do you do? You screw it up and ruin my day."

I stood silently. I'd learned a long time ago that the best way to shut Geneva Barton up was to let her burn out on her own. Giving Geneva any excuses for my tardiness would only extend her tirade. I stared down at the black asphalt, resigning myself to the fact that this was one of many outbursts I'd endure today. I'd suck it up, knowing the less I said, the less she'd attack me.

"Maybe if you hadn't been so busy getting completely trashed last night this wouldn't have happened," she said.

My stomach burned with hot anger. I swallowed down my words, along with the bile threatening to spew all over her expensive pantsuit.

Then it happened.

I felt him before I heard him, his presence enveloping me like a warm blanket.

"Maybe if you wouldn't have left her all alone outside a nightclub, where some random dude tried to shove her in a cab and would have probably raped her if I hadn't shown up, this wouldn't have happened. Ever think about that?" Rory's deep voice growled from behind me.

I turned.

Skater Boy glared at Geneva, just begging her to say something. He was defending me, just like Dana always did, a feat I'd never mastered myself. I wondered why I'd always felt the need to keep the peace in my family.

When I heard nothing from Geneva, I turned.

Instead of the usual menacing gaze she always gave me, she was smiling at Rory. Her eyes swept over his body in a predatory fashion. You'd never know she was about to get married in less than six hours by the way she was molesting him with her eyes.

Geneva pushed past me and stopped directly in front of Rory.

"And who might you be?" she asked, her voice raspy and sensual.

This was her predatory voice, the one she used to lure in the prey. Rory didn't stand a chance. He'd fall into Geneva's trap just like all the other guys I'd ever shown an interest in.

"I'm her date for the evening," Rory said without missing a beat.

Wait? My what?

Geneva pointed at me, her face wrinkled like she'd sucked on a lemon. "You're going with *her*?"

"Yep." Rory smiled.

"Why?" Geneva threw her head back, her lip curling.

"Look at her." Rory moved his hand up and down my body, his eyes drinking me in. Slowly, his delicious lips curled into a devilish smile.

I sang inwardly at the joy of being the object of his affection. He was picking me. *Me*. Not Geneva.

"She's a knock out," Rory said. "Hell, I'm just happy she said yes. She's totally out of my league." Rory's eyes locked on mine, holding my gaze.

He was serious. He actually thought he wasn't good enough for *me*.

"You can't be serious," Geneva said, eyes wide. "Her?"

"Oh, I most certainly am serious." Rory snaked one arm around my waist, pulling me close.

I instinctively wrapped both my arms around his lean torso. God, his hard body felt good against mine. I marveled at how well we fit together.

I took a moment to commit every detail to memory. This moment was surreal. I was Cinderella, and the wicked stepmother —or stepsister in this case—was getting kicked in the stomach by Prince Charming.

Geneva's eyes narrowed, her nose wrinkled as her cosmetically-altered lips curled with disgust. The look was priceless, one I hadn't seen in a long time.

Skater Boy leaned closer, his jaw flexed. He wasn't done with Geneva yet.

"Don't you have a groom, or a bridesmaid, or a photographer somewhere to bitch at instead of Hindley?" He shooed her away with the flick of his wrist, like she was a pesky gnat.

I bit back a laugh.

Wait, he'd remembered my name. And it sounded delectable from his mouth.

Geneva's cheeks flushed red and her jaw tightened. No one ever dared talk to Geneva Barton that way. God, I'd never wanted a camera so bad in my life.

Rory's arm tightened around my waist as he glared at Geneva. I could hear his silent words. *Go on, nobody wants you.*

Even if Skater Boy drove off right this very second and I never saw him again, I would remember this moment forever. It was the first time I could ever recall that Geneva Barton wasn't going to get what she wanted. Rory wanted me, not her.

I tightened my hold around Rory, dragging him closer as we stood here together. I silently dared Geneva to say another word. Today, *I* was getting the prize, and he came in the form of a gorgeous, sexy-as-sin man.

Steam practically spewed from Geneva's ears, she was so livid.

I laughed to myself. If I didn't know better, I would have sworn I saw piss running down the side of Geneva Barton's over-priced, ivory linen pants.

CHAPTER 8

RORY

DANA'S BEEMER SHOOK as I slammed the door shut. I was furious with Hindley's sister for making her feel like shit.

Geneva was a bully, just like Timmy Dubowski, and there was nothing I hated more. I hoped Hindley would find a way to shove that spider somewhere in that bitch's lunch, or preferably up her ass.

I touched the spot on my cheek where Hindley's lips had kissed me moments earlier. Closing my eyes, I remembered her beautiful smile as she'd steadied herself on my shoulders.

I'd inhaled her scent, my arm tightening around her waist.

She'd stretched up on her toes and leaned in close, to whisper in my ear. "I owe you one."

My dick had gone hard as stone. Images of her body—

"Hello," Dana yelled beside me. "Earth to Rory."

I jumped in my seat. "What?" Shit, where was I?

"So, you going tonight?"

"Going where?"

"To the wedding?"

"Oh, umm…I don't know." Did I want to get involved in this family's shit show? Probably not.

"But you just told Geneva you were Hindley's date for the evening. I think those were your exact words."

Shit, had I really said that? I'd been so furious with Geneva, I wanted to protect Hindley.

"You have to go, man," Dana's said. She sounded desperate and her plea hit me hard in the gut. "If you don't show up, Geneva will crucify her."

"Why?"

"Geneva *hates* Hindley."

"But they're sisters."

"By marriage only," Dana said, her lips pursed.

"Why does Hindley hate her sister?"

"Stepsister," she corrected. "Don't ever call Geneva Hindley's sister in front of her or she'll rip you a new one."

"Which one, Hindley or Geneva?"

"Both."

"Wow. They hate each other that much?" I definitely did *not* want to get involved.

"Geneva hates Hindley. Always has, ever since their parents got together years ago." Dana shook her head. "I don't know why. Geneva's pretty much gotten anything she's ever wanted, the spoiled little bitch."

"I know why she hates Hindley," I said quietly.

"What does that mean?" she asked.

I turned and studied Dana, unaware until that moment how attractive she was.

Her blue eyes reminded me of glacial water I'd seen once at a competition in Switzerland. Her eyes stood in stark contrast to her olive skin-tone and jet-black hair. The dimples that drilled into her cheeks anytime she smiled could slay a man.

Dana was definitely a hottie by any guy's standards, but she didn't hold a candle to Hindley. Not to me anyway.

Hindley's long blonde hair and dark chocolate eyes were a startling contrast. And those rosy-red lips practically begged a man to devour her. Just thinking about the smooth, creamy skin of her thighs had me about to lose my shit. I'd had a difficult time sleeping last night, picturing those long, toned legs wrapped around me—

"Hey!" Dana shouted.

Shit. I'd done it again.

"You want her, don't you?" Dana nudged my arm.

"No," I shot back a little too quickly. Maybe I did want her, but I'd never admit it. And I'd never act on it.

Judging from Hindley's house last night, it was easy to see the woman was a Braniac. Her shelves had been stacked full with some of the biggest books I'd ever seen. And her table was littered with all kinds of papers and files, important looking shit, not that I'd read them.

Dana laughed. "Liar."

I stared out the front windshield, afraid I may give myself away if I looked at her. I liked Hindley, more than I should.

"You should come tonight," Dana said.

"You're wrong, I really shouldn't." There were a million reasons why I shouldn't go to this wedding tonight.

"Whatever." Dana pulled out into the road. "Where to?"

I rattled off Leif's address and sunk back into my seat, reaching for my phone. I slid my hand into my pocket but instead, found something else—the one reason I knew I should go tonight. Pulling out the spider from my pocket, I opened my hand and stared down.

"What time should I pick you up tonight, One-Nighter?"

I glanced over at Dana.

She was staring down at the spider in my hand, a slow smile spreading across her face. Her blue eyes rolled up to meet mine as two huge dimples appeared on either side of her face.

Shit.

Clutching the spider in my hand, I knew in that moment I was going to this fucking wedding, like it or not. If for no other reason than to make sure Hindley was safe. Seeing Geneva piss all over her designer dress would be a bonus.

◠

I squirmed on the wooden pew, tugging at the collar of my shirt. I was going to pass out if this shit didn't start soon. Well, if I died at least I was in a church.

"Stop." Dana swatted my hand away, straightening my tie. "You look good, One-Nighter. Chris is going to have a shit fit. So is Geneva. I can't wait." Her shoulders shook with laughter and I couldn't help but join in. "That bitch has it coming." Dana was just as protective of Hindley as I was becoming.

"Chris is her ex, right?"

She nodded.

"He's that bad?"

"He dumped her in front of half the student body in college on Valentine's Day. Who the fuck does that?"

There was a time and a place to cut a woman loose, but in front of a crowd wasn't one of them.

"All because she wouldn't put out. I'd call that a major douche bag, wouldn't you?"

"Are you serious?"

"Totally."

"Uh, yeah." I nodded. "Total asshole."

Hindley's refusal to consummate their relationship had obviously damaged Chris's delicate ego. He hadn't wanted to just hurt her, he'd wanted to crush her. What better way to do that than through public humiliation? I hated him already. Bully.

Digging in my pocket, I rubbed the plastic spider. I silently vowed to shove his dick in the dirt tonight. If for no other reason than to give Hindley the revenge she deserved.

"Oh, here they come." Dana rubbed her hands together and rolled her lips like she was about to devour a delicious meal.

I couldn't help but laugh. I liked this girl.

The attendants marched down the aisle and a stab of disappointment hit my chest when I realized I'd only see the backside of Hindley. Well, I wasn't exactly disappointed. She had an ass that could stop traffic, even on a slow day.

"This shit is ridiculous," Dana said.

The couple in front of us jerked their heads and glared at Dana.

Dana raised her hands and scowled. "What the fuck are you looking at?"

They shook their heads and mumbled something about irreverence before turning back to watch the ceremony.

I chuckled.

"Now you know why they didn't invite me." She laughed.

"Are we wedding crashers?"

"No, you're not. Geneva allowed Hindley to bring one guest. Their parents shelled out an ass-load of money for this shin-dig, so I said, fuck it, I'm going."

"Are you her one guest?"

"I was." She smiled deviously. "But now that Hindley brought you, I couldn't resist showing up for the show."

"What show?"

Dana glanced up at me through her long, dark lashes and laughed, almost cackling. She was definitely a witch, a good witch, but still.

A surge of anxiety shot through my body, similar to the one I experienced right before a competition.

Dana stiffened next to me. "I can't believe that bitch did this," she said through gritted teeth as she lifted up to see over the couple in front of us. "She must have changed the lineup today."

"What are you talking about?" I searched the church.

"Up there." Dana nodded toward the front. "Hindley was supposed to be the second bridesmaid in the lineup. Her mom arranged the girls in order of height. But obviously Geneva changed them up at the last minute. Now Hindley is the last bridesmaid. That bitch," Dana growled.

"What's wrong with that?"

"Geneva paired Hindley with Chris."

"Who?"

She glared at me over her shoulder as if I was clueless, which I was. "The douche bag who dumped Hindley in college." She snapped several times. "Keep up, man."

"Her sister actually knows the douche bag?"

"Geneva's fiancé does, supposedly." Dana rolled her eyes. "Geneva couldn't wait to put that asshole in the wedding party once she found out Chris had humiliated Hindley. That slut did this on purpose. Now Hindley has to actually lock arms with that prick and wear a smile on her face while doing it." She shook her head. "Fucking whore. I'm going to kill Geneva, I don't care what Hindley says."

I made a mental note never to piss off Dana. "Calm down, tiger." I placed my hand on her shoulder and gently pushed her down into her seat.

Thankfully, the ceremony concluded quickly. When the minister pronounced the couple man and wife, they turned to face the crowd. Everyone cheered like they were at the Super Bowl. Geneva and her groom quickly descended the stairs and rushed down the aisle toward the back of the church as if the place was on fire.

Just as they reached our row, I noticed Geneva slow. She turned her head toward me and...winked.

What the fuck? Had she winked at me? I glanced behind me. Nope, no one. She'd definitely been winking at me, on her wedding day. This was seriously one fucked up chick.

I shook my head in disbelief and focused on the remainder of the wedding party now marching down the aisle. As each couple approached, my body vibrated with anticipation as I waited for Hindley.

Finally, she appeared, like a goddess. She was breathtaking, dressed in a corseted, strapless dress the color of a new copper penny. The design showcased her perky tits and small waist. Her long blonde hair fell over her bare shoulders in thick waves. Unfortunately, the dress fell to the floor, covering her best assets. Her long, lean legs.

My fingers twitched as I remembered the delicious softness of those smooth legs under my hands when I'd accidentally grazed mine against them last night. Okay, so maybe not so accidentally. My dick swelled thinking of how much I'd wanted to suck and lick those pretty little blue toes. Right before I threw her legs over my shoulders and—

"Oh, shit." Dana shoved my arm. "She's not doing well."

I focused on her face. Lines creased her forehead and the edges of eyes. She looked paler than normal. My gaze moved to her partner and instantly I understood the reason for her distress.

The Douche Bag.

He clutched her arm, rubbing her hand as he gazed down at her like he wanted to eat her alive.

Fucker.

Now I was glad I'd come. My need to protect Hindley wasn't surprising, but the twinge of jealousy in my chest was.

As if hearing my silent thoughts, Hindley turned her head, her gaze finding mine as our eyes locked. Her full lips spread into a magnificent smile and her dark brown eyes sparkled, lighting up her entire countenance.

God, she was beautiful, inside and out.

My own face split wide with a huge, dopey grin. A surge of desire shot through my veins. My body thrummed with excitement, the high better than any drug I'd ever taken or any contest I'd ever won.

"So, where's the reception?" I asked Dana, never taking my eyes off Hindley until she'd escaped through the back door.

"Dude, what the hell was that?"

"What was what?" I looked down at Dana.

"What the fuck just happened between the two of you?"

The high from earlier evaporated. "Nothing," I said.

Nothing could happen between us. As much as my body desired Hindley, my mind warned me not to try. We were from different worlds. I didn't need the drama of her life, and I'd never burden her with the secrets of mine.

"Nothing," I repeated. "It was nothing."

I sat back on the pew, releasing a heavy sigh. Sitting in a church where most people found peace, I'd never felt more defeated in my life.

CHAPTER 9

RORY

As we stepped into the grand ballroom of one of Austin's most exclusive hotels, I realized Dana hadn't lied. Hindley's parents had spared no expense for this wedding. I'd never seen anything like it.

Tables lined the entire ballroom, each covered with a starched, white linen table cloths. Massive flower arrangements, some almost as tall as I was, sat in the center of each table. They looked more fitting for a casket than a wedding.

Yards and yards of satiny material billowed from the ceiling, tied together in the center by a huge crystal chandelier. Soft pink lights strategically placed around the perimeter gave the room the feel of a sexy jazz night club.

At the front of the room, I noticed a stage and dance floor. The letters G and S were illuminated on the center with specialized lighting. Good God, these people had more money than sense.

The inadequacies of my childhood washed over me and threatened to pull me under. I seriously considered bolting. Then Hindley's beautiful face flashed in my mind, those chocolate brown eyes holding me captive. I had to see her one more time.

I walked up to a table just outside the ballroom and froze.

"Name please?" a young brunette sitting behind the table asked.

A cold sweat broke out on my forehead as I fisted my hands. These were name cards.

"Don't bother looking for yours," Dana said, strolling up beside me.

"What?"

"They just added you today so you won't find your place card here."

"What are you talking about?" God, I was stuttering, I was so nervous.

"Your table assignment," she said, nodding toward the cards. "Haven't you ever been to a wedding before?"

"Yeah, but they were usually at a courthouse or somebody's backyard."

She laughed but stopped abruptly. She covered her mouth when I stared down at her. "Oh, shit, you're serious?"

I nodded.

Her blue eyes went wide. "I'm sorry, I didn't mean—"

"It's all right." I was used to being judged. I could tell from Dana's expression she'd meant no harm.

"Come on." She grasped my hand and pulled me toward the end of the second table. "Here. You look in this row for my name and I'll look in these over on the other table. I think they're in alphabetical order. It's Dana Di Grazio. D-I capital G-R..."

Her words faded away, deafened by the pounding of my heart. My palms broke out in a cold sweat. "Uh, I have to take a leak," I mumbled. "I'll be right back."

"Oh, here it is." She held up a place card, waving it in the air. "We're at table fourteen. I'll see you inside."

"I'll follow you in."

She glanced back at me, her brows furrowed. "I thought you had to pee."

"Well, I don't want to miss seeing Hindley come in."

She smiled, deep dimples drilled into each cheek. "I bet you don't, One-Nighter. If y'all didn't have sex last night, you sure as hell did back in that church." She giggled. "How sacrilegious. I loved it. Maybe I should start going back to church."

I chuckled. Dana was bad, in a good way, and I was already falling a little in love with her, in a sisterly sort of way. My chest clenched at the thought of sisters, but before my thoughts could spiral into darkness, the DJ announced the happy couple had finally arrived.

I turned my attention to the back of the room and searched the large crowd of attendants. Finally, I saw her and my breath caught. She was even more beautiful close up.

Hindley searched the room like I had moments before, her brows furrowed. Was she looking for me? God, I hoped so.

Look at me, I called out silently.

As if hearing my plea, her eyes found mine. A slow smile spread across her face as she walked toward me. She jerked to a stop just before she'd reached me, as if she'd slammed into an invisible wall.

"You came," she said softly, staring up at me.

I couldn't tell if it was a statement or a question.

"Yeah." I smiled. "I did."

Her face washed red as she stared down at the carpet. Was she being shy now?

I lifted her head with my finger and waited for her eyes to meet mine. "I had to get my spider back."

She giggled.

Something prickled in my chest at the sound of her laughter. Warning bells sounded in my head. I was quickly becoming addicted to this girl. Her ability to quiet my racing mind was unnerving.

"Or did you already use it?" I asked.

"I'll never tell." She moved in closer, leaning against me.

The scent of her perfume tickled my nose. Fuck, she even *smelled* amazing.

"But if I were you," she whispered, "I'd stay away from the wedding cake."

I pressed my hands to my legs to keep them from grabbing her by the waist and sweeping upstairs to one of the hotel rooms. My desire to fuck her senseless in all kinds of crazy ways that I knew would drive us both insane was slowly taking over.

"You didn't!" Dana shrieked.

Hindley shrugged her shoulders. "Maybe." She and Dana burst into laughter.

I stood stock still, willing my dick to calm the fuck down. There was a bar in the back of the room. Maybe a walk around the place would help cool my libido. Besides, Hindley could probably use a little liquid courage.

"You guys want something to drink?" I asked.

Dana grinned, a deviant twinkle in her blue eyes. "Why don't y'all get me a bottle of the most expensive champagne you can find?"

"You know Paul is paying for this wedding, not Geneva?" Hindley asked.

"In that case, give the bottle to Geneva." Her smile grew as she leaned in closer. "But be sure to shake it up first then point the bottle right at that bitch's smug face before you pop the cork."

"Dana." Hindley swatted her arm. "It's her wedding day."

Dana rolled her eyes. "Oh, please, like this shit is going to last. Besides, she deserves a lot worse than champagne in the face for that little stunt she pulled with Chris."

Hindley stiffened and her smile fell.

I slipped my hand into hers and gently squeezed. "Come on. Let's go."

Hindley looked down at our joined hands, her long lashes spread across her cheeks like dark fans. Slowly her gaze swept up my body, drinking in every inch of me.

I swallowed down my desire and forced my dick into submission.

When her eyes finally met mine, she sucked in a breath. Her chest rose high, accentuating those perfect tits in her corseted dress. Her examination of my body was one of the most erotic things I'd ever seen or been a part of in my life—and I'd done some crazy shit, so that was saying something. Everything from my waist down cried out in agony, begging for release.

"You two are doing it again," Dana said.

"Doing what?" Hindley asked.

Dana nodded toward us. "Optic copulation. You were doing it at the church too."

Hindley's brows pinched together. "Optic what?"

"Optic copulation. Eye fucking each other."

"Dana," Hindley growled, her eyes darting around the room.

"What? I'm not the one doing it. Unfortunately." Her shoulders sagged.

I bit back a laugh, but failed, chuckling under my breath.

Hindley narrowed her eyes. "Don't encourage her."

Apparently, Hindley didn't see the humor. That only made me laugh harder.

"Come on." She tugged on my hand. After several steps, she glanced back at me. Her long blonde hair slid over her bare shoulder and tumbled down her bare back, caressing her ivory skin. I'd never been more jealous of hair in my life.

I'd been wrong earlier. *This* moment, *this* woman—walking gracefully across a room, so completely unaware of her own sensuality—was the most erotic thing I'd ever seen. My half-mast cock was now flying at full-staff. A raging hard-on pressed painfully against the zipper of my dress pants.

Hindley nodded toward Dana, unaware of my discomfort. "I'm sorry about her."

I couldn't answer, I couldn't think. All the blood from my brain was pulsating in my dick. Hindley was like a wet dream come to life.

Had it really been less than twenty-four hours since this girl had been down on all fours in front of me, puking her guts up all over the sidewalk? I realized in that moment, Hindley had been just as appealing to me last night, drunk as a skunk as she was right now. Her beauty transcended the physical realm.

"Rory?"

God, my name rolling off her tongue was like healing music, better than any song I'd ever downloaded.

"Rory," she said louder, tugging my hand.

"Oh, uh," I stuttered like a horny teen, "I'm sorry."

"This is my stepfather, Paul Barton."

Stepfather? Did she just say stepfather? Oh, fuck me.

"Paul, this is Rory."

I shook my head like a cartoon character trying to clear my mind.

"Hello, Rory."

Oh, shit. What was I supposed to say now? It wasn't like I could tell him what was really on my mind.

Hello, sir, it's nice to meet you. I was just eye fuckin' your daughter two minutes ago and fantasizing about dragging her upstairs and sinking my dick in her so far she wouldn't walk straight for a week.

No. Definitely couldn't say that.

I glanced down and saw his hand held out. Jeez, how long had he been standing there like a dope?

I grasped his hand and shook. "Hello, sir." My voice cracked like a pubescent boy.

He gave me one solid shake that was firm but not overbearing.

I studied Hindley's father. He was a well-built man with thick, dark hair graying on the edges. He wasn't as tall as me, but he was in decent shape and could definitely kick my ass. Probably would if he knew what I was fantasizing about doing to his daughter, or her doing to me with those full pink lips.

As if reading my mind, her father's grip tightened and I winced. "Does Rory have a last name?" he asked, his eyes never leaving mine.

Hindley's eyes widened.

Shit. She didn't know my name.

Paul kept one hand fisted around mine as he brought his other up to my shoulder, squeezing to the point of pain. He leaned in and brought his face closer to mine, speaking slowly and softly.

"Perhaps by the end of the evening, you'd be so kind as to properly introduce yourself to my daughter before you peel that banana in your pants and try to feed it to her again, okay, player?" He slapped my shoulder once, releasing my hand and stepping back.

I stood in stunned silence, praying my mouth wasn't on the floor. I wasn't fooling anyone at this fucking wedding, least of all Hindley's father.

The worst part of all was the fact that he obviously believed Hindley and I had already slept together, without knowing one another. Anyone could tell just from looking at her that Hindley wasn't that kind of girl. Me? Well, that was a different story.

Her father gave me a nod that clearly said, *Leave my daughter alone, asshole,* before turning toward Hindley, gently caressing her shoulders. "You look stunning tonight, sweetheart. You're stealing the show."

Pride and adoration shone in Paul's eyes. Hindley was obviously special to him and I'd fucked up, royally. Not that it mattered, I'd already decided Hindley and I had no future. But a guy could dream.

Paul lightly kissed her cheek and Hindley's face beamed. She adored her father, anyone within fifty feet could see that.

"Don't let her drink too much, Rory," Paul said, glancing back at me as he let Hindley go. "She doesn't hold her liquor well."

Hindley cut her gaze toward me and we both stifled a laugh. "I don't think I'll be drinking again for a while, Paul," she said.

"Yes, so I heard." He winked at Hindley.

He didn't seem pissed that his daughter had gotten so shit-faced drunk last night that she'd allowed a total stranger to take her home. In fact, he seemed tickled to know his daughter had tied one on. If he only knew the real story, he wouldn't be happy at all. Paul would be just as furious as I had been.

"Well, you two have fun tonight." Paul's gaze travelled up and down my body as a slow smirk spread across his face. "But not too much."

I laughed to myself. So, Paul Barton had a sense of humor. Good to know.

"Paul!" Hindley shrieked. "You're as bad as Dana, I swear."

"Nobody's that bad, Hindley." Paul snorted.

Hindley nodded. "True."

Paul turned to face me. "Take care of her, Rory With No Last Name." Before I could respond, Paul Barton disappeared into the sea of guests. And I stood, speechless, trying not to feel like the degenerate that I was.

"Hey." Hindley tugged on my hand. "What's wrong?"

I looked down at her.

Her brows were furrowed, her lips pressed tightly together.

"Nothing." I shook my head.

"Please don't let Paul get to you. He loves intimidating people." She smiled, patting my chest.

The warmth from her hand spread through my body, heating up my midsection.

"He's a great guy, once you get to know him," she said.

"Who?"

"Paul, silly." She swatted my chest.

"Yeah, easy for you to say. You weren't the one he was grilling." I rubbed my hand. "And the dude has one hell of a grip."

"Well, thankfully for you, you're not asking for my hand in marriage. You're just my stand-in guy for tonight, right?"

Hindley's words sobered me. I was her stand-in guy, not a stand-up guy. I didn't belong in her world. I was here to protect her from her bitchy stepsister and jerk-wad of an ex-boyfriend. Nothing more.

"Oh, no." She covered her mouth and her eyes went wide. "That came out wrong. I'm sorry," she whispered.

"Sorry for what? You're right. It's not like I'm going to ask you to marry me." I laughed nervously. "Well, not tonight anyway."

Hindley remained quiet for several moments, her eyes searching mine. "You're not just a stand-in, Rory. Not to me. I hope you know that," she said quietly, gliding her fingertips up and down my arm.

Her touch had my dick swelling to painful limits. I wondered what those fingertips would feel like gliding over my bare chest, and lower. Fuck.

Her brown eyes held mine, the depths of remorse surprising me. "You're much more than that to me," she said. "I tried to make a joke but obviously it wasn't funny and I apologize. I'm not really a funny person. I hope you'll forgive me."

I stared at her, at a loss for words. I wasn't used to receiving words of apology from women. It was usually me asking for their forgiveness.

"I do care about you, Rory," she continued. "And no matter what you tell yourself, I know you care about me too or you wouldn't be here tonight. Or last night."

Hindley was the most genuine, honest, real person I'd met in a long time.

I didn't respond. I had no smart-ass comeback or words of self-deprecating sarcasm. Instead, I turned to the bartender, ignoring her comments before I did something really stupid. Like kiss her.

"A glass of champagne and two waters please," I said. Hindley didn't need any more alcohol tonight.

The bartender nodded. "Sure thing." He moved quickly, pouring the drinks and setting them on the bar.

I slid a fifty-dollar bill toward him.

He waved off the money. "Thanks, man, but it's an open bar."

I fished in my wallet and pulled out a twenty instead, stuffing it in his tip jar. "Thanks."

"No, thank you." The bartender smiled before moving down to help another couple.

I turned and held out a water toward Hindley.

She was staring at me, one hand held to her chest, her head tilted. "That was really nice."

"What?" I glanced over my shoulder. "The guy's a bartender. That's how he makes his living."

"I know, but that was a lot of money for one drink."

Did she think I couldn't afford a fucking drink? I may not be as rich as some of these assholes in this ballroom, but I made decent money doing what I loved.

Hindley squeezed my arm. "Hey," she whispered, waiting until my eyes caught hers. "I'm sorry. I didn't mean to insult you. It was a nice gesture to offer him so much money, that's all I meant. I grew up with rich, entitled people, and now I work with them. It's nice to be with someone who's so down to earth."

I slipped an arm around her waist and pulled her close. "No, I'm sorry," I said, surprised at how easily the words rolled off my tongue. I usually made no apologies for the way I lived life.

Her warm, chocolate brown eyes searched mine before her lips spread in a slow smile. Her head fell against me, her cheek pressing against my chest.

Something painful squeezed my heart and I couldn't breathe. I wondered if this was how the Grinch felt when the villagers of Whoville welcomed him in after having been such a shithead for stealing all their Christmas gifts.

Having Hindley cuddled against felt...natural—like home, a home I'd been searching for my entire life. I pulled her closer.

She raised her head and her body stiffened. "Oh, crap."

I released her and stepped back, afraid Paul had finally come back to kick my ass. "What?"

"It's my ex," she whispered. "He's on his way over here."

I snaked my arm around her waist again and drew her close. Her body molded against mine as she wrapped her arms around me like we'd been together for years. This felt right. Too right.

I watched as a tall, lanky dude approached the bar. I recognized him from the service earlier. He looked like a snotty, rich boy, his nose so high in the air he'd drown if it rained.

Dipshit stared me up and down and curled his lip. I thought he might actually call security and have me tossed out. Judgmental prick.

My protective nature kicked into high gear. I squeezed Hindley. "Follow my lead," I whispered in her ear.

She shivered in my arms. Good girl.

Dipshit stopped at the bar, completely ignoring us. He sighed audibly, as if he were bored with the whole event. "What brand of Chardonnay do you have?" he asked.

Chardonnay? Seriously? I snorted. The kids from my old neighborhood would have beat the fuck out of me if I had ever asked for a bottle of wine at the E-Z Mart.

Dipshit glanced toward me, raising a perfectly manicured brow. The fucker probably had it waxed during his facials. "Something funny?" he asked.

Oh, yeah, asshole. It's about to get *real* funny up in here. This guy was a total prick. Rubbing his dick in the dirt was going to be like shooting fish in a barrel.

When I said nothing, he turned his attention to Hindley. His pervy gaze roamed up and down her body. His look of lust from earlier was gone, replaced with disgust, as if she were beneath him. Probably because she was wrapped around a prick like me.

I pulled her closer and smiled when she tightened her grip around me.

"Thanks for walking with me today, Hindley," he said, his words sounding as insincere as the look on his face. "I'm sure it wasn't easy for you, given our history."

I glanced down at Hindley and bit back another laugh. What a fucking moron. He'd thrown away the most valuable thing he'd ever get in his pathetic little life.

Hindley shrugged, her body stiff, eyes dulled with pain. "Anything for Geneva, right?"

Fuck this. It was show time.

"Baby," I said in a whiny voice, "how much longer do we have to stay?"

Hindley gazed up at me, her head tilted, brows furrowed. God, I hoped she would play along.

"I'm sorry, babe. It's just that you look so fucking hot in that dress," I said, practically growling. My eyes devoured her body. "I don't know how much longer I'm going to be able to keep my dick in my pants without blowing a load all over this ballroom."

Dipshit choked on his wine, spitting his drink all over his over-priced tuxedo.

Hindley bit back a laugh but raised a brow, cautioning me.

She may be worried about this fucker, but I wasn't.

"Rory, I don't think you've met Chris." Her voice sounded even and unaffected, as if my raunchy comment was something she heard every day.

"Hey, man." I grabbed some napkins off the bar and held them out. "May want to wipe that." I nodded toward his chin.

He snatched the napkin from my hand and wiped his face, then his tuxedo. He didn't even glance behind him when he tossed the crumpled napkin toward the bartender like he was a peon.

He stared at me, then down to my outstretched hand like I had a disease before finally shaking.

His hand was small, cold, and clammy, probably just like his dick.

I smiled, realizing just how easy it was going to be to take this asshole down. "It's nice to meet you. Chris, Putz-man, is it?" I knew his real name but thought Putz-man was a better title for this douche bag.

Hindley snorted and turned her face into my chest.

I squeezed her, biting back my own laugh.

Slowly she raised her head. "Sorry," she said, biting her lip as she fought not to laugh again.

"It's Putman," Dipshit said, annunciating his name. Like it mattered.

"Oh, yeah, sorry about that, man." I slapped his shoulder, nearly knocking him over. "I've heard a lot about you."

He smirked. "So, Hindley still talks about me, huh?"

"No, not Hindley." I shook my head. "She's never told me about you."

Dipshit's smile fell.

"Dana was filling me in on the way over here," I said. "She told me what a major dumbass you are."

He choked on his Chardonnay. Again. "Excuse me?"

Here it was, my chance to shine. I was about to make this fuckwad regret ever hurting Hindley.

"You know, Putman," I said, scratching my chin, "my dad used to take me fishing when I was young."

"How wonderful for you." He rolled his eyes.

Fucker.

I continued, unfazed by his disinterest. "I always wanted to keep every fish I caught, even the small ones. I'd be so stoked, all that adrenaline pumping through my veins. You know what I mean?"

"No," he said, but leaned in closer. He was interested, and that was all I needed for bait.

"But my dad was smarter than me." I tapped my temple. "Most dads are, right?" I had no fucking clue what most dads did. I'd never met mine. And I sure as shit had never been fishing. "Anyway, my dad would always talk me into throwing the small fish back, no matter how much I begged. You know why, Chris?"

Dipshit leaned back against the bar, crossing his arms over his scrawny chest, one brow raised. "No, why?"

I smiled. Dick face had taken the bait, so like any good hunter, I went in for the kill.

"My dad told me that if I threw the small ones back, in a year or two they'd grow to ten times their size." I stared at Chris, wanting to drive my point home. "He promised that if I was patient and waited for the fish to grow, we would come back in a few years and catch them. He said they'd so big by that time, we would easily win any tournament we entered."

"Okay." Dipshit tilted his head and thrummed his fingers as if I were wasting his time. "That was a riveting story."

What a prick. I'd never wanted to punch someone in the face so bad.

"And your point is?" he said in his whiny little voice.

I stepped in closer, my eyes boring into his with my most intimidating glare. "My point is, *dipshit*...you weren't patient. You gave up on Hindley too soon. I didn't. I waited for her, waited for her to grow into the beautiful woman she is today." My eyes roamed over Hindley's incredible body. "And damn, she was worth it," I added, meaning every word.

I tugged Hindley as close to me as humanly possible. "You see, Chris, I captured her, body and soul, and now she's *my* grand prize." I drew in a deep, steadying breath. My next statement would be his undoing, and possibly Hindley's. "Me and my dick thank you for being the biggest dipshit on the face of the earth."

His mouth fell open, as did Hindley's I was pretty sure.

I narrowed my eyes. "You're a complete moron. This chick's a fuckin' monster in the sack, but you'll never know what you threw back. I promise you though, every night, and sometimes twice on Sundays, me and my dick sure as shit do."

I turned to Hindley. I'd pushed her well past her comfort zone. She was a sophisticated woman and probably completely mortified by my words. She wouldn't stay quiet. She would feel the need to make excuses. I had to keep her from talking if my words were going to have the maximum effect on Dipshit.

My eyes lit up in amusement when I realized the best way to keep her mouth shut was to cover it with mine.

CHAPTER 10

HINDLEY

THE MOMENT RORY'S lips touched mine I knew I was in trouble.

The sane part of my brain—the one that had finished college despite all the odds, the one that had been accepted into law school and passed with almost flying colors—said push him away. Slap his face and escort him out of the hotel. But the other side of my mind—the irrational side, which was rarely used—screamed, "Live in the moment, Hindley. For once, forget about the future and stop doing what everyone expects you to."

That side of my brain was winning the war raging inside me.

The pressure of his lips against mine was a perfect combination of tenderness mixed with raw animal desire. Everything about this man was delicious, unlike anything I'd ever experienced in my life.

His tongue parted my lips, asking me for more.

My mouth opened and I moaned when his tongue seductively stroked mine.

Sometimes people talk about seeing fireworks when they kiss. That didn't happen for me with Rory. I felt the fireworks, the explosion pulsating between my legs with a need so deep I couldn't breathe.

I wrapped my arms around his neck, pulling him closer. My

tongue pressed deeper, my mouth begging for more. I was certain that my response was polar opposite to what Rory expected.

In response, he groaned into my mouth, tilting his head to deepen the kiss.

The vibrations from his deep voice sent me over the edge. My hips pressed against him, delighting in the feel of his hard, lean body. Suddenly our kiss went from make-believe to full-on desire.

Rory's arms tightened around my waist. He pulled me flush to his body as if he were trying to make me part of him. His hands travelled my back, one moving up to tangle in my hair, the other slipping down, cupping my butt. He squeezed and pulled me up, rocking his body into mine, nearly lifting me off the floor.

I knew I should stop. This was inappropriate, for a number of reasons. None of which came to mind at the moment.

Rory thrust his hips into mine and I could feel how hard he was. For me.

Something inside my body burst with need. Instead of pulling away like the old me would have, I wound my fingers into his thick hair, gripping him tight

Our kiss deepened and desire surged through my veins, pooling between my legs. I feared I might spontaneously combust with need. I'd never felt this out of control, this desirable, this desperate, in my life. It was addictive, and I didn't want it to end. Ever.

"Get a room!" someone shouted.

I stumbled backward, breaking our kiss. My head spun and I blinked several times, my eyes unable to focus on anything. I felt drunker from one kiss with Skater Boy than I had from all the tequila I'd drank last night.

I stared down at my dress, unable to meet Rory's gaze. He was probably disappointed. I didn't have a lot of experience with men. I straightened the twisted material of my dress and smoothed back my hair. I needed to compose myself before I dared look at him.

Slowly I raised my head.

Rory's lips curled into a devilish smirk. His blue eyes twinkled with mischief, as if he'd gotten away with the most diabolical crime. Actually, he had.

I'd never kissed anyone like that in my life, let alone in a crowded room full of stuck-up socialites. I should have been ashamed, mortified, humiliated even. But all I could think of was how sensual the experience was, how wanton Rory made me feel, and how much I craved his mouth on mine again.

"Nice, Drunk Girl," he said, his voice deep and raspy.

I exhaled a deep sigh of relief. He wasn't disappointed, thank God. I stepped closer, my thumb trailing across his bottom lip to wipe away my gloss. Even though I knew it wasn't a good idea to touch him again, I couldn't resist.

I moved to pull away but Rory grabbed my hand, lifting it to his mouth. I stood paralyzed, my eyes locked on his lips as they gently pressed his mouth against the inside of my wrist.

I shivered as goose bumps spread over my heated skin. Parts of my body that had laid dormant for years suddenly throbbed with desire. Rory's kisses were erotic and forbidden, everything I knew nothing about.

I had to get the hell out of here before I threw myself in his arms and begged him to take me right here in the middle of the grand ballroom. "I, uh," my voice broke, "I, I'm going to go to the ladies' room and freshen up my makeup."

I turned to leave but Rory tugged me back, his fingers slipping under my chin. He lifted my face, forcing me to look up at him. I knew it wasn't a good idea. He was like the sun, a blazing fireball. If I stared too long, I might go blind. Or worse, be burned alive.

Unable to stop myself, my eyes found his. The light blue from earlier had turned a deep sapphire. His expression was wicked, and delicious. Rory had a way of drawing me in to his sexual vortex. If I wasn't careful, I'd be swept away.

"Okay," he whispered in a husky voice.

My insides melted and I nearly orgasmed from that one word.

"Don't be gone long though." His lips turned up into that half-grin I was already growing addicted to.

My face burned with embarrassment, afraid he could read my thoughts.

"I don't know a soul here except Dana," he said, "and from the looks of it, she's about ready to explode on both of us."

I glanced over my shoulder.

Dana stood next to our table, two thumbs ups as she dry-humped the air. "Get it, girl!" she shouted.

Oh. My. God.

I ducked my head and raced toward the exit, praying Rory wouldn't follow. I wound my way through the hall until I found the bathroom. Pushing the door open and walking inside, I leaned against the wall with a huge sigh. What the hell had I just done?

"Are you all right?" someone asked.

I glanced down.

An older woman sat on a stool next to the vanity. Trays filled with perfumes, lotions, and candies sat beside to her. She held out a small tin. "Do you need a mint?"

I shook my head. What I needed was a shot of vodka. My stomach rumbled at the thought. Maybe not. That's how I'd gotten in to this mess in the first place.

"Are you sure?" she asked.

I nodded, still unable to speak after my kiss with Rory. Had it been real? Or was it just for show? Probably just for show. Why would Rory want to kiss me? Especially after last night. I shook my head. It didn't matter anyway.

A toilet flushed at the far end of the bathroom just before the door of the handicapped stall swung open with a bang.

I jumped.

"*Oh, Dios mio*," the older woman said, clutching her chest.

Geneva waddled out, hands fisting the front of her wedding dress as she lifted the material off the floor.

"Geneva, wait!" Wendy yelled, stumbling behind her as she lifted the rest of Geneva's massive dress over her head. You could barely see the poor girl through all the satin and tulle. The two stumbled and nearly fell over. It looked like a bad comedy sketch from *I Love Lucy*, and I couldn't help but laugh under my breath.

Geneva's gaze snapped to me. "What's so funny?"

"Nothing," I said, swallowing back another giggle. I leaned over the vanity and stared at my reflection. My face was flushed rosy pink, my hair a ratted mess. Touching my kiss-swollen lips I realized I looked thoroughly ravaged, and I loved it. I couldn't hold back my smile.

"Aren't you even going to congratulate me?" Geneva asked, interrupting my thoughts.

"Congratulations," I said, keeping my gaze fixed on the mirror. Reaching inside my dress, I pulled out a tube of pink lip gloss.

"So, who's this new love interest?" Geneva said. "He's hot. Even though he was a complete dick to me before my luncheon."

"He's super hot," Wendy added.

My wand of lip gloss stopped mid-way to my mouth. Had Geneva and Wendy seen Rory and me kissing? Oh, shit. What if Paul saw Rory and me making out? Or worse yet, my mother?

"Hindley," Geneva said.

I smoothed the gloss over my lips and twisted the cap back on. "He's just a friend." It wasn't a lie.

"I've never kissed a friend the way you kissed him."

Crap, she had seen us.

"I tell you though, I wouldn't mind kissing him," Geneva said under her breath.

"Geneva," Wendy swatted at her, "you just got married."

"Just because a girl's on a diet doesn't mean she can't look at the menu. Am I right?" Geneva laughed, the sound echoing off the tile walls.

My eyes stayed glued to the mirror.

"I'm kidding," Geneva said, "jeez, lighten up."

I wanted to believe her but I'd grown up with Geneva Barton. I knew exactly what she was capable of and wouldn't put kissing another dude on her wedding day past her.

"You look good tonight," Geneva said.

I turned, my eyes wide with shock. Compliments from Geneva were rare, and usually came right before she did something nasty to me.

"Probably because I picked out the dress." She snorted.

I turned to face her, trying to mask my surprise. "Thanks."

"So, tell me about your *friend*," she said sarcastically. "Besides being an ass to me. Is he good in bed?"

"He's just a friend, Geneva," I repeated.

"So, who is he? You were sucking face with him pretty good out there."

"Just a guy."

Geneva stepped closer. "Where'd you meet him?"

Oh, no. How the hell was I supposed to answer that question? I was a horrible liar. I decided to go with a form of the truth. "I met him at a bar." Even though I don't remember it.

"Last night?"

The bathroom door flung open with a bang, saving me from answering.

We all turned.

"What's up, bitches?" Dana's voice echoed through the bathroom.

My saving grace. Again.

Dana strolled toward us, one perfectly sculptured eyebrow raised in mischief. "Congrats there, Gen. Looks like you got yourself a real fine man there. I'm kind of jealous." Dana smiled but I could tell it wasn't genuine. You could barely see either of her dimples.

The woman had a gift for sounding sincere when she was really full of crap. Most people never knew but I could smell Di Grazio bullshit from a mile away.

"Thank you," Geneva said, her comment sounding more like a question. Obviously, she couldn't tell Dana's shit from her shine.

"Don't you love Hindley's new beau?" Dana said. "Damn, he's fine."

"He sure is," Wendy said.

An evil smile spread across Geneva's face. "I was just asking Hindley where they met."

"Oh, he's my cousin's friend," Dana said without missing a beat. She was a natural born liar but only utilized the skill for the greater good of mankind, namely me. Tonight, I was glad she'd mastered the art of ambiguity. "I introduced them a few weeks back and they've been inseparable ever since."

"Why am I just now hearing about him?"

"Probably because if you met him before you got married, you'd try to ride his skin bus to Tuna Town."

I rolled my eyes. Dana could be so crass.

Geneva laughed.

Dana leaned in closer. "Although this morning, he pretty much shut you down. You definitely won't be getting a ticket to ride on that meat wagon." Dana stepped back, fanning her face. "Ouch. That must have hurt like shit when he set your ass straight, huh, Gen?"

Geneva's eyes narrowed as her face flamed red. I feared she might stroke out.

Dana played with one of the bottles of perfume. "He's the reason Hindley was late to your luncheon you know."

Oh, crap. This was off the script. What was she doing? Geneva was a master bull shitter and could smell a phony story from a mile away.

I turned, begging Dana with my eyes not to say more.

"What do you mean?" Geneva asked. Great. We'd awoken the beast.

"Well," Dana stepped closer, "when I busted in on them this morning—let's just say the pay-per-view sex channel looked like Sesame Street compared to those two, if you know what I mean." Dana waggled her brows and gave Geneva an innocent wink that was anything but. "They were fuckin' like two dogs in heat."

"Dana!" My voice echoed off the bathroom walls. I was more than mortified. I was furious. I didn't want anyone to think I'd been intimate with Rory, especially Geneva. Not only was it untrue, it gave Geneva too much information, information that she would use against me one day very soon, I had no doubt.

Geneva leaned back on the bathroom counter, hands crossed over her chest. "Well, well, look at you, Hinny Bin. Looks like you've finally taken a trip to the wild side. Although I must say, I'm surprised you could do anything at all last night, you were so hammered. Isadora said she saw you puking your guts up in the bathroom."

Before I could make excuses, Dana started in again. "Hindley was so wasted last night, Rory had to come pick her up."

"His name is Rory?" Geneva asked.

"Yeah."

"Rory what?" she asked.

Shit. I really needed to find out this guy's last name.

Dana continued as if she hadn't heard Geneva's question. "Rory wasn't too happy with you when he got to the club. Said he couldn't believe you'd left her all alone."

Geneva glanced at me. "You should have told me you were leaving."

She'd seen me leave.

"Well, it doesn't matter," Dana said. "Apparently, Rory's got some special tonic that helps with hangovers."

"I wish I had some of that this morning," Wendy said. I'd completely forgotten she was in the room. Poor thing was nearly covered by Geneva's huge dress.

Dana nodded toward me. "It obviously worked for Hindley because this morning he was on her hot little body like a monkey on a football. She was happily taking it too. And I mean *all* of it, if you know what I mean." Dana dry humped the counter.

"God, you're so foul, Dana." Geneva's faced bunched.

I had no idea why Geneva pretended to be offended. She had a wild side to her that could be just as vulgar. She just never showed her dark side to high society.

"Thanks," Dana said, smiling, dimples on display. "Coming

from you I consider that a compliment, Mrs. Stanley Winston."
Dana paused and looked at me.

"The third," we said in unison.

Geneva's eyes darted between the two of us, knowing we were being sarcastic. "Fuck you both." She pushed past us, stomping toward the door, nearly knocking over the attendant and all of her belongings. "Watch it you idiot." She glared at the woman. "If you get anything on this Mauro Adami wedding dress, I'll sue this whole damn hotel, and you personally. This is imported Italian silk, you imbecile."

The woman recoiled, crossing her arms over her body for protection.

Geneva had a way of evoking fear in almost anyone with one lethal glare. Everyone except Dana Di Grazio. And now Rory With No Last Name.

"Congratulations again on your wedding!" Dana shouted as Geneva rushed through the swinging door. "I'm sure you'll be very happy." The door closed just as Dana turned toward me. "In hell that is," she added, giggling hysterically.

"Why the hell did you tell her about Rory?"

She patted my shoulder. "Calm down."

"I can't calm down. You know Geneva will use that information against me. And it's not even true. I didn't sleep with him. Paul knows I don't even know his last name."

"What?"

"And now she's going to tell him we've been dating for weeks." God, now I was rambling.

"I'll go smooth it over with your dad."

Tears burned the back of my eyes.

Dana squeezed my shoulders. "Hey, it's going to be okay."

I stared down at her, wanting to believe her.

"Look, I'm sorry. You know I love to get Geneva all worked up. I'm sorry it came at your expense. I'll go tell her I was yanking her chain if you want me to."

"Forget it. She'll just figure out another way to screw me over no matter what you say."

"Are you sure?"

I nodded. "Yeah, I'm sure."

"Okay, good." Dana hopped up onto the counter and leaned her back against the mirror. She crossed her arms over her chest. "So. Now that we've got your evil bitch of a stepsister out of our hair, tell me about that kiss." She waggled her brows and smiled, her deep dimples on display.

I laughed and jumped up beside her, proceeding to tell her everything. Just like I always had since we were seven years old.

CHAPTER 11

HINDLEY

"I'M STARVING," Dana said as we returned to the ballroom. "Are they serving food yet?"

"You're always starving." I laughed. Glancing down at her petite frame, I shook my head. "I have no idea how you stay so tiny."

She reached down and cupped her large breasts. "I've got to eat enough to keep these girls happy."

"Yes, we wouldn't want your boobs to starve."

"Exactly," she exclaimed. "You *so* get me, girl."

"We get each other." I smiled at the truth of it.

"True, true." Dana stood high on her heels. "Hey, where's your boy?"

I glanced around the room but didn't see Rory anywhere. If he were smart, he would have left by now. My chest tightened at the thought. As much as I didn't want to admit it to myself, I wanted to see him again. "I don't know."

"Well, I'm hitting the bar. Do you want anything? Water, soda, a shot of tequila." She laughed.

I rolled my eyes. "God, no. I'm going to sit down."

"That kiss took it out of you, huh?" Dana waggled her brows.

"Something like that." Between my hangover, the kiss with

Rory, and my confrontation with Geneva earlier, my body was wiped. All I wanted to do was go home and crawl into bed. My mother would never allow me to leave early though.

Dana waved her fingers. "I'll meet you back up at the table."

"Okay, see you in a bit." I walked toward our table, still searching for Rory. I lifted a silent prayer that Geneva hadn't actually spoken to him. I wouldn't be surprised if she'd already made a move on him. Nothing shocked me about my stepsister any more.

Our table was completely empty, including the chair next to mine. Rory had definitely left. Feeling defeated, I sank down into my chair. Why was I surprised?

"Seems like your gentleman friend is very popular with the kids."

I turned to find my mother standing next to me, staring at the corner of the room.

"Where?" I asked.

"Over there." She pointed toward the back of the ballroom as she sat down next to me.

Glancing over my shoulder, I saw Rory surrounded by several boys. His feet were straddled as if he were on a surfboard, his hands spread wide as he spoke.

The boys watched with rapt fascination.

One of the smaller kids tugged on Rory's suit jacket.

Rory turned and glanced down, smiling at the young boy as he bent down on one knee beside him.

The boy's eyes widened, his mouth hanging open in obvious awe.

What in the world?

The boy held out a magazine and pen.

Rory took both with a smile, talking to the kid for a few moments before scribbling something on the cover. Before Rory could finish, another boy shoved something in his face and Rory signed it too.

What was going on? Was Rory someone famous? Obviously,

these kids thought so. Then I remembered, I still didn't know his last name.

"Not too bad with the ladies either," my mother said.

I stared at my mother, wondering what she was talking about

She was gazing at the bar where several women were shamelessly gawking at Rory like he was a male stripper. My body heated with a surge of jealousy I'd never experienced.

"It's all right, sweetheart." My mother patted my knee. "It's obvious to everyone that you're the object of his affection. Tonight," she said under her breath.

"What is that supposed to mean?"

"That kiss was something else, huh? I haven't seen passion like that since Paul and I started going out."

Gag. The thought of my mother and Paul sucking face turned my stomach almost as much as the tequila last night.

It hadn't escaped me that my mother had completely ignored my question. It was a specialty of hers, sweeping things under the rug and ignoring the elephants in the room.

She let out a loud sigh and sank back in her chair. "Makes me wish I was twenty again." Her green eyes glazed over with a dreamy look, and I knew my stepfather couldn't be far away.

I followed her gaze, not surprised to see Paul standing a few tables away. With dark hair, blue eyes and a body that could still knock down a man half his age, I had to admit that Paul Barton was attractive.

My mother was drawn to more than just Paul's good looks. He was intelligent and walked with confidence, not in a conceited way. And despite his teasing with Rory early, he was a kind man, forgiving, unable to hold a grudge, unlike his daughter. I had to admit, my mother had chosen well.

I was actually jealous of my mom and Paul in many ways. The fire and passion they'd found in each other years ago had never faded. After almost fifteen years of marriage, they still acted like teenagers in love—sometimes teens in heat. The only thing Geneva and I had in common was our mutual mortification of our parents' make-out sessions.

As if feeling my mother's gaze, Paul turned his head, his blue eyes connecting with hers. They were half-lidded and darker than usual.

Oh, God. I quickly looked away. What had Dana called it earlier? Eye copulation? Yeah, they were definitely eye fucking each other.

"So, tell me about this boy," my mother said, once she'd gotten her fill of her husband. "Where did you two meet? Paul said you don't even know his last name, but Geneva says you've been dating for a few weeks. Which is it?"

With each new question, my head spun. What could I tell her? Not the truth. I blinked several times, trying to construct a believable story.

"Hindley?"

I stared at my mother. "Truth?"

"Always." She smiled and rubbed my arm.

I realized this wasn't an interrogation, she was truly interested.

What could I tell her that wouldn't make her freak out? Nothing, I decided, so I went with a watered-down version of the truth. Raising my hand, I brought my pointer finger and thumb close tougher. "I may have gotten slightly inebriated at Geneva's bachelorette party last night."

"I heard it was more than slightly." She laughed.

"Good news travels fast, doesn't it?"

"Were you all right?"

"No. Geneva and her gang of misfits got me smashed, then left me all alone."

My mother rolled her eyes.

I never understood why my mother always believed in Geneva's innocence even when presented with the evidence of her deceitfulness.

"Anyway," I rolled *my* eyes, mirroring her gesture, "I got sick in the bathroom so a nice woman helped me outside. And that's where I met Rory." I neglected to tell her about Gap Boy or the fact that Rory spent the night in my bed.

"You met him outside a bar, Hindley?" she practically shrieked. "What were you thinking? And then you bring him here, to your sister's wedding?"

Fury exploded inside me. How dare my mother be so judgmental. "Geneva left me last night, *Mother*. All alone," I said through gritted teeth. "What part about that don't you understand? She knew I was plastered, hell I think she did it on purpose, and yet she still let me leave the club with a total stranger."

"What?" my mother said.

I ignored her. "Then some guy who'd tried to feel me up on the dance floor decided to follow me outside the club and start rubbing his hands all over my body."

My mother gasped, her hand covering her mouth, eyes wide. "Oh, God, Hindley."

"Yeah, Mom. He'd called a cab and was going to throw me into the backseat and take me to God knows where to do God knows what. Thank God, Rory stopped him."

Tears filled my mother's eyes as the familiar expression of guilt washed over her face. Part of me felt bad for scaring her but she needed to understand once and for all. Geneva and I would never be friends.

"Why do you always think Geneva is such a frigging saint, Mom?"

"I don't think she's a saint."

"Well, I don't care what you think. Rory helped me when my own stepsister wouldn't. That's all you guys need to know about him."

"Why are you getting so upset?"

"Why?" I laughed sarcastically. "Maybe because somehow I knew you were going to twist this around and make Rory look like the bad guy. He saved me, Mom. Geneva didn't." Tears burned my own eyes as I suddenly realized what could have happened to me last night if Skater Boy hadn't intervened.

My mother grasped my hands, pulling them into her lap and bringing me closer. "I'm sorry, honey, I didn't mean to upset you. It's wonderful that he took care of you and I appreciate him for that."

"Well, you should. And you should stop judging him. I know that's what you're doing."

"Honey, I just want the best things in life for you."

"How do you know this guy isn't the best thing for me?"

"Hindley, you don't even know the boy's last name. What kind of a man doesn't properly introduce himself to a woman? For all we know he could be—"

"Don't." I yanked my hands free.

"I'm sorry, sweetheart," she whispered, fumbling with her hands, "I didn't mean that he was—"

"What do introductions have to do with anything, Mom? That doesn't prove what kind of man Rory is. Manners mean nothing. I think we've both learned our lesson on that one."

My mother's green eyes met mine and held for a heartbeat as we both relieved memories best left unspoken.

"Look, Mom, Rory saved me last night. That's all you need to know. It doesn't matter what his last name is or what he does for a living, how much money his bank account has." I was tired and hungry and still hungover. My poor mother was about to get the brunt of my frustrations if she didn't let this go.

"Good evening, Mrs. Barton," a low voice spoke behind me.

I didn't need to look to know it was Rory. His deep, sexy tone was a siren call to me. I turned and stared up at him, struck dumb by his predatory, protective gaze. The usual glimmer in his eyes was dimmed with guilt.

Heat crept up my face as I wondered how much of our conversation Rory had overheard.

He reached for a chair and scooted it next to mine before slowly sitting. The material of his jacket caressed my bare shoulder as his long legs spread wide, pressing against my thigh.

Scorching heat pooled between my legs and chill bumps spread across my body like wildfire.

His warm arm wrapped around my shoulders as his thumb drew sensual circles against my bare shoulder

My body blazed with desire and a slow throb pulsated low in my core. I sat up taller, feeling empowered just by Rory's presence.

"You're right, ma'am." Rory finally spoke. "It was wrong of me not to properly introduce myself to Hindley last night, or to you and your husband tonight."

I was grateful he hadn't told my mother that he couldn't introduce himself to me last night because I was drunk as a skunk. Once again, Rory was protecting me, sacrificing himself to save my reputation.

He held out his free hand to my mother. "I'm Rory Gregor, ma'am."

Gregor, I repeated to myself. Rory Gregor. Why did that name sound familiar?

My mother glanced down at his extended hand then lifted her gaze. She smiled, an adoring, genuine expression of delight, before placing her perfectly manicured hand in his. "It's very nice to meet you, Rory Gregor. Please, call me Caroline."

They released hands and we sat in awkward silence.

"I spent the night with your daughter," Rory said.

Oh, shit.

My mother's eyes widened as they darted between us.

Rory held up a hand. "But we didn't do anything. I found her outside of a bar last night, completely inebriated and all alone as a man attempted to push her into a cab."

My mother's face crumpled, her chin quivering as she reached out and squeezed my hand.

"Realizing how intoxicated she was, I thought it best if I try to get her home and make sure no one else tried anything with her. We rode in a cab to her house, and with the help of her neighbor, I was able to get her safely inside."

I stared at Rory, speechless. I couldn't believe he was telling my mother *everything*.

"I stayed the night only to make sure she was all right." He continued. "Her friend Dana was kind enough to invite me to the wedding tonight. Your stepdaughter, Geneva, was very rude to Hindley this morning before her luncheon and I thought it best if I accompanied her tonight, to make sure no one else hurt her. Especially since your stepdaughter had obviously left Hindley in harm's way last night."

My mother and I sat in stunned silence.

Rory's admission was surprising, his raw honesty completely unexpected.

When I'd awoken with him in my bed this morning, something had warned me that Rory was probably a player of the worst kind, one who would want to tout his sexual exploits. But that wasn't the man sitting beside me now. He was defending my honor, in front of my own mother, even if it cost him his own.

A small smile spread across my face. Rory Gregor was an honorable man worthy of anyone's respect.

He glanced down at me and graced me with a small smile before looking back at my mother. "That's the truth, ma'am. That's how Hindley and I met. I'm sorry if I or anyone else gave you the wrong idea about our relationship. It was never my intent to do so."

Rory squeezed my shoulder.

I fought the urge to crawl into his lap, straddle his hips and finish our make-out session from earlier.

The most touching part of his story was his courage to tell my mom exactly how Geneva had treated me today. Anyone listening could hear he was just as upset as I was. His words were a quiet warning to my mother. He would not allow Geneva to put me down again.

My insides fluttered like a stupid, love-sick girl. Excitement coursed through my body as I considered the possibilities with Rory Gregor.

My mother stood.

Oh, crap. What was she going to say?

Rory stood with her. My Skater Boy had manners.

I jumped from my chair as well, fearing I may have to protect him from my mother.

"Well," my mom smiled, staring at me as she tossed a lock of hair over my shoulder, "it's very nice to meet the young man who took care of my precious daughter." She looked up at Rory. "I'm delighted that you came tonight, Rory Gregor. I truly hope you'll stay and enjoy the rest of the evening, as a personal friend to our family."

Personal friend? What did that mean?

"Thank you, ma'am," Rory said. "I appreciate your hospitality, but it's not necessary." He gazed down at me, that delicious smirk spreading across his face. "I would have taken care of Hindley regardless of the reward."

Wow, that was good.

"Well, again," my mom said, "I'm glad to meet my daughter's knight in shining armor. Enjoy yourself tonight, Rory." She winked.

Was she flirting with him? I grabbed Rory's hand, tugging him toward the dance floor, afraid of what Caroline Hagen-Barton might say next.

"Rory promised me a dance," I said over my shoulder in explanation.

Rory stared at me like I was crazy, which I was. He'd never promised to dance with me, but I had to get him away from my mother. Dancing seemed like the best way to do that.

"Nice to meet you, Caroline," Rory called over his shoulder.

I yanked him harder.

"What's wrong with you?" He laughed, tugging my hand to stop me.

I turned and sucked in a breath when he wrapped me in his arms.

"I can't believe my mother winked at you."

"I'm irresistible." He smiled.

I had no doubt of that. "She told us to *enjoy* ourselves tonight. You know what she means, right?"

Rory howled with laughter, his amusement only frustrating me more.

"It's not funny," I said.

"What?" Rory raised a brow. "Your mom winking at me or her wanting you to *enjoy* yourself with me tonight?" He rolled his hips into mine.

I gasped.

He chuckled, a low throaty growl, his blue eyes locked on mine.

My heart raced, blood pulsating through my body with desire. Suddenly the thought of *enjoying* myself with this man tonight didn't seem so embarrassing.

"Thank you," I whispered.

"For what?" He twirled us around the floor with ease.

"For talking to my mom."

"I have a way with women." He winked.

"Yes, I know," I said quietly, my gut clenching. I tried not to think of all the women he'd probably *had his way with*.

Rory pressed his lips against my temple. "Only you tonight, Drunk Girl," he whispered in my ear.

I felt myself falling a little more for Skater Boy.

"Thanks for explaining everything to my mom, especially about Geneva. She has a hard time seeing Geneva's faults."

"Your sister's a real bitch."

I stared up at him, eyes narrowed. "*Step*sister."

"Okay," He laughed, pulling me closer.

I leaned in to his warm embrace with a heavy sigh, grateful for his strength.

"Are you tired?" he asked.

"Yeah, it's been a long day."

"Are you ready to go home?"

"I wish I could." I said.

"Why can't you?"

"I have to stay until they leave."

"Until who leaves?" Rory asked.

"The newlyweds," I said sarcastically.

"Why? Who cares?"

"My mom will have a hissy fit if I leave now. It's not worth listening to her fuss."

"Maybe I could talk to her. I have a way with women." His lips curled up in a mischievous grin.

I swatted his arm. "Stop." God, I wanted to kiss him so bad. "I'll suffer through it. Like I always do," I muttered to myself.

"Hey."

I glanced up, surprised to see Rory's brows furrowed, his lips pressed in a hard line. "If you want to leave, just leave."

I smiled, squeezing him tight. "I'm good here, thanks."

He laughed, the vibrations ricocheting through my own body.

"You're a good dancer," I said after several moments of silence.

"Thanks. So are you? But I'm sure taking pole dancing classes helps you." He chuckled.

"Shut up." I swatted his arm again, searching the room to see if anyone else heard him.

"Quit hitting me." He jerked me close.

I stiffened in surprise, my breath catching in my throat.

He gazed down at me, leaning in closer as he stared at my lips. "Relax," he whispered, his blue eyes growing darker.

Kiss me, I willed him.

"So, I'm assuming the socialites don't know about your classes?"

"I don't take classes," I said. "It was a party for Geneva."

He leaned closer, his lips a whisper's breath away from mine. "If you say so."

I gulped. "I do, say so, I mean," I stuttered, my voice squeaking.

Rory pulled back, taking with him the promise of a kiss I'd been silently begging for.

We moved gracefully around the dance floor for several moments in comfortable silence.

"Hey," I said, "who were all those kids around you earlier? And what were you writing down for them?"

The music came to a stop and Rory pulled me off the dance floor, ignoring my question. His fingers intertwined with mine as we walked out of the ballroom and down a hallway toward the lobby.

"Hey, what's going on?" I asked, my feet stumbling as I tried to keep up with his long strides. "Where are we going?"

He came to an abrupt stop and I bumped into his back.

He turned to face me. "You were right. It's been a long day. I'm beat."

So, this was it, the brush off. Well, I deserved it. He'd had to put up with me and my crazy-ass family for as long as he could stand it. No one would blame him for bailing. Least of all me.

"Oh, uh, okay." I stared up at him.

His eyes darted around the lobby, like he was searching for someone.

"I'm sorry," I said.

He stilled and stared at me. "For what?"

"For..." I paused, trying to think of the right words. "You've done a lot for me today, Rory. Well, last night too, even though I can't remember it. I wish there was a way I could repay you."

"Stop letting your sister get under your skin. That's how you can repay me."

"She's my *step*sister," I reminded him. "And what the hell does that mean?"

"Look, Hindley, you're an amazing woman. I can tell from the short time I've known you. Someone like your *step*sister doesn't deserve your energy. So, quit giving it to her. Eventually, she'll run out of steam and crash and burn all on her own. She'll end up destroying herself, instead of destroying you."

I stood in stunned silence. His candid words were surprisingly poignant. It seemed Rory Gregor knew me better than some people who'd known me my entire life, my mother included.

"Wow," I whispered, shaking my head.

"What?"

"No one's ever said that to me before. Thank you," I said quietly.

"You're most welcome." His deep, gravelly voice brushed over my skin like a sensual touch.

I stared into his brilliant blue eyes, lost in the desire of his gaze. My legs suddenly felt weak, and I feared I may actually fall on my ass. All I wanted was one more kiss.

"Would you like to go to dinner?" I blurted out.

He stepped back, eyes wide.

Oh, shit. Why had I asked him that?

"I mean, you don't have to, I just thought—"

He pressed a finger to my lips and smirked. "I'd love to go to dinner with you."

I swallowed hard, forcing myself not to suck his finger into my mouth.

Rory reached inside his jacket and pulled out a cell phone, tapping the screen several times. "Here." He held the phone out to me.

I glanced down at the screen. He'd already created a contact for me. "Who's 'DG'?" I asked, staring up at him.

He laughed. "It's you, Drunk Girl."

"Me?" I asked, touching my chest.

"You were pretty drunk last night."

"You know I have a name, right?"

His blue eyes sparkled with mischief as his lips twisted up in a lopsided grin. "I know you do."

I shook my head, laughing as I typed in my cell phone number. I added my real name, just in case he forgot who 'DG' was. I fought the urge to scroll through his contact list to see how many Drunk Girl numbers he had.

Without thinking, I hit the 'Add Photo' button and turned around so I was leaning against his chest. Holding the phone out in front of me at arm's length, I smiled. "Say cheese."

Rory leaned in closer, resting his chin on my bare shoulder. The scent of his cologne tickled my nose, and other parts of my body.

"Cheese," he whispered in my ear.

Holy. Shit.

My body shuddered and I nearly dropped the phone. That one word held the most sensual, erotic promise I'd ever heard. My insides throbbed with desire. I wanted this man. Bad.

Fumbling with his phone, I looked down at the screen, so dazed and disoriented, I had no idea if I'd even taken the picture.

"Here," he said, gently sliding the phone from my hand. "Looks like you got it." He slipped the phone back in his jacket.

I stood silent, mouth gaping like a moron. His sensual promise rang through my mind.

"Are you all right?" he asked.

I heard the question but couldn't answer. I was intoxicated by the moment, and aroused beyond belief.

"Hindley."

"What!" I jumped, shaking my head.

"What's wrong with you?"

"I'm not sure," I whispered, staring up at him.

He smiled, his devilish grin spreading wide across his face.

I swooned and nearly passed out.

"So," he said, "tomorrow?"

"What?"

"Dinner?"

"Oh, uh, yeah." I shook my head. "That sounds good. Tomorrow."

"What time?"

I mentally ran through my schedule. "Oh, wait, I completely forgot. I have to work most of the day tomorrow, but I should be free by the evening."

"You work on Sundays? It's the Lord's day you know." He chuckled.

My legs wobbled as his laughter vibrated over my skin. Jeez, I needed to calm down.

"Well," I said, "when you get shit faced on Friday night and stuck with a bunch of snooty, rich people on Saturday, you have to work on the Lord's day to catch up."

His smile broadened and two small dimples I hadn't noticed early appeared around the edges of his mouth. God, he was gorgeous

"Yeah," he said, "I guess those things can make taking Sunday off pretty difficult."

"But I should be done by eight o'clock. I'll make sure of it." God, I sounded desperate, even to myself.

"That sounds good," Rory said. "What do you do anyway, for work I mean?"

"Oh, I'm an attorney."

His smile fell and something in my gut clenched.

"Don't tell me you hate lawyers too." I laughed nervously.

He didn't laugh. He didn't speak. His face was like stone, all amusement from earlier gone.

I instantly regretted telling him.

A lot of people didn't like attorneys. Usually, I didn't tell anyone about my profession right away to avoid this type of judgment. But considering what Rory and I had been through in the last twenty-four hours, I figured he knew me well enough not to judge. Apparently not.

"Well, I better go." His voice was cool, his body stiff as he reached down and kissed my cheek. His lips barely brushed my skin. The interaction was a far cry from the smoldering kiss we'd shared earlier.

What the hell had just happened?

"Um, okay?" I said, unsure of what else to say. "I'll see you tomorrow." It was more of a question than a statement.

He gave me a small nod and without another word, turned and walked toward the revolving door at the front of the hotel.

I stood silent, watching him disappear into the night, confused, and a little pissed off if I were honest. After several minutes of trying to figure out what the hell had just happened, I gave up and walked back toward the ballroom.

If Rory was this moody it was better to say good-bye now. He was probably a player anyway. And everyone knew once a player, always a player.

Halfway down the hallway, I stopped, refusing to take another step. I wasn't giving up, not this easily. I wanted to know what was wrong with him, and I wasn't willing to wait until tomorrow night to find out, if he even called then. Rory was a good guy. Last night and today proved that. I didn't want to lose him. Not like this anyway.

I turned on my heels, determined to live in the moment for once in my life. My high heels clicked on the marble floors as I entered the lobby, my eyes darting around the area.

I spotted Rory outside, his shoulder casually leaning on the glass wall. One ankle was crossed over the other in an 'I Don't Really Give a Fuck' kind of stance. He looked like James Dean, minus the leather jacket—sexy and confident, with a touch of bad boy.

I noticed he was talking to someone. A woman. A beautiful woman. Who was standing close, too close.

Panic washed over me.

The woman laughed at something Rory had said, her head falling back as her long dark hair gently blew in the evening breeze.

Rory smiled, his eyes staring at the sultry curve of her throat.

I recognized that look. I'd been the object of his predatory gaze just moments before.

Once a player…

Reaching inside his jacket, Rory pulled out his phone. Relief flooded me when I realized his intent. He was going to call me. Rory tapped on the screen multiple times.

I waited, but the phone tucked inside my dress never rang.

Rory smiled adoringly at the woman, holding out his phone to her.

The woman took it without hesitation, returning his expectant grin.

A sharp pain hit me square in the chest, robbing me of breath. My stomach clenched and I fought back a wave of nausea. The scene was eerily similar to our interaction less than five minutes ago. How stupid could I have been to actually think I'd captured Rory's attention for any length of time.

I choked down tears as the familiar pang of rejection slammed into my body. Turning quickly on my heels, I rushed down the corridor to the ballroom.

I refused to cry. I'd shed too many tears over situations far worse than this in my life. Rory didn't deserve my tears. This weekend was a reminder of why I wasn't spontaneous, why I kept my life orderly and neat. Why I guarded my heart.

Rejection hurt. Especially from someone I was really starting to fall for.

CHAPTER 12

RORY

I sat in the glider on Leif's back porch, my fingers absently thrumming the armrest. I was restless and irritable. Nothing new, some would say. I'd been unable to sleep the night before. One word still rattled around in my brain.

Lawyer.

She's a fucking lawyer.

Of all the things in this world Hindley could have been, she chose an attorney.

In my vast experience with lawyers, from the courtroom to the boardroom, they'd only been interested in two things—putting me jail or fucking me over. Usually both.

Hindley was too gentle, too naive to be an attorney. She obviously let people walk all over her instead of exploiting them, like most attorneys did. Didn't that go against the first commandment for lawyers—Screw over others before they screweth unto you.

I laughed to myself, setting back in the rocker. Gazing out over the railing, I watched as the sun set slowly over the Texas Hill Country. It was hot as hell but I had to admit, the scenery was breathtaking. I loved living in Southern California, but I could get used to Texas too.

Antsy to move, I stood and walked across the deck to the railing, leaning over and staring out at Leif's property.

I stared down at the skate park sitting adjacent to his house. He'd built it himself, or rather, his company, Fly By Night Skate Parks had. Leif was a master designer and built skate parks all over the world. The one in his yard was no exception.

Maybe a ride on my skateboard would help me shake off these nerves. I'd ask Leif to join me. Skating with my best friend always seemed to relax me.

I smiled, thinking back to how I'd met Leif and his family.

Leif's parents had followed him to a local skate park in Denver to watch him practice one day. His father, Jack, said once he saw me skating on the course that day, he'd known I had the potential to go all the way.

When Jack and his wife Kara had approached me, I didn't mention I'd just gotten out of juvie and homeless. Turns out, I didn't have to. They'd seen right through my tough exterior and taken me in, no questions asked. They treated me as if I were their own, and slowly I became theirs.

Eventually I shared my story with them. How I'd left home when I was sixteen, the day my stepfather decided to teach me a lesson about "putting my shit up," as he'd called it. He was drunk, as usual, and had come home and tripped over my skateboard. Instead of using his belt or fists to teach me a lesson, my skateboard became his weapon of choice that day.

Something inside my mind had snapped, like the trigger on a loaded gun. I don't know if I was trying to protect myself or my board, but suddenly I became the aggressor. All the years of pent up frustration, all the abuse and neglect I'd endured, came flying out through my fists.

I'd wailed on my stepfather, not stopping until the cops were on top of me, yanking me off. My mother told the cops to take me away, asked them to press charges. She never once felt the need to tell the officers about the years of abuse I'd suffered at her husband's hands.

The courts had been equally as unkind, partnering me with a court-appointed attorney who was more interested in meeting his tee-time on the golf course than defending me. Of course, my priors didn't help—vandalism, minor in possession, possession of a controlled substance with intent to sell. I knew it looked bad but what no one in the court system understood was that I had no other way out, no way to escape the hell I was living in except with drugs.

Until the Jennings.

Through hard work and practice, under Jack's training, I worked my way up in the amateur standings of skateboarding. By the time I was seventeen, I was getting major recognition by some big-name manufacturers. On my eighteenth birthday, I signed my first major deal and officially went pro. I celebrated by getting high as fuck on several lines of coke and screwing two random chicks I met at my signing party—but I tried to forget that part. Some habits died harder than others.

The money and the notoriety of being a professional athlete proved to be a lethal combination for me. I found myself on the bottom of a jail cell more than once on my way to the top. Sponsors and endorsers didn't enjoy bailing their star athletes out of jail. I was quickly let go from most of my contracts.

In the end, it proved to be for the best. I found out later that my agents and attorneys had screwed me over, working very lucrative deals, in their favor. Leif's father had tried to warn me, but I was a dumbass teenager, smitten with the idea that I was going pro. I thought I knew it all.

I laughed out loud at the memory. I'd been a complete dumbass.

Now, here I was, twenty-six years old and starting over. I was working hard to make a comeback in a sport that loved underdogs. This time I had no problems admitting I didn't know jack shit.

I was working my ass off, training and entering every major competition I could find. I was slowly rebuilding my reputation as a talented skateboarder. Companies were taking notice, companies like River City Skateboards here in Austin.

This time I'd taken Jack's advice and hired an attorney who understood my limits, personally and professionally. I was on my way up the ranks, and fans were stoked. They loved the Bad Boy Turned Good Guy story.

Even though I'd been clean for several years, I hadn't lost all my bad boy traits, evidenced by my actions with Hindley. I still had anger issues and used women for my own pleasure. Not that I didn't satisfy their needs too. I mean, I wasn't a total prick.

None of that mattered though, not compared to the one secret that threatened to ruin me if anyone found out. I wouldn't be able to save myself or my sobriety if the public knew the real me.

My palms grew damp and my heart pounded hard in my chest just thinking about reviewing the contract tomorrow. How could I admit to my new sponsor, or anyone else for that matter, that I was functionally illiterate?

I couldn't. That was the simple answer. And so I hadn't. Only Leif, his parents, and my attorney knew I couldn't read.

I wasn't completely illiterate. I could read a few words, mostly small ones. I faked my way through the rest most days. I recognized things, like brand labels at the grocery store or street signs on the roadway. It didn't mean I could read them. I just remembered them. My mind memorized pictures and symbols, not words.

Putting words and phrases together had always proven difficult for me. Instead of trying, I'd dropped out of school when I was released from juvie and run away, hoping no one would ever discover my secret.

Throughout the years, the Jennings had tried to help, especially Kara. Nothing ever worked. I couldn't focus or concentrate long enough. And the techniques she used only confused me more. No matter how much I tried to tell people, they never understood that what they saw on the paper wasn't what I saw. Eventually, I gave up, and so did everyone else.

Now in my mid-twenties, I was too ashamed to ask for help. If I walked into an adult learning center at my age, potential sponsors and endorsers would drop me like a bad habit. Not to mention what social media would do. I'd be crucified.

Luckily, the few who knew about my illiteracy loved me enough to keep my secret. It wasn't easy, and I'd surprised myself by keeping my secret as long as I had. It's amazing the things people are willing to overlook when you're a successful athlete making a shit ton of money.

I still lived in constant fear though, afraid people would find out my secret and reject me like my own mother had.

I walked back to the glider and sat, watching the sun vanish over the hills. I wanted to disappear with it.

I closed my eyes as images of Hindley's beautiful face ran through my mind. Her satiny hair, those luscious curves, and perfect tits. But it was her smile that had me completely captivated.

God, I was becoming obsessed with the girl, which was completely out of character for me. Usually I had sex with a chick once or twice and we were done. No lingering thoughts, no day dreaming about her hair or her smile, for fuck's sake.

From the beginning, Hindley had been different though. Our relationship hadn't begun because of my desire to fuck her. Although that would be nice too. No, I'd been drawn to Hindley because she needed me, she needed my protection. Not a lot of people needed me. It was a good feeling.

As much as my body craved her, life had taught me I'd never have her. Hindley's kind didn't mix with mine. An attorney from high-society and a skateboarder from the mean streets of Denver? Please. I laughed. Not going to happen. Ever.

As much as my head said no, my body refused to listen. I couldn't let her go. I wanted to see Hindley again. I *needed* to see her again. Hear her sexy voice.

I drew my phone from my back pocket and found her contact information with ease. I stared at the photo she'd taken of us. Instead of looking at the camera, my eyes had been glued to her beautiful face. She was breathtaking. She drove me crazy.

I scrolled down further and found the contact information from the woman I'd met outside the hotel shortly after I'd left Hindley. No, ran away from Hindley was more like it. I was ashamed just looking at the chick's phone number.

I'd memorized her name and assigned her an acronym, as I did most people. But honestly, I probably wouldn't recognize her if I ran into her on the street.

By contrast, I had every facet of Hindley seared in my mind. From the way she twisted her hair when she was nervous, to the dimple in her chin that formed only when she smiled, to the soft tender skin of her lips. I was infatuated with everything about her. My need to see Hindley again scared me almost as much as going to my contract review meeting tomorrow.

My finger hovered over Hindley's number on my screen as I mentally listed off reasons why I shouldn't call her—she was rich, she was refined...and she was a fucking attorney.

I scrolled down to Mandy's number. I'd entered her as "HH" for Hotel Hottie. She seemed a much better fit for someone like me, if our conversation last night was any indication. She'd laughed at my sexual innuendos, even rubbed against me like a cat in heat. She'd displayed all the typical signs of a woman up for whatever kinky shit I wanted to do in bed that night. In the end I'd walked away, Hindley's scent consuming me.

I toggled between the two numbers, Drunk Girl and Hotel Hottie, my mind racing. Sweat beaded across my brow. I'd never been this torn between calling a woman before in my life. Before I could change my mind, my finger swiped across her name.

I listened anxiously as the line rang. If she didn't answer, I vowed not to leave a message. That would be my sign that this entire idea was a mistake.

After only one ring, she answered. "Hello."

My palms broke out in a cold sweat.

"Hello?"

"Hey, uh, it's Rory. Sorry I'm calling you so late." God, I sounded like a nervous teenager. What the fuck was that about? "I was wondering if you still wanted to go out this evening?"

With little coaxing, she agreed, despite the late hour. After finalizing our plans, I walked back inside Leif's house.

"Hey, man, can I borrow your motorcycle?"

He glanced over the couch, smiling. "Got a hot date?"

"Maybe."

"Girls don't like to have helmet hair, you know. Better take the Mustang?"

Leif had a vintage 1966 Mustang convertible that he and his father had completely restored. It was his pride and joy, his "Baby Girl," as he called it. There was no fucking way I was taking that thing out on the road.

"We're just meeting at the restaurant," I said. "I'm not picking her up. I'll take the bike, if that's okay."

Leif shrugged. "Sure, man. I'm just glad you called her. She sounds like a decent chick from what you've told me. You need a decent chick in your life."

I chuckled under my breath. Did I deserve a decent chick? Probably not, considering I was anything but. Didn't stop me from wanting it though.

"Oh my God," Leif said, "stop already. You deserve a decent chick."

"So do you, Leif."

Leif choked on his drink. "Uh, yeah, sure, man." He laughed nervously, quickly turning back toward the television.

What the hell was that about?

"Keys are on the hook by the garage door," he said. "Drive safely."

I had no idea what had just happened but figured it was best to let the comment go.

I walked into the garage and pulled the helmet over my head. Straddling the bike, I fired up the engine, waiting as it warmed up.

You need a decent chick in your life.

Leif's comment rang through my mind. I didn't even know how to treat a decent chick if one ever gave me the chance. Should I try?

Part of me wanted to. But I was afraid. And when I was afraid, I did stupid shit.

Securing the strap under my chin, I opened the garage door and eased the motorcycle out onto the driveway. A pang of unease hit my chest.

Shit. Had I called the right woman?

I turned the bike onto the street and twisted the throttle, speeding away into the night.

Too late now.

CHAPTER 13

RORY

I STOOD OUTSIDE THE RESTAURANT, wondering what in the hell I was doing here. Was this really a good idea? Should I even go in? Probably not.

Figuring I'd come this far, I swung the door open. Mariachi music blared from inside as the smell of stale tortilla chips assaulted me.

A large Hispanic woman approached. She wore a bright yellow dress with detailed embroidery. Her hair was slicked back in a neat bun. "Table for one, sir?"

Her accent was heavy but thankfully, I lived in Southern California so I was used to the language barrier. I even spoke a little Spanish.

I shook my head. "Um, no. I'm meeting someone at the bar."

"Of course, sir." She swung her arm toward the back of the restaurant. "The bar is that way. I'll make sure she knows you're here when she arrives. It is a woman, yes?"

I laughed out loud. In Austin, no one assumed.

"Yes, a woman," I said. "Thank you."

I weaved through the restaurant and found the bar. Taking a seat on one of the stools, I glanced around the area. It was busy for a Sunday evening.

The bartender stopped in front of me. "What can I get you, sir?"

"Just water."

"Tap or bottle?"

"Tap is fine," I said.

"Comin' right up, sir." After a few moments he returned, placing the glass of water on the bar, along with a basket of tortilla chips and salsa. "Anything else?"

"Not right now, thank you."

"Rory!" A woman's shrill voice echoed behind me.

I swiveled on my stool and stared blankly at the woman fast approaching. I swallowed hard. Shit.

She slid up next to me, her hand resting on my arm. "Thanks for calling me."

"Uh, sure." I ran a nervous hand through my hair.

I'd made a mistake, a *huge* mistake. I should have never called this chick. I needed to get the hell out of here. Fast.

"I can't stay long though," I said. "I've got an early meeting in the morning."

She placed both hands on my knee and squeezed, slowly pushing them apart. Her fingers crept up my thighs, moving toward my dick.

I was surprised to feel nothing stir below my waist. Unlike Hindley, who's simple smile from across a crowded room could make my dick hard as stone.

Hotel Hottie leaned in close, her fake boobs practically mashed against my chest.

"It's all right," she breathed into my ear. "I don't need long. Not with you."

I drew in a deep breath, assaulted by her floral perfume. My gut twisted with nausea.

Two days ago, I might have accepted the chick's invitation for sex. She had a centerfold's body that any man would give his left nut to be inside of. Staring into her sea-green eyes, all I could think about was how different she was from Hindley, and how much I wanted her to get the hell out of here.

Why had I called this chick instead of Hindley?

"What's wrong?" she asked.

I shook my head. "Nothing."

"You want to go back to my place?"

"No, I don't think so." I nervously rubbed the back of my neck. I had so fucked this up. I knew I would. "In fact, I shouldn't even be here tonight. I'm sorry."

She stared at me, brows furrowed. "What do you mean? Why?"

"Look, I just need to go." I reached into my wallet and dug out a twenty, throwing it on to the bar.

"Are you fuckin' kidding me?" She glared at me, nostrils flared. She looked like a cat about to be stuck in a tub of water.

Oh, shit.

She fisted both hands and placed them on her hips. "You call me up and tell me to meet you in half an hour. I bust my ass to get my shit ready and look halfway decent, thinking you wanted to take a roll in the sheets. And now," she waved her hand around the restaurant, "I haven't even had one drink and you say you're already leaving? What the fuck is up with that?"

Nice mouth, Cinderella. Do you blow guys with that dirty thing?

"Look, I'm sorry," I said. "Honestly. I should never have called you. Stay here, order whatever you want. I'll leave the bartender some cash for you."

"I don't need your fucking cash, you prick. I'm not a prostitute."

Yep, real classy. Nice call.

I drew in a deep breath, reminding myself that I was the one who'd fucked up, not her. I blew out a slow breath, ready to make amends. "Look, all I can say is, I messed up. I made a mistake. I never should have called you. I'm sorry. Tell me if you're staying and I'll buy you a drink."

"Hell yeah, I'm staying. I didn't get all dolled up on a Sunday night just to sit at home and watch TV."

I waved down the bartender and gave him a one-hundred-dollar bill. "Give her whatever she wants, just make sure she takes a cab home. Make sure she gets home safe, okay?"

God, what was it with me and needing to make sure women were safe? I stiffened. I knew exactly what drove my desires.

The bartender surveyed the chick sitting next to me. His eyes traveled up and down her body as if to say, "You're seriously leaving this hottie?" He grabbed the hundred from my hand and nodded once. "Sure thing, man, no problem."

I slowly turned toward the woman, afraid of what I might find. "Look, I really am sorry. I know you're a nice person, but I have to get up early tomorrow. Sorry I wasted your time."

She cut her eyes over the rim of her drink as she held it to her lips. Slowly lifting her other hand, she raised one red-tipped finger, one very *significant* finger, and shoved it in my face. "Screw you, asshole."

"Nice," I said, shaking my head as I turned to leave. I had no one to blame but myself for this mess. As usual.

What the hell had I been thinking?

Last night, this chick had seemed like a classy lady. She'd been standing outside one of Austin's most expensive hotels, for God's sake. Obviously, I'd been a poor judge of character. Nothing new there.

Maybe if I'd been wrong about Hotel Hottie, I was wrong about Drunk Girl too. Maybe Hindley wasn't your typical attorney. Maybe I could trust her. Maybe we weren't so different after all.

That was a lot of *maybes* to bank on. I wasn't a guy who based his life on chance.

A huge smile spread across my face. I needed to see her, settle this once and for all.

I pushed open the restaurant door, feeling more confident than I had since I met Hindley. A cool bite of night air slapped me in the face. The dip in temperature was unusual for this time of year in Texas.

I pulled my phone out of my pocket and looked at the time. Ten twenty-eight.

It was too late. I shouldn't do it. I scrolled through my contacts, staring down at Hindley's beautiful face.

Fuck it.

I pushed her number, praying she'd answer. I needed to talk to her. I needed to hear her voice. I needed to say I was sorry for not calling earlier. After the fourth ring, her phone clicked over to voicemail.

"You've reached Hindley Hagen. I'm sorry I missed your call. Please leave a message at the tone."

I hung up without leaving a message and talked myself out of immediately calling back just to hear her voice again. I swung my leg over the seat of Leif's bike and started the engine. The seat vibrated as I sat and thought about what to do next, where to go.

Suddenly a destination came to mind. Without a moment's hesitation, I kicked the motorcycle in to gear and sped away into the night.

Before I even realized what I'd done, I found myself sitting outside a familiar duplex. I parked the bike well beyond the streetlamp, careful to stay in the shadows.

God, I was so fucked up in the head. Seriously, what was wrong with me? This chick was driving me insane.

I noticed a small light illuminated one of the windows on Hindley's side of the duplex. She was home.

I ducked down in the shadows like a total perv. I'd come this far, why not go all the way with psycho stalking.

I tried to remind myself that it was too late for a visit, but as usual, I didn't listen to my own warnings. It didn't matter. I was a selfish prick. I'd already gotten Hindley under my skin. There was no way to relieve the itch until I scratched.

I punched her name on the screen and held the phone to my ear. The call went directly to voicemail, not a single ring. What the fuck? Was she was rejecting my phone calls? Now I was pissed.

Without thinking, I jumped off the bike and stalked toward her front door. I stopped, mid-way, wondering what in the hell I was doing. Did I actually expect her to open the door? She better not. It was nearly midnight. And if she did, what the hell was I going to say?

As much as I wanted to leave, I couldn't. Hindley was like a drug, and I was already addicted to her. I needed a fix. The more she eluded me, the more I wanted her.

It was official. I'd completely lost my shit. Over a girl.

I held my breath as I stepped up on the porch, praying she'd answer. What would I say if she did? I'd basically stood her up. My insides clenched with an uneasiness I wasn't used to.

My hand hovered in front of her door as I blew out a shaky breath. Shit. I'd never been this nervous in my life, especially over a chick. Finally, I said, fuck it, and knocked on the door.

If she didn't answer, I'd leave and never come back, never call her again, I promised myself. I shook my head. That was a fucking lie. I'd bash her door down if she didn't answer, I was that addicted.

There was no answer. I wasn't sure if I should be thankful or pissed. Instead of debating, I peered through the small window in the door. It was covered with material, but I could see movement inside. She was home. But wait, if she was home, why wasn't she answering the door? Or my calls?

Suddenly, a disturbing scenario flashed before my eyes.

What if she was in there with someone else? What if she was hooking up with some other dude in there?

Nausea had me almost doubled over, and I thought I might puke. I couldn't bear to think of another man holding her, caressing her, kissing her. Those were *my* lips. I could still feel them pressed against mine last night as our tongues danced in an erotic beat of pure lust and desire.

I'd sucked face with a lot of women, for a multitude of reasons, but none had ever affected me the way Hindley's had. Her kiss had made me feel complete, whole, alive for the first time in a long time. And the best part was, she'd kissed me back, with a passion and a desire that matched my own.

God, I sounded like a character from a fucking Nicholas Sparks movie. But it was the truth.

Hindley was different. I knew it the minute I'd uncovered those delicious blue toenails. She was a rare breed. And that's why I was standing out here in the cold, on her front porch, like a lunatic at eleven o'clock in the evening. I just prayed she would answer the door.

Seconds turned into minutes as I waited for her to answer. Blood rushed through my veins and my heart nearly beat out of my chest. I feared I may stroke out. I raised my hand and knocked a second time.

Finally, the dead bolt clicked. I held my breath as the door creaked open.

And there she was.

Her long blond hair was pulled back in a ponytail, a pencil tucked behind one ear. Visions of her the night we met tumbled through my head. Unlike the first time I'd seen her, tonight she wore black-rimmed glasses that gave her a naughty librarian look. Her face was free of makeup and I thought I'd never seen her look more beautiful.

My eyes scanned lower.

She wore a T-shirt with Hello Kitty printed on the front and matching Hello Kitty flannel boxer shorts, revealing her long, toned legs. That could be fun, I thought.

Hindley cleared her throat.

I glanced up, staring into her brown eyes. They were darker now and narrowed.

She leaned against the doorframe, staring at me, expressionless.

Oh, shit. This was worse than I thought. I could handle her being pissed at me. I'd dealt with that emotion from people most of my life. What scared the hell out of me was the look on her face now. Or lack thereof. She was unresponsive, her emotions hidden. The fun-loving Drunk Girl from yesterday was gone, replaced by someone I didn't know. This was her attorney look.

"I'm sorry to come by so late," I blurted out, trying to break the spell. "It's just that...I was trying to call and you didn't answer, and I started to get worried about you, and well..." I sounded lame as shit, even to myself.

She cocked her head and raised a brow, the arch peeking over the frames of her glasses. "Really?" she said sarcastically, drawing out the word.

Yep, this was way worse than I thought.

"What, you don't believe me?" I asked.

"Rory, what do you want? It's late and I still have a lot of work to do."

"I thought you said you'd be done by eight." I smiled, going for the innocent look.

Her face remained impassive.

Obviously, I was failing miserably.

Her lips pressed in a tight line as she scowled at me

My head dropped to my chest and I stared at my dingy boots. "I'm sorry," I whispered, unable to meet her gaze.

"For what?"

I looked up.

Her scowl was gone but her expression was still lukewarm at best. I had one shot with her. Honesty. I would go with honesty.

"For not calling you tonight like I said I would," I finally answered. "I asked you out to dinner and then I never called you. I'm sorry for that."

She nodded and grabbed the edge of the door. "Apology accepted. Now, if that's the only reason you came, I need to go. It's cold out there and I'm tired." She took a step backward and prepared to shut the door.

I stuck my foot out, stopping her. "Wait, Hindley."

"What?" she barked out.

I stood silent, unable to answer.

"What the hell do you want from me, Rory?" she half-shouted.

I expected her to be upset, disappointed even, sure. But this reaction was different, something I was unaccustomed to. She was furious, and it wasn't because of one missed call from me. Something else had happened to Drunk Girl tonight.

"What's going on with you?" I asked quietly.

"What's going on with me? What's going on with *me*?" she repeated, laughing sarcastically. "You're seriously going to stand there and ask what's wrong with *me*?"

"Can I come in and talk to you for a second?"

"No, you can't come in." She grasped the door, preparing to shut it.

"Why?" I asked, moving closer.

"You apologized, I accepted. We're done. You've absolved yourself, you're cleansed. Happy?"

Her eyes glistened with tears.

Shit, she was going to cry. I felt like the biggest asshole alive.

"No, Hindley. I'm not happy," I said, lowering my head. "I'm not happy at all." Out of all the shitty things I'd done in my life, this was at the top.

When the door didn't slam in my face, I glanced up.

Hindley stared down at her hands, fumbling with the drawstring of her pajama shorts. Slowly, she lifted her head and she stared at me, as if trying to gauge my sincerity.

We stood silently, me patiently waiting, for once. I needed her to believe me.

"I'm sorry," I whispered.

Her lips opened as if about to say something.

I leaned forward. A thrill of hope shot through me when she didn't step back. It felt like that first hit of an illicit drug, burning through my veins. Hindley was going to give me a chance.

The porch light from next door flickered on, startling us both.

"Hindley," a familiar voice called out from around the hedges, "is everything all right over there?"

Hindley pushed past me, wrapping her arms around her body. She leaned over the edge of the porch. "Yeah, I'm fine, Frannie, thanks."

Red's face peeked around the bushes.

"Oh, hey, Lover Boy." Red smiled. "Finally back for more, huh?" She waggled her brows.

Hindley looked at me then to Red. "You two know each other?"

Red and I nodded.

"Well, he's just leaving." Hindley placed her hands on my chest and shoved me off the porch.

"You might want to rethink about letting this one go, Hindley," Red said. "I mean, how many guys find a totally smashed chick on the street and work their asses off trying to get her home safely without getting anything in return?"

Hindley's brow furrowed. "What do you mean?"

"He brought you home. Didn't even know where you lived. He came knocking on our door to make sure this was your address before he carried you inside. It took him a lot of work to get you home safely, trust me."

Thank you, Red.

"He did?" Hindley's gaze moved from Red over to me. The look of confusion on her face, mixed with shock, had the earlier expression of contempt disappearing.

"Uh, huh," Red said. "He even carried you inside. It was so romantic."

Hindley's big brown eyes met mine. "You carried me in?"

Of course, she wouldn't remember how she got in bed that night.

"Yep," Red said. "He sure did. You were toast, girl." She laughed. "You couldn't have walked if you had to. Who knew you had a wild side, Hindley?"

A flush crept across Hindley's cheeks and she grimaced.

I could take embarrassed. At least she wasn't glaring at me anymore.

"Well, good night then." Red waved. "See you in the morning, sunshine." Red glanced over at me. "Maybe you too, Lover Boy." Her eyes twinkled with mischief before she disappeared around the corner, laughing all the way. Within seconds, her porch light clicked off.

It was just Hindley and me, standing in the cold night air, staring at one another.

Her body shivered.

I reached out and rubbed her arms up and down, trying to warm her. "Come on," I said, pushing her back inside. "This is ridiculous. You're freezing out here."

She glanced over her shoulder. "I can't believe how cold it is outside."

I walked her inside, with surprisingly no resistance, and shut the door. Locking both dead bolts, I turned to face her.

"Why did you lock us in?" she asked.

Her question surprised me. Why wouldn't I? "Because I want to talk, and unlike you, I'm not nearly as trusting of the human race."

"Rory, I wasn't kidding. It's late, I'm tired, and I've still got a shit load of work ahead of me." She motioned toward her dining room.

I turned and studied her table.

Her laptop sat open at one end, surrounded by piles and piles of paper littered everywhere. A plate with several slices of pizza sat off to the side.

"Did I interrupt your dinner?" I teased, but quickly remembered I was supposed to take her to dinner tonight. The reason she was eating pizza was because of me. I glanced back at Hindley.

She stared down at the floor, hands fisted by her sides.

I released a heavy sigh. It was official. I was the world's biggest prick. "Look, Hindley, I wanted to come by tonight to apologize. I needed to see you."

Her head lifted and she glared at me. "That makes absolutely no sense, you know that right? I mean, last night you said you wanted to go out with me, but then you never called. Instead, you show up hours later and say, 'I need to see you,' whatever the hell that means." She lowered her voice, trying to mimic mine.

I clenched my teeth to keep from laughing. "Was that supposed to be me?"

Her eyes narrowed but her lips twitched with amusement.

I couldn't hold it any longer. A small laugh burst out before I could stop it.

Hindley balled up her fist and hit my arm. "Shut up." Her lips pressed in a tight line as she tried to stifle her own laugh.

The tears from earlier were replaced with a glimmer of amusement. Relief flooded me.

I decided the best way to play this now was casual. Act like nothing had happened. Pretend I hadn't been the biggest douche bag ever.

"What kind of pizza is this?" I asked, strolling over to the kitchen counter. I couldn't care less if it were covered in dog shit, I was going to eat. Especially if it meant I could stay here a little longer with Hindley.

"What are you doing?"

I glanced over my shoulder. "We're having dinner."

"No." She fisted her hands on her hips. "*You're* being a jackass and eating *my* dinner."

"Either way, we're both hungry. Can you take a break for ten minutes and eat with me?"

She stared at me, studying me, assessing me.

Afraid she may see the real me, I diverted my gaze.

"Hold on." She sprinted down the hallway.

My gaze followed her. Something in my midsection stirred to life as I watched her tight little ass run down the hall. I seriously thought about dropping my plate and following her but before I could take a step, she'd returned.

Her sexy body was now covered with a ratty robe, and her blue toenails were covered in bunny slippers.

Well, shit. So much for ogling her while I ate.

She'd released her ponytail and blonde hair fell in waves over her shoulders. I couldn't help but hope she'd done it for me. She may be trying to detour me but she actually looked hotter than ever.

I scooped up several slices of pizza on a napkin for myself and grabbed her plate from the table. "Let's sit over there." I nodded toward the living room.

She hesitated, clutching her robe tighter.

I shrugged and moved toward the coffee table, not bothering to ask permission. In my life I'd always found it easier to ask for forgiveness than permission.

I plopped down on the sofa as if I'd lived here for years. Picking up a piece of pepperoni pizza, I shoveled a bite in my mouth. I hadn't realized how hungry I was. "So, do you own this duplex?" I asked around a mouth full of pizza.

"Don't do this, Rory."

I glanced up.

Hindley held out a bottle of water and a napkin.

"Do what?" I choked out in between bites, wiping my mouth.

"Don't start this small talk crap. It doesn't suit you."

I swallowed the pizza. It felt like a boulder going down. "What does that mean?"

She sat on the chair opposite me, the one I'd put her down on when I'd brought her home from the bar. "I know who you are."

"Who am I?" I asked nervously. Maybe she'd discovered I was a professional skateboarder. She probably thought I was a loser, completely beneath her. Which was somewhat true. Especially after the way I'd treated her tonight.

"You're a player."

"A player?" I laughed.

"Yes. A player." She pulled her pizza apart and picked at the crust.

She was nervous, and defensive, and I was the reason why. I hated myself for being the source of her pain.

"I saw you last night," she said, still staring down at her pizza.

"Where?"

"Outside the hotel, with that woman. I saw you take her number." Her eyes rolled up to meet mine, all amusement gone. "Just like you did me."

Oh, fuck. Hotel Hottie. She knew about Hotel Hottie.

I swallowed hard. A tight band of guilt cinched around my chest, making it hard to breathe. Shit. Shit. Shit. I'd been prepared to grovel, I'd even been prepared to beg, but I wasn't prepared for this.

"You have one chance to get this right, Rory." Hindley sat up straight, shoulders stiff, eyes unreadable.

I knew she was right. If I fucked this up, if I gave her a wrong answer, this shit between us would be over before it began. How was I going to explain why I'd taken another woman's phone number and called her instead of Hindley?

"Just answer one question," she said calmly.

Sweat beaded on my forehead and I rubbed the back of my neck. Shit, I was going to fuck this up. "Okay," I finally said.

"Why did you run last night when I told you I was a lawyer?"

That was it? That was her one question I had to answer?

I held my breath. Answering Hindley's question would be much more difficult than explaining why I took another girl's phone number. The answer involved my past, and I didn't want to go there. Not with Hindley.

I placed my pizza back on my napkin on the coffee table, suddenly losing my appetite. I leaned back against the sofa, rubbing my palms over my jeans. What could I tell her that wouldn't make me look like a bigger asshole?

The truth? I bit back a laugh.

Tell her what? That I was a juvenile delinquent, a hot-headed punk who'd seen the inside of a courtroom more times than a classroom? That I was a dope head? Tell her I had to constantly check myself to make sure I didn't go over the edge?

Yeah, definitely not the truth.

Wait, did I even want to go down this road for a chick? Yeah, yeah, I did. In the end, I decided a watered-down version of the truth would be best.

"Rory," she called quietly, patiently.

I drew in a steadying breath. My stomach cramped in knots, the pizza threatening to return. My eyes met hers and I prayed she would believe me and not run like all the others had.

"I guess," I said, running a hand through my hair, "I guess I've just had bad experiences with attorneys in the past and I'm a little leery."

"That's not all, and you know it." She stared at me with those attorney eyes, the ones that demanded the truth, no matter what. Shit.

"If that's your answer, then you need to leave. Now." Rather than stand and escort me out, she leaned back in her chair as if awaiting a good story, and slowly crossed her legs. Her robe fell open, revealing long, silky-smooth legs.

I clenched my teeth to bite back a moan. All I could picture were those long legs wrapped around my waist, her lips pressed to mine.

"So, is that your answer?" she asked, her head tilted.

Her question woke me from my lurid thoughts. "Look, Hindley, I've got a tainted past. Can we just leave it at that?"

"Why didn't you call me tonight?"

Fuck.

"I don't know." It wasn't a total lie. "I guess I figured you deserved better than me."

"Did you call her?"

"Who?"

"You know who."

I stared down at the coffee table, afraid to meet her gaze. "Yes," I whispered.

"Did you take her out tonight?"

"We met for drinks, but I left as soon as she got there."

She nodded. "Well, I'm sure you had a nice time." She stood and grabbed our pizzas, quietly leaving the room.

My head sunk into my hands and my fingers pulled at my hair. I'd completely blown it. One chance and I'd choked. I'd lost tournaments and competitions because of one bad trick. And now I'd lost her.

I glanced up when I heard her return. I didn't know whether to be ecstatic or scared shitless.

She walked toward the door and undid both locks. Turning the door handle, she pulled the door open. A gust of cold wind whipped through the room. But it was nothing compared to the icy glare she gave me.

"It's late, Rory. You need to go." Her voice was flat but author-itative.

I'd fucked up. Majorly. But I didn't want to leave. I wasn't even sure I could leave her.

I rose from the sofa, realizing this was it. I'd never see Drunk Girl again. My heart sank. I'd never experienced this kind of rejec-tion and pain before. I walked past her but stopped in front of her. I couldn't leave, wouldn't leave, without touching her one last time.

Taking her hand in mine, I brought it up to my mouth, brushing each knuckle with my lips.

Her eyes widened, and she sucked in a breath.

She was definitely affected. Unlike at the wedding though, there was a coldness in her expression. She was closing herself off to me. I wasn't entirely sure I could coax my Drunk Girl out but I wanted to try. As long as she didn't object, I'd push on.

My fingers trailed up the sleeve of her robe until I reached her shoulder. With the back of my hand, I gently brushed her hair back, revealing her soft, supple neck.

Slowly her tongue peeked out and she licked her lower lip.

My dick went rock hard, picturing those lips wrapped around me. I sucked in a breath.

Her gaze moved down to my lips. God, I wanted to kiss her but I needed to go slow.

I slipped my hand around the back of her neck, surprised she didn't protest.

Instead, she leaned into my embrace.

With my eyes trained on hers, I stepped closer, looking for any sign of opposition. When I saw none, I gently slipped my free hand around her waist and drew her in to me. I stilled when her full breasts molded against my chest. She wasn't wearing a bra.

Fuck.

I studied her face for any signs she wanted me to stop.

Her eyes were half-lidded and glazed over, mouth open as her chest rose and fell against mine.

She wanted this, and so did I.

Moving slowly, afraid I would scare her, I lowered my head and covered her mouth with mine.

A delicious warmth spread through my body as she pressed into me. Her lips spread opened, and I took what she was offering, my tongue gently caressing hers. The heat of her hands burned through my shirt as her fingers wrapped around my shoulders.

Hindley's touch was like heaven and hell. I wanted more but I needed to take this slow.

Her hands wound into my hair, pulling my face closer to hers.

Despite my intent to go slow, our kiss quickly progressed from desire to primal hunger and I lost all control. I couldn't think, couldn't breathe. I was consumed with everything about her.

Her hands slid down to my chest and she shoved me away.

I stumbled back, heaving for breath. What the hell?

Hindley recoiled, her eyes wide as she pressed a fist to her mouth. "Go, Rory," she whispered, so low, I could barely hear her.

Shit. Had I read her wrong? I'd thought she'd wanted me as much as I wanted her.

I nodded once and stepped out onto the porch. "I'm sorry," I said as I turned to face her. I couldn't help myself. I wanted to see her one last time.

One hand covered her throat, the other pressed against her stomach. The corners of her mouth were tipped up in a smile so small I may have missed it if I hadn't been searching for any clue that she still wanted this.

I'd affected her. Whatever this was between us, it wasn't over, and we both knew it. My face split into a shit-eating grin and I wondered if I should go back in for another kiss. Before I could move, she shut the door in my face.

Her dead bolt clicked and relief flooded me. At least she'd be safe tonight.

I stood on her porch, staring dumbly at the door. Would she really give me a second chance? That kiss sure as shit said yes. And so did that smile.

Suddenly the porch light clicked off and I was surrounded by the night. Unlike the other times in my life when the darkness had consumed me and I felt lost and alone, this time I was filled with something new, something different. Hope.

CHAPTER 14
HINDLEY

I COULDN'T BELIEVE what I was looking at. I'd been staring at it for so long, my eyes were seeing double. Why hadn't I noticed it last night after he'd left? I prided myself on details. I was a contracts attorney, for God's sake. Well, for now anyway.

It wasn't like contract law or tort litigation had been my passion in law school. My desire to be a prosecutor had fueled my need to finish law school.

During the summer of my first year, I interned at the local District Attorney's office. I quickly realized I'd never survive criminal law. I'd wanted to do some good, help contribute justice to a system that had been unjust to me. But in the end, the work had been too overwhelming—the crime scene photos, the victims' statements, the police reports. It had triggered too many memories and had nearly been forced to drop out of law school.

After graduation, I still hadn't settled on one particular area of law. Thankfully, Paul introduced me to one of his financial investors at a party, Mr. Aston Stedwick.

Mr. Stedwick was the founding partner at Stedwick and Nigh, a prestigious Austin law firm. We'd had an impromptu interview right there at the party. I must have impressed him because two days later, Mr. Stedwick called and offered me a position with the firm.

I didn't want to let the firm down. And I didn't want to disappoint Paul. I mean, he wouldn't mind if contract law didn't turn out to be my cup of tea, but I couldn't leave Mr. Stedwick high and dry if I didn't like the work. Paul needed Mr. Stedwick's investment if he was ever going to recover from the economic downfall his own company had suffered over the last few years. I couldn't afford to disappoint either of them.

The starting salary was decent for a first-year lawyer. I made enough to put a good down payment on my duplex and stash the maximum amount in my retirement account, my 401K, and a separate annuity. I was planning for the future.

I'd learned my lessons about living in the moment and being careless. Every move I made now was calculated, precise, and planned. My life didn't have room for surprises anymore.

Until now. This wasn't a surprise. It was an oversight, a huge one, on my part.

I studied the document for the hundredth time.

The majority of the contract was boilerplate. I'd worked hard over the last three months, drafting the verbiage with Michael and Luis, my two other associates. We'd ensured the words were written to protect both parties, whether we represented them or not. Today though, I wasn't concerned about anything other than the name in front of me.

How could I have let my personal feelings get in the way of my professional judgment?

I'd been pouring over the contract all day yesterday, well into the night. I knew exactly why, and I was furious with myself. Why hadn't I seen it before?

I didn't know if I was more upset with Rory for coming to my house for a late-night booty call, *after* he'd called a complete stranger to go out with instead of me. Or at myself for dreaming of him last night, of our parting kiss. I was so mad at him, so hurt by his dismissal, yet in one kiss he'd essentially wiped away all my anger and disappointment.

I clicked the internet icon on my laptop and let it toggle over to the pages I'd pulled up earlier this morning. It was him, definitely him.

My gaze darted to a stack of papers on my desk. It was right there, literally in black and white. The title of the document, 'Sponsorship Contract', was the same as all the other signings I'd been a part of since I'd drafted the original copy.

The Sponsor name was no surprise either, 'Kopra Enterprises, LLC'. We'd drafted several legal documents for them in the past, including an Article of Incorporation when they'd decided to grow their company.

This was the third sponsorship contract I'd personally worked on with them under their subsidiary company. Maybe that's why I'd skimmed over it so hastily. I wasn't representing the Sponsee, I was representing Kopra.

No, all of the rest of the text on the document was common, no surprises. The only thing different was the 'Sponsee Name' and it had my head spinning. The man Kopra Enterprises wanted to sponsor, the man whose name appeared before me on all these legal documents, was the only difference.

Rory Gregor.

Rory. Friggin'. Gregor.

I'd been sitting at my desk for over an hour, staring at the name. I had no idea what to do. I'd been so caught up in the particulars of the terms of the contract that I'd completely neglected to associate Rory's name on the contract to the one who'd sucked my face last night.

How could I trust myself with this contract if I couldn't even notice something as major as that? What should I tell Michael and Luis? Should I even tell them I knew Rory?

Yeah, I knew him, those lips especially.

Oh, God, what would Mr. Stedwick say? He'd probably fire me on the spot. And worse, pull his investments from Paul's company.

I would just play dumb, act like I didn't know Rory, that would be best. But wait, what if Rory didn't play along? Oh, shit, I was screwed.

I looked down at my watch, relieved to find I still had an hour to figure out what the hell I was going to do. I needed help. And there was only one person who could fix this. I picked up my phone and dialed Luis's extension.

"What's up, girl?" Luis asked in his sexy Spanish accent. "You ready for the meeting?"

"Um, about that. I need to talk to you."

"Ut oh, that doesn't sound good. What's going on?"

"Do you have a second to talk?"

"For you, *cariña*, I have a lifetime. I'll be right there."

Luis Marquez was an angel fish in a sea of blood-thirsty sharks, a beauty inside and out. I feared one day he may be eaten alive by those he worked for. He never seemed to mind though.

I had no idea why he'd ever pursued a law degree. He had so many other strong talents. Even at Stedwick and Nigh though, he'd managed to climb his way up the corporate ladder nicely. He always told me, "Girl, my taste is too expensive. I need a profession that can support my extravagant tastes."

Luis was a triple threat—funny, smart, and gorgeous. The problem was, he knew it. With bronzed skin and eyes that looked like melted caramel, he had every woman—and gay man—in the office swooning.

Luis swung my office door open. "What's up, *mí amor*?" In other law firms, his actions toward me could have been construed as sexual harassment. Given the fact that one, Luis was gay and two, that was his nature, I'd grown accustomed to it. In fact, a large part of me loved that about Luis. His terms of endearment were a welcome part of my day.

"I think I may have a problem with the Kopra contract."

"What's up?"

"I know the Sponsee." I pushed the front page over to him.

Luis and Michael had shown extreme trust in me over the last three months. They allowed me to draft the contracts pretty much on my own. Michael was the closer, the negotiator, and Luis dealt with the personalities, the 'divas' as we liked to call them.

Luis was already familiar with both parties we'd be dealing with today. He prided himself on intel and was good at it. More than anything, he wanted this new division to prosper and grow. Despite his lackadaisical attitude, Luis had goals. Becoming a partner by the age of thirty-five was one of them.

Stedwick and Nigh was venturing into a new area in the sports industry called attorney-agent representation. It brought together the best of both an attorney and an agent for the athlete, things that used to be standalone positions.

Not only was an attorney-agent someone who was familiar with all aspects of the law, they were also able to promote the athlete and stay on top of any legal issue that may surround them.

It was the latest trend in sponsorship contracts and it was a very lucrative deal. An attorney had the potential to make much more than just a standard fee. Their earnings were directly tied to the athlete's success, if written correctly. It was an area Mr. Stedwick was *very* interested in, hence his presence at today's meeting.

Luis shrugged. "So what, he's a professional athlete. Most people who haven't had their head up their ass for the last five years know who Rory Gregor is. He's got like a zillion X Games medals, for God's sake."

"Well, that's the thing. Up until two days ago, I'd never heard of him."

"So, what's the problem?"

"I *know* him," I said, willing him to understand my insinuation.

Luis perched high on the edge of his seat and covered his mouth with his hand. "Uh uh. Girl, tell me you did not tap that?"

"Luis." I batted my hand.

"No, seriously, do *not* tell me. I mean, I want you to tell me, but professionally, please don't. I wouldn't blame you though. He is *muy caliente.*" Luis fanned his face. "I would too, if I thought I stood a chance."

"I didn't 'tap that.'" I used air quotes. "We just kissed. Twice," I muttered.

"Twice," he practically shrieked. "I know there's more there, girl, I can see it in your eyes. Spill." He pushed back in the chair and folded his arms over his chest as if he were preparing for a tantalizing movie.

I started from the beginning, not sparing a detail. Well, maybe a few details, like how completely smashed I'd been.

Luis rubbed his dark hair with both hands as he rolled his eyes up toward the ceiling. "*A Dios, mío.* Holy hell, baby girl. We have us a real problem here."

"I know." I bit down on my thumb. "I can't go into these negotiations."

"I'm not talking about the negotiations. I'm talking about you." He pointed straight at me.

"What about me?"

"You're already over the moon for this guy. It shows in your face, in your whole damn countenance. Every time you say his name, your eyes light up and you get this adorable crinkle in your nose." He reached over the desk and touched my nose.

I swatted him away.

Luis laughed and fell back in his chair. "I've never seen you like this before, *cariña.* You look good wearing a little lust on you."

I threw a paper clip at him but missed. "That's not true." I was good and pissed at Luis. Not for his comments, but because deep down, everything he said was true.

Even after all the things I'd learned about Rory on the Internet, after all I'd experienced with him personally, a ball of lust still burned deep in my belly for the man.

"Look, I'm not saying you can't play with him on the side," Luis said. "Just be careful. I think he's way beyond you though."

"What the hell does that mean?"

"Don't get defensive." He held up a hand.

"I'm not getting defensive. First." I ticked off on one finger. "I can't have any sort of relationship with him other than professional because that's my job. Second, I still wouldn't involve myself with him even if I didn't represent his sponsor. Have you seen all the shit he's done?" I turned my laptop around and scrolled.

Rory had become a pro skateboarder at age eighteen, which was remarkable apparently. Yet in less than four years' time, he'd not only managed to lose all his money, he'd also broken four endorsement deals, gotten arrested twice—once on a drug charge—and screwed every prostitute looking bimbo in the lower forty-eight.

When it came to men, I'd never quite been sure what my 'type' was, but I definitely knew what my type wasn't. And it wasn't Rory Gregor—at all—at least not on paper. In person though, it was a much different story.

I couldn't wrap my head around the fact that the punk pretty boy I read about in countless stories on the Internet was the same man I'd met just two days before. That man was caring, kind, and protective.

Of course, he'd also stood me up and took another woman on a date so, no, definitely not my type, at all. Period.

"Yeah, I knew about this," Luis said, turning the laptop back around. "He was a crazy kid and did some serious damage to his reputation." Luis stared at me. "How did you not already know this? I mean, I know I'm the one who schmoozes the client, but you're so detail oriented. This surprises me, Hindley."

He wasn't reprimanding me, but his words of consternation hurt. I prided myself on my work. Luis's and Michael's approval were huge to me. I'd disappointed him and I couldn't hide my shame.

"I don't know." I shook my head. "I'm worried, Luis."

"Why?"

What could I say?

"You've got it that bad, huh?"

I glanced up. "What do you mean?"

"Baby girl. The guy's a solid fox, no doubt. He's talented as shit and poised to be the next great skateboarder of all time. And he's changed."

"I don't think so. Did you not hear my story? He took another chick's phone number seconds after taking mine. He promised to call me and instead, called her. Once a player, always a player."

"That's not true. Look at me." Luis waved a hand down his body.

"You're different." I smiled

Luis had been quite the player himself when he was single. But three years ago, he'd met a man who changed him.

Teddy had been patient with Luis, watching countless times as Luis sabotaged their relationship. Instead of bailing, Teddy had helped Luis, shown him where his demons were, and helped put them to rest. In the end, Luis was a different person and was able to love Teddy with his whole heart. Something apparently, he'd never been able to do before. Luis credited Teddy with all their success.

"No, I'm not," Luis said. "I'm no different than Rory Gregor. Except he's white and straight." He laughed to himself. "I *was* a player, sweetheart, plain and simple."

"Not as bad as this guy though," I said, pointing to my laptop.

"Trust me, if I'd been given all the money, notoriety, and free ass that boy had handed to him at eighteen, I would have been worse."

I rolled my eyes, all the while knowing, in my heart it was true. Luis had been bad.

"Look, Hindley, people change, they evolve. The guy fucked up. It doesn't mean that's who he is now. Once upon a time we were all Neanderthal cavemen, dragging our knuckles across the vast terrain." He straightened his tie and tugged down on his suit jacket, completely smitten with himself. "Oh, wait, I forgot. You white people hate the word evolution."

I couldn't help but laugh. Luis was anything but politically correct.

"But look at us now. Civilized creatures. You'll do fine, sweetie." With his final words of wisdom, he pushed up out of my chair and headed for the door.

"Wait!" I felt as desperate as I sounded.

He turned to look at me, those hazel eyes full of hope and

promise. "Hindley, you have killer instincts, you've just never trusted them. What do your instincts say right now? What is your gut telling you?"

"I don't know."

"Yes, you do."

I dropped my gaze and nervously twisted my hands, afraid to look him in the eyes. I knew what my gut was telling me and it scared me to death.

"Until you admit it to yourself, there is nothing I or anyone else can do to help you. If you like this guy, then don't let his past stop you from at least exploring your options."

I could hear the sexual innuendo in his voice and my head snapped up.

He gave me a wink and a huge smile. "Just don't tell me about it. At least, not in the office." He poked his fingers in his ears and began humming, "lah, lah, lah," as he walked out of my office.

I loved Luis. He always knew exactly what to say, and he was right. No matter what the Internet said or what had transpired yesterday, my gut told me Rory was a good guy. He was on his way back to the top of his profession and it seemed like he'd learned from his past mistakes.

Last night was probably a slip up. He'd acted squirrelly when I'd told him I was an attorney at the wedding. And he admitted he didn't have a good history with them. Maybe I'd spooked him and that's why he'd turned to the other girl and blown me off.

I couldn't help the niggling feeling in my stomach though, telling me not to pursue this. I wasn't Rory's attorney, but I was an attorney for the company he was representing.

I straightened the papers on my desk as I continued working on a few more changes to the contract. Legal jargon should cure my woes.

Rory's attorney had drafted the original sponsorship contract but I found it to be riddled with all kinds of loopholes that definitely didn't benefit Rory or River City Skateboards. Several times while reading through the contract I wondered where the guy had received his law degree. Probably some minuscule island in the Caribbean.

Rory had a right to know that perhaps his attorney wasn't working in his best interest. Maybe Mr. Stedwick was right. Athletes *did* need better representation but I didn't want to be responsible for Rory Gregor. I couldn't. I was already developing feelings for him and there was no way I would be able to keep a clear head around him. Somewhere along the way, my personal feelings would jeopardize my professional decisions and in the end we'd both lose.

CHAPTER 15

HINDLEY

"THEY'RE HERE," Michael called from my doorway.

I glanced up.

He stood and studied me for a moment. "You ready?"

Shit. Luis had told him everything. Well, maybe not *everything*, but enough for Michael to be concerned.

"Yeah, I'm ready." I drew in a deep breath and slowly exhaled, willing the butterflies in my stomach to calm the hell down.

Michael looked me up and down. "You look like you're about to throw up."

"I feel like it."

"You can't go in there like this, Hindley. Go to the bathroom and freshen up. Splash some water on your face. Throw on some lip gloss, or whatever it is you girls do, then meet us in the main conference room in five minutes. Luis and I are going to go in and make introductions."

I stood and shook out my hands.

Michael's eyes travelled the length of me, assessing me. He was probably trying to decide whether or not I could stand up to the challenge. I could, and I would. I had to prove myself to him, show him that he could count on me, even when the situation was less than perfect.

"Five minutes," he repeated more sternly, then turned and left my office.

I darted out of my office and all but ran to the bathroom. I prayed Rory Gregor wouldn't see me vomit, again.

After fortifying myself in bathroom with a silent pep talk, I made my way to the conference room. Standing just outside, I smoothed my dress and smacked my lips together. I'd applied a light coat of gloss and a little mascara, but other than that, I was going for *au naturel* today.

I took in a deep breath through my nose and grabbed the door handle, putting on my best game face. As I exhaled, I turned the knob and pushed the door open, knowing that what lay inside may very well eat me alive.

The first person I noticed in the massive boardroom was Mr. Stedwick, sitting at the head of the table. Even though I'd expected him to be present, my heart still hammered in my chest. Slowly I took in the rest of the room.

Luis and Michael were in their usual seats, their faces mirroring my nervousness.

Mr. Stedwick stood and motioned toward me. "Gentlemen, you've met Mr. Marquez and Mr. Perkins. I'd like to introduce you to another associate here at our firm, Ms. Hindley Hagen."

I plastered on what I hoped was a smile to hide my nervousness. "Hello," I said to no one in particular.

A man across the table from Luis stood. "Hello, I'm Jack Jennings, Rory's manager." He was well dressed in a pullover shirt and slacks. His dark brown hair was graying around the temples and the creases around his brown eyes had me guessing he was in his late forties or early fifties. He was a handsome man, very fit, with a smile that immediately put me at ease. I wondered if he was Rory's father.

"Nice to meet you, Mr. Jennings," I said, taking his hand in mine.

He gave me a firm but not overbearing shake. "Please, call me Jack."

I nodded and smiled as some of my tension eased.

As Jack sat down, the gentleman next to him stood and held out his hand. "I'm Eugene Albright, Rory's attorney. You can call me Gene-O."

Gene-O was more rotund than Jack, and much shorter. He wore a navy suit that looked to be a size too small. His jet-black hair was slicked back but a few pieces had fallen around his face. I noticed a slight sheen of sweat on his brow. Overall, he looked disheveled and a bit nervous.

I shook his hand, not surprised to find his palm damp and his grip loose. Paul had always taught me to make my first impression from a person's handshake. My first impression of "Gene-O" was that Rory was in trouble if this guy was representing him.

I held my breath and let my gaze shift to the final person in the room. My heart beat wildly with fear, the sound roaring in my ears. I drew in a sharp breath when my eyes connected with his.

God, he was beautiful, just as I'd remembered, only better. Dressed in a blue, button down dress shirt that matched his eyes, he literally stole my breath.

His eyes were wide with surprise but a small smile played on his lips.

This was it. The moment of truth. He was either going to go ballistic and bust me, or act as if he didn't know me at all. I wasn't sure which would hurt me more.

Rory tilted his head, extending his hand. "Hello, Hindley. It's nice to see you again."

His tone was cordial but not familiar. Either he couldn't care less or he was a great actor.

"Oh, you two know each other already?" Mr. Stedwick asked.

"Yes," he answered before I could. "I had the pleasure of meeting Hindley Friday evening when I was out with friends."

Oh, thank God, he wasn't going to go into more detail about our *meeting*.

Rory nodded toward his hand.

"Oh, uh, yes," I stumbled, "Nice to see you as well." I slipped my hand into his and as our palms touched, a bolt of electricity ran up my arm.

He gently squeezed my hand and released me but not before his thumb trailed slowly across my fingertips. Goose bumps skidded across my flesh. I felt the loss of his touch down to my toes.

God, what was I doing? This was a professional meeting. I had no business thinking about what his hands would feel like on—

"Well, how delightful." Mr. Stedwick's voice woke me from my lurid thoughts. "Perhaps that will help these proceedings go more smoothly." Mr. Stedwick eyed me for several seconds, his gaze assessing.

Oh, God, did he know?

I ducked my head, smoothing my skirt flat against the back of my thighs as I took a seat next to Luis.

"Nice to meet you all," I said, glancing around the room. My eyes briefly stopped on Rory. I wasn't surprised to find him studying me. The butterflies in my stomach from earlier turned into bees, stinging me relentlessly.

Once I settled into my seat, I noticed the owners of River City Skateboards weren't at the table. This was their contract negotiation with Rory.

Bernard "Bucky" Kopra and his wife Pena were the founders and co-CEOs of Kopra Enterprises, River City Skateboard's parent company. They were two of the nicest people I'd ever met, always more concerned about relationships than the bottom line.

Bucky and Pena first retained the firm several years ago when they filed for a corporation status. Their company was growing exponentially and they wanted to protect everyone associated with the family. Having worked with them twice before, I was very familiar with their company, as well as with them personally.

Before I could question their absence, Mr. Stedwick spoke. "I'm sorry Bucky and Pena couldn't join us this morning. Apparently, their daughter was ill last night and had to be rushed to the hospital."

"Oh, no," I said. My eyes shot wide as I stared at Mr. Stedwick.

He shrugged and glanced around the table as if he couldn't care less. Wait, was he…smirking?

I turned to Michael.

His head was down, his face impassive.

An ache in the pit of my stomach warned me something wasn't right.

Mr. Stedwick was lying. I didn't know why. If something had happened to Bucky or Pena, or one of their children, I would be devastated. The fact that Mr. Stedwick may be exploiting them by lying about their children had my blood boiling.

I would never wish harm to any one of them, least of all their children. And I certainly would never use it as leverage at the negotiation table.

"Is everything all right?" Rory asked. "Is their daughter going to be okay?" He was genuinely concerned and something warmed in my heart. He was always the protector.

"Yes, she'll be fine," Mr. Stedwick answered as if the situation was nothing more than a stubbed toe.

"That's quite all right," Gene-O said. "I don't think it's necessary that they be here for this portion. We're still ironing out the details. As long as you know their wishes and they're present for the signing, we should be fine today."

Gene-O spoke with empty authority, as if he was in control of this meeting.

Obviously, he had no idea who Mr. Aston Stedwick was. Gene-O would never be in control, not sitting here in the conference room of Stedwick and Nigh. Especially with the founder and senior partner personally present and seated at the helm.

"Shall we begin, gentlemen?" Michael opened up his portfolio and pulled out the contract.

I stood and passed out copies to everyone at the table. As I handed Rory his contract, his eyes locked on mine and I was surprised to see him smile. I sat quickly, staring down at the contract to avert my eyes.

"I believe Ms. Hagen has made quite a few changes to your

original contract, Mr. Albright," Michael announced. "I'm going to let her review those first, then we can start our negotiations." Michael's tone was firm and confident, which surprised me. I wasn't as experienced as Gene-O Albright, but I could tell by the verbiage in his original document I was already a much shrewder attorney.

I straightened the copy in front of me and cleared my throat. "As you can see, Mr. Albright, I've made quite a few changes to your original document. I felt it was lacking in specifics that would protect and benefit both of our clients."

I spent the next half hour going over all the changes. I tried to be as specific as possible. At sporadic intervals, I would take a breath and glance up. Every time Rory was staring at me. He had an unnerving glimmer in his eyes that gave me a sense of confidence.

"I think the biggest change you'll find is in the Incentives Clause on page fourteen," I continued.

All the men flipped through the pages, but I noticed Mr. Albright reach over and turn Rory's contract for him. He pointed to the exact spot on the paper where we were. It wasn't unusual for clients to be lost in these negotiations so the act didn't completely surprise me but it did seem somewhat odd that he actually turned the pages for Rory. I let the thought go and continued.

"I don't think the incentives are specific enough for either client to fully benefit," I said.

"Are you referring to your firm benefiting, Ms. Hagen?" Gene-O said.

Was he insinuating that we were trying to take advantage of everyone? It was his dumbass document that was so screwed up. How dare he make it look like I was exploiting Rory or the Kopra's.

Rather than confront him in front of my bosses, I continued as if I hadn't heard him. "If Mr. Gregor continues to perform at the level he's at, we're assuming his victories will only increase over the next year."

I'd done my research before the meeting, and although I found lots of knocks in Rory's personal armor, professionally his performances were stellar. He was extremely talented. The critics made it clear they believed if Rory stayed on task, he'd climb the rankings over the next few months and be back on top.

I'd also had a chance to watch videos of him skateboarding. I had to admit, he was amazing. He made the sport look effortless, and everyone knew that was the sign of a well-trained athlete.

"We believe it's in the best interest of Mr. Gregor *and* River City Skateboards to tie those victories into the incentive clause," I said.

"Well, that's unusual." Jack cleared his throat.

His manager's remark startled me.

"What's that, sir?" I asked, looking up from the contract.

"An attorney representing the sponsor who actually tries to negotiate a better deal for the *athlete*," he said.

I stared at Jack. "Although I know Mr. Gregor is currently represented by Mr. Albright, it's not the Kopra's position to hold him back. If there is a way they can help Rory succeed, they will." I glanced around the room, surprised to find every eye on me.

Even Rory's

I turned my attention to Jack. "This isn't about taking from Rory," I said, "it's about being mutually beneficial to all parties. Believe me, if Mr. Gregor is successful, everyone in this room will be too. It behooves us all to support him in any way possible. Incentivizing this contract for him only means we're allowing him to perform and be rewarded when he's successful. After all, it's he who's doing all the work, not us."

The room fell silent and I feared I'd overstepped my bounds. Glancing toward the head of the table I saw Mr. Stedwick staring at me, brows raised with a small smile.

Well, at least he wasn't pissed. He seemed…intrigued.

I felt a sense of pride wash over me. I wanted Mr. Stedwick to know that I had drafted a sound document that protected not only Kopra Enterprises, but also Rory Gregor. And if I could do it for Rory, I could do it for other athletes who chose our firm. At least, I thought I could.

I wasn't entirely sure that my need to make sure Rory was compensated fairly wasn't tied directly to my feelings for him as a man though. I needed to keep my motives in check going forward.

"To be honest, Mr. Albright," I continued, "I was surprised at how poorly your contract was written in Rory's favor. As his legal counsel, it's your job to not only protect Mr. Gregor, but to also negotiate the best deal for him."

Gene-O sat back, folding his arms over his chest.

"Not only were the performance incentives lacking in specifics," I continued, "but you also failed to allow Mr. Gregor to approve any and every advertisement or promotional product distributed by River City Skateboards. Believe me when I say River City has no intentions of maliciously harming Rory in any way. If he looks good, they look good. However, I would have expected you to understand that and draft a contract that protected him, regardless."

All eyes in the room were locked on me, a few jaws lax, including Mr. Stedwick's.

Oh, shit, now I'd done it. I truly had overstepped my bounds by calling out a seasoned attorney, no matter how inept he was.

Gene-O's face turned bright red and his eyes burned with so much fury, I feared they might actually cross. If looks could have killed, I'd be dead.

I'd attacked him, called him out in front of fellow professionals, and even his own client. I couldn't stop myself though. It was obvious this idiot didn't give a rat's behind about Rory's compensation, which was surprising. The better Rory did, the more money Gene-O would make, if his contract had been drafted correctly.

Michael was going to kill me. He hated insubordination most of all. I was out of line, and there was no doubt in my mind he would call me on it. He may even fire me as soon as I left the room. Hell, he might do it right here in front of everyone. That would serve me right.

Mr. Stedwick would probably back him, and he'd have every right. It wouldn't just hurt me, it would destroy Paul if I got fired.

He'd basically finagled me into this job. Mr. Stedwick might even be so pissed he'd pull all his investments from Paul's real estate holdings.

Shit. Shit. Shit. I was so screwed. When would I learn to control my mouth?

Mr. Stedwick broke the silence, speaking directly to me.

I clenched my hands and held my breath, preparing for the words, "You're fired."

"I think your changes and concerns are very valid, Ms. Hagen," he finally said.

Wait? What?

"I'm sure Mr. Gregor and Mr. Albright appreciate your diligence to negotiate the best possible deal for all parties. Am I correct, Mr. Albright?"

I suppressed the smile threatening to spread across my face. I'd done a good job, a damn good job, and I deserved the praise.

Gene-O's grimace faded as he realized Mr. Stedwick supported my changes. I couldn't blame him for being pissed. He'd basically been served his ass by a lowly first year attorney.

From the corner of my eye, I saw Michael and Luis both biting back smiles. Their delight thrilled me. It was validation that I was well on my way to becoming a good attorney. Even if contract law hadn't been my first choice, I was happy that all my hard work and diligence was paying off. It didn't hurt that the senior partner was witness to my efforts either.

My thoughts quickly turned to Rory and I wondered what his reaction to my outburst would be. Would he be upset? Surely not, I was working a deal in his favor.

Suddenly a chill ran up my spine. I raised my lids and peeked at Rory through my lashes. My insides fluttered when I found his bright blue eyes fixed on mine.

He was wearing that sideways grin that I was slowly becoming addicted to. I was already halfway gone for the guy.

He looked happy, maybe even impressed with my work. For some reason it was *his* approval I most wanted.

"Well, if everyone is in agreement," Michael said, shoving the contract into his portfolio, "then we'll make these changes and have a finalized version for you by tomorrow." He glanced at Gene-O. "Should we deliver it to you personally, Mr. Albright?"

"You can have it delivered to our house," Jack said.

Our house? Did Rory have a house in Austin? That was a surprise.

"That sounds wonderful," Michael said, seeming pleased. "If you'd like to stop by my assistant's desk on the way out and give her the address, we'll be sure to messenger it over tomorrow. After you have a chance to review the changes, we can schedule another meeting with all of us to sign the final documents."

I wouldn't be at the signing. Those were all Luis and Michael. My chest seized with pain at the realization that this would be the last time I ever saw Skater Boy. Images from the Internet of the life he'd led before flashed through my mind. Maybe it was best we part now.

My conversation with Luis played through my mind. *People change, they evolve.* Even Luis had experienced his own transformation once he'd met the right person. Was I the right woman for Rory? Did I have what it took to reform him, transform him? Did I even want to?

No. Hell no.

Then I remembered his kisses. A slow smile spread across my face. My fingertips brushed softly against my lips as I remembered how delicious his mouth felt pressed against mine.

I turned to leave, keeping my head down to hide my expression. I didn't want him, or anyone, to see me like this, so affected by his presence. But if this truly was the last time I'd ever see him, I wanted just one more glance at his gorgeous face.

I lifted my head and stared at him. One look and I knew it had been a mistake. He was staring right at me, his bright blue eyes drinking me in. The sunlight danced across his gorgeous face, bringing out the highlights in his dark blond hair. I felt like that chick from the Bible who looked back at the city and instantly turned to a pillar of salt because she hadn't obeyed God.

We stood, silently staring at one another for several heartbeats, a million words left unspoken.

Slowly his eyes traveled down my body.

His gaze stroked my body like fingertips, heating my skin.

I was glad I'd worn my best dress, a form-fitting Vera Wang, and high heels.

His eyes finally met mine and he lifted a brow, gracing me with a small smile.

My body tingled, and the butterflies that had once resided in my stomach were now flying south to other parts of my anatomy. If I didn't get out of this conference soon, I'd throw him down on the table, rip off all his clothes, and beg him to make love to me in every way imaginable.

Rory reached for me but I tucked my arm into my chest and turned, ducking my head in shame. Had I really just pictured us naked on the conference table? Yes, yes I had.

This man was dangerous. I had to escape. Knowing better than to look back, I rushed out the door, racing to the only place where I'd be safe from his touch. The ladies' bathroom.

CHAPTER 16

HINDLEY

MICHAEL AND LUIS treated me to a celebratory lunch. They talked non-stop about what a fantastic job I'd done in the meeting.

Even I was surprised at how aggressive I'd been. I'd never negotiated like that before. Actually, I'd never negotiated at all. Had Rory changed me? Had he allowed me to tap into my never-before-seen predatory side? My cheeks heated thinking about how delicious he looked today, sitting in the boardroom, smiling at me.

My office phone rang and I jumped in my seat. I picked up the receiver. "Hello."

"Miss Hagen, it's Donna Friar."

Donna Friar? That was Mr. Stedwick's personal assistant. What could she possibly want from me? Before I could think of an answer, she continued.

"Mr. Stedwick would like to see you in his office at two."

Oh, shit. This was it. He was going to fire me. "Um, okay."

"I'll let him know to expect you," she said.

"Yes, thank you." There was silence on the phone. "Good bye," I said hesitantly before I realized she'd already hung up. The woman carried about as much personality as a thumb tack. That didn't mean she didn't intimidate the crap out of me, and most of the office staff. Everyone except Luis.

I sat at my desk, anxiously awaiting our meeting. There was no use in starting anything new, I was a nervous wreck. At one fifty-five, I reapplied my lip gloss and made my way to the elevators.

Michael was standing in the foyer. "You ready for this?" he asked.

"Ready for what? What's going on?"

"I don't know. Either we're both being fired or we're getting big fat raises. I'm thinking it's raises because Mr. Stedwick never does the firing. It's always HR."

After waiting almost fifteen minutes outside Mr. Stedwick's office, Donna escorted us in.

His office was huge, as big as my side of the duplex, and sat in the corner of the building. He had a breathtaking view of the rolling hills of central Texas on one side and downtown Austin on the other.

"Please, have a seat." He motioned us to two high-backed leather chairs in front of his desk.

I couldn't wait to find out why he'd called us here. I had to explain myself. I had to absolve Michael. "First, I want to apologize about this morning, sir," I said. "I know I was out of line and I should have discussed the changes with Michael beforehand. I had no right to assault Mr. Gregor's counsel. Please believe me, Michael had no idea I was going to be so forward."

"Well," Mr. Stedwick leaned back, "if Mr. Perkins deserves none of the blame as you suggest, then it would stand to reason he deserves none of the accolades as well."

"I don't understand, sir."

"Rory's manager called me an hour after our meeting. Apparently, they haven't been happy with Mr. Gene-O Albright's performance for a while."

The way he said the man's name told me he had no respect for the attorney either.

"After hearing how passionate you were about protecting Rory, they began to rethink not only their choice of attorney, but their choice of agent, as well."

"So, wait a minute. You're not upset with me?"

"On the contrary, Hindley. I'm extraordinarily pleased with you. Your tenacity has proven beneficial, not only to this firm, but to Mr. Gregor as well. They've asked to retain our firm as their legal counsel for all contracts."

My gaze snapped to Michael. Both of our mouths were slightly ajar as we fought to hide our excitement.

"Don't be bashful, Hindley. This is something to celebrate." Mr. Stedwick smiled. "This is exactly the type of business our law firm has been trying to attract. When word spreads of your tactics to negotiate for the other side, I have no doubt other athletes will line up behind Mr. Gregor. You've done a great job, Hindley."

I couldn't hide my joy any longer. Mr. Stedwick was proud of me so certainly I deserved some self-praising too. I allowed myself this rare prideful moment of honor as I let the realization of my success sink in.

"Here." He pushed an envelope toward me.

"What's this?"

He remained silent, waiting for me to open the envelope. I pulled out two large, laminated cards that read 'VIP Event Pass - River City Skateboards Pro-Am Tournament', attached to red lanyards. "What are these?"

"Those are two passes to Rory's next competition. Actually, it's not a competition. Apparently, a friend of his designs skate parks and has his grand opening this weekend. The venue set up a pro-am tournament to showcase the new park. Rory is the headlining pro. His manager sent over two passes for the weekend event. What do you know about skateboarding, Hindley?"

"Honestly, not much, sir."

"They'll have a trade show at the convention center in downtown San Antonio starting Friday afternoon. The competition will be held all day Saturday, followed by a party that evening. These are all excellent opportunities for us. I want you to attend all three events and bring along a friend, preferably a female."

A female? That was weird.

"I want you to learn as much about the extreme sports industry as you can," he said. "Mix and mingle with other pro skaters, and find out who the next up-and-coming amateur athletes are. I want this firm to be representing more athletes like Rory."

Skateboarding? Was he serious? I had to learn about skateboarding for my job as an attorney? It didn't make any sense at all. But who was I to argue?

"If we're going to represent them, we need to know how best to do that. I think Rory will be an excellent source of information for you."

Oh, shit. Hang out with Rory?

"But why me?" I asked. "I just draft the contracts. Why not Michael or Luis? They're senior associates."

"It's obvious you already know him. He seemed comfortable with you," he said. "And he was pleased with your efforts on his behalf today. I have no doubt he'll learn to trust you, if he hasn't already."

Should I tell him that Rory trusts me a little too much? Not if I wanted to keep my job.

"Why can't I take Michael or Luis with me to the event? Why another female?"

Probably because he was used to being surrounded by groupies. The thought of Rory with other women made me physically sick.

"I think Rory's manager is leery of attorneys," Mr. Stenwick said, "especially after Mr. Albright's abysmal performance today. I can't say I blame him. I think the fewer attorneys present, the better. I also think fitting in as a friend rather than legal counsel will go a long way with Rory's team."

"I think Michael or Luis should go, sir, not me."

"Impossible."

"Why?"

"They specifically asked for you."

"Who did?"

"His manager. He was impressed with your negotiating skills

and made it very clear that if they retain our firm, they want you to handle all of Rory's contracts."

I could barely think when I was around Rory Gregor. Now they wanted me to be his legal representation? How would this work? It wouldn't. I would never be able to do this. I had to refuse. Rory Gregor would ruin me. He'd eat me alive and spit me out and never give me a second thought.

Sensing my apprehension, Mr. Stedwick continued. "Hindley, I don't have to tell you how important this is to the firm. I'm not really asking you to do this."

His insinuation hit me square in the gut. If I didn't take on Rory as a client, my future with the firm would be in jeopardy. And possibly Paul's investment.

I had no choice. Once again, I'd be living my life for someone else, trying to make someone else happy instead of myself. My life would not be my own.

But then again, ever since I'd seen Rory Gregor in my bed, taken in his tantalizing tattoo, his mesmerizing eyes, and his rock-hard body, I'd known somewhere deep inside me on a spiritual level that I'd already lost myself to him.

The first time his lips touched mine, I'd felt like a polarized magnet drawn to something deep within him, a moth to a flame destined to burn alive. I'd tried to pull away, but it had been impossible. His sexual energy was too strong for someone as naïve as me.

There was no doubt in my mind Rory had sent those passes to me on purpose. In the game of sex and passion, Rory Gregor was a professional and I didn't stand a chance. My only hope was that he wouldn't completely destroy me.

CHAPTER 17

RORY

"Dude, will you calm the fuck down?" Leif said. "You're making me a nervous wreck."

I raked a hand through my hair. "I am a nervous wreck."

"You'll be fine."

"I'm not nervous about that." I nodded my head toward the stage as we stood behind a curtain. "Well, I am."

"You know I'm here. There won't be any surprise questions, I promise."

I squeezed Leif's shoulder. "I know, man. I know. Thanks."

"Then what is it?"

I clasped my hands behind my neck, glancing up at the ceiling as I let out a heavy sigh. Leif was my best friend. He'd stood by me for years and held on to my deep, dark secret, protecting me ever since I'd known him. The stress I put on him was unfair, but I didn't know what else to do. We were brothers. He'd do anything for me if I asked him.

"It will be okay, man."

I nodded, trying to convince myself he was right. I wanted to see Hindley so badly, it actually hurt somewhere deep inside. I'd never felt like this way in my life, never experienced this kind of longing, and it scared the shit out of me.

It was more than Hindley that scared the shit out of me. I shook out my hands and glanced around the curtain. The trade show floor was packed and as usual, I was ready to piss myself thinking about sitting at a table fielding questions.

Reporters would shove magazines at me and ask me to comment on articles or the sport in general. Fans would hand me letters they'd written me and want me to read them out loud. The entire time on stage would be a major cluster fuck for me. It was a good thing I didn't drink any more because if I did, I'd be three ways to shit-faced right now.

Usually Jack sat with me and interceded when problems came my way. It looked natural to have him close by. He was my manager. But tonight, Jack was out of town and Leif was joining me for the panel discussion. This was his big event, it was his skate park's grand opening. Thankfully he was leading the symposium. Leif would never let anything or anyone jeopardize my secret.

"She'll be here, man, relax," he said.

I didn't even have to tell Leif who I was thinking of. "How do you know?"

"My dad made sure."

"I know he sent the passes, I asked him to. That doesn't mean she'll use them though."

Leif smirked.

"What?"

"My dad told the attorney dude that you specifically asked for Hindley to represent you."

"I did ask for her." After the shit-show they'd called a contract negotiation where Hindley basically handed my attorney his ass, I didn't trust Gene-O anymore.

"Dad said she totally crushed poor Gene-O."

"You should have seen her, man. She was a beast in that board-room. She tore his ass apart. I actually felt kind of bad for him. I mean, he's always been decent to me. Plus, he's protected my secret with a vengeance, so I never faulted him for not being the *best* attorney."

"I can't believe he was being such a dumbass about your contracts though."

"You know my reputation. I was lucky to get anyone to sponsor me at all, let alone represent me. Beggars can't be choosers."

"No, but they can at least trust their attorneys to get them the best deal possible, given their current ranking."

"I'm only ranked sixth right now."

"Only? Some kids would kill to *only* be in sixth place."

"I was on top once, remember? Being in sixth place is like not even showing up for the event to me."

"Whatever." He rolled his eyes.

I felt like an ungrateful douche bag. Leif had always loved to skate, but he didn't have the talent to compete at the pro level. I'd always thought it a blessing. He created some of the best skate parks in the world, and he made a shit load of money doing it.

"Look, I'm sorry, man," I said. "I didn't mean it that way."

Leif nodded.

"I just know that skating isn't her thing. I'm afraid she won't show and I really want to see her, to thank her for..." I couldn't go on.

"What?"

"For believing in me. For fighting for me."

"I do all those things for you, man."

"Yeah, but you don't have long blonde hair, a body made for sin, and legs to die for."

"I don't know." He pulled up his jeans to reveal one scrawny leg. "These legs look pretty good if you ask me."

I stared at his leg then up at his face. We both burst into laughter.

"Look, don't worry, man. My dad said her law firm wants to get involved in this type of law."

"What type of law?"

"Representing sports figures."

"That's not what they do now?"

"I don't think so." Leif shook his head.

"Damn, she could have fooled me. She sounded like she'd been doing this shit for years. My dick got hard just watching her fight for me. I could barely stand up to leave, it hurt so bad."

Leif choked and spewed Red Bull all over the stage. "That was," he coughed, "graphic." He wiped his mouth with the back of his hand. "She must be hot."

"You have no idea, Leif." I closed my eyes, thinking back to our meeting earlier this week. "She was wearing this tight-ass red dress and these fuck-me pumps. She looked like a naughty librarian or something."

I opened my eyes.

Leif stared at me, brows raised.

"What?"

"Just, be careful, man."

"Whatever." I knew what Leif was saying. Don't fuck this up. But I couldn't help it. I couldn't get Hindley out of my mind no matter how hard I tried. And I'd tried.

All I'd been able to dream about after our meeting was throwing her sexy ass down on that fucking conference table and ripping that dress off. I'd throw those shoes over my shoulders and drive into her, hard and fast, just the way I knew she'd want it.

I honestly didn't know how any of those attorney bastards got any work done looking at her all day. The thought had seized my balls with red-hot jealousy that day. Even now, the thought of any man lusting after Hindley had my blood boiling.

I cracked open a Red Bull and swallowed down half the can in one gulp. Because of my addictive personality I didn't drink them a lot. Red Bull had been a good sponsor in the past and I hoped maybe if I proved myself worthy, they'd support me again.

I'd managed to fuck up a lot of endorsement deals when I'd gone off the deep end years ago. I had to get my shit together now and make up for lost time. If I wanted to keep training at the level, I needed in order to become number one again, I would have to secure more sponsors and major endorsement deals. I believed Hindley could do that for me, and there were very few people I believed in.

I was stoked to have River City Skateboards sponsor me. The contract was solid. Hindley had made sure. But I needed at least two more major deals by the end of the summer if I wanted to keep skating.

Most people didn't realize that it took a butt load of money to be an independent pro athlete. I didn't have a team or a franchise backing me. If I failed, a lot of other people did too. At least with the River City deal, they were providing all my equipment. That would definitely help with some of my expenses.

"Anyway," Leif said, "I'm pretty sure her law firm is foaming at the mouth to have you. Dad told them you like her."

"What!" I darted around the backstage area. "Why the fuck did he tell them that?"

"Calm down, ass wipe. He told them you like her, *professionally*. You admire how she defended you and fought for your fair share of the earnings."

"Oh. I do."

"My dad said the firm wants to learn the industry. The owner dude is kind of chomping at the bit and offered up Hindley. Trust me, if she wants a future with her law firm, she'll be here."

"Dude, I didn't want it to go down like that."

"Like what?"

"I didn't want to force her to come. I wanted her to *want* to come, *want* to learn more about my sport, especially if she's going to represent me."

"Hey, whatever gets her here, right?" He smirked.

I shook my head. I didn't want to force Hindley to do anything. That wasn't my style. If she felt pressured, she'd resent me, and that was the last thing I wanted.

Leif looked down at his watch. "Dude, we've got to go. You ready?"

"I guess."

"Let's give these people a show." He waggled his brows.

I laughed out loud.

It always surprised me how supportive my fans had been over the last few years as I worked hard to straighten out my life. People said it was because my skills were unsurpassed, but it was more than that. They were rooting for me. My fans were there for me, and this time, I wasn't going to disappoint them.

Leif's voice boomed over the PA system and broke through my thoughts.

I glanced up and saw him sitting down at the table.

"Ladies and gentlemen, I want to welcome you to the River City Skateboards' Pro-Am Tournament and Trade Show."

Cheers erupted in the auditorium.

"My name is Leif Jennings, owner and lead designer of Fly By Nite Skate Park Developments. I want to extend my sincere thanks to River City Skateboards for sponsoring this event."

More applause echoed through the room as people made their way closer to the stage.

"Thanks," Leif said. God, he was built for this shit. If he wasn't such a talented designer, I would definitely have pegged him for PR work.

"I'd also like to thank all our pro skaters who have joined us this weekend, as well as some up-and-coming amateurs who will also participate in this symposium," he said. "If you haven't already given your questions to Mr. Chip Billings, please do so now. He's standing here at the front of the stage. We'll try to answer as many of them as we can."

I smiled to myself. Leif had purposely had all the questions written down and filtered through one person so I wouldn't be surprised. He'd always had my back.

I searched the crowd for Hindley as Leif continued to introduce all the skaters. As much as I didn't want her to be forced to come, I couldn't deny that I was happy to know she would be here.

"And finally," Leif said, "I'd like to introduce a man who needs no introduction. Currently ranked at number six but climbing the charts by kickflips and tailslides…"

Leif's voice faded into silence when my eyes found her at the back of the auditorium.

She stood tall, her blonde hair pulled back in a high ponytail. She loved those damned ponytails, and surprising to me, I loved her in them too. I fantasized about holding on to her mane of hair as I took her in every sexual position imaginable.

Her eyes darted around the enormous convention center. She looked as nervous and out of place as a whore in church. I wondered why she was so anxious. She should try being up here on stage. Now more than ever I longed to be off this stage and down on the convention floor next to her.

"Rory!" Leif shouted over his shoulder as he covered the mic.

Oh, shit. How long had he been saying my name?

I walked toward the chair he held out. Just before I sat, I scanned the back of the auditorium. My heart dropped when I didn't see her. She'd probably left after taking one look at the freak show that was my life.

We skateboarders and our fans were an interesting bunch of misfits no doubt. But we were also a family, for lack of a better term. If this girl couldn't find a way to fit into skating, then anything I wanted from her would never work.

After an hour of the typical questions and my usual answers, the symposium ended. Thankfully with no surprises. I spent the rest of the evening signing autographs and taking pictures with fans. Usually, I didn't mind it at all, but tonight I had one mission on my mind, and being with all these people in a crowded convention center wasn't it.

The last fan strolled away from the stage, my clumsy signature adorning his River City skateboard. I stretched my neck, glancing up for the first time in two hours. The show floor was nearly empty. I checked my watch. It was ten thirty. The trade show ended at nine. I was sure Hindley was long gone now.

With a long sigh, I gathered all the markers I'd used to sign fans' souvenirs and stacked them in a neat pile. I pushed back in my chair, a heavy weight of disappointment in my chest. Usually interacting with the fans at an event had me high as a kite. But not tonight.

"You're a pretty popular fella," a familiar voice said behind me.

I recognized the Southern accent. My pulse raced as I glanced over my shoulder.

She'd changed her outfit. Her hair, no longer in a ponytail, hung loose in soft waves that caressed the swells of her breasts. She wore a pair of dark blue skinny jeans that showcased her long, lean legs. Bright yellow DC brand high tops adorned her feet. The fitted top she'd worn in earlier had been replaced with a River City Skateboards T-shirt.

Hindley made a dramatic, sweeping turn, showing me her backside. And it was a magnificent backside. She slowly swept her hair from her back and glanced over her shoulder. "Do you like it?"

I stared at her ass.

"Rory."

Oh, shit. "What?"

"Do you like it?"

"Yeah, I like it."

Hindley laughed. "The T-shirt."

"Oh." I forced my eyes higher. The graphic on her shirt was the silhouette of a girl with a ponytail doing a kickflip. Words spanned across the top but I didn't know what the fuck it said. My heart pounded in my chest. I prayed to God she wouldn't ask me to read it.

"Well?" she asked, biting her lip.

My dick swelled. Shit, she was hot as fuck. I forced myself to look out her outfit objectively. The clothes seemed inappropriate for someone as rich and sophisticated as Hindley. But honestly, she looked like heaven, adorned in the clothes of my lifestyle.

"I like it." I smiled, pretty sure she knew I meant more than just the outfit.

Her face blushed red.

Yeah, she knew. "You stayed," I said.

"I wanted an autograph." She smirked, her eyes dancing with playfulness as her long lashes batted against her pale skin. She held out a black felt tip pen and rested her chin on her shoulder, brows raised.

Was she...flirting with me? Blood pulsed in my midsection as images of her chin resting on my thigh with her plump mouth taking my—

"Rory."

I coughed and bent over. My dick was hard as stone.

"Are you okay?" She stepped closer.

"Are you serious? You want my autograph?"

"Oh, very. I didn't stand in line for two hours for nothing. Here." She held out the pen as her big brown eyes rolled up to meet mine.

Fuck.

I struggled to draw in air. "You're, um," I sputtered, "you're sure?" My voice cracked like a pubescent teen's.

"Um hum," she murmured, batting her eyelashes, her huge doe eyes shining back at me. "Please." She turned around to give me access to her entire back.

Holy. Fucking. Shit.

The dull ache in my pants was becoming a painful throb. She was definitely flirting. And I was totally okay with that.

I steadied my hand around the marker as I moved closer. Placing my free hand on her shoulder to anchor myself, my thumb caressed the exposed skin on her neck.

She sucked in a breath and stiffened under my touch.

I inwardly gave myself a high-five. I affected her as much as she did me. My fingers brushed against her hair as I leaned in closer. Christ, she smelled fucking amazing, and her hair was like satin.

Before I could conjure any more X-rated thoughts, I scribbled my name as quickly as I could, knowing if I didn't back away from her soon, I'd throw her down and rip off all her clothes and bury myself deep inside her.

My erection was now to the point of pain. I started counting backward from a hundred and thought of the old lady at the grocery store by my house. She had more hair on her chin than I did.

"Are you okay?" Hindley asked.

I jumped. Shit. She was talking. I shifted on my feet, thankful my woody was finally going down. "Yeah, I'm good. Just tired."

"Oh, I'm sorry. I should get going."

"Are you hungry?" I blurted. I didn't want her to go. "Because I'm starving. All I had was a corn dog at lunch. Do you want to go get something to eat?"

"No," she said, "I had a funnel cake and shared some nachos with Dana earlier."

I looked past Hindley and saw Dana talking to a few pro skaters who were performing tomorrow. "Looks like she made some new friends."

Hindley glanced over her shoulder. "Yeah, Dana always finds friends somewhere." She turned to face me, a pinched expression on her face.

Was she pissed? At me? There was definitely more going on behind those brown eyes. If I didn't act soon, I was going to lose her to some invisible force.

"She's an outgoing girl," I said.

"I know." Hindley stared back at Dana and rolled her eyes. She wasn't angry; she was envious.

"You take your time getting to know people," I said. "It doesn't mean one is better than the other. They're just…different."

She stared at me, her eyes filled with a haunting mix of gratitude and fear.

I wrapped an arm around her shoulders and drew her in close, thinking all the while she'd fight and try to escape.

Instead, she wrapped her arms snuggly around my waist and laid her forehead on my chest.

"Come on, let's go, lovers." Dana's voice cut through our

moment of intimacy. That little pixie cock blocker was starting to annoy me.

As if coming to her senses, Hindley pushed me away with such force I almost stumbled back. She glared at me, as if I'd done something sordid and disgusting.

I didn't know what to say to make her feel better, so instead I acted as if nothing had happened, as if there'd been absolutely no connection between us. "I'll see you tomorrow?"

"Yeah," she nodded, "I'll be here."

Her feigned expression of excitement mixed with her monotone voice were proof that being at a skateboarding exhibition wasn't anything remotely close to what she wanted to do this weekend. I didn't care. As long as she was here, as long as she saw me in action, I'd take it.

I knew Hindley had probably seen a shitload about me on the Internet, most of which wasn't even true. Those asshole reporters thrived on blowing shit out of proportion to get readers to buy their rag mags. The look on her face when she'd walked into that conference room earlier this week reflected it and I'd been on a recon mission ever since.

I hoped that if she saw me in my element, successful at something and not fucking everything up, then maybe she'd give me a second chance. I couldn't rely on my skills as a decent human being to win her back.

"Where are y'all staying?" I asked.

"We're not. We're going back to Austin tonight," Hindley said. "Then I'll drive back down tomorrow."

I glanced over at Dana then back to Hindley, surprised and disappointed that she wouldn't be spending the night.

"I have to work tomorrow, *Cheater*," Dana said, one brow cocked high above her blue eyes. She was pissed. At me. Hindley must have told her I called another chick last week. I didn't even remember the woman's name now. Last weekend, Dana had been my ally. Gaining back her support was recon mission number two.

"Dana!" Hindley said.

"What?"

"It's okay," I said, "I deserve it."

"No, you don't." Hindley's eyes narrowed.

"Where do you work?" I asked. I'd never thought of Dana working before. She'd said her Beemer was a gift from her parents so I'd assumed she was independently wealthy like Hindley. I, of all people, should know better than to make assumptions.

"Denny's," she answered.

I burst out laughing. "No, seriously. Where do you work?" I glanced between the two of them and noticed neither were laughing. I stilled, my mouth clamping shut as my face heated with embarrassment. Shit, she wasn't kidding. "Um, sorry, I guess I thought—"

"Well, that's probably your problem, *player*." Dana narrowed her eyes. "Trying to think when your mind's not used to it."

"Ouch," I said, understanding clearly now that she was not a woman to be fucked with. I'd insulted her. If I couldn't get Hindley's best friend back on my side, I'd never have a chance with her. I had to make this right, sooner rather than later.

I walked toward Dana and stopped in front of her. She was so short so I had to strain my neck to look down. "Look, Dana, I'm sorry. You're right, I am an asshole, in more ways than I'd like to admit. I made an assumption and I judged you. It's something I'm all too familiar with. I hate it when people do that to me. I never meant to insult you and I hope you'll forgive me."

She slugged my arm with her fist.

I was caught off guard by how much it hurt. This girl was packed with dynamite and I was totally afraid of her. How could someone barely five feet tall be so intimidating?

"Don't worry about it. All's forgiven, One-Nighter."

"I thought that wasn't my name any more because, you know." I nodded over to Hindley.

"Oh, yeah, that's right. You failed to seal the deal, didn't you, Cheater?"

Hindley rolled her eyes, but I saw the hint of a smirk lurking.

Dana stepped in closer, cupping her mouth.

I leaned in closer.

"Maybe after this weekend, I'll call you All-Nighter, yeah?"

I straightened, not sure how to react. Was she calling me a man-whore?

She winked at me and flashed a bright smile.

Did this pint-sized vixen actually *want* me to sleep with Hindley?

"What the hell did you say, Dana?" Hindley half shouted.

"I told him to keep his dick in his pants if he didn't want me to chop it off. He has a lot of explaining to do."

"He doesn't have *any* explaining to do." Hindley scowled at Dana.

"Of course, he does," Dana answered. "I mean, who does shit like that?"

"Look, I fucked up, Dana. Plain and simple. I wish I had a better explanation than the fact that I was a dick, but I don't."

Her eyes rolled up to mine and she gave me another wink just outside of Hindley's view. Her nose wrinkled and she had the distinct look of mischief in her blue eyes.

Suddenly I realized this show wasn't about me. Dana was trying to rile Hindley up to make her defend me. I wasn't sure if I loved Dana or loathed her for it. I was already familiar enough with Hindley to know that when she became agitated or passion-ate, her lips seemed to find mine, so I settled on loving Dana.

"Dude, we need to get back to the hotel," Leif said behind me. "You've got an early morning tomorrow."

I glanced over my shoulder and saw Leif carrying several bags. I rushed to his side and took two off his shoulders. They were heavy as shit. "What the hell is in here?"

"Stuff." Leif nodded toward Dana. "Hey."

"Leif, this is Dana."

Dana stuck out her hand.

Leif looked her up and down like he was afraid to touch her for fear of being attacked, but slowly shook her hand. "Cool eyes," he said.

"Thanks."

"And this is Hindley." I swung my arm toward Hindley.

Leif's eyes went wide as he stared from Hindley to me. "Nice," he mouthed.

"Hindley, this is my best friend Leif. Jack's son."

"Oh." Hindley nodded. "Yes, I met your father earlier this week. He's very nice. It's good to meet you, Leif."

"Nice to meet you too." Leif took her hand in his. "I've heard a lot about you."

"Well, don't believe a word of it. Unless it was good." She laughed.

The throaty vibrations of her laughter reverberated through my body, making my dick throb in pain.

She took his hand in both of hers and smiled. I recognized the gesture, and the expression. I'd found an ally in Dana, and Hindley had found one in my best friend too.

"I'm sorry, I didn't mean to keep y'all," Hindley said. Her Texas drawl made me crazy and had me dreaming of all kinds of sordid pictures of her body wrapped around mine.

Leif turned from Hindley then back to Dana. "Where are y'all staying?"

"We're actually heading back to Austin tonight," Hindley answered.

"No, we're not!" Dana shouted from behind us. She held up her phone in victory, as if she'd conquered Spain. "They just called me. Said they found a replacement. I'm good until Sunday morning." Her eyes held a mischievous glimmer.

I looked from her, to Hindley, then over to Leif. All three remained surprisingly quiet. Was I the only one who found this change of events odd? I expected Hindley to argue, but instead she stared at her best friend in disbelief. Dana had found a reason to stay in San Antonio–Leif Jennings.

"Where do you work?" Leif asked.

Oh, shit. She was going to rip him a new one man if he laughed.

"Denny's," Dana said, her answer begging him to make fun of her. I prepared myself for World War III, knowing she'd tear his ass up and feed it to him if he even thought of laughing.

"Oh, cool. I'm starving. Can you get us a discount if we find one here in San Antonio?"

And just like that, the pair walked off the stage, talking and laughing as if they'd been lifelong friends.

I glanced at Hindley. The resigned look on her face broke my heart. She shrugged her shoulders, her lips curling into a painful smile that didn't warm her eyes.

"Always makes a friend wherever she goes." She laughed quietly, but I could hear the disappointment in her voice.

"And you take it slow," I reminded her. Her gaze met mine and I found myself lost in her chocolate brown eyes. She looked scared, vulnerable. I could sense that no one else had ever dared to peer so deep.

She ducked her head, breaking our gaze and backed away like a frightened animal.

If I approached too fast, she'd attack, not out of anger, but in defense, in fear. I could see she'd been hurt in the past, like me. That fact made me want her even more. I never wanted anything or anyone to hurt her again.

I lifted the bags higher on my shoulder and walked toward the steps. I wanted her to know I meant no harm. If she wanted to wait, I'd be patient. It went against every natural habit in my being. I was an instant gratification kind of guy in every part of my life, not just sex. But if Hindley was scared, I'd wait.

God, was I thinking about having sex with my attorney? That was so fucked up. There had to be a law against that.

I glanced back over my shoulder, staring at her intently. She was lost and I wanted to bring her back, back to me. "Hey," I called out, waiting until I had her attention. "I wanted to say thank you."

She clumsily followed me toward the edge of the stage. She was having trouble walking in her new shoes. DC shoes were big and bulky and probably weighed as much as she did. It was amazing to watch her plunge head first into my world right in front of my eyes though. I was her Skater Boy and something inside me wondered if maybe she could be my Skater Girl. Could she grow to love this sport as much as I did? God, I hoped so.

"You're welcome," she said quietly.

Her throaty reply had my dick buzzing again. It was bizarre. I didn't need to tell her *why* I was grateful, she instinctively knew. She understood that I was grateful she'd stood up for me in a way no one ever had before.

"I owed you one, remember?" she said.

"Why?" I reached back, offering her my hand to help her down the stairs. I laughed silently, watching her clunk down each step.

"Any man who holds a girl's hair back when she's vomiting and practically makes her stepsister piss on herself from humiliation deserves to have proper legal representation." She smiled.

I felt something in my heart squeeze.

"Plus," she said, "I know how much you hate attorneys so I wanted you to know that we're not all ambulance chasing vultures."

We reached the bottom of the stairs and she stopped directly in front of me.

Our eyes locked and I felt that pull, the one that always came right before my need to kiss Hindley and get her into all kinds of kinky positions. *Go slow. Go slow. Go slow.*

I took a small step backward, trying to distance myself. "We're even."

Her brows creased. She was confused by my actions. I couldn't blame her. Hell, I was too. She'd expected me to go in for the kill but I'd resisted. She looked...disappointed. Should I go for it?

Jack's words rolled through my head. He always told me, "When in doubt, leave it out." He used the mantra for training purposes, reminding me that during competitions, if I wasn't completely sure about a trick, I shouldn't do it. In the end he said

I'd be rewarded for the tricks I did well and not judged for the tricks I screwed up.

I'd been judged all my life for the fuck ups I'd made. I wouldn't be able to stand it if I looked up in the stands and saw Hindley's disapproving gaze. As much as I wanted to slip my arms around her waist, press my body against hers, and cover her lips with mine, I had to wait. I wasn't completely confident that's what *she* wanted. If it wasn't, she'd run. And I couldn't take that.

I drank in her body, enjoying the masterpiece that was Hindley Hagen. She was breathtaking. "I like your Skater Girl look." I winked. "It suits you."

She shrugged her shoulders in a shy way that I was beginning to recognize and appreciate.

"Really?" she asked.

Her question was so innocent and fresh.

She pointed her toe and flexed her ankle, showing me both sides of her shoes. Grabbing her shirt by the hem, she stared at the graphic. "I wasn't sure if I could pull it off."

"Hindley, you could wear a garbage bag and still be the most beautiful woman in the room."

Her eyes flashed up to mine and we were lost again.

I hoped she could hear the sincerity in my voice. God, I wanted her so badly. It was taking all the strength I possessed not to drop these damn bags from my shoulders, grab her up, throw her on the stage, and screw her senseless.

Go slow. I reminded myself. I also reminded myself that I was an extreme sports athlete. Slow wasn't in my vocabulary.

Her eyes glowed with a look of hunger that mirrored my own but still I pulled back.

"So, you gonna get the Grand Slam?" I changed the subject, giving myself time to tame my dick to a size that would allow me to walk again without limping in pain.

She ducked her head but not before I saw it flush with color. Had she been thinking dirty thoughts too? God, I hoped so.

"What are you talking about?" she asked.

"At Denny's." I reached back and took her hand. "The Grand Slam? I love that dish." I tugged her close and felt an odd sense of satisfaction and familiarity as we walked out of the convention center hand in hand.

Her lips twisted into a small smile.

God, I wanted to kiss them again.

Go slow.

Go slow.

Yep, still wasn't working.

CHAPTER 18

HINDLEY

"I TOTALLY DON'T GET IT." Dana spoke around a mouthful of breakfast taco.

"What's there to get?" I stared down at my coffee cup before taking another sip. I didn't want her to 'get' anything.

Instead of answering her, I studied the skate park Leif had designed. The course was huge, taking up at least three acres. Half of the park looked like a giant empty swimming pool with humps of varying shapes and sizes. The other side contained several sets of staircases with railings and side boards. All in all, the area looked like a chaotic mess to me, but the participants warming up seemed to love it.

Dana swallowed her food. "Uh uh. Don't do that."

"Do what?"

"Play all cute and innocent like you don't know what the fuck I'm talking about." She wiped her mouth with a napkin. "That shit doesn't fly with me and you know it."

I sat my cup beside me on the bleachers and stared at her. "What do you not get?" I didn't have to ask her; we'd been best friends since we were kids. She got me.

"First, you say Rory doesn't mean anything to you. Then, you say you're totally attracted to him but you're not going to do anything with him. And now you're all upset and pouty because he didn't ravish you last night when you gave him the thumbs up."

"I'm just saying that I don't understand him."

"Do you want him or not?"

I closed my eyes and tipped my face toward the sun as I let Dana's question roll through my befuddled brain. I knew the answer, I just didn't want to say it out loud.

It was a gorgeous morning, perfect for the day's skating event. We sat in the VIP bleachers in the middle of the skate park Rory's friend, Leif, had designed. The park was filling up fast with spectators and fans, more than I ever thought would show. It was only 8:45 a.m. and already there were hundreds of people packed around the perimeter of the park.

"I want him," I finally answered on a sigh, unable to look at her. The revelation was more to myself than to Dana. I opened one eye and peered down at her.

She bobbed her head in approval, working to stifle a laugh. She already knew my answer before she'd even asked the question.

"I want him," I repeated, "but I can't have him."

"Why not?" she asked, shoving the last bite of her breakfast taco in her mouth.

Dana never ceased to amaze me. She was tiny, just over five feet tall and barely a hundred pounds, but she ate like a horse and never gained an ounce.

"Is it because he's a skater boy?"

I laughed. She was right, I'd never been attracted to the 'Bad Boy' type of guy, but that wasn't why I wouldn't allow myself to even think about being with Rory Gregor. "I can't be with him because I represent him. We have a professional relationship."

"So?"

"So, I could lose my job if we did anything else."

"Only if you get caught." She winked as she sucked on her straw. Her efforts were in vain, she'd drained the cup dry moments earlier. She shook her cup, refusing to believe it was empty before cutting her blue eyes back to me. "Do you like him?"

I rolled my coffee cup back and forth in my hands, trying to think about my answer. Of course, I liked him, but I couldn't allow myself to feel for a client. Especially one as sexy and sinful as Rory Gregor.

"It doesn't matter if I like him or not," I finally answered. "To me, he has to be off limits."

"So why were you so upset that he snubbed you last night?"

"Just because I can't do anything with him doesn't mean I don't *want* him to want me."

She rolled her beautiful aqua blue eyes in disgust. "You're sick, you know that?"

"What?"

"Did you hear yourself? I thought you were a feminist."

"I'm a realist."

"Well, Miss Realist, reality is, he's totally hot for you."

"Really?"

Dana snapped her gaze back to me.

I'd answered too quickly, and I was pretty sure my voice cracked it was so high. Dana could always see right through me.

"You're pathetic."

"How do you know?"

"How do I know you're pathetic?" She laughed sarcastically. "Because you look like a giddy schoolgirl who found out through the playground grapevine that little Johnny has a crush on you."

"No, how do you know he's hot for me?" I batted my eyes, striving to appear coy, but Dana knew me better than anyone else on earth. I *was* pathetic.

"First of all, let's get one thing straight," she said. "It is beyond me why you don't see how gorgeous you are. You still see yourself as the dorky sister of Geneva Barton, but that's not who you are any more. Hell, you were *never* that girl. Even back then you were beautiful and Geneva knew it. That's why she always put shit in your head to make you feel bad about yourself."

Dana was right. In high school, I had been heavier and had always been self-conscious. When I was a teen, people always told me I had a beautiful face, but I chose not to believe them. That was something you told a fat girl to make her feel better.

Sensing my insecurities, Paul had invited me to compete in a father-daughter triathlon my senior year to boost my confidence. He'd been competing for years but I was reluctant, not because I didn't think I could do it, but because it was for fathers and daughters.

Even though I felt awkward, I agreed and three months later and twenty pounds lighter, Paul and I finished third in the competition and I'd been running ever since.

When we crossed the finish line at our first triathlon, I made my mind up that day that I was a different person, inside and out. Yet here I sat, seven years later, still stuck in my self-deprecating thoughts, wondering why Rory Gregor didn't find me attractive. I was very close to soaking my misery in a huge funnel cake.

Dana's voice broke through my morbid thoughts. "Plus, Leif told me Rory was a nervous wreck yesterday waiting for you to show."

"Really?"

"Yeah. I think he wants to make a good impression with you, you know, because he fucked up so bad in the beginning. Plus, the way Leif talked, I don't think Rory feels like he's even in your league, or has a right to pursue you."

"That's ridiculous."

"That's what I told him. I said, hey, if you knew *half* the shit Hindley's done, you'd say she's way beneath Rory."

"No, you didn't."

"No, I didn't, but it's true."

"Definitely." I nodded. "If he only knew." Truth was, I didn't want him to know what I'd been involved in, or what had happened to me. I knew he'd judge me and that's why I never told anyone what I'd been through. Only my mom, Paul, and Dana knew my history, and even *they* didn't know *everything*.

"You and Rory are actually perfect for each other."

"Why do you say that?"

"You're both running from your past, trying to escape being judged by people you couldn't give a shit less about."

"That's not true."

"Yes, it is. Why won't you sleep with Rory?"

"Well, for one, because he's never asked me."

"Please. Whatever." She rolled her eyes so hard, I thought they may fall out of their sockets. "You won't sleep with him because you're afraid your law firm will fire you. You're afraid Rory will judge you. It's the biggest fuckin' lose-lose scenario I've ever seen."

I took in a deep breath, trying to comprehend Dana's statement. I was so busy worrying about what other people thought about me that I was letting my life pass me by.

"Fuck everyone else," Dana said. "What does *Hindley* want?"

I couldn't help but laugh at her question.

"What's so funny?" she asked.

"Luis asked me the same question."

"And what did you tell him?"

"I told him I didn't know."

She shook her head as if I were a lost cause.

"I know." I smiled. "Luis said I already knew what I wanted. I just wouldn't admit it to myself."

"And that is why I am clinically depressed," Dana said.

"Why?"

"I'm depressed because Luis is gay. He's the perfect man for me, except the whole gay thing." Dana giggled.

"I don't know if you need Luis. It seemed like you and Leif were getting along pretty well last night."

Her eyes light up. "He is cute, isn't he?"

I laughed.

It wasn't a question, it was a statement and I could tell she liked him. That one fact made me happy.

Dana had had a string of not so nice guys from her past. She always put out a sense of self-confidence and assurance. But since the death of her parents more than six years ago, I knew her acting out came from a place of self-loathing rather than self-reliance like others thought.

From the outside, Dana's crass personality looked like confidence, but I knew her actions were a defense mechanism. She felt alone, and lonely, even though she was surrounded by people most of the time.

Her bright blue eyes grew bigger and I followed her gaze, not surprised to see Leif walking toward the grandstand.

"Hey!" he shouted, waving at her.

"Hey," she said, holding up one hand.

I bumped her shoulder. "Now, who's being pathetic?" I wanted to give her more grief but I lost my breath when I saw the man following close behind Leif. Rory. And God, he looked amazing, every bit of the professional athlete that he was.

He wore blue jeans and a bright yellow T-shirt that was baggy but still showcased his muscular physique. The shirt bore the River City Skateboards logo as did the black helmet he held in his hand. His shoes were black suede with a yellow DC logo, like the ones I had on yesterday. The color reversal put an idiotic grin on my face.

Slowly his eyes caught mine and he stopped. His mouth spread wide in a beautiful grin showcasing two small dimples at the edge of his lips.

I held my breath, wondering what he'd do next.

His clear blue eyes sparkled in the morning sun and I lost myself in their pull. The warmth of his gaze spread through my body and pooled between my legs.

He climbed the stairs, two at a time, making his way to our row, his smile growing bigger. Just before he reached our row he stopped in the aisle.

He turned his attention to Dana. "Hey." He nodded once.

"Hey, man." She held out a fist. "Good luck today."

Rory smirked and hit her small fist with his rather large one. "Thanks."

Oh, crap. They'd bonded. I didn't stand a chance with this man now. Dana was going to help him get into my panties no matter what I did. My body hummed with desire as I imagined Rory Gregor inside my panties.

Finally, Dana scooted back.

Rory slid in next to me.

My pulse raced at his nearness. "What are you doing up here?" I laughed awkwardly.

He wrapped one arm around my waist while the other held his helmet and skateboard.

I was about to protest but before I could do anything, he tugged me close to his side and dropped his head so his lips were only inches from mine.

I inhaled deeply. His aroma was intoxicating, a mixture of soap, sunshine, and Rory. I gripped his arms for support as I gazed up into his blue eyes.

"You look amazing," he whispered.

His breath caressed my neck and my skin prickled. I gazed down at my clothes. I was wearing yellow shorts with a fitted, red, spaghetti strapped tank top and tan sandals, nothing earth shattering by any means.

He pulled away and his gaze followed mine, sweeping my body from head to toe.

It felt like he was devouring me with his eyes, and I loved it.

He leaned in. "Thanks for coming," he said close to my ear, his broad smile revealing how grateful he was.

"I had to."

His delighted expression vanished.

He'd taken my comment the wrong way. "No, I didn't mean it like that. I *wanted* to come, I *wanted* to see you skate. I just meant..." I hesitated, trying to choose my words carefully. "I meant, I had to come see you skate because I've heard how good you are from so many people. I *wanted* to see you skate, Rory."

I placed my hand on his chest and something clicked inside me, like I'd been connected to my missing piece.

"I had to see you, for myself," I said.

His eyes flashed with satisfaction as he nodded.

Thank God, I'd recovered. The last thing I wanted to do was upset him before his big event.

"Well, Drunk Girl, I hope you like what you see." His tone was laced with sexual innuendo, and I was surprised that it didn't offend me at all. He bent lower and whispered in my ear. "Because I sure like what I see."

Before I could respond he was gone, flying down the staircase as fast as he'd appeared. He stopped occasionally, taking pictures with fans and signing autographs.

"What the fuck did he say to you," Dana asked, "because you just had a major ear-gasm?"

I shook my head, trying to focus on Dana's voice but couldn't. "What?"

"Rory. What did he say?"

"What do you mean?" I asked, still lost in Rory's sexual vortex.

"He whispered something in your ear that made you come right here in front of God and all these spectators, no question about it."

"Dana! Shut up!" I bumped her shoulder with my arm.

"It's true, isn't it? I bet you need to go change your panties, don't you?"

I searched the area, ensuring no one had heard her. "Dana, shut up."

"What? I'm jealous. I bet that man can tear it up in bed," she growled and pumped her hips.

"Seriously, Dana, shut up."

"If you don't give up the poo-nanny to him, I will."

I shook my head. It was pointless trying to quiet Dana Di Grazio once she'd started a rant, especially when it was about sex. She was a semi-nympho but I'd be lying if I didn't admit I was somewhat jealous.

I wasn't well versed in the art of sex. In fact, I could claim only two conquests to my lowly existence.

Dana had always said there was something wrong with me, and she was right, I'd been scarred. Not to mention that my last boyfriend was pretty vocal about how bad I was in the sack.

If Rory took me to bed, he'd be disappointed too and would run away faster than he could get his boxers back up. That didn't make me want him any less though. It meant I had to work harder to stay away from him.

I turned my attention back to the event and watched as some of the skaters began moving around the course. The pro-am was amazing. I'd never seen anything like skateboarding. It was astonishing what these guys could do with a board and four wheels.

I felt smaller than an ant for judging the athletes the way I had. This was a bona fide sport, no question about it, and for the first time since Rory had been thrust upon me as a client, I was actually excited to learn about the skateboarding industry.

My eyes scanned the crowd and I was surprised to discover it had almost tripled in size, with well over a thousand screaming fans surrounding the entire park. They were yelling at the top of their lungs, chanting Rory's name and growing anxious to see him, and so was I.

Dana bumped my elbow and nodded toward the crowd above us. "This dude is for real. Listen to the crowd going nuts for Rory."

I had to admit, it felt like we were at a small rock concert. People of all ages were out watching this event.

I glanced around the park and saw spectators hoisting signs with Rory's name on it. My head turned and I smiled when I spotted a girl behind us, maybe sixteen or seventeen, holding a poster that read, 'I love U, SK8R BOY.' She'd drawn an actual heart to replace the word 'love' and plastered a huge lipstick smeared kiss inside the heart.

A pang of jealousy surged through me at the thought of someone else calling Rory 'Skater Boy'. It was *my* term of endearment.

Mine? Where had that come from? Rory was a client, not a possession.

Someone announced Rory's name.

The fans stood and looked toward one end of the skate park.

Suddenly, out of nowhere, Rory came sliding through an enormous cement cylinder and started his run.

I watched in awe as Rory flew over every obstacle with ease. I soon realized that every area of the park had been carefully designed by Leif and his team with great skill and intent. Each competitor had used almost every surface to do some type of death-defying trick and Rory was no exception.

The other skaters had done well, performing tricks that were definitely impressive, especially the other pros, but they were nothing compared to Rory. His skills proved why he'd once been on top of this sport and there was no doubt in my mind he'd be there again. Only this time, I'd take him there.

CHAPTER 19

HINDLEY

"Holy shit, Hindley, look at yourself," Dana said.

"What?" I asked, looking down at myself.

"Your skin. It looks like you're on fire."

During my shower I'd noticed the hot water had burned my shoulders but the way Dana was talking, I must be blistered. I stepped back into the bathroom and turned on the fluorescent lighting.

"Oh my God, Dana." My entire chest practically glowed, the skin was so red, except for two small white lines over my shoulders where my spaghetti straps had been.

"Holy shit, Hindley," Dana said, standing behind me in the bathroom. "This is bad."

I glanced at her reflection in the mirror. "What am I going to do, Dana? I have to go to this banquet tonight. I'm supposed to make contacts with other skaters and vendors. Mr. Stedwick will have a fit if I'm not there." Tears pooled in my eyes and before I could stop them, one rolled down my cheek.

"Okay, calm down," she said in a reassuring voice. "We'll figure out something." Before she could disclose her bright idea, she was gone.

Unable to look at my reflection, I followed her out and plopped down on the bed beside her.

She held the hotel phone to her ear. "Um, yes, do you have a pharmacy nearby?"

I touched my chest. Heat radiated from my skin before I even touched it. I swallowed down a sob. I couldn't lose it now.

"Oh, really?" Dana grinned at me. "Here, in the hotel? Is it open?" She paused and I felt my heart kick in to overdrive. "Oh, great, thanks." She replaced the receiver and popped up off the bed. "They have a store here in the hotel. I'll go down and grab some aloe vera lotion. Hopefully they have some with lidocaine, and you'll be good as new."

"Thank you," I sighed in relief. I stood and walked back into the bathroom to finish getting dressed.

Dana gasped.

"What?" I turned to face her.

"Uh, nothing, it's nothing." Her wide eyes and lax jaw were in stark contrast to her statement. She darted toward the mini fridge and began pillaging through the contents.

I must be just as red in the back. God, what was I thinking today? I was whiter than a sheet of paper. I knew better than to sit out in the sun all day without sunscreen but I couldn't help it. Rory had mesmerized me and I hadn't wanted to leave.

I'd stayed well after the event was over, watching him sign autographs and pose for photos. I'd been surprised at the number of fans he had. And it hadn't escaped my notice that many of them were beautiful young ladies. An unfamiliar ache of jealousy burned in the pit of my stomach.

I unwrapped the towel on my head, willing away my unwarranted feelings. I had no hold on Rory. Plus, those women were a great demographic to reach out to. Yeah, sure, I was concerned with marketing him.

I let my hair fall loose against my back but sucked in a breath. God, even my hair brushing against my skin hurt. I slowly combed the long tresses out, taking extra care not to scrape my back.

Dana stepped into the bathroom and sat a tumbler filled with some kind of amber liquid on the counter.

"What's this?" I asked.

"It will help with the pain."

"What is it, Dana?"

"Just drink it."

I lifted the tumbler and was assaulted with the aroma of strong alcohol. Usually I didn't drink before an event but at this moment, I didn't care. My back was already throbbing in pain. Experience had taught me it would only get worse as the evening went on. Without another thought, I cocked back my head and downed the contents in one gulp. The burn of the alcohol was nothing compared to the burn on my shoulders.

"Nice." Dana smiled. "Now, take these," she held out four orange pills in her hand, "and drink this whole bottle of water before I get back."

I grabbed the pain relievers from her palm and popped them in my mouth, swallowing them down with half the bottle of water.

"You'll be fine," she assured me, stopping her hand just before she patted my back. "Oh, shit. Sorry."

"Dana, what am I going to do? Everyone will want to shake hands and hug." Tears pricked the back of my eyes.

"Don't worry, sweetie, the alcohol and pain relievers will kick in soon. You'll be fine. Finish getting ready and I'll be back soon to help."

"Okay," I said, fighting back my emotions. She ducked from the bathroom and I heard the hotel room door shut. I turned and stared at my reflection in the mirror. My face wasn't burned, thankfully. I'd at least been smart enough to wear a hat. I gave a small shrug, resigning myself to the fact this was going to be a long night.

I was almost done drying my hair when I heard a knock on the door. Dana must have forgotten her key. Again. She was such a scatterbrain sometimes.

I tightened the towel around my body then swung the door

open. "Did you forget your key?" I laughed but stopped short when I saw who was standing just outside.

Rory stood tall, looking as delicious and hot as he had at Geneva's wedding. He was dressed in a suit, obviously for the banquet, which surprised me. I figured most skaters existed in jeans and a T-shirt all day long. But seeing him standing here before me in a platinum gray suit and starched white dress shirt, I was thankful that tonight he'd dressed up.

He wasn't wearing a tie and his top button was undone, revealing a dark patch of skin at this throat. My eyes roamed over his body. His suit was form-fitting and tailor made, hugging every curve. He looked edible. All I could think about was what a fool I'd been to be so drunk with him that first night after the club.

"Shit, Hindley." He gasped, his face bunched in what looked like pain.

His statement was like a bucket of ice water on my libido and I instantly snapped out of my erotic fantasy.

"What were you thinking?" he asked.

I sensed the real question he was asking. Why hadn't I taken better care of myself? The same question had been running through my mind all day. I sure as shit didn't need his reminder of how careless I'd been. Tears burned my eyes and I turned to leave, closing the door.

"Wait." He reached out and grabbed my shoulder.

"Owe!" I winced in pain.

"Oh my God, I'm so sorry, Hindley." He slipped into the room and scooped me up, gazing down at me. His blue eyes burned with remorse and sadness. "I didn't mean to hurt you, Hindley. I'm so sorry."

He'd mistaken my tears for physical pain. I remained silent. It was better he not know how disappointed I was. I was being ridiculous anyway.

He gently placed me on the bed and sat down beside me. "Here," he said, pulling a small bottle from his pocket.

"What's this?" I grasped the bottle from his hand, and when I did my fingers brushed against his skin. Fire raced through my body, burning me more than the sunburn.

"It's a special lotion I use when I get too much sun," he said. "It's a mix of aloe, lidocaine, and extra emollients that will help with the pain and discomfort."

"How did you know?"

"I saw you this afternoon when you got back to the hotel. I was going to stop by earlier because I knew you'd need it. But then I ran into Dana downstairs and she told me. I'm sorry, Hindley."

I stared at him. "Why?"

"I should have told you. I should have reminded you to put on sun block."

Why did he seem so hurt? "It's not your responsibility to take care of me."

He grimaced and jerked back as if I'd slapped him.

"I'm sorry, I didn't mean it like that. The sunburn, it just...hurts."

"Yeah, I know. Trust me." He gave me a lopsided grin and I felt the tension between us melting away. "Here, turn around. I'll put some on your back."

I hesitated for a moment. Did I really want him rubbing lotion on my skin? No. Definitely not. Not because of the physical pain his touch might bring, but because of the desire I knew it would spark inside me.

The bed gave way as he stood up. "Lay down on your stomach," he said with such an air of authority, I immediately complied.

Before I could second guess myself, he was on top of me, his legs straddling my rear end.

His weight on top of me sent my mid reeling and I immediately began to panic. Oh, God.

"Push up," he instructed.

My breathing grew shallow and my fingers clutched the comforter.

"Hindley." Rory's gentle voice rattled in my mind. He sat up, taking some of his weight off me. "Push up, babe."

"Wh-what?" I stuttered.

"Push up so I can pull the towel down and get to your back."

"I don't, I don't think—"

"Don't think, babe, just do."

Okay, that sounded simple enough. Don't think, just do.

He leaned closer, avoiding contact with my skin as he whispered close to my ear. "Push up, Mr. Krabs."

"Who?"

"You know, Mr. Krabs, the lobster on Sponge Bob. He owns the Krusty Krab."

"No." I shook my head.

"He's a lobster. You're as red as he is."

"Oh." Without thinking any more I did as Rory asked and lifted up.

"You seriously don't know Sponge Bob."

"No." I shook my head.

He laughed as he slid the towel down my back, almost to the crack of my ass, much further than necessary.

Chill bumps skittered across my skin.

"We'll have to watch it some time." He placed his warm hand in between my shoulders, gently pushing me down into the mattress.

Panic rose inside me again but I breathed through the fear. As my breasts grazed the silky comforter my fear was soon replaced with a rush of electric heat that quickly pooled between my legs. I realized then I was completely nude underneath this towel.

The bed dipped.

I darted over my shoulder, wondering what Rory was doing. I watched in mild fascination as he removed his jacket, tossing the coat onto the bed beside mine. He carefully unbuttoned his cuffs and rolled the sleeves up to his elbows.

His eyes met mine and I saw a hint of wickedness in his gaze. The bad boy had returned but this time I wasn't so scared.

He repositioned his body on top of me. I was surprised at how comfortable it felt, how well we fit together.

I closed my eyes and allowed myself to enjoy the moment. I

wasn't used to letting others take care of me but I had to admit it felt kind of nice.

Rory's hand gently slid across the nape of my neck and draped my hair to the side to expose my entire back.

I shuddered at his touch. Heat raced down my spine and coiled in my belly before quickly spreading south, settling between my legs with a slow burn. I'd never been this turned on in my life.

"Damn, Hindley, you're hot."

I let his words roll around in my head, enjoying the compliment. "Thanks," I said quietly.

"I bet your body temperature is up a full degree or two with this sunburn."

Wait, what? Body temperature? Oh, God, he wasn't talking about me being sexy, he was being literal. I was so embarrassed I pushed up off the mattress.

"What are you doing?" he asked.

"Just leave the lotion, Rory," I said through clenched teeth. "Dana can put it on when she gets back."

He pressed his body into mine, trapping me underneath him.

Tears stung my eyes as the buttons on his shirt gouged the sensitive skin on my bare back.

He lowered his chin, the rough growth of his beard abrading my shoulder.

"You're hurting me," I said. "Let me up."

"Listen to me, Drunk Girl," he whispered, not budging. "You know I think you're fuckin' hot as hell."

I squeezed my eyes shut and sagged back onto the bed.

"Can't you feel how sexy I think you are?" He pushed his hips into my back.

Oh, my Lord. His massive erection settled between my open legs. I had affected him. I smiled inwardly, realizing I had just as much power over his physical body as he had over mine.

"That's my Drunk Girl," he murmured in my ear, his warm breath caressing my neck.

Goose bumps spread across my body.

"Now relax and let me put this lotion on you." His lips caressed the area below my ear.

I sucked in a breath and something exploded…down there. What the hell?

"Relax," he murmured.

The tension in my body melted away as his surprisingly gentle hands spread lotion across my back and shoulders. It was so soothing and sensual that I almost had an orgasm without him being anywhere close to my private parts.

I didn't have much experience with orgasms, my other two sex partners being much more selfish in the bedroom—taking from me what they could and not giving much in return. Before I could relive any more unsatisfying memories, Rory's weight lifted off me. I was surprised how disappointed I felt.

"Roll over," his deep voice said behind me.

Not understanding, I pushed up and wrapped the towel around my body before sitting up. He was sitting on the other bed, facing me. "What?"

"Roll over, so I can do your front."

"Uh, no. But thanks, I can do the front." I reached across to take the bottle from him.

He yanked it out of my reach and his gaze fell to my lap.

My eyes followed his and I froze when I realized what he was looking at. My towel barely covered my girlie parts. My gynecologist hadn't even seen that much of my hooter. I shot up like a rocket, trying to make a beeline for the bathroom.

Rory caught me around the waist and tugged me between his legs.

My entire body heated with embarrassment when I realized how close his face was to my vajayjay. Shit, shit, shit.

I made to move but he put his large hand over my stomach and gently pushed me back. He stood and I had no choice but to back up. I jolted to a stop when my legs hit the other bed.

Rory stared down at me, our eyes locked. I noticed his were

darker, a deeper blue mixed with brown flecks that were strangely hypnotic.

"Lay down, Hindley," his baritone voice commanded.

I had no choice but to obey. Slowly I lowered to the bed and laid down on my back.

His predatory expression reminded me of a wild animal on the prowl as he climbed on top of me and straddled my hips. Surprisingly enough, I *wanted* to be devoured.

My body hummed with desire even though I clutched my towel tighter around me. I'd never felt so aroused, especially with a large man straddling me, basically holding me down. I should buck him off and tell him to leave, but I couldn't.

I knew what Rory was going to do, and despite my better judgment, I was going to let him. For better or for worse, I was about to expose myself to this man who'd captured my heart some time ago.

I closed my eyes, embarrassed by my primal need. But mostly I was ashamed of what he would discover underneath my towel, what he would find deep inside my soul if I let him in.

"Open your eyes, Hindley."

His breath washed warm against my skin and I shivered. He was close, closer than I wanted him. When I finally opened my eyes, his beautiful blue ones stared back at me. He searched my face, asking the silent question I didn't want to answer. I couldn't speak.

"Do you want me to put lotion on your body, Hindley?"

I'd never heard anything so erotically inviting in all my life. My legs were wet, and it wasn't from the shower. I couldn't find my voice. All I could do was nod.

"Yes?" he questioned.

I nodded again but he still wasn't satisfied.

"I need to hear your answer, Hindley. Out loud."

Oh, shit, Oh, shit, Oh, shit. He liked dirty talk.

I drew in a deep breath and closed my eyes, not knowing if I could even talk like that in my head, let alone out loud. I was horrible at the act of sex itself, so I was pretty confident I'd fail miserably at trying to *talk* dirty.

"I'm only going to ask you one more time, Hindley."

Shit. His voice was stern but compassionate, filled with desire and need, all for me.

"What do you want me to do to you?" he asked.

Oh, God. I blew out the breath I'd been holding on to and offered up an answer, hoping it would be good enough for him. "Rub lotion on me," I squeaked out, peering up at his eyes. "Please."

His eyes glowed with a chilling look of satisfaction as a devilish smirk slowly spread across his face. "All you had to do was ask." He chuckled.

His deep, low growl sent vibrations straight between my legs.

"Where do you want me to rub lotion, Hindley?"

Oh, shit. Please don't do this, I silently begged. The way he kept emphasizing my name sucked me in. I swallowed down my fear and embarrassment and finally answered. "Here," I said, pointing to my red chest.

He complied and gently applied lotion to my chest, just above the towel. "Only there?" he asked, his lips curling up in a grin.

"My arms too, please."

"Of course. Anything for you, Hindley."

His words bordered on sarcasm but I didn't care. When he took each arm into his hands and held them with such care, I felt like a small child being tended to. Never had I received a more nurturing, caring touch. I was lost.

After gently rubbing lotion onto both arms, Rory placed my wrists above my head. The movement caused the knot in my towel to pop open, exposing the skin between my breasts. Thankfully most of my chest was covered.

He leaned down so that his cheek was resting on mine, his lips caressing my ear. "Anywhere else...Hindley?"

My body convulsed and I was pretty sure I'd had another spontaneous ear-gasm from that one question. This guy was good with words. There was no stopping my body. It was on fire, and not from the sunburn.

"Well?" he asked.

I swallowed back my fear. Unable to speak, I nodded.

"Where?" He breathed against my neck.

I closed my eyes, petrified to look, afraid this was a dream.

"Everywhere," I finally spoke, my eyes still screwed shut.

He leaned back on my hips and his fingers skimmed across my chest, slowly pulling my towel apart.

The cool air of the hotel room gently caressed my breasts, instantly hardening my nipples. His fingers brushing over my body set every nerve ending on fire. My insides pulsated with need.

Just as quickly as the desire came, it fled as my mind took me back to another place and time. I froze, panic setting in when I realized there was no hiding myself from him. Instinctively, I slapped my arms down to cover my body.

He grabbed my wrists and tugged them back above my head.

My eyes flew open and I struggled to breathe.

"Look at me, Hindley."

I did as he asked and when I looked into his eyes, they were darker now, yet strangely alluring.

"I'm not going to hurt you," he said quietly, calmly.

I blinked up at him.

"Do you believe me?"

I did, but I couldn't force the words so I nodded instead.

"Words, Hindley."

I stared at him, willing him to hear the words.

He cocked a brow.

"Yes, I believe you," I whispered.

He grinned, his smile lighting up the entire room. And just like that, my panic attack was gone.

"I'm safe," he said. "I'm not going to hurt you."

I nodded. "Okay."

"Now, I'm going to put your arms back above your head. Don't move them, all right?"

"Why?" I asked.

"Because I said so. Okay?"

The gentle tone of his voice was in direct opposition to the possessive look in his eyes. For some inexplicable reason, I felt safe with Rory though.

"Okay," I said.

Never had I seen such desire on a man's face. And it was all for me.

"Good girl, Hindley." His eyes turned a shade lighter.

I smiled inwardly, surprised by how much his approval meant to me.

Slowly he lifted his body off mine and I immediately felt his loss. Before I could miss him too much, he returned.

His hands smoothed lotion between my breasts, teasing me, tempting me. "You said everywhere, right, Hindley?"

I closed my eyes, embarrassed by the answer I wanted to give. "Um hmm," I finally choked out, nodding my head. This was so bad, so very bad, but so good too.

"Open your eyes, Hindley. I won't tell you again."

My eyes shot open at his command. God, was he a Dom? First the hands, now this.

I'd read about dominants and S&M stuff, I mean *Fifty Shades of Grey* had pretty much put that crap out there on the open market for chicks to talk about in the grocery store checkout line. I'd never understood the fascination, but here in this moment with Rory, I definitely wanted to keep going, and that surprised me most of all. I'd never thought of myself as kinky.

"Where do you want me to rub the lotion?" he whispered in my ear. "Be specific, Hindley."

Shit. He wasn't going to let me point. That's why he'd put my hands above my head. He likes to talk dirty. I couldn't do it. I wouldn't do it. This wasn't me. I raised from the bed, attempting to get away.

Before I could lift my head, his mouth covered mine, his tongue caressing mine. He pushed me down, keeping me under his control.

I was surprised that old instincts didn't kick in that would force me to fight back. Instead, I wrapped my arms around his neck and held him tight to me, my mouth matching his kiss in passion and intensity. He wanted it rough, I could tell, but he was holding back. And surprisingly, I was disappointed.

"Don't leave me," he whispered against my lips.

Where had that come from? Two seconds ago, he'd been dominating me, and now he was pleading with me to stay. "I'm not leaving," I answered softly.

"I meant in here," he said, touching my temple. "Your mind left me. It's just as important to me as your body. I have to have both to have you."

Oh, Lord, he was good. He'd said exactly what I'd needed to hear.

"Where did you go?" he asked with genuine concern.

I knew exactly what he was talking about, but I had no answer, at least none that I was willing to share.

He splayed his fingers on my bare stomach, inching them lower. His lips left mine and skimmed across my burnt chest, leaving a trail of kisses before traveling down my body.

My body quivered and I worked to stay still.

His mouth moved to my breast and his tongue began stroking my nipple back and forth as his teeth clamped down, tugging on the puckered peak.

I gasped and let out a small moan. God, it all felt so good, this man and his amazing mouth. The way he commanded my body with such ease frightened me, but was exhilarating at the same time. An intense tingle shot straight between my legs when his hand cupped my other breast and rolled my nipple between his fingers. I melted into his touch, feeling a sense of safety and desire that I'd never experienced before.

He placed his knee between my legs and spread them wider.

His mouth left my nipple, but was quickly replaced by his other deft fingers as his lips worked their way down toward my navel.

Oh, shit, Oh, no, not there, no. My body stiffened.

"Rory, please, no," I begged, trying to stop him. I wiggled and pushed against him. No one had ever done this before and I was still embarrassed of my nakedness. My heart beat hard and my breaths became shallow. A full-on panic attack threatened.

Rory sat up. "Hindley, look at me." His voice was softer than before, full of care and concern, void of any dominance.

I couldn't look at him. Not like this, completely naked on a hotel room bed. I was too embarrassed and ashamed. No one had seen this much of me, physically or emotionally.

He took my chin and gently turned my face toward him. "Hindley, please look at me."

His words were whispered, his concern evident with every syllable. I didn't have a choice. He wasn't going to stop until I opened my eyes.

Slowly I lifted my lids. His gorgeous face stared back at me, his expression filled with adoration and respect. He revered me. My heart ached with sheer bliss.

His eyes roamed over my entire body.

I sat still, holding my breath. My lungs burned as I anticipated what he might do next.

His thumb gently stroked under my eyes, wiping away my tears. I didn't even know I'd been crying.

"Hindley." He waited until my eyes were on his, making sure he had my full attention, before continuing. "You." He leaned down and placed a soft kiss on my lips. "Are." Kissed me again then stared down at me like I was priceless, precious. His. "Beautiful," he finally said, smiling.

Rory Gregor was a living, breathing oxymoron. He was a professional skateboarder, a bona fide player of the most dangerous kind. He was a delinquent, a trouble maker, a punk—all by his own admission—and he made no excuses for it. Yet, here in this small hotel room, he was kind and caring, offering up something I'd searched for probably my entire life if I was honest.

No doctor, therapist, or counselor had ever been able to give me this. No drug or self-help book had ever provided me with this much relief from the pain I'd lived with for years.

I'd hidden my true identity from people in hopes of escaping the demons that lived inside me. Yet, here I was, lying completely exposed to this man, both physically and emotionally, unafraid of what he would find. For the first time in my life I felt free, and that made me feel beautiful.

"There she is." He smiled.

"Who?" I asked.

"My Drunk Girl. She's back." His thumbs ran across my cheeks and down to my lips.

I giggled like an idiot.

"I don't know who's told you differently in your life, but they're wrong, Hindley." He was so genuine and gentle in this moment. "You are beautiful, inside and out."

"Thank you," I whispered.

His eyes swept over my body in a predatory fashion. "I've seen the outside." He lowered his head to my waist, his lips twitching in anticipation.

I was under his spell, hypnotized by everything about this man.

He dragged his lips across my abdomen.

Small goose bumps rose to the surface of my skin. His touch was exquisite and I couldn't remember why I'd tried to stop him before.

"Now I want to see the inside of you."

"I'm not on the pill," I blurted out.

"You don't need to be on the pill for what I'm about to do."

"Wait! What?" I lifted up.

"Hindley, you're fuckin' hot, and sexy as hell, like no one I've ever seen before," Rory said. "Now, close your mouth and lie back like a good little girl so I can eat you out and make you come so hard, you forget about everything in your life but me."

What?

No one had ever spoken to me like that before in my entire life, and I loved it. I had no choice but to collapse back on the bed and let this man take over.

Surrendering control didn't come naturally for me, but Rory was making it easier and easier. I covered my face with two pillows, knowing full well I'd need them to hide my beet red face and deflect my screams.

"Eyes, Hindley," his deep voice commanded.

I startled, afraid to look at him. I knew there was no escaping this man. Somewhere deep inside me, in a place I didn't even know it existed, I found the strength to be brave for once in my life. Slowly, I pulled the pillows away from my face.

He sat up on his knees, gazing down at me like I was a goddess. He was unwilling to let me cower behind my fears. "There is no shame in this body, Hindley," he spoke, running his fingers along my hips. "I refuse to let you act like there is."

How could he do that? How did he know exactly what I was thinking?

"You don't have to look at me," he spoke gently, "but you have to look somewhere, because I know when your eyes are closed, you close yourself off from me. There's no way I'm taking you there if you're not one hundred percent with me."

Well, there you go. He'd put it all out there. He wasn't going to let me run. There was a part of me that hated him for it, hated him for exposing me and making me work on my issues. Especially when he was sitting between my naked legs.

Rory taking control was actually freeing though. I wanted that in my life. I needed to be free, to finally let go of my past and stop living in fear.

A smile spread across my face as I ran my hand through his messy blond hair.

"Okay," I whispered.

"That's my Drunk Girl." He winked.

I loved his term of endearment. It reminded me of the first night I'd met him.

"Now, if you'll excuse me," he said, a hint of mischief in his eyes, "I believe you asked me to rub lotion on you." He paused. "Everywhere."

"Not with your tongue!" I shrieked.

"Would you like me to use my tongue, Hindley?"

The way he said *use my tongue* definitely made me want his tongue, anywhere on my body. How could I acknowledge that out loud though? I couldn't. Drawing in a deep breath, I nodded.

"Tell me exactly what you want me to do," he said.

Oh, shit. I closed my eyes, but quickly opened them when I remembered his warning from earlier about closing myself off to him when he couldn't see me.

You can do this. Something deep inside me echoed again. *You can do this.* It was Rory's voice, encouraging me.

With an unsteady voice, I spoke the words I never thought I'd ever recite. "I want you to eat me out and make me come so hard that I'll forget about everything but you." I fell back on the bed with a giggle and let my hands fall above my head

"That's my Drunk Girl," he said as his face lowered between my legs. His warm breath caressed the sensitive skin of my inner thigh, sending shivers up and down my body. When his mouth pressed against me, it felt like heaven, he felt like heaven, and for the first time in my life, I truly felt beautiful.

CHAPTER 20

RORY

"I can't believe you had sex with her," Leif growled from the driver's seat as he glared out of the windshield.

"For the hundredth time, man, I didn't sleep with her."

He remained unmoved by my words. It was obvious he was never going to believe a word I said.

"If you screw this up, Rory, so help me God."

"What?"

Leif shook his head in frustration.

I laughed.

"Have you ever heard of anyone being allergic to latex?" I asked.

"What?"

"Latex. Have you ever heard of anyone being allergic to it?"

"What the hell does that have to do with you and Hindley having sex?"

"She can't use condoms."

Leif yanked the steering wheel and cut the car across three lanes of traffic. Horns blew all around us as we veered off the highway and skidded to a stop on the shoulder.

I fell forward, but was thankfully held in place by my seat belt. Otherwise, Leif's quick detour would have had us both flying through the windshield. Unfortunately the contents inside his car didn't fair so well.

Leif shoved the car into park and unlatched his seat belt. Before I could ask him what the hell was going on, he was halfway in my seat grabbing at my neck.

"What the fuck, man!" he shouted.

Leif was smaller than me, but I was surprised by the amount of strength he showed as he gripped my neck.

"You dumb motherfucker," he growled. "I swear to God, Rory, if you get that girl pregnant, I will kill you with my bare hands."

"I did not have sex with her, man!" I shouted, pushing out of his hold.

"You're a fuckin' liar. I know you. That's how you operate."

I pushed him in the chest, hard enough to send him back in his seat. "Well, I didn't operate like that this time." I held back the smirk threatening to form as I thought of Hindley's naked body sprawled out on the bed, watching her quiver and shake from my oral skills.

Leif shoved my shoulder and held me against the door. I instantly snapped out of my erotic memories. "Your shit eatin' grin says otherwise," he said.

"Dude, seriously, I didn't have sex with her. Let. Me. Go."

His hand fell away, but his sour look stayed.

"She can't use condoms."

"Who can't?" Leif said.

"Hindley."

"What?" he yelled. "You fucked her with nothing?" He sagged back against the door, raking a hand through his dark hair. "God, I hope she's on the pill."

"She's not on the pill either."

The words were out before I even thought about how guilty I sounded. I knew my declaration would push Leif over the edge. I tensed, waiting for his first punch. It never came.

Instead, Leif took in a deep breath and settled back into his seat.

He exhaled slowly then a loud click echoed through the car. It was the locks. He quietly opened his and stepped out.

Shit. I sat for a few moments, wondering what the hell he was doing. Suddenly, my door flew open.

Leif grabbed a fist full of my shirt and dragged me from the car before I could stop him.

My ass hit the ground with a hard thud. Now I was pissed.

Suddenly he drew back a fist.

Leif and I'd had physical altercations before but not like this and definitely not over a chick. Instinct and experience had my hand flying up to stop him seconds before his fist pounded my face.

What the fuck?

I took my free hand and punched him in the chest, shoving him away from me and into the car door. He rebounded and slid to the ground. I stood, dusting off my ass. "What the fuck was that, Leif!" I shouted above the road noise.

He sat on his ass, staring down at the ground, arms propped on his knees.

"Leif!" I yelled again.

He remained unmoved.

Panic set in at the thought that I may have actually hurt my best friend. I squatted down in front of him and wrapped both hands around his shoulders, shaking him. "Leif, what the fuck is wrong with you?"

"You can't do this, Rory," he said.

"Do what?"

"You can't screw this up, man." His eyes met mine. "You've got one shot with these endorsements. This girl is different. She's not like the others. She's a fuckin' attorney. She's *your* attorney, Rory."

His words hit me like a hard punch to the gut. Hindley was out of my league. I knew that, and apparently Leif did too. The fact he verbalized it hurt me more than the realization itself. It was one thing for me to be self-loathing, but for my best friend to actually say I wasn't good enough for Hindley either only confirmed what a failure I was.

"Just get in the car, man." I extended my hand to help him up.

He took my hand and stood, staring at me for several seconds before releasing me.

I watched as he made his way around the car then I slid into my seat. It had been a long time since I'd felt this low about myself. I stared through the front windshield, thinking about how little my best friend thought of me.

No one needed to tell me Hindley Hagen was too good for me, least of all my best friend. I'd been telling myself that since the moment her neighbor told me she wasn't "that" kind of girl.

Leif slid into his seat and started the engine.

I stared out at the long highway before us. "Look, man, I know she's out of my league," I said. "I get that." I glanced down at my hand. My right thumb pressed circles on my palms. It was a nervous tic I'd developed years ago. A therapist that Jack and Kara sent me to said it was a coping mechanism I'd developed during my violent adolescent home life.

"What the fuck are you talking about, Rory?"

I turned.

Leif stared at me, his brows furrowed.

"Hindley," I said. "I know a loser like me has no right to even look at her, let alone try and get in her panties. Don't you think I've told myself that a thousand times?"

Leif's head fell back on the seat. "You're a fuckin' idiot, man."

Idiot. Idiot. Idiot.

I stiffened and fought to push down the rage building inside me. Out of all people in my life, Leif understood the most how traumatizing that word was to me, how much it could utterly destroy me.

My folks had called me an idiot, among other things. My teachers had called me an idiot. The judge who sentenced me to juvie even called me an idiot a time or two. It was a red-hot button that conjured up all types of emotions and feelings I never wanted to have again.

"I know you hate that word," Leif said, "but I'm not going to apologize for it because that's exactly the way you're acting. Like a fuckin' idiot."

I closed my eyes, trying to steady my breathing and keep the demons at bay. My head throbbed and my hands clenched into fists. I was losing the battle. I just hoped Leif didn't say the word a third time.

"It is beyond me why you think any person is out of your league," he said. "That's not what I meant at all and you know it."

I blew out the breath I'd been holding and tried to relax my body but images of my childhood continued to race through my mind.

All I could hear was my stepfather.

You're a lying sack of shit, and the only thing anyone will ever do with a piece of shit is flush it down the toilet. So that's what I'm going to do to you.

Then he'd thrown my Buzz Lightyear in the toilet, peed all over it then forced me to get it out with my bare hands.

"Don't go there, Rory." Leif's words broke through my thoughts. "I mean it. I'll get out of this car again and kick your ass if you let that shit hole of a human being you called stepfather bring you back down. There is no one," he poked my shoulder with a finger, "and I mean *no one* who is out of your league. You're in a league of your own, man. Look at you. You're talented as shit, you have money, and have the potential to make an ass load more."

Even though his words were true, my stepfather's abusive words were never fully silenced.

"And you're sexy as hell." He punched my arm.

I was jolted from my dark memories. I turned, catching his jovial smile, the one I'd come to expect from my best friend. We both burst into laughter and instantly the tension was gone. That's what Leif did for me.

"Well, you're right about one thing," I said.

"What, that you're sexy as hell?"

I shook my head, chuckling. This was the Leif I needed in my life. "Yes, that I'm sexy as hell."

"And you do have the potential to make a shit load of money, Rory. That's what I meant."

Leif was right. I'd pissed away so much money in the last eight years, it sickened me. And now, here I sat on the edge of a come-back with the potential to make it all back, plus tons more.

Money wasn't what excited me any more though. True, I needed it if I wanted to continue to compete at the professional level, but that's not why I skated.

Skating was my drug of choice now. The sport was addicting, the thrill of competing, the excitement of being the best at some-thing. There was nothing like it.

For me, skateboarding was liberating. Being out on the course, jumping over the rails and ramps—just me and my board, soaring through the air—freed my mind and allowed me to let go of all my anxieties, fears, and insecurities. It was the only time I truly felt good about myself.

"That's why you can't fuck this up, man," Leif said.

"I know," I sighed.

"I'm serious. Hindley is your new attorney. She's not one of the countless bimbos you bring home, screw, then toss out the next morning."

"I know," I repeated under my breath. I couldn't fuck this up, but not for the reasons Leif thought.

This girl was different and I'd known it from the moment I'd discovered those enticing blue toenails the night I undressed her when she was three sheets to the wind. Then, when I'd woken up beside Hindley the following morning and found her admiring my body, something inside me lit on fire, something I'd never experi-enced before, something I couldn't quite explain. I didn't want to lose her. I couldn't fuck this up. Yet, somehow, I knew I would.

"Her law firm is big time, man," he said. "They'll treat you right, and I know they'll negotiate the best deals for you. But if you hurt Hindley, if you screw this up, the firm is likely to drop you like a hot potato and word of that will spread like wildfire. You know that, right?"

Leif didn't need to remind me how fast bad news worked its way through the media. We were all acutely aware of their inaccuracies and the lack of journalistic excellence when it came to a juicy story line.

He squeezed my shoulder. "You need these endorsements to stay in the game, man."

His emphasis on the word 'need' was a sobering reminder of how much I'd fucked up in the past. I'd lost so much on my way down two years ago that I'd almost sold my house in California to pay for my expenses. Thankfully Jack wouldn't let me. He said my house was an investment worth keeping and he didn't want me to jeopardize my future. Instead, he took a major cut in salary to let me keep living my dream.

Jack and Kara were good that way, they were my surrogate parents, had been for ten years and I couldn't let them down. Not this time. I had the potential to make millions with some of the deals Hindley would negotiate for me. Yet here I sat, selfish as ever, wondering how I would ever be able to walk away from this amazing woman who made me feel things I'd never experienced in my life.

"She's different, Leif."

"She's way different," he confirmed. "And she's off limits, Rory. You need to get that through your thick, fuckin' head."

"I know, I know. You don't have to tell me again. I know my place in this world and it's not with a girl like Hindley Hagen."

"Man, you're a fucking—"

I held up my hand, threatening to punch him in the face if he said 'idiot' one more time.

"Well, you're acting like one," he said. "That's not what I mean though."

"But it's true."

"What?"

"There's no way I could ever be in her world."

"What world? What are you talking about?"

"Look at her, Leif. Hindley's beautiful, she's brilliant, she's educated, and she comes from a family of money, power, and wealth. She oozes refinement from every pore of her body. I can't even fuckin' read, man."

"Yeah, she's hot and her parents are loaded, but from what Dana told me, they're definitely not perfect. And I have a feeling that her dad's money has purchased a lot of cover-up to hide their flaws."

"What does that mean? What did Dana say?"

"She didn't say anything specifically, but I could tell that Hindley and her family are anything *but* perfect. She did say that Hindley put herself through law school, and she refuses to take any money from her dad, so there goes your whole loaded theory."

I sat back in my seat, sorting out what Leif had revealed. I'd known from the beginning Hindley was a hard worker, but why wouldn't she let her father pay for law school when he obviously could? She had something to prove, just like me. The thought made me want her even more.

"Besides," Leif continued, "even if they all were perfect, that shouldn't mean shit to you. You *totally* have the right to be with someone like Hindley."

"Then why are you having such a shit fit?"

"Because after Tuesday's meeting, not only will she be your attorney, she'll be your agent too. Fucking this up with Hindley doesn't mean you'll get a psycho bitch stalking you for a month. It means you could lose endorsement deals and be sued by her firm."

"I never thought about that."

"You never do. That's why I'm here."

I wanted to let Hindley go, I needed to, for both our sakes, but all I kept picturing were her giant chocolate eyes from last night.

The way they pierced through my hard exterior as she lay sprawled out on the bed, completely bared to me, not just physically.

All I could remember was how fucking hot she looked, entering the grand ballroom later that evening in that tight, little black dress, her ass as round and firm and juicy as a sun-ripened watermelon.

All I could feel was her skin on mine as I caressed her arms in the elevator after the event was over. The way her perfect hips ground into my dick as we rode back up to our rooms after the party had ended.

And all I could smell was her delicious hair as I nuzzled her neck and wrapped my arms around her waist before she opened the door to her hotel room. I could still hear her contagious giggles when I swatted her ass and watched helplessly as she batted her eyes and tentatively but firmly shut the door in my face.

There was nothing about this girl that didn't completely and totally transfix me. Even though I knew I should, something inside me wouldn't let her walk away from me, no matter who she was or how much I thought I may hurt her.

"Just please tell me you didn't screw her with no protection."

"First of all, it's none of your business what I did or didn't do with her last night."

"Your business is always my business."

Leif was right. Even though it was his father who technically was my manager, I'd always involved the entire Jennings family— Jack, Kara, and Leif—when making business decisions. Four heads were better than one, especially in my case.

"Second," I continued, "we didn't do anything."

"Well, you sure as hell better not if she's not on the pill. And what's up with the latex?"

"She's allergic to it."

"And?"

"And, condoms are made out of latex, you idiot."

"Now who's insulting who?"

"I think it's whom." We both burst into laughter, knowing I had no idea what was grammatically correct. Hell, I probably couldn't even spell 'whom'.

"So, if she's not on the pill and she can't use condoms then you better stay the fuck away from her."

We drove in silence for miles as I thought about staying away from Hindley. I'd never be able to muster that much strength.

"So what does she use," Leif asked, "for protection, I mean?"

I thought back to our conversation last night when Hindley panicked, thinking I wanted to have sex with her. It had never been my intention in going up to her room last night, I'd just wanted to give her the lotion. I knew firsthand how painful sunburn could be and I didn't want her to go through that, not if I could help.

But when I saw her hot little body wrapped up in nothing but that towel, other parts of my anatomy took over and I couldn't stop myself. Memories of our night together flooded my mind...

"Why aren't you on the pill?" I asked Hindley as she lay on top of her bed in the hotel room.

"Estrogen and I don't mix," she said.

I stared in confusion.

"The female hormone, estrogen," she said. "That's what's in the pill that stops you from ovulating."

I sat silent, still not understanding and feeling dumber by the minute.

"Ovulating is when you release an egg and then—"

I held up a hand. "Got it."

She laughed.

I was actually thankful for her sex-ed lecture. Finding out she wasn't on any type of birth control had essentially reduced my hard-on to a limp noodle.

But then I removed her towel and my hands roamed all over her gorgeous body. In true Rory fashion, my stiff soldier returned for battle ten times more aggressive.

I'd hoped tasting her would be enough to sedate my boy, but who was I kidding? Hindley Hagen had been a buffet that I couldn't get enough of. She tasted better than Kara's homemade buttermilk pancakes on Sunday morning, and that was saying something.

My senses were on fire for her. My dick actually ached to be inside her, but the panic in her eyes after I'd given her the release she'd craved told me something else was going on. I had to put my One-Eyed Milkman back in the fridge.

"What's wrong, Hindley?"

She sat up and clutched the towel tighter as if disgusted with herself for what had happened.

"Hey?" I reached out to stroke her arm but she flinched. Ah, shit.

"We shouldn't have done that," she said quietly.

"Why?"

Her eyes darted between mine like a caged animal awaiting slaughter. An emotion that looked a lot like regret flashed in her eyes. God, please don't let it be regret, I prayed.

I knelt in front of her and wrapped my arms around her waist, giving her some sense of safety. For the first time in my life, I had more concern for the well-being of a woman than for my own selfish need to be inside her. If this wasn't what she wanted, if she didn't want to have sex with me, then it wasn't going to happen.

I braced myself, preparing for her dismissal, for her inevitable rejection. As I gazed up at her face, I saw something else entirely, something I wasn't prepared for. Her once bright brown eyes pooled with tears.

"I can't use condoms," she said with great effort, falling onto the bed. She remained motionless, staring at the ceiling.

There was more going on inside that beautiful mind of hers than just a fear of condoms. I didn't know if she was trying to avoid me or keep her tears at bay but I knew her eyes wouldn't lie to me.

I stood up and leaned over her, placing my face within inches of hers. I needed to make sure I was the only thing she could see. Slowly I cupped her face with my hands, holding it firm to ensure she couldn't look away.

Tears still glistened in her wide eyes and for a second, I rethought my plan.

"Hindley," I said quietly as if I were coaxing back a frightened kitten. "If you're not on the pill and you can't use condoms, does that mean you're not, sexually active?"

She slammed her eyes shut and struggled to free her face from my grip but I held on tighter. I wasn't going to let her run. My heart ached as two lone tears rolled down her cheeks.

Fuck, was she a virgin?

I needed to find out what was going on before I lost her again. I couldn't take this power position, hovering over her if I wanted the truth. I released her face, letting my hands skim across her neck as I sat down beside her, folding in my leg so we were as close to one another as possible without touching.

"Hindley," I said, "what's going on? Talk to me."

Her fear was almost a palpable thing in the room, anxiety seeped from every pore of her body. I needed to reassure her, convince her that I wouldn't hurt her like someone else obviously had before.

My stomach churned in disgust, thinking about anyone intentionally hurting her. Who had it been? The asshat from college her sister matched her up with at the wedding? An old high school boyfriend? Shit, maybe it was even her birth father. She never talked about him.

My mind reeled with endless possibilities as my hands clenched into fists, a sense of protectiveness surging through me. I didn't have time to think about it though. I needed to bring her back.

I reached out and gently stroked her hair as I placed a small lock behind her ear. She was wounded, and like any wild animal, I had to wait and let her come to me. So I did. We sat in comfortable silence for a moment before she spoke again.

"I'm allergic to latex," she finally said, her eyes closed. "I can't use regular condoms."

That's it? That's all?

I ached inside for the shame she obviously carried, but I couldn't understand why. I caressed her jaw with my knuckles then wrapped her chin in my hand again and turned her face toward mine. Her eyes were still screwed shut.

"Look at me, Hindley," I said softly.

She immediately complied and my dick twitched at her obedience. *Not now, boy.* Her eyes were blood shot and swollen and...mesmerizing.

For a minute, I couldn't think, I couldn't breathe. I wanted to stare at her forever. "I don't care, Hindley," I whispered. Her face softened and I was reassured that she felt a little safer with me. "Why are you so upset?"

"Because I know you're used to women just, like, lying down and spreading their legs for you," she said. "I'm not like that." She jerked out of my hold and turned away from me.

"I never thought you were like that, Hindley."

"But that's exactly what I did," she said through a muffled sob.

I heard the shame in her voice and refused to sit by and let her feel this way, not when I didn't share the same sense of guilt. I laid down beside her, putting my face in front of hers, careful to keep my hands to my side. When I finally settled, I noticed her cheeks were stained with tears. I was lost in her pain, confused by my own sense of empathy.

"Hindley," I spoke gently, "did I do something to you that you didn't want me to?"

She hesitated.

I held my breath, fearing there was a small chance that perhaps in my selfishness, I'd pushed her too far.

Her luscious lips curled into a small smile and instantly my anxiety evaporated. She'd wanted what I gave her just as much as I'd wanted to give it.

"Well," I said, "if I wanted to and you wanted me to, why should you feel ashamed?"

She shrugged, her eyes looking anywhere but at me.

I sensed her disconnecting from me physically and emotionally, but I wouldn't let her. "Look, Hindley, I'm not a saint, you know that. Hell, half the world knows that. I've screwed a lot of women and I'm not proud of it."

She flinched at my words and scooted out of my reach.

Anger swelled up inside me. I was trying to help Hindley cope with her unfounded emotions but honestly, the entire scene was starting to piss me off more than I wanted to admit.

"Look at me, Hindley," I said sternly. I didn't mean to sound so demanding, but there was something about her that brought out the dominant side of my personality.

I needed to maintain control and order in my life. That's how I'd fashioned my comeback in professional skateboarding. Hell, it was the only way I could survive now. Yet, with this woman, I'd never felt more out of control in my life. The realization scared the living shit out of me.

She turned her head and faced me.

Hindley was unaware of my need to control her, but a sick part of me loved her reaction. It excited me to know that even in her embarrassment, she wanted to obey me. It shouldn't have, but it did. I was a sick fucker. My past had molded me into this person who needed control in order to survive.

"Putting my mouth between a woman's legs isn't something I make a habit of doing with just anyone," I said.

That part was true. I may be considered a certified muff-diver with the ladies, but that didn't mean I ate out every chick I screwed. In fact, I couldn't remember the last time I had.

"I think it's a very personal act," I said, "at least for me it is. I know you're not the type of woman who goes off and has casual sex with random men you meet at bars. You proved that on the first night we spent together."

Her eyes widened and I knew I'd hit a nerve I hadn't intended. Oh, God. she's a fucking virgin.

"Has anyone ever done that to you before, Hindley?" I asked. "What I just did, you know, oral sex?"

She jerked away from me, trying to stand.

I grabbed her hips and hauled her back down.

"I don't want to talk about this, Rory." She squirmed in my hold.

"Are you a virgin, Hindley?"

"What?" She recoiled. "No, I'm not a virgin, that's idiotic."

My body stiffened and my hands fell away at her offensive slur, but I couldn't focus on my self-esteem issues right now. This was about her.

"Why would you even ask that?" she asked. "This was wrong. It shouldn't have happened. I'm sorry I let it get this far."

I was losing her, I was losing my Drunk Girl, and I couldn't sit here and watch her escape. Experience had proven that she responded to my dominant side, so even though it went against my better judgment at the moment, I switched tactics.

I pulled her onto the bed and rolled on top of her. "Are you, Hindley?"

"Am I what?"

My dick twitched at her raspy voice. She may have been going for innocent, but she was failing miserably.

"Are you really sorry about what I did? Are you sorry that I put my tongue between your beautiful legs and ate you out like an all-night buffet? Because it didn't *sound* like you were sorry when you were screaming my name."

"That's what I'm talking about." She attempted to shove me off.

I sank deeper into her, my hips pushing into hers.

Her breathing accelerated, her chest rising against mine. "I can't do this, Rory."

Ah, who the fuck was I kidding? She was so far out of my league. Of course, she couldn't do this. She'd never wanted me from the beginning and I was a fool, a gigantic dumbass, to think I had a chance. Something in my mind snapped. I rolled away, shoving off the bed to stand.

She grabbed my wrist, tugging me back down.

My dick jerked at her touch and my pulse raced, in what? Excitement? Anticipation? No, fear.

"It's not what you think, Rory," she whispered.

I didn't want to see her beautiful face for fear it would express her rejection and remorse for what we'd done. I couldn't help myself though. I needed to see her like I needed air. I slowly turned and my gaze met hers.

Her bright eyes were darker now and half-lidded, filled with longing and desire. This wasn't a rejection, this was an invitation.

"I want you," she said, "like really, *really* want you. Even though we shouldn't."

Okay, that was two "*reallys*" so that had to mean something, right? Forget that she said we shouldn't. Suddenly a feeling of dread washed over me. I sensed there was more she needed to say, something I didn't want to hear.

"But I'm not on the pill and we can't use regular condoms, so it's a no go."

Still, there was more she wasn't saying but I refused to ask any more questions, not when she'd declared she wanted me, *really, really* wanted me. I couldn't help but smile.

"Whatever?" She rolled her eyes but I saw the smirk on her face.

"So, if you're not on the pill and you can't use condoms, what do you use?" I asked. My stomach cramped at the thought of Hindley with any other man. It wasn't like me to act like a possessive chick but everything was different with Hindley. Before I knew it, my mind had wandered to the dark side, wanting to pummel any man who'd ever had sex with her, let alone hurt her.

Her face was expressionless, her eyes void of the brilliance from earlier. Something had happened to her. Instantly my green-eyed monster disappeared. Her expression spoke of memories too difficult to speak of. She was scared, damaged, just like me. No wonder I was so drawn to her.

I wanted to be with Hindley any way I could. I wanted to protect her, comfort her, and wash away all the hurt from her past. If that meant we could never have sex and all I would ever be able to do was rub lotion over her sexy body, I would be okay with that. Hell, I'd get excited about that. I had to be with her, next to her, holding her.

I'd never had a relationship with a woman that wasn't sexual, except with Leif's mom, Kara. Suddenly I realized how special Hindley was becoming to me. Wanting to be with her, even if it meant we couldn't have sex, was huge for me. I wanted her, I needed her, just for her, not for what she could give me in return.

"Look, Hindley, I'd love to have sex with you, don't get me wrong, but if you can't, you can't."

Her eyes flashed with something that looked like hurt.

I cringed, realizing she'd misunderstood me, again. Verbal communication was obviously not our strong point. "I'm sorry, that sounded bad. I just meant that with you, it's not about sex."

Her brows rose.

"I mean it is, I want to, it's just…"

She pushed her fist to her mouth to hold back the laughter, but failed. "I can have sex, Rory, God. I just need to use special condoms, non-latex, that's all."

All sorts of sordid fantasies flooded my mind. I felt like a six-year-old on Christmas morning, looking at his brand-new bicycle, giddy with wild anticipation of the adventures that lay ahead of him. I coughed with embarrassment, realizing how shallow I was. Knowing I could have sex with this wanton Goddess was like heaven, and I had a difficult time containing my joy.

"Um, where do you get these special condoms?" I asked, trying to keep my tone indifferent. I didn't want to appear too eager, even though my dick was throbbing like it'd been beaten with a hammer.

"I usually order them online."

"And you have some here?"

Without warning, her fist flew up and hit me square on the arm.

"Ouch!" I yelled in actual pain, rubbing the spot where her fist had made contact. This girl was strong.

Note to self—don't piss her off.

"Unlike you, I don't walk around with a box of condoms in my purse." She laughed.

"I don't have a box of condoms in my purse."

She tilted her head and cut her eyes up at me.

"What?" I shrugged. "I don't have a purse." But I did have a box of condoms. At home.

She laughed.

"So you really don't have any special ones with you?" I asked.

"No, Rory, I don't have any with me."

"Did you leave them all at home?"

She shook her head.

"Then where are they?"

"Probably still at the store," she said.

"You don't have any of your special condoms, at all, anywhere?"

She shook her head again as she stood. Walking toward the closet, she removed her dress from the rack and laid it down on the bed.

Well, it was going to be a long night in a cold shower for me.

"Shit!" she said.

"What?"

"My dress."

"What's wrong?"

"My legs are beet red."

"And?"

"This dress is above the knee. I'll look ridiculous, like I've been down on my knees all night."

I fought to stifle a laugh but failed miserably.

She pointed at me with a stern face. "That's not happening, Rory."

"Ever?" I asked in genuine disappointment.

She remained silent, her face passive, but her pouty lips shifted ever so slightly.

Confirmation. Hindley had a freaky side. Maybe no one had discovered it before, but it was there. My One-Eyed Milkman was back out of the fridge and ready for action. I inched toward her.

She stuck her palm in my face. "No, Rory. I need to fix my dress."

I laughed and pressed her body against the wall with relative ease, holding her in place with my hips as I pressed my hands on either side of her face.

Her eyes grew darker, lust filling their brown depths. Her breathing accelerated, her chest heaving, pushing her full breasts against me. She wanted this, and I was going to give it to her. A low growl erupted from my throat as I watched her grab at her towel.

"You didn't answer me, Hindley," I said.

"What?" she breathed out against my neck, her response barely above a whisper.

I dragged my lips down the nape of her neck, just below her ear. "Are you saying your knees will never be red because you knelt down in front of me and sucked me off?" Her body shivered against me and my dick jutted out so hard I thought I might explode right here in my pants. "Well, I'm waiting for your answer, Hindley." I growled.

She shook her head, her hair rubbing against my face. I wasn't sure if her movement was an involuntary reaction to my voice or an actual answer.

I drew in a deep breath, inhaling her scent as my mind swirled from the intoxicating aroma. No woman had ever affected me like this. I was pretty sure what her answer would be but I needed to hear her say it, out loud. My lips turned up in a victorious smile. I was the predator going in for the kill.

"Say it, Hindley."

She shook her head again.

"Say it," I demanded, brushing my lips against her soft skin, coaxing her to tell me the truth. Just thinking about her sucking my dick had me about to blow a wad.

"Say what?" she panted. Her breath caressed my shoulder, making it impossible to move with the painful throbbing in my pants.

"That you'll never get down on your knees in front of me, put your face between my legs and suck my dick until I come all over your pretty little mouth." I knew I was being crass and crude but something told me Hindley liked it down and dirty no matter what she appeared like on the outside. I needed to hear her say it, even if she was afraid to admit it out loud.

Her body vibrated against mine. I imagined how hot and wet she was, all for me. Hell, I was about to come all over the entire hotel room if she moved against me one more time. She responded to my commands in a way no other woman ever had before and I loved it.

I dropped my hand and let it slide up her leg, raising the towel as my fingers crawled further, feeling for myself how turned on she was.

"Rory, please," she whispered.

My hand stopped between her long, lean legs. I tilted back to gauge her reaction. Was she serious? Did she really want me to stop, or was she just overwhelmed with desire? When I peered down at her face, I wasn't surprised to find her eyes closed, the expression she wore one of pure ecstasy. In that moment, she was mine.

My lips brushed against hers and I smiled when she kissed me back. "Please what, Hindley?" I murmured, my fingers moving against her center.

"Oh," she moaned, rocking into my hand. "Please, not tonight."

Those were my affirming words. She wasn't saying no, she was saying, not *now*. My lips crushed down on hers as I tugged her leg and guided it around my waist

Her arms slid around my neck as she molded her body to mine, pressing into me. We couldn't have sex tonight but it didn't mean I wouldn't try to get as close to her naked body as possible.

I thrust my thick erection between her legs.

She moaned against my mouth and rubbed against me.

Fuck.

"Knock, knock!" someone yelled. Dana. Fuck.

This chick was the biggest fuckin' cock blocker I'd ever seen in my life.

Hindley pushed me off so hard, I bounced onto the bed, landing flat on my back.

That's when I noticed her towel. It was lying on the floor. In our tangle of lips and legs, it must have fallen off. I knew Hindley didn't want to look like 'that girl'.

Without thinking, I flew up from the bed and grabbed the towel. I shoved it in her hands then darted to the other side of the room, struggling to catch my breath. The painful throbbing in my dick was making it difficult to even breathe. I mustered all my strength and painted on my most innocent looking face, knowing I was failing miserably.

"Well, well, well, what do we have here?" Dana asked, surveying the room.

"Hindley needs to fix her dress," I said, guilt oozing from every syllable. "She, uh, asked me to look for a needle and thread." My voice broke. God, I sounded like a pubescent boy. The gig was up.

One perfectly groomed brow arched high above Dana's arctic blue eyes. "Oh, really? I'm surprised she didn't ask you to look in her suitcase where she always keeps her sewing kit." Dana reached inside Hindley's bag without looking and pulled out a small container. She held it high in the air, her eyes darting between me and Hindley.

This girl was a master at breaking my balls. The gleam in her eyes proved that humiliating me brought her immense pleasure. I wanted to hate her but I couldn't find it in me. Dana was a dynamo and her saucy attitude made it nearly impossible to do anything but love her. Plus, she was the gatekeeper to Hindley. I shook my head in defeat.

Hindley tightened the towel around her with one hand then snatched the sewing kit from Dana. "Thank you," she said, scooping up her dress. She stomped off into the bathroom and slammed the door.

That was my cue to exit. I'd seen a lot of girls do the walk of shame, all thanks to me. This was the first time I could ever remember having to do it myself. It felt awful and I was ashamed I'd ever made any girl feel this used. I slinked by Dana and opened the door.

"We'll see you downstairs, One-Nighter." Dana giggled as she slammed the hotel room door in my face.

I stared at the empty hallway. What was I doing here? Hindley wasn't a random sex kind of girl. I'd known that from the beginning. I'd be damned if I was going to make her into one now, not that she'd let me. The painful swelling in my pants made it harder and harder to abide by the rules.

"Rory!" Leif shouted from the driver's side of his car.

I jumped, jolted from my elicit memories of last night. "What?"

"Where were you?"

"A million miles away," I said under my breath.

"Please, man, don't do this."

"I know, I know, you've said it already. She's off limits. She's my attorney."

"It's not just that, man." He released a heavy sigh.

"What are you talking about?"

He shook his head and gripped the wheel tighter. "Nothing, man, forget it."

"I'm not gonna forget it, you brought it up. What the hell are you talking about?"

"Hindley's different, for a lot of reasons."

I stared at him, brows creased. What the hell was he talking about? "I know, you don't have to tell me."

"Yeah, I think I do."

I stared at him, waiting for him to continue, but he didn't. "So what? Are you going to tell me why?"

Leif glanced over at me. "I don't know all the reasons, not for a fact. I just know that after talking to Dana yesterday, it's clear that Hindley's been through a lot."

"A lot? Like what?"

He didn't answer.

"Just say it, Leif."

"I don't know, I can't. Dana didn't explain it, it's just a feeling I got listening to her talk about Hindley."

"What did she say?"

He stared straight ahead at the road.

My heart pounded in my chest. The thought of anyone hurting Hindley, physically or emotionally, had me clenching my fists. "What *exactly* did Dana say?" I asked in a tone I hoped would make Leif realize I was tired of playing this roundabout game of his.

"She said that Hindley's been through a lot. She emphasized a lot."

"I know the asshat boyfriend in college humiliated her."

"I think it's more than that, man. It's like Dana was warning me, or silently asking me to warn you."

"Warn me about what?"

"Do you like her?" Leif asked. "You know, *like* her, like her."

"What are we, in third grade again?" I laughed. "Yes, I like her."

"Then leave her alone." His voice was flat, void of emotion. "I don't think she can handle someone like you, Rory."

What the hell did that mean?

I stared out the window as I watched the cars pass us by, surprised at my best friend's words.

Leif had so little faith in me, and the truth was, I had little faith in myself. But I had all the faith in the world in Hindley. She was strong, braver than even Dana knew, and although I realized I shouldn't, I wanted her. I needed Hindley. And I'd never needed anyone. Ever.

The logic and warning of Leif's advice shouted, 'Leave her alone!', but with every fiber of my being I knew I wouldn't. I couldn't. She was my drug, already pumping through my veins. I was addicted. And that thought more than any other scared me to death.

I'd fought addiction for years and won, but Hindley Hagen was slowly becoming my new drug of choice. Even though she wasn't illegal, I had no doubt she was lethal...at least for me.

CHAPTER 21

HINDLEY

I GLANCED at the clock on the dining room wall. It was just after eight in the evening. I couldn't believe how long I'd been working at my sewing machine. Almost four hours. No wonder my neck was killing me.

I pushed back from the table and stood up, stretching like a cat. I was working on a maternity set for a girl at work. I'd never made maternity clothes so this pattern was pretty stressful.

I'd been sewing since high school, more out of necessity than desire. Shopping for clothes back then was a daunting task, given the fact that I was twenty pounds heavier. Nothing ever fit right, and when I couldn't drag a zipper all the way up or watched in horror as the pant sizes got bigger and bigger, it sent me spiraling in a shame game that left me shoving another big, fat cheeseburger in my mouth.

One day, after spending a depressing afternoon at the mall, humiliating myself at several stores who catered to girls who ate for lunch, I schlepped back home and threw myself on my bed. I silently cried, hoping no one would find me, especially Geneva.

As I sat there wallowing in my self-pity, I decided if I couldn't find clothes to fit, I'd just make them. I purchased a small sewing machine at a second-hand store and made a few pieces of clothing on my own.

My mom was supportive. She hated seeing me so upset. All she'd ever wanted was for me to love myself. She even bought me one of the nicest sewing machines on the market, the one I still used today. And she purchased bolts of material so I could create all kinds of clothing.

People gushed so much over my first shirt, I kept sewing and before I knew it, I had a complete wardrobe that fit me perfectly. People even bought pieces for themselves.

At first, sewing had been a hobby, but as I moved on to law school, it actually became a way for me to pay the bills. I'd stay up late at night and wake up early in the morning to create new looks for all kinds of people.

The work was interesting and I loved designing clothes, but sewing was much more than that for me. It was an escape, a way to forget about all the bad things that had happened in my life. Creating new clothing gave me a sense of accomplishment and pride like nothing else ever had. I could get lost for hours on one pattern. As proven tonight.

There was plenty of light outside despite the late time. The added daylight was a benefit of the late spring in Texas.

I bent down under the table and gathered the scrap pieces of material on the floor. Ideas spun in my head of what I could make with the remnants. I hated to let anything go to waste. Maybe I'd make a baby blanket.

My cell phone rang, scaring me. I jumped and hit my head on the table. I rubbed the tender spot on my scalp as I backed from underneath with the pieces I'd gathered.

I was embarrassed to admit that I'd been anxiously awaiting a phone call from Rory. Dana and I had returned from San Antonio earlier this morning. I felt like a stupid girl in middle school, waiting for the boy I'd been pining for to call. In actuality, that's exactly what I was. It wasn't my proudest moment.

It wasn't like I'd actually had sex with Rory, but we'd done enough to make my face flush with embarrassment.

I should have been more upset with myself. He was my client. Instead, I'd actually lain awake in the hotel room last night, lusting over him.

I'd replayed every moment, remembering the way his hands had roamed all over my body, the way his touch set my skin on fire. Worst of all, I wanted him again, even more now. The release he'd given me was an escape I didn't even know I'd longed for. I wanted that freedom again. I craved it. With Rory I wasn't afraid of sex, which was unusual for me.

I reminded myself that being with Rory Gregor wasn't a good idea though. If people discovered our relationship, they'd soon delve in to my past and find it as sordid as his. I'd worked too hard and too long to overcome my past. I couldn't afford to risk it. Not now, not ever.

The problem was, I'd felt a connection with Rory that was undeniable. I'd seen the same demons of insecurity haunting his eyes that lived in mine.

Mr. Stedwick believed in me, enough to give me this opportunity. I couldn't screw it up. Which meant I couldn't do anything else with Rory besides represent him, legally.

A sense of purpose filled me as I thought about doing battle for Rory. Something deep in my heart told me no one had ever fought for him, not enough to make a difference anyway.

It was wrong and went against all my better judgment, but I still wanted him despite my pep talk. I craved him in a way I'd never felt before. I had a deep seeded desire to help ease his insecurities, to make him feel as special as he'd made me feel last night. His soft words and gentle touches made me realize there was so much more to my Skater Boy than met the eye.

My Skater Boy? God, this was worse than I thought.

I'd always feared being judged by others, especially given my past. But Rory made me feel like no matter what I'd done, I was special and deserved to be treated with the utmost care. And it was for that reason that I found myself hanging by the phone all afternoon, now late into the evening, waiting to talk to him. I wanted to feel that rush of belonging, of being treasured and cherished. It was new and I wasn't ready to let it go, despite my better judgment.

My phone continued to ring. I searched for the phone, fearing he'd hang up before I could answer. I was such an idiot. It probably wasn't even him. After the fourth ring, I found the phone hiding under piles of material on the table. I didn't even have time to look at the caller ID before I answered.

"Hello," I said, out of breath.

"What are you doing, skank?"

I sighed heavily when Dana's voice echoed on the other end. "Nothing," I said.

"Still no word from Clam Diver?"

"Who?"

"Clam Diver. Muff Muncher. Furburger Flipper."

I sat in silent humiliation. Why did I think it was a good idea to tell Dana *everything*?

"You know," she continued, "Rory 'Mack the Muff' Gregor."

"I knew I shouldn't have told you what he did. You're sick. You know that, right?"

"Are you kidding me? It's been months since I've had someone lick my beaver."

"Dana!"

"What? Do you know how depressing it is that now I have to live out my fantasies through you? Who would have ever thought it?"

"This is a disgusting conversation."

"Why? Are you embarrassed because of my colorful terminology or because Rory ate at the Y?"

I hung my head in defeat, rubbing my temple as a migraine threatened. "Both."

"Don't be." She laughed. "Do you know how long you have to be with a guy before he goes down on you?"

"Obviously, it takes way longer than any guy I've ever been

with since no one's ever done that to me before," I said. God, I was pathetic. Suddenly, all I could think of was Rory's past sexual experiences. I was just another notch on his bed post. His lack of communication was evidence of that. What had I been thinking, getting naked with him last night?

"Oh, yeah," Dana said, "I totally forgot, your old lovers, Shit-for-Brains and Dick-Smaller-Than-My-Forefinger never did get you off, did they?"

Again, I wondered why I told her everything. *Because she's your best friend.* I reminded myself. We'd never been able to hide things from one another. Not to mention, I was so inexperienced, I needed her help to navigate the turbulent waters I called sex.

Dana had been the one who'd explained how to put a condom on. She was the one who'd told me how to hold a guy's penis and how to work it. She was even the one who'd helped me find alternative condoms when I'd discovered I was allergic to latex.

When I was seventeen, I had my wisdom teeth removed. As soon as the oral surgeon put on the plastic gloves, I could feel something in my body react to the smell alone. I dismissed it as nerves. Once he touched the gloves to my lips though, everything changed. Within seconds, I looked like Angelina Jolie on Botox.

Even as I prepared for my first sexual encounter with Tim Moffit in college, it had been Dana who'd reminded me of my latex allergy, which included most condoms. And it had been Dana who'd taken me to the sex shop to look for alternatives.

That's where I met Regan Jackson, owner and operator of 'Sex World', a small sex shop in downtown Dallas. Her store wasn't far from the university I attended. The boutique specialized in anything from vibrators to party favors to latex-free condoms. I'd been embarrassed as hell to go into the store at first but my upcoming sexual escapades had required it.

When I walked inside, I'd been shocked to find the store was like any other specialty shop in downtown Dallas, minus the dildos and crotch less panties in the window. The boutique-style shop was clean and upscale, and Regan was a hardworking, honest business owner.

That was the day I discovered how judgmental I'd been my entire life. After that, I'd vowed never to be such a sanctimonious, holier-than-thou twat again. Dana and I struck up a friendship with Regan that still remained to this day. Judging Regan and what she did for a living had been an eye opener for me.

You'd think after all these years of having a friend like Regan in the sex shop industry I'd have been more comfortable with the act of sex itself but I wasn't. I had too much to overcome. Regan would rant and rave about what a beauty I was. Of course, I never believed her. She'd said a girl as pretty as me with my body as sexy as mine should be on stage making money with what God gave her. She was certifiably crazy.

My thoughts came back to Rory and what a mistake this was to get involved with a client. Then Regan's words of advice rumbled through my head and I laughed.

Honey, if it feels good, it's legal and don't hurt nobody, then get on board and take the ride.

She was a mentor and a hero to me in so many ways.

"What's so funny?" Dana's voice interrupted my thoughts.

"Regan."

"What about her?" she asked.

"I was thinking what a hoot she would get out of me. Knowing so much about sex but still being so embarrassed by Rory's act."

"You can't even say it, can you?"

"Say what?"

"What he did to you."

"No, I can't." My face flushed with embarrassment. "Why is that such a big deal to you?"

"Oh, it's not a big deal to me, I'm just joking with you," she said. "But judging by what you said he wanted last night, you better start getting comfortable with talking dirty."

"Why do I tell you everything?"

"Because you love me."

"I do love you," I said, "but there has to be a better reason than that, to go through the humiliation you're putting me through."

"Ah, I'm sorry, Hindley. You know I'm just busting your chops. I love the fact that you've found a guy who's obviously willing to put your needs above his own. And it sounds like he's pretty well versed in the art of—"

"Stop. Don't say it any more."

She giggled.

I couldn't help but laugh with her. "You know I can't do this."

"Why?" she asked.

I pulled at the hem of my shirt. "You know why."

"Oh, the whole, *I'm his lawyer* thing?" she said, sarcastically. "Whatever."

"It's not whatever. I took an oath."

"No, you didn't."

Okay, she was right, I didn't take an oath, per se. "Dana, I could lose my job."

"So? You're not that crazy about it anyway. Look, I'm telling you from experience, Hindley, if you can find a guy who, one, is willing to go down on you, and two, does it with as super skills as you said Rory did, then you better keep him. Or at least ship him over to me when you're done."

"Rory doesn't keep women; he uses them."

"Leif didn't make it sound like that."

"What did he say?"

"He said Rory has commitment issues. I don't think he *uses* women, not like you think anyway."

Dana shared some of the conversations she'd had with Leif over the weekend with me on the drive home this morning. He'd confirmed that Rory was a player. He'd never been in a committed relationship. The revelation stung more than it should have, and I couldn't help but feel cheap and used. And yet, I was still pining for his call.

Did I have any room to judge though? I mean, I knew going into it he was a player. And it wasn't like I was asking him for forever. I just wanted for-right-now. That's exactly what he'd given me.

"I didn't mean to upset you, Hindley."

"You didn't," I said. "I'm a big girl and I took it for what it was."

"And what was that exactly?"

"It felt good, no one got hurt, and it wasn't illegal so I went along for the ride."

Dana snorted as Regan's words rolled off my tongue with ease. "That's true, but I know you, Hindley. You don't just buy a ticket for one ride. You want a season pass to the whole fucking amusement park, don't you?"

I nodded, frustrated that she knew me so well. I wasn't looking for Mr. Right Now, I was looking for Mr. Right. Rory didn't fit that bill, but it didn't mean I wanted to get off the ride. Not yet anyway. That one thought scared the shit out of me.

Rory was different in so many ways. He had the potential to not only hurt me, but completely destroy me if I let him. I was hiding under the facade that this relationship was about work, that I was letting him into my life because I represented him now.

The sobering truth was, I was falling for him, fast. I was on the edge of a high cliff about to jump into a dangerous sea that could destroy me. Instead of running the other direction, all I could think about were his beautiful blue eyes, his amazing body, his golden blond hair, his adorable dimples, and his tattoo. Oh, that tattoo.

My Skater Boy. It was wrong to claim him but who was I kidding? I was already hopelessly lost.

"Just take it slow, Hindley. Maybe Leif was wrong. Maybe he hasn't met the right girl yet."

"Yeah, right." I snorted. "You've dated tons of players like Rory Gregor. Has one of them ever stopped their promiscuous ways to settle down and make you an honest woman?"

She laughed.

We both knew the answer. Once a player...

My other line beeped.

"Hold on " I held the phone away from my face and sucked in a breath when I saw the caller ID. "Holy shit, it's Rory," I said, bringing the phone back to my ear. "What should I do?"

"Do you want to talk to him?"

"I don't know."

"Yes, you do."

I sat in silence. I knew, I just didn't want to admit it to myself.

"I'll talk to you tomorrow." Dana laughed.

Without another word, the line switched over and immediately, I heard his deep raspy voice.

"Hello? Hindley?"

I held my breath, afraid that he would hear me breathing.

Ride the ride, Hindley.

"Hello." I said, as if I didn't know who was calling.

"Oh, uh, hey. It's Rory. I wasn't sure if you were there or not." He sounded…nervous.

"Oh, sorry. I was on the other line."

"Do you need to go? I can call you back. Or you can call me back. Whatever works for you."

I smiled to myself. His uneasiness echoed through the phone line. The thought that Rory Gregor was nervous talking to a woman—to *me*—made my heart sing. I thought of what Dana said, 'Maybe he hasn't found the right girl'.

"No, we're good," I said. "It was just Dana. She's gone."

"Oh, okay. How is she?"

I smirked, thinking of all the vulgar ways she'd described Rory's actions last night. If he only knew.

"What's so funny?" he asked.

Had I laughed out loud? "Dana."

"Let me guess," he said. "You told her about last night and she was being sick and twisted about it, like only Dana can be."

I chuckled. "Pretty much."

"There's nothing more amazing to me than the sound of your laughter, Hindley."

I sucked in a breath. His words sounded genuine, not like a line, and took me totally by surprise.

"So how many different ways did she describe cunnilingus?" he asked.

"What?" I shrieked. Yeah, old Rory was back.

"That many, huh?"

"You guys are sick."

His deep, rich laughter echoed through the air.

The vibrations pulsated between my legs. I clenched my thighs together. He had the sexiest laugh.

"So, what are you doing?" he asked.

"Right now?"

"No, ten minutes ago, dipstick."

I sat in stunned silence. Was this joking Rory?

"Yes, I mean right now, silly." He laughed.

I wasn't sure how far I wanted Rory Gregor into my life, but letting him know about my hobby seemed innocent enough.

"I'm sewing."

"You sew?"

"No, dipstick." I repeated his words. "I'm sewing when, in fact, I don't sew."

Silence rang through the line. For a split second, I thought I might have offended him.

"I see I have my hands full with you, Hindley."

His growling laughter did something to my insides and I wasn't sure how to respond. I was a sheep and he was a wolf and it was only a matter of time before he devoured me. Although, last night he'd pretty much made a buffet out of my body. And I loved it.

I decided to play his game. It was a dangerous one, and I risked getting hurt, but for once in my life I was going to try and get the upper hand.

"Yes, you do, Rory," I said. "You'll always have your hands full with me."

His sexy moan rumbled through the phone.

My insides tightened with desire.

"Oh, God, I hope so," he whispered in a husky voice.

I closed my eyes, letting his words feed the deep need pulsating through my body, especially down there. Dana was right, I was pathetic. I couldn't even think dirty words, let alone say them.

"Do you want to get something to eat?" he asked.

Okay, here was my chance to walk on the wild side, to enjoy the ride, as Regan said. I drew in a deep breath to calm my racing heart. I exhaled and said, "I have something you can eat."

Oh. My. God. Did I just say that out loud? Yes, yes I had. And it had come out with no thought. Well, okay, there'd been thought, but it came out. I'd never talked like that with anyone, ever.

Rory moaned. I was poking the beast.

"Pizza!" I shouted. "I want pizza to eat."

"Oh, I don't want pizza now," he said in a low voice that sounded sexy as hell. "I had something entirely different in mind to eat tonight, Hindley."

Holy hell, the way he said my name turned my legs to jelly. I nearly orgasmed right here on my sofa.

"Well," I said, "all I want is pizza and that's all you'll get from me." I wanted to add 'tonight' but I knew I'd taken him too far already.

"So can I come over?"

Oh, shit. He wanted to come over? I'd just revved him up. If he came over now he'd try to start something. And I wasn't entirely sure I'd say no. I cleared my throat. "That's probably not a good idea."

"Why?"

"I'm your attorney and it would be wrong for us to…" I couldn't even finish my own sentence.

"I believe we crossed that line last night in your hotel room."

"It shouldn't happen again."

"But you know it will," he said. There was amusement in his voice.

He was right. Even as I said it shouldn't happen again, even as I pushed him away, I was already braver with Rory than I'd ever been with anyone else in my life. That realization and the power it brought was intoxicating.

I wanted to push past my limits, not just sexually. Rory made me...brave. I was tired of being afraid of sex, of my job, of people, of life in general. Getting involved with Rory wasn't technically illegal, but it was definitely frowned upon in my profession. If word got out that I was involved with a client, it could ruin both of us.

"This isn't a good idea for either one of us, Rory."

"Why?"

"I could lose my job. And you could lose millions of dollars in endorsement deals if anyone finds out. Sponsors don't like to see their star athletes dipping their pen in the company ink."

"Did you just say dip my pen in your ink?"

"Yes, I did just say that." It sounded cliché, but I meant it.

"No one will find out, Hindley."

"How do you know?"

"You taste too good for me to give up. I'll do whatever you say just to be with you."

I gasped in shock, and excitement at his declaration. A lot of girls would probably be offended by his statement, but to me, it was one of the sweetest, most erotic things anyone had ever said. I wanted to say yes to him. My body was screaming for another night with Rory but my brain was in the way.

I sat for several heartbeats, angel on one shoulder, devil on the other.

"Hindley?" he spoke softly, his silent "please" ringing through the phone.

I caved. "Pick up some food on your way over. I'm starving."

"So am I," he growled.

God, I was in so much trouble. My body trembled with anticipation. "I'll see you soon," I said, clicking off the phone. I sat in silence for several moments.

I'd just invited the Big Bad Wolf over for dinner, and I had a feeling I was the main course.

CHAPTER 22
HINDLEY

"So, what are you working on?" Rory asked as he walked around my table. He picked up various scraps of fabric, inspecting each piece.

"A woman at work is pregnant," I said. "I'm trying my hand at a maternity top for her."

"That's cool."

I pushed the material aside and cleared a spot for us at the end of the table. I sat down our plates and two water bottles. "What's cool?" I asked.

"That you're making something for her. You know, using your talent for someone else."

"You do it too." I remembered reading about Rory's generous donations through the years to various children's organizations, ranging from cancer treatment to after-school programs for at-risk youth. It was another facet to him that attracted me to him.

Somewhere beneath the bad boy facade hid a generous man. I wanted to draw him out, let the public meet the real Rory Gregor.

"What?" he asked.

"You donate your money to worthy causes."

"How did you know about that?" He leaned away, his lips pursed as he glared at me.

Suddenly, I wondered if this was something I should have mentioned. "I read it on the Internet."

"You can't believe everything you read on the Internet," he said.

"I also saw photos."

"It's not that big of a deal."

He was modest, almost shy. Nothing was fitting the bad boy image displayed all over the Internet. Now I was overcome with the need to find out who Rory really was behind the tough facade.

"So what do you want?" he asked. "Beef with broccoli or Kung Pao chicken?"

"Is the chicken super spicy?"

He picked up a piece and popped it in his mouth, sucking off the sauce on his fingers.

My girlie parts tingled. God, this was worse than I thought if just watching him eat could bring me close to orgasm.

"It's pretty spicy," he answered, oblivious to my desire.

"I'll have the beef then."

He scooped out the beef and broccoli for me. "You don't like spicy?"

"I do, but my stomach doesn't."

"Why?"

"I had ulcers as a kid," I answered flatly, hoping he wouldn't ask more.

"I didn't know kids got ulcers." He scooped out his own plate full. "You must have worried a lot."

"I guess I did. I still do."

"Why?"

I shrugged. "I don't know."

"You're a control freak." He smirked.

"Me? Don't you have that backward?" I laughed. Sitting down in the chair, I motioned for him to take a seat next to me.

"What do you mean, I have it backward?"

"You were pretty domineering in the hotel room last night." I wanted to wait for a more opportune time to discuss his issue of dominance but now was as good as ever. There was no way I'd let him put me on a leash or whip me.

"I can be," he said, stuffing food in his mouth.

"So are you in to that, you know the whole bondage and S&M stuff?" I waited as he chewed.

He swallowed and laughed. "You girls read too much *Fifty Shades of Grey*."

"You didn't answer my question."

"Define 'into that.'" His voice was flat, his face void of expression.

Shit, he *was* into that stuff.

"I mean, do you get off on beating chicks, tying them up, leading them around on a leash? You know, that sort of stuff."

"Why? Would that turn you off?" he asked, his brow raised in playfulness.

"Well, it wouldn't exactly turn me *on*, being led around like an animal."

"But you'd like to be spanked?" His lips curled in a devilish smirk.

Dammit. He was too cute for me to concentrate.

I pushed my food around on my plate. "I'm just saying, I'm not in to that stuff, so if that's what you need to get your rocks off then you can forget this." I motioned between us.

He reached across the table and grabbed my hand.

I jerked it away and stood, heading for the kitchen. The idea of violence in the bedroom was not appealing to me.

I wandered around the kitchen like a caged animal, flipping open cabinet doors, mindlessly scanning the shelves for nothing in particular. I held on to the handle tight and inhaled deeply, blowing out a slow breath as I tried to stave off the anxiety attack threatening.

Suddenly strong arms slid around my waist as a familiar scent accosted my senses. Rory's presence jolted me from my thoughts. His rough whiskers skimmed my still sunburned shoulders as he nuzzled my neck.

My eyes fluttered closed and I leaned into him without even thinking.

"Hey," he whispered, drawing out the word.

There was something about his voice that soothed me, like he understood what I needed. Within seconds, my breathing evened, matching his. My hands settled on his arms still wrapped around my waist. Being held by Rory, leaning into him like this, felt perfect. I wondered if he felt it too.

"I'm sorry," he whispered, his breath caressing the skin of my neck.

I shivered. His words were a salve to my injured soul. I hadn't heard apologies much in my life, and certainly not from the people who'd actually hurt me. Somehow, those two words coming from Rory's mouth filled a need in me I hadn't ever realized I craved. I felt…almost whole again.

I turned in his arms, my hands sliding up his broad shoulders. My gaze caught his. I watched his blue eyes dart between mine. His body pressed into mine as he breathed in and out. My breasts rubbed against his chest, my nipples tightening with desire.

He pulled me closer, his erection hard to miss against my hip.

I pressed up on my toes and kissed the hollow of his neck. God, he smelled good, and he tasted good too. I ran my lips up his neck, spreading kisses along the way.

His head rolled to the side, giving me better access. The deep rumble of his moan gave me courage.

My hands moved to the nape of his neck and I ran my fingers through his unruly hair. The soft strands were just long enough to tug. Touching Rory, tasting him, listening to his heavy panting, felt like heaven. I was affecting him.

"Don't be sorry," I whispered in his ear.

"If you don't have any condoms and you're not on the pill, I'm *really* going to be sorry if you don't stop what you're doing."

I giggled.

He grabbed me around the waist and lifted me up on the counter.

I yelped in surprise. I wasn't a small girl, so being manhandled was a surprise.

He spread my legs and pressed against my center, his erection rubbing against my thin shorts. He thrust his hands into my hair and before I could argue, his lips crashed down on mine.

I wrapped my legs around his waist, drawing him nearer as I opened my mouth and took him in.

He slid one hand down my shoulder.

I winced in pain.

"Oh, God," he said, "I'm sorry, I forgot about your sunburn."

I didn't want another apology. I wanted him.

I slid my arms around his neck and pulled him toward me, my legs tightening around his waist again. He rubbed against me several times and I moaned when he hit the spot that sent me flying.

His hands ran up the back of my shirt and his nimble fingers opened my bra with little effort.

I tugged at the hem of his shirt. Understanding my desire, he grabbed a fist full of fabric at his back and yanked the T-shirt off with ease, tossing it on the counter beside me.

God, he was beautiful, his body sheer perfection. Who knew a skateboarder could be so ripped?

Tentatively, I placed my palms on his muscled chest, enjoying the warmth of his tanned skin. Slowly my palms moved down toward his tattoo, my fingers tracing across his ribs. I peeked up at him.

His eyes were darker and heavy lidded as he stared down at me.

"My Skater Boy," I whispered, tracing the words on his abdomen.

Rory flinched as if I'd electrocuted him and stepped back.

I sat on the counter, my legs spread wide open, Rory now out of my reach.

His head fell to his chest and he stared down at the floor.

"Rory," I called out, reaching for him.

He stepped back even further. "We can't do this," he whispered. He reached around me for his shirt and quickly pulled it over his head.

He was rejecting me. Of course, he was. I was surprised to find his dismissal hurt more than I'd anticipated.

Hot tears burned my eyes and before I could will them away, they streamed down my face. Dammit. I dashed them away with the back of my hand and jumped down from the counter, quickly refastening my bra. How could I have been *so* stupid? Again.

I turned and dashed toward the dining room but before I could make it out of the kitchen, he caught my wrist.

"Let me go!" I yanked my hand out of his hold. It slipped and I slammed it against the door frame with a loud thud. Searing pain shot up my arm. I bit down a scream, afraid I may have broken it. There was no fucking way he was going to see how much he'd hurt me, physically and emotionally.

I bent over and gritted my teeth, holding back the tears. Tucking my hand protectively into my body, I drew in deep breaths.

"Oh my God, Hindley." He rushed beside me. "I'm so sorry."

Another apology. How many was he going to extend tonight?

"Let me see it." He reached for my hand.

I shoved past him and stalked toward the refrigerator. Opening the freezer with my good hand, I dug through the contents until I found a bag of mixed vegetables. I sat it over the back of my throbbing hand and kicked the door closed with my elbow.

After several silent moments I glanced up.

Rory stood in the middle of my kitchen, his huge presence taking up more than just the physical space. The fear and regret in his eyes warned me he had no plans of letting me leave, not without talking first. I didn't want to talk, not now, not ever. I just wanted away from him.

"Get out of my way, Rory," I said through clenched teeth. I moved to walk around him but he reached for the bag. I jerked away from him.

"Hindley, stop!"

"What the fuck do you want?" I yelled back. "You did this to me." I held up my hand.

His eyes went wide, pain etched across his face as his head fell to his chest and he stared down at the floor. He raised his hands and clasped them behind his neck, his thumbs digging into his head. My words were harsher than I'd intended and obviously wounded him terribly.

God, what had I done? He hadn't meant to hurt me, not intentionally. I didn't know a lot about Rory but I knew he wasn't abusive. That's probably how he'd taken my words. Because that's exactly what I'd said.

"I'm sorry," I said, "I didn't mean what I said."

He lifted his head, his eyes still pained. "You can't put the ice pack directly on your skin," he said. "That's what I was trying to tell you. It will burn your skin."

I nodded, unable to speak.

With his shoulders slumped, he moved toward me. "Here, let me wrap it in this towel and then you can put it back on your hand yourself."

I held out the bag of vegetables and watched as he wrapped a dish cloth around the bag before handing it back. His gaze travelled to my hand and I heard him gasp.

I glanced down at my uncovered hand. Shit. A huge purple bruise had already formed from my mid-knuckle, spreading out to my wrist and growing.

"Oh my God," he whispered, taking a step back. His eyes darted from mine down to my hand and back.

I snatched the bag and towel and covered my hand. "It's not your fault, Rory," I said quietly. "It was an accident."

He pulled back, physically and emotionally. I didn't want him to leave, not like this.

"Rory." I grabbed his arm with my good hand to get his attention. "You didn't do this to me. I'm sorry I said that." I walked closer, thankful when he didn't back away.

His eyes stayed glued to my hand.

I released his shoulder and held my injured hand closer to my body, trying to hide it. "Come on, let's finish dinner."

His eyes finally met mine. "I don't think that's a good idea, Hindley." He turned to leave.

"Why?" I asked, reaching to stop him. The bag of frozen vegetables fell to the floor.

"I'm not good for you, Hindley. Just look at your hand." He knelt and picked up the bag. Rewrapping the towel, he held it out to me.

I didn't take it. Instead, I held out my bruised hand, silently asking him to take care of me, again. When he didn't stand, I sunk to my knees so that we were at eye-level.

I looked deep inside his eyes, willing him to stay with me, not just physically. "Stay," I said. I couldn't let him leave thinking he'd hurt me on purpose. "We can review your contract. It will be a business dinner. You need to look at it anyway, right?"

His face went ashen and he stiffened.

What was going on with him? I didn't want to lose him so I rose, hoping he'd go with me.

He remained kneeling, his gaze glued to the floor.

I reached down and slid my hand under his jaw, raising his head. His eyes were closed. "Rory, look at me," I said in my sternest voice.

He didn't move.

"Rory. Look at me," I demanded. "I won't ask you again." I echoed his words from last night, surprised at how easy my dominant side appeared.

His eyes darted up to mine. A thrill raced through my body when I realized how much power I had over him. As much as he held over me.

"Stand up," I said in a low, monotone voice.

Cautiously, he stood until he was at his full height, towering over me. There was no way I was going to let him intimidate me now. My technique was working, even if I didn't one hundred percent believe I had a dominant side.

"You're right," I said, staring up at him. "We can't do this."

His shoulders slumped and his lips pressed into a firm line. Was he...disappointed?

"I'm your attorney," I said, "you're my client. Any relationship other than that would be inappropriate, right?"

He nodded.

My gut told me Rory had probably been trampled on his entire life. I'd recognized his damaged soul the first night we met. I knew exactly what it felt like to be used by others for their own selfish gain. I'd closed myself off from most people. Unlike me, Rory had fought back, using women, booze, drugs, fame, even money to ease his pain. We were birds of a feather, but our coping skills were different. I couldn't let him leave, not like this.

I slipped my good hand into his and dragged him toward the dining room. I slid out his chair. "Now, have a seat."

He willingly lowered himself.

"Do you like hard copy or screen version?" I asked.

"What?"

"Your contract. Is it better for you to look at it in hard copy or on the computer?"

He swallowed hard and turned his head, averting his gaze.

I was losing him, again and had no reason why.

"Just email it to me," he said, moving to stand, "I'll look at it when I get home tonight."

I pushed him down. "No. I'm *your* attorney. There are several points we need to review together, not on your own. I'm sure you've read lots of contracts before, but this one is different, a lot different."

I marched over to the living room table before he could escape and picked up his file. Carrying it back to the dining table, I strengthened my resolve to keep him here, at least until he could calm down and read through his contract.

"Scoot over." I nudged him, scooting my chair so we were sitting side-by-side. Our arms brushed against one another and just that one touch made my body burn with need. Stupid, stupid girl.

I recalled his rejection earlier, specifically how much it hurt. I would embrace the pain and allow the memory of his words to keep me strong, keep me fighting for him professionally, as his lawyer. Nothing more. Taking a deep breath, I pulled out the large contract. I noticed him squirming from the corner of my eye. "What's wrong?"

"It's just…" He rubbed the back of his neck, a move I recognized he did when he was nervous. "Jack usually reviews these for me."

"You don't review your own contracts?"

"No."

That's weird. "Why?" I asked.

"I get…" Beads of sweat gathered above his brow. God, he was freaking out.

"Rory, what's wrong?"

"It's all so confusing, you know," he pointed to the contract, "all that legal-ease shit."

"I know exactly what you mean." I laughed, remembering how lost I was the first year of law school. "Understanding legal documents takes time," I explained. "Hell, I've been to law school and this crap still doesn't make sense to me sometimes. That's why I've drafted yours so it's not so confusing. This is actually my first attorney-agent contract. I wrote it myself, so of course I'm quite proud of it." I glanced at him.

He sat quietly, his face giving nothing away. Where was my old Rory. *My Rory?* Not good.

"Hey," I bumped his shoulder, "I'm *your* attorney. I'm here to help *you*, Rory, not confuse you. That's my job."

He nodded but remained silent.

"If something doesn't make sense then tell me and together, we'll sort it out," I said. "That's why I'm here, to protect you. Only you."

I did want to protect him, and not just legally.

He glanced down at my injured hand and stiffened beside me.

The bruise was practically glowing a deep purple. I jerked it away and slid it under the table.

Leaning across me, he took my hand and gently placed it in his. Mine looked so small and delicate compared to his mammoth-sized one. He brought my hand up to his lips and pressed feather-light kisses across the bruise.

I closed my eyes and bit my tongue, holding back a moan. He may not want me physically but obviously my body hadn't gotten the memo. Dammit. Everything this man did turned me on like no one I'd ever met.

"I hurt you," he said quietly against my hand.

His tone was achingly sad. It was clear Rory had a tormented soul created by a life he wasn't willing to share. My heart literally ached for him.

"I'll always hurt you, Hindley," he whispered.

My eyes fluttered open and I stared into his blue eyes.

"I won't mean to, but in the end," he paused and I held my breath. "In the end, I'll hurt you."

I pulled my hand back but he held it tighter, staring like it was a precious jewel.

"What does that mean?" I asked.

His downcast eyes remained fixed on my hand as his fingertip gently traced the bruise. "I fuck up everything I touch."

"All the more reason to work harder this time, Rory." Maybe he thought I meant the skating, but I also meant me, maybe he could try harder, with me.

"If I hurt you again, like this," he continued, holding up my hand, "I'll never forgive myself, Hindley. Ever."

I yanked my hand away from his, upset at how I'd been reading this whole scene. Maybe I was wrong. Maybe he'd never wanted me at all.

"Look, Rory, I don't know what's happened in your life to make you feel so shitty about yourself, but trust me when I say this, I know exactly how you feel. If you hurt me, I'm a big girl, I can take it. What I can't take is your on again, off again bullshit."

His beautiful blue eyes searched mine, looking for something I wasn't sure I could offer. Permission? Rejection? Slowly, he slid his hand into my hair, bringing my face close to his, that infamous predatory look spreading across his gorgeous face.

"Who knew Drunk Girl could be so forceful," he whispered against my lips.

"Who knew Skater Boy could be so sensitive." I smiled, pressing my lips to his.

This kiss was different, not as passionate or as desperate as our other kisses. I wasn't sure if that was a good thing or a bad thing. Part of the embrace felt like a new beginning but mostly it felt like good-bye.

Rory shifted away, and just like that, our moment was over. Brushing away a lock of hair from my forehead, he traced the entire strand with his fingers before his hand fell away. "I think I should probably get going."

I tried to hide my disappointment and push down all my old insecurities of abandonment. It was useless. This was good-bye and I knew it.

"All right," I said, swallowing down the emotions threatening to break me. I scooted my chair back and stood to walk him out. Obviously what we'd felt for each other earlier was over. It was for the best.

I was his attorney. He was my client. I was still a woman though, deeply moved by this sexy, vibrant, virile man and most of me couldn't help but feel disappointed and hurt by his rejection.

"Here," I said, shoving the contract at him.

He looked down at the document like it was a snake ready to strike him.

"You need to read over it, Rory, before you sign. With or without me."

"That's what I pay you for," he said with a nervous laugh.

And there it was, spelled out in plain English. 'That's what I pay you for.' He was *paying* me for my services. I was an employee. Nothing less, nothing more.

I shrugged. "Even still, you should read over it and let me know if you have questions. If you still don't want to, even after I've advised you that you should, you'll find I've labeled it with idiot proof tags at all the places you need to sign. Don't sign until Tuesday though. We need witnesses and a notary."

He grabbed the contract from my hand and folded it in half, shoving it into his back pocket. He clenched his jaw, his eyes hard and...cold.

"What's wrong?" I asked.

"Nothing." He stomped to the front door and ripped it open, stepping out onto the porch. "I'll see you Tuesday."

I followed but before I reached the door, he'd slammed it shut in my face. *What the hell was that?*

I didn't have to ask myself twice. My eyes burned with tears and I cursed myself for being so stupid by expecting more from a man, from anyone.

I'd misunderstood Rory's affections, thinking he could change me, make me start living instead of just existing. I only had myself to blame. I was the one who'd told him we could only be attorney and client. God, I was turning psycho.

I plopped down on the sofa, my arm falling over my eyes and swallowed back the tears. What a fool I'd been.

I sat for several moments in silence as tears fell down my cheeks. Dammit. There was only one person who could help.

Picking up the phone, I dialed her number. I hiccupped a sob just as she answered.

"Ah, fuck me, what happened now?" Dana said, her voice full of attitude.

"Nothing," I stuttered through my tears.

"That little prick," she cursed under her breath. "I'll be over in ten."

The line went dead and I rolled over on the couch, burying my head in the cushions as all my old insecurities came crashing down. How had I let this man get into my head? I'd been doing so well for so long. Yet, within the span of a week, I was right back where I started, flailing like a wounded duck, on the verge of spiraling out of control again.

I sat straight up, willing myself to be strong. I could do this on my own. I had to. I dialed Dana's number again, waiting for her to answer.

"I'm headed out now," she said. "Are you hungry?"

"Don't come over."

"Why?"

"I need to do this on my own, Dana. I need to learn how to fight back by myself."

"Are you sure? You know I love you, I'll be there in a heartbeat if you need me."

"I know and I love you for it, but I've got to learn how to do this on my own, without help, you know?"

"I do know, sweetie," she said, "and I'm proud of you. I'm worried about you, that's all."

"Don't be."

"Why? Have you been watching Doctor Phil again?"

I laughed. "No. I've been letting one guy get into my head, and even though he crushed my heart, he also made me feel brave and confident for the first time in a long time. That felt good. I can do this."

"You still feel brave and confident even though this dill hole is the reason you broke down and had to call me tonight?"

"Yep," I answered with confidence. "Even though he's the reason I broke down. Ironic, huh?"

"Ironic that this little prick would be the one to help you get over his own douchey maneuvers? Yeah, I'd call that pretty damn ironic."

We both laughed.

"I'm proud of you, Hindley," she said. I could hear the smile in her voice. "You are brave, and strong, and smart. So many things I wish I was, and probably everything Rory wishes he were too."

"But you are. You both are all those things."

"And so are you, sweetie."

I smiled, realizing for once that maybe she was right, maybe Rory was right.

"So did y'all do the nasty?" She giggled. "Is that why you're so upset? Was it horrible?"

"No!" I yelled. "I doubt very much that doing the nasty with Rory would be anything but horrible."

"Yeah, you're probably right. He's probably hung like a horse. Most pricks are. I'm sure he knows exactly what he's doing in the bedroom too. Especially if he macks the muff as well as you said he did."

I grasped my head and shook it. "I don't know why I even told you that."

"Because you tell me everything."

"True." I nodded.

"You want to talk about it?"

"There's not much to say. I know he wants to be with me. He works so hard at making me feel special and beautiful and all the things a girl wants to be. But then, I don't know, it's like he pulls away."

"It's probably better this way, don't you think?"

"Why? You don't think I can handle him?"

"Why would you say that?"

"Because I wonder if I could handle him," I said, sinking into the sofa. "I'm pretty inexperienced, and it's all over the Internet that he's been with tons of women. What could I offer?"

"I thought you said you were going to work on your self-esteem. Putting yourself down doesn't help anything."

I nodded even though she couldn't see me. "You're right, but it's true though. I don't have much experience."

"Then let him teach you."

"He doesn't want me. Besides, you just said it's better if we don't get involved."

"Well, that's the whole attorney-client thing. But the more I think about it, the more exciting it sounds. Like one of those soft-porn movies they show on late night cable."

"Why do you love those channels so much?"

"Because I don't have a love interest in my life right now. I haven't had sex in weeks and it's killing me," Dana sighed. Going more than two days without sex was a long time for her. "Do you know how much it sucks having to live vicariously through you? I never thought I'd see the day."

"What about Leif?"

"Leif's gay."

"What? He told you that?"

"No," she said, "he didn't have to."

"What makes you say that?"

"Experience."

"Just because he didn't try to get in your panties in the first twenty-four hours of meeting you doesn't make him gay."

"No, but it's definitely a mark against him."

"I think you're just saying that because you like him," I said, "and you're afraid of those feelings because he's not pursuing you."

"Maybe, we'll see. Time always tells with the homos."

"Dana, that's awful."

"What? It's true."

"I'm talking about calling him a homo."

"Why? That's what he is."

"First of all, you don't know that Leif is gay," I said. "Second of all, that's a derogatory term. You wouldn't like it if someone called you a WOP."

"Wow, you are being feisty tonight, aren't you? I like the effect Rory is having on you. Even though he's making you cry your eyes out tonight. Twat head."

"I'm not crying my eyes out."

"Not now."

"That's why I called you." I fumbled with one of my throw pillows. "I knew you'd make me feel better."

My phone beeped and I pulled it from my ear. Staring down at the screen, my mouth fell open.

Rory.

"Shit," I said.

"What's wrong?"

"It's Rory."

"Are you gonna answer?"

"I don't know." I chewed on my bottom lip. "I'm still pretty raw."

"Well, if you need me, call me. I'm not doing anything except changing out the batteries in my vibrators."

I laughed, knowing she was probably telling the truth.

"Love you, Dana."

"I love you too, Hindley. Tell Douche Bag I said hi."

CHAPTER 23

RORY

"Fuck, fuck, fuck!" I slammed Leif's door closed and chucked his keys on the entryway table.

"I take it dinner didn't go so well?" Leif laughed.

I walked into the living room. "I totally fucked up, man."

Leif switched off the television and turned around to face me.

"Want a drink?" He held up a tumbler filled with an amber liquid.

"What the fuck, Leif?" He knew I hadn't had a drink in over two years.

"Relax, man. It's just apple juice."

I scraped a hand through my hair and fell on to his sofa with a sigh. "Don't fuck with me right now, man. I'm a nervous wreck."

He sat up straight. "What the hell happened?"

"I hurt her."

"Well, we knew that was coming. That's why I told you to leave her alone, fuck-face."

I glared.

He shrugged. "Well, I did."

"Whatever, man. No, I mean, I physically hurt her."

"What the fuck, Rory?" Leif lurched for me.

I pushed him away. "It was an accident, man. But still, she hurt her hand."

"God, how could you be so fucking stupid? I told you not to mess with her. She's your fucking attorney, Rory."

Something inside me snapped. I flew toward Leif, jumping on top of him as I cocked my fist, readying to beat the shit out of his fat mouth.

Someone's hand wrapped around my arm and yanked me off. Only one person would dare touch me when I flew into a rage. Jack Jennings.

"Rory!" Kara shrieked. "What are you doing?"

I fell back and scraped a hand down my face. God, what *had* I been about to do? Kick the shit out of my best friend. And now I'd scared the shit out of Kara too. I jumped from the sofa and practically ran through the back door, slamming it behind me. I paced around the deck like a caged animal, breathing hard, fighting the urge to roar.

Unable to hold back, I threw my head back and yelled up to the sky. "Fuck!"

Jesus, what the hell was wrong with me?

I shuffled to the railing and leaned on my elbows. I lifted up a silent prayer of help to no one in particular. What in the fuck was going on with my life? I hadn't felt this out of control in a long time.

A warm hand pressed against my back. Kara had followed me out. She was the only person who could calm me down when my brain exploded.

She stood beside me, silent. She didn't have to speak. She'd been talking me off the ledge for years.

Any other mother would have knocked the shit out of me for nearly beating the shit out of their son, but not Kara. I was as much a son to her as Leif. There was nothing she would ever do to hurt me or make me feel worse, no matter how stupid my actions were or how much I deserved it.

Kara had worked years building up my self-worth, and up until this moment, she'd done a pretty good job. But the fact that I'd hurt Hindley physically, and probably emotionally, had my stomach in knots.

I stared out at the horizon. The sun had finally set and the colors that filled the night sky were as mixed as my emotions. "I hurt her, Kara," I finally whispered. "Physically."

She remained silent.

"I'm pretty sure I hurt her emotionally too."

She continued rubbing slow circles on my back and remained quiet. This was Kara. She allowed me the time and space to exorcise the demons of my soul. No judgment. It was called unconditional love, and I'd never known it until I met the Jennings. But most days I still had a hard time believing I deserved it. Today was one of them.

"I didn't mean to hurt her, Kara," I said. "It was an accident, but still." Something welled up inside me and burned my throat. It felt like a sob, but I hadn't cried in, well, ever. I fought to push down the emotion but before I could blink them back, tears rolled down my face.

I turned to face Kara, not surprised when she took me into her small arms, holding me close as I released years of pent up anger, frustration, and hostility.

She remained silent, her comforting hands rubbing my shoulders back and forth. I trembled in her hold and she held me tighter.

We stood locked together until the tears subsided and the tension in my body eased.

I pulled away and stared down at her, shocked to find tears in her eyes too. Well, shit. Now I could add Kara to my growing list of people I'd hurt tonight.

She reached up and stroked my cheek, wiping away the tears. "I think we both needed that," she said, leading us to the glider. "Sit."

I fell into the seat with a heavy sigh. Spreading my legs wide, I settled my elbows on my knees as I held my head in my hands.

She nestled in beside me, sitting sideways and folding her legs underneath her so she could look directly at me. She remained quiet, giving me the time I needed to process everything. That was her way.

Kara never pushed me. She knew I was a wounded animal, and she'd always taken the 'wait and watch' approach when it came to my welfare. When everyone else in my outer circle of friends poked and prodded, trying to uncover my demons, Kara remained still. She'd found a way to reach me, to quiet the monsters in my head.

There was only one reason I wasn't in prison, or dead...Kara Jennings.

My only regret was letting her down by pissing my life away. Not once had she ever acknowledged her disappoint in me. She understood I had enough self-loathing to last a lifetime. I'd spent many an hour wondering how different my life would have been if Kara Jennings had been my birth mother from the start.

I blew out the breath I felt like I'd been holding since I left Hindley's. "She's different, Kara. I don't know how to explain it, other than, she's different." I turned and stared at her.

A small smirk spread across her face.

"What?" I asked.

"Nothing." She shook her head.

"That smile is definitely something."

"I'm just waiting." She shrugged. "I want to hear more about this girl who's so different."

"What's up with the smile?" I nodded toward her face.

"Can't I be happy that you've finally met someone who's different?"

I'd never stopped to think of Kara wanting me to find someone special. I'd always assumed she was resigned to the fact that I'd be a 'One-Nighter' the rest of my life.

"You want me to find someone, don't you?" I asked. "Someone to settle down with?"

She took my hand in hers. "Rory, I just want you to be fulfilled, mentally, physically, and spiritually."

Kara and Jack weren't religious fanatics but they did believe in spiritual gifts and atonements. I'd never swung one way or another, but I'd always noticed how content they were, in life and in love.

"How do I get that?" I asked. "Fulfillment, I mean?"

"Only you can answer that one, sweetheart."

I rolled my eyes. "A likely answer."

"What? It's true."

"Says the woman who's fulfilled."

"I can't argue that." Her head fell back, eyes closed. She drew in a deep breath.

I envied her and Jack so much. They had peace, something I'd never even knew existed before I'd met them.

"What?" she asked, never opening her eyes.

I'd always found it strange how attune Kara was to me. She and I were connected. I'd known that since the first day I'd met her. That's the only reason I went home with them that first day they found me. Kara and I weren't related by blood, but by spirit, and that thought had always brought me some semblance of peace during my darkest times.

"I like her, Kara."

She opened her eyes and stared at me. "I know you do, sweetheart. You didn't have to tell me that. It's written all over your poor, pathetic little face." She smiled and ran a hand through my hair.

"Whatever." I laughed, swatting her away.

"So, tell me about her, this girl who's so different. Why do you like her, Rory?"

I'd never slowed down enough over the past week to think about *why* I liked Hindley. Maybe answering Kara's question would help me find some sort of peace when it came to my life.

"Rory, close your eyes," she instructed.

I knew she'd never let me escape until I followed her command, so I did as she said and closed my eyes.

"Picture the first time you saw her."

I snorted.

"What's so funny?"

"She was drunk as a skunk when I met her," I said. "I called her Drunk Girl because she was too smashed to even tell me her name." My eyes flew open and I stared at Kara. "I didn't do anything with her, I swear. I took her home and made sure she was safe. That's all."

A huge smile spread across her face. "Of course you did, sweetheart."

Her belief in me was a salve to my heart.

"That's why she's different to you," she said.

"Why?"

"You want to take care of her, don't you?"

I thought about her question. Did I want to take care of Hindley? I had tonight. I shook my head, dismissing the memories of her bruised hand.

"And tonight, you hurt her," Kara said. "It goes against everything you feel for her, everything you hold dear."

I closed my eyes, Hindley's face flashing before me, the look of anguish and disappointment in her eyes turned my stomach.

Kara squeezed my arm.

I opened my eyes and stared up at her.

"Rory, we all hurt each other. Jack has torn my heart to shreds numerous times, as I have his. It's part of the process of love."

"Love," I snapped. "I don't love her."

"Not yet." She winked.

"What does that mean, not yet?"

"It means that this is the first girl you've ever seen potential in. The girls you've been with in the past have been superficial. It's been easy to escape unharmed. You've never let them in so they never had the chance to hurt you. Right?"

I nodded. "I guess."

"But now you've met this woman who wants more, who you want more with, and it's scary and exciting all rolled up into one."

"I don't want more with her."

She raised a brow.

Yeah, I did. And that was the problem.

"And now, all your insecurities are floating to the surface," she said, "just like I'm sure hers are."

I'd never thought about Hindley having insecurities like me. She always seemed so confident and self-assured.

"No one's perfect, Rory, no matter how it looks from the outside," Kara said. "Trust me. And I'm sure if you got to know her better, you'd find she's just as self-conscious and vulnerable as you are. If you hurt her tonight then those insecurities are going to drown her until you make it right."

"What does that mean?"

"It means that she probably has low self-esteem, so anything you've done tonight to prove her self-deprecating image is right, the more she'll beat herself up. You have the power to hurt her. You should know that better than anyone. Even if you don't like her or don't see it going any further, you have to make this right with her or she'll beat herself up all night."

"She's stronger than that, way stronger. Trust me. She doesn't need a guy like me to make her feel better about herself."

Kara reared up on her knees. "That's bullshit and you know it, Rory Gregor."

Oh, shit. I scooted back. Kara never cussed. In fact, she hated it when Leif and I went at it, and she definitely never raised her voice in anger.

"I did not raise you to think so little of yourself, and it offends me that you would. Get on that phone and make this right with that girl or I will come back out here and beat you senseless, which by the sound of it won't take long." She popped up from the glider and stomped toward the door.

"She's my attorney, Kara."

Within seconds, Kara was back at my side, her hand resting softly on my shoulder. "First and foremost, she's a woman. She has needs and desires, like all of us."

I turned and stared up at her face, not surprised by the motherly love and affection radiating from her eyes.

"Attorneys are a dime a dozen," she said. "A girl who makes

you feel different, who makes you question everything in the past, isn't. You owe it to yourself, and to her, to find out why." She reached down and cupped my face. "And you are as worthy of love as she is, my dear. Don't ever let anyone make you think differently." She reached down and kissed my cheek.

"But I can't read, Kara."

"Then tell her."

"She's an attorney," I said. "My attorney. I can't."

"Why?"

"If she laughs at me, if she leaves me because I'm stupid, I'm not sure I could take it."

She grabbed my chin in her hands and yanked my face toward hers. "You are not stupid, Rory Gregor. Why do you think so little of yourself and this girl?"

I shrugged.

She squeezed my chin then released me. "If she does any of those things then that will give you the answer you're looking for. From the look in your eyes and the way you're fretting though, I don't think that's the reaction you'll get from her. You'll never know unless you tell her."

My gaze fell to the ground, embarrassed by my own illiteracy and lack of education.

"Rory Gregor, look at me."

Kara was in no mood to be fooled with tonight, I could tell by her tone. My gaze snapped to hers as I prepared myself for her wrath.

Her hands were fisted on her small hips, a fire in her eyes I hadn't seen in a long time. "Reading does not make you a man worthy of a woman's love, do you understand me? Did you ever stop to think maybe this girl needs you?"

"She doesn't need anything, Kara. She's rich, beautiful, and smart."

"Maybe she needs more. Maybe she needs purpose, confidence, and self-assurance, like you. Maybe you can give that to each other."

Her body relaxed and she came to sit next to me again. "Rory, you can't sit on the sidelines wondering 'what-if.' You've taken risks your whole life, most of which have paid off in the end. Don't stop taking chances just because you feel inadequate, not with this girl anyway. She's different, right?"

I nodded. Hindley was *so* different.

She punched my shoulder. "Let her prove it then. Let her show you how different she really is. She sounds amazing and I think you'll be surprised at how much she needs you." Kara stood and moved toward the house again.

"Kara," I called out, just as she'd reached the back door.

She gazed over her shoulder. "Yeah, sweetie?"

"Thanks."

"You know I'm always here for you, Rory. Always have been…"

"Always will be," I added.

She smiled and gave a wink. "You bet your bottom dollar, buster. They gotta get through me first." She stabbed her chest with her thumb.

I laughed. Kara was almost a foot shorter than me but one of the fiercest people I knew. "Thanks."

"That's what moms are for." Before I could acknowledge her comment, she closed the door. Kara was my mom, in every way.

I pulled my phone from my pocket and scrolled the contacts' list until Hindley's beautiful face appeared.

I still didn't feel worthy of her, especially since I'd hurt her physically and emotionally. But Kara was right. I couldn't sit on the sidelines and wonder what-if. That wasn't my style.

Being with Hindley, sharing my secrets with her, was a chance I had to be willing to take. I drew in a deep breath to calm my racing heart as my finger pressed her name.

CHAPTER 24

RORY

I SAT and waited as her phone rang and rang, the sound grating my last nerve. Why wasn't she answering? My anxiety was through the roof and I seriously thought I might throw the phone over the railing if she didn't answer soon. Finally the ringing stopped and I held my breath.

Silence filled the space.

What the hell?

"Hello?" I said.

Nothing.

I pulled the phone away from my face and glanced at the screen. The call was still connected.

"Hindley?" I said.

Still nothing. I was just about to hang up and try again when I heard her voice

"What, Rory?" Her voice was deep and raspy, like she'd been crying. Fuck.

I swallowed down a ball of fear, wondering what the hell to say next.

"Um, hi," I finally spoke.

No response.

This was not good. Her silence spoke volumes. I had a lot of ground to make up for.

"Did I disturb you?" I asked.

"I was talking to Dana."

Dana? Oh, shit. I was screwed.

"Well, I can call you back if you want. Or you could call me back." I raked a nervous hand through my hair. Fuck. I sounded like a pathetic middle schooler prank calling his crush.

Just grow a ball sack and tell her already.

"No, it's okay," she said. "I hung up with her already."

I waited for her to say more but nothing came. More awkward silence.

"I, uh…" Christ, was I stuttering now? "I wanted to call and tell you I was sorry."

"For what?"

For what? Where should I start? There were so many things.

"First," I said, "I'm sorry about your hand. I truly am." Emotions choked me and I pulled the phone away, clearing my throat. "Does it, uh, feel better? I mean, is it still sore?"

"It's all right. I took some Ibuprofen."

"You should keep ice on it, to help with the swelling."

"You're speaking from experience?" she asked.

"I've had more bruises, contusions, concussions, and broken bones than I want to remember."

"Oh my gosh, that's horrible. Seriously?"

"Oh, yeah."

"How many bones?"

"Well, let's see." I let out a long sigh and leaned back in the glider, kicking my feet out in front of me. I placed my free hand on the back of my neck, trying to remember.

"That many, huh?"

"Oh, yeah. Comes with the territory, I'm afraid. I still can't bend my left pinky."

"What happened?"

She sounded genuinely interested so I continued. "I came down wrong from a spin on a half-pipe and landed on my hand. Hyper extended my pinky."

"Stop!"

"What?" I sat up.

"Oh, that is so gross. Don't tell me any more. That made me want to vomit."

"I'm sorry." I chuckled. "But you did ask."

"I know. I don't know why I did. I get queasy from stuff like that."

"Then you probably shouldn't come to any competitions because stuff like that happens all the time."

"I know," she said. "I saw the videos. Plus, some of those amateurs bit it big time at the Pro Am."

"That's because they're knuckle heads."

"What makes you say that?"

I crossed an ankle over the opposite knee. "They shouldn't be trying out stupid shit like that for a show. The fans didn't come to watch us fall on our asses."

"What's wrong with falling?"

"Nothing, when you're legitimately skating. But a Pro Am is for the spectators, not a time for us to practice new moves."

"Well, I kind of liked the fact that they went all out." I could hear the smile in her voice.

"I thought you said you didn't like watching stuff like that, watching people break their fingers and arms and wrists and—"

"Stop."

A low laugh escaped before I could silence myself.

"Why do you enjoy upsetting me so much?" she said.

Her question took me by surprise. I didn't know if she was serious or not.

"I didn't know I was upsetting you," I said.

"Yes, you did. You totally did. And you love doing it."

"No, I don't." My words were harsher than I'd intended, but I wanted her to know the truth. "If I upset you, it's never on purpose, Hindley. Ever." There was a long pause and I had no idea what to say next. "Are you still there?"

"I'm here."

"What are you thinking?"

"What an oxymoron you are," she said.

I wasn't sure what an oxymoron was, but it had the word "moron" in it so that couldn't be good. "I'm not an idiot, Hindley."

"I never said you were."

"I'm not a moron either."

"I never said that you were. God, calm down, Rory." I could hear the exasperation in her voice. "I said you were an *oxy*moron. You know, a paradox."

What the fuck was she talking about, a paradox? There was no way we could be together. Hindley was light years ahead of me in intelligence. Shocker. Why had I even tried? I was about to say good-bye and hang up when she continued.

"I mean, you're a walking, talking contradiction."

"What the fuck is that supposed to mean?" Now I was fuming. She'd personally attacked me and like a wild animal I lashed out.

"Don't get pissed off and go all cave man on me," she said, her voice steady and calm. "I meant that at any given moment, you can be kind, caring, and sensitive. Then you turn faster than you do on your skateboard and become mean and selfish, shouting out profanities that would make a customer at a biker bar red with embarrassment. Like now, what you just did."

"Are you making fun of me?"

"Man, what is wrong with you?"

"What?"

"First, you come over here and get me all sexed up on my own kitchen counter. Then you pull away and storm out of my house, pissed off like I've done something to offend you. I think it was pretty obvious I was putting my junk out there for you to take, and instead, you—"

"I can't read," I blurted out.

"What?"

I sat in silence for a long moment, staring up at the sky. What the hell had I just done?

"I can't read," I repeated.

"At all?"

"I can read some stuff, but not much. It's the longer, more complicated stuff that's confusing. You know like books, newspapers, websites. That kind of stuff."

"And contracts?"

"Yeah. Contracts. Especially contracts."

"Is that what this has all been about?"

"What?"

"You," she said, "acting all angry and defensive one minute then sorry and apologetic the next."

"Yeah, probably. I guess. I mean, that's part of it."

"What's the other part?"

"I'm still trying to figure that one out."

"Well, when you figure it out, let me know so I can act accordingly."

There was a long pause filled with deafening silence. It felt like I was losing her.

"How can you have survived this long without reading?" she asked, her voice void of judgment.

I sat on the glider, staring up at the stars. How *had* I gotten by this long without knowing how to read?

"That came out wrong, Rory, I'm sorry," she said.

"Don't be, I know what you meant. You'd be surprised how far an insane amount of money and talent can get you."

"How did you graduate high school if you couldn't read?"

"I didn't."

"You didn't graduate high school?"

I shook my head as if she could see me.

"So, that's it," she said.

"That's what?" I asked.

"I graduated college and law school. That's why you feel inferior, isn't it?"

"You're also talented, achingly gorgeous, rich, and smart."

"Please, don't let me stop you." She giggled.

Her laughter was like sweet music to my ears, an indicator that maybe there was a chance for me, for us.

"Well," I paused, as if I had to think of more. "You're kind, and sweet, and sexy, and funny and beautiful. And you taste like heaven."

"Okay, now you're making me blush."

"Why?"

"Because I'm pretty sure half that stuff isn't true."

"Why do you do that?"

"Do what?" she asked.

"Put yourself down."

"Same reason you do, I guess."

We sat in silence, processing her revelation.

"Have you tried to read," she asked, "you know, since you became an adult?"

"I've tried. Leif's mom, Kara, worked with me for a while, but I couldn't concentrate."

"What do you mean?"

"It was like we were looking at two different things. Like I was seeing a square and she was trying to make me see a circle. I ended up more confused and frustrated than when we started. Eventually, I gave up and thankfully she didn't push me."

"How do you get by, I mean, when you have stuff you need to read?"

"Leif and his parents help a lot. And my attorney. The one you got fired."

"I didn't fire him." She laughed. "He sucked. Your manager fired him."

"Well, good or bad, he held my secret for years, so I have to give him props for that."

"Aren't you scared?"

"Of what?"

"Of people finding out?"

"Are you kidding," I said, "I'm terrified."

"Were you afraid of me finding out?"

I sagged back into the glider, sighing. "Afraid doesn't even begin to explain how I felt about you finding out. I think paralyzed with fear and scared shitless would about sum it up."

"So why did you tell me?" she asked.

"Kara told me to."

There was silence but I could hear her breathing.

"Leif's mom," I said, "my manager's wife, Leif and Jack and Kara Jennings. They're my family, my surrogate family."

"What about *your* family?" she asked. "Your mom and dad?"

"Long story."

"What did Kara say that made you tell me tonight?"

What could I say? How could I answer her without giving away everything and exposing myself to heartache and ridicule? "She said I had to take a chance. On you."

"And?" she said.

"And what?"

"Are you glad you told me?"

"That depends."

"On what?"

I rubbed a hand through my hair. "On how you act toward me, now that you know."

"Well, I haven't slammed down the phone, so that has to count for something, right?"

The lightheartedness of our conversation returned.

"I guess."

"I'm in awe of you actually," she said.

"Why?"

"I can't imagine how difficult this has been on you all these years. Reading is something I've taken for granted. I'll never do it again."

There was something in her voice but it didn't sound like pity. I smiled.

"So, how do you get by?" she asked.

"What do you mean?"

"Like at the grocery store, or at a restaurant, or at an autograph signing? I'm sure people put stuff in front of you all the time asking you to read it."

"For grocery stores and stuff like that, it's pretty easy. There are enough pictures and I have them memorized so I know how to tell a can of soup from a can of dog food."

We both laughed and immediately my heart felt lighter.

"I can read a little," I said, "just not long, complicated sentences, or stories with big words. And smart phones have been my saving grace. There are all kinds of apps on the phone now that help me read and write."

"That's kind of cool, I guess."

"Not really. It's stressful as hell. I try to avoid situations where I think that might happen. But if I can't, I make sure I have Leif, Jack, or Kara with me."

"Who else knows?"

"Besides you? Just the Jennings, and Gene-O."

"Seriously? That's it?"

"That's it."

"What about your agent back in California?"

"He probably knows, but it's not something I've ever confessed like I am with you."

"So why are you telling me?"

Her question was genuine, not accusatory.

"Because you're my attorney and eventually it's going to come up."

"Like tonight when I tried to get you to review the contract?"

"Yeah," I nodded, "stuff like that."

"Why did you leave all pissed off tonight?"

"That's a different story."

"You called me."

I drew in a deep breath, wondering if I wanted to share all my secrets with her tonight. Deep inside, where no one had ever ventured before, I knew I trusted her. She didn't trust me though, not yet. Being vulnerable, opening myself up to her with no guarantees, scared the shit out of me.

Then the realization hit me like a blow to the chest. I was afraid. Afraid of this girl. Because like it or not, Hindley Hagen had the power to destroy me.

"Look, Hindley, I don't trust a lot of people."

"I can tell." She snorted.

"How?"

"Your ability to go from zero to a hundred in about two seconds is one of them. I wish I could run as fast as your mind switches gears."

"You run?"

"Don't change the subject, Rory," she said. "Why don't you trust people? And why are you taking a chance on me?"

"It's hard to be vulnerable."

"You don't have to tell me."

"Tell me something."

"What?"

"Tell me something that makes you vulnerable, to me," I said. "I've shared something with you, now it's your turn." There was silence on the other end and I feared I may have pushed her too far. "It's okay, Hindley. I'm not going to tell anyone."

I heard her intake a breath before she finally spoke. "I'm not as experienced as you are. Sexually. And that scares me. I don't know why."

That was a revelation. Nothing in our past make-out sessions had ever indicated she was anything *but* experienced. Shy maybe, but inexperienced? No way.

"Are you serious?" I asked.

"What does that mean?" she asked in a huff.

I didn't like that she was getting defensive. "First of all, don't do that."

"Do what?"

I could picture her sassy little lips puckering up, getting ready to spew something hateful. "Don't get defensive. We're being vulnerable here so cut me some slack." I waited for her rebuttal but when I heard none, I forged on. "What I meant was, that to me, I have found you anything *but* lacking in the sexuality department."

"Really?"

I smiled, picturing how adorable she probably looked right now. "You have no idea, do you?" I asked.

"What?"

"Hindley, you're fucking sexy as hell, and you kiss like a prisoner on death row."

She giggled. "That's a visual."

My chest ached and heat radiated through my entire body. Her laughter did something to me, on the inside. The sound eased the pain that always lived just under the skin.

"I hope that's a compliment," she said.

"Yes, that's a compliment. The way you move your body is…" I didn't know how to finish. "Let's say that my dick gets hard just thinking about you."

"Like right now?" she asked coyly.

"Uh huh," I hummed.

The melodious sounds of her continued laughter had my dick throbbing painfully. I was relieved to hear the return of the confidence in her voice and couldn't help but feel partially responsible for her new-found self-assurance. I'd helped her believe in herself and that was unusual for me.

Her voice broke through my thoughts. "What if I helped you?"

"Helped me? With my hard-on? You could come over here and relieve the pressure under my zipper."

Her laughter rang through the night sky.

"Tempting," she said, still laughing, "but no. I meant, maybe I could help you learn to read."

"Doubtful."

"Why?"

"Kara is one of the most patient people in the world. If she couldn't help me, then there's no way you can."

"I did some tutoring when I was in college," she said. "You might be dyslexic."

"They already tested me for that."

"Who did?"

"My high school."

"You can never trust their tests. They're skewed to give false answers. There are more than thirty different learning styles. Those tests only pick up a few types of dyslexia. Most can never be discovered through standard tests, if at all."

"You sound pretty knowledgeable about it."

"I don't know if I'm knowledgeable, but I know a little. And I have a thing for learning about new stuff."

"Does it bother you?"

"What?"

"The fact that I can't read."

"No."

I smiled when I heard no hesitation in her answer.

"But," she said.

"But?"

"I can only imagine how stressful this is for you," she said, "and that makes me sad. I don't want you to feel that way. I want you to see yourself the way everyone else does. The way I do."

"And how is that?"

"Confident, charismatic, charming, talented."

"Go on." I grinned, repeating her words.

"Sexy, sensual, hot as hell."

"You think I'm hot as hell?" The fact she said it out loud floored me. "Well, Miss Hagen, I believe you're becoming braver, aren't you?"

"Sounds like you're rubbing off on me."

I didn't need to explain, she understood what I was talking about. I wanted her to feel as confident in her body as she wanted me to feel in mine. We both had something to prove, if to no one else but ourselves. She'd opened herself to all types of replies and my wicked self couldn't resist engaging her more.

"Oh, I'd like to rub off on you, trust me, Hindley."

Her laughter rang in my ear and my heart tripped in my chest. I felt more alive than, well, maybe ever.

"I'm serious," she said.

Could she really help me read? Did I want her to?

"All right," I said.

"You'll let me try?" Excitement buzzed in her voice. "Really?"

I was surprised by her response. "As long as you stop when I say stop and you don't judge me."

"I would never judge you, Rory."

"I know. That's why I told you."

"Thank you. Thank you for trusting me with your secret," she said quietly. "I swear, I'll never tell anyone, unless you want me to."

Assuring me of her loyalty wasn't necessary. I knew she would hold my secret close to her heart, that's the reason I'd shared it with her. It touched me immensely though to know she was grateful for my trust.

"Hey, Rory."

"Yeah?"

"You know I'm not as perfect as you seem to think I am. Please stop putting me up on that pedestal, because I can guarantee you, I'm going to fall. And when I do, it will hurt both of us."

"I'll try, Hindley. That's all I can promise."

"That's enough. For now," she said.

"Good night, Drunk Girl."

"Good night, Skater Boy."

I sat on the phone, waiting for her to hang up, but silently hoping she wouldn't.

"Are you going to hang up?" she asked.

"I was waiting for you to."

"Where are you?" she asked.

"At Leif's, on his back porch."

"You're outside?"

"Yeah. It's a gorgeous night." We sat in silence. "I wish you were here."

"Me too," she said. "What would you do if I was there?"

Ah, she wanted to talk dirty. I was on board if she was.

"I'd sit you on my lap so you could feel how hard my dick's been since I left your house. Do you know how fucking difficult it is to ride a motorcycle with a chubby?"

"A what?" She laughed uncontrollably.

"A boner, a trouser tent, a throbbing meat whistle."

She snorted. "You've been hard that long?"

"Longer."

"How's that possible?"

"I have no idea," I said, shaking my head, "but it hurts like hell."

"Well, if I were there, I would kiss it and make it all better."

I groaned, and maybe growled. "If you keep talking like that I'm going to drive back to your house and drop you to your knees like a sinner in church."

"Maybe you should."

"Hindley?" I admonished.

"Yes, Rory?"

"Good night."

"Good night, Skater Boy."

Without another word, the phone went dead and my dick throbbed so hard I thought it might actually explode.

For better or for worse, I was committed to her now. My secret had been revealed, but strangely enough I felt relief. I could finally breathe easy, knowing I wouldn't be rejected or humiliated by the one person who could destroy me.

My admission hadn't even fazed Hindley. In fact, she'd wanted to help me. She'd wanted to protect me from everything and everyone who threatened to humiliate me. She was actually concerned for my well-being and had nothing to gain personally by doing so. I was in awe of her, again.

Kara was right. Hindley and I needed each other, and I couldn't ever remember needing anything or anyone before in my life. The thought should have scared the shit out of me but instead I felt a deep calmness.

My feelings of inadequacy ran deep and I feared I may never truly outrun them. The images and memories of my childhood were so ingrained in my way of thinking, I thought it unlikely I'd ever change.

And then I'd met a brown eyed drunk girl who made me rethink everything. I just hoped I wouldn't hurt her in the process.

CHAPTER 25

HINDLEY

"WHAT ARE YOU LOOKING AT, doll face?"

I jumped in my chair at Luis's words.

"What's wrong?" he asked, genuinely concerned that he'd frightened me.

I quickly minimized the Google web search page I was looking at, 'How to teach adult learners to read.' "Nothing," I said, sounding as guilty as I was.

He arched one eyebrow but didn't say any more. "So, are you ready for tomorrow's signing?" he asked. "You ready to become a sports agent?" His smile broadened as he used air quotes around my new title.

"I'm still an attorney, Luis."

"Yes, you are that indeed." He sauntered around the chair in front of my desk with grace and ease then flopped down like a wayward teen. He was such a contradiction, suave and refined one minute then brassy and uncouth the next. "what were you looking at? Market research for skateboarding?"

"Yes." It wasn't a total lie. One of my web page tabs was on various market strategies for extreme sports products, including snowboarding, motocross, and skateboarding. I had no idea there were so many facets to this industry and so much buying potential.

"And?"

"And, what?"

"You were obviously looking at something else," he said. "What gives? Doing more Rory research?" He smirked, wiggling his brows.

"He *is* my client, isn't he?" My phone pinged with an incoming email. Shit. I grabbed it from my desk and punched in my password, surprisingly giddy when I realized the new message was from Rory. It was short and simple and I wasn't surprised.

<Lunch?>

"Who is it?"

I didn't answer.

"Let me guess. Rory?"

I glanced up and met Luis's gaze. He stared at me, judgment in his eyes.

"He wants to have lunch today, right?" he asked.

I didn't want to divulge any information that might jeopardize my job, but I was a hopeless liar. Besides, it was just lunch, between an attorney and her client, what could be wrong with that?

"How did you know?" I asked.

"That goofy ass smile on your face for one. I was a player too, remember, Hindley?"

"Do you think he's playing me?" I panicked, my voice shallow, breathy, and…desperate. After last night's admission, I believed Rory's feelings for me were genuine. But Luis had been a certified player at one time, and if anyone would know the signs, it would be him.

"No. I think he's probably nervous about tomorrow."

"You think so?" I was embarrassed at how relieved I felt. Maybe Luis didn't realize where our relationship was headed.

He let out a wry laugh as he rubbed a forefinger against his chin.

"Why would Rory be nervous?" I asked, changing the subject to hide my anxiety.

"The boy has the potential to earn millions and he's putting all his eggs in your basket, so to speak."

I blushed.

"Oh, God, Hindley, tell me his breakfast sausage has not been in your biscuit."

"No!"

"Oh, thank God," he sighed and leaned back in his chair.

"Why?"

"Because this is business, Hindley. Serious business. This could cost the firm and Rory millions if you're not careful."

"I'm surprised, Luis. I expected you of all people would support me if I wanted to give my biscuit away."

Luis had badgered me constantly over the three months I'd been at the firm, wondering how someone like me could be sexually inactive. "It's a crime against nature and human sexuality for you not to be doing the horizontal hula on a regular basis," he'd offered in jest.

"Believe me, I'd love for you to give your biscuit away to any eligible man in the world, you know that," Luis said. "Just not to Rory Gregor."

I slumped in my chair, sighing in disappointment at Luis's disapproval.

"You told me to have fun a few days ago," I said.

"Changed my mind. When's he going back to California?" he asked.

I had no answer for Luis, and his question only reminded me of the bleak situation I was facing. What *did* my future with Rory hold? Was there even a future for us?

"I don't know. I assume tomorrow after he signs the paperwork."

Luis pushed out of my chair and knocked his knuckles on my desk. "Just think about what I told you, doll face. I'd hate to see you holding your broken heart in the unemployment line when all of this is said and done."

I stared up at the ceiling, trying to put Luis's comment into perspective. I reminded myself that he didn't know Rory like I did. His warning did make sense though and I couldn't ignore it, not completely. "I hear you, boss," I said. "Loud and clear,"

"Hindley." Luis paused at the door.

I glanced at him.

His caramel brown eyes held my gaze. "I don't want to see you get hurt, baby girl, financially or emotionally."

"I'm fine," I offered up meekly, afraid to tell him it was too late for that.

One perfectly groomed brow rose above his eye as he cocked his head.

"I promise."

"Good. Stay that way, beautiful." He nodded and gave me a classic panty-dropping Luis Marquez megawatt smile and playful wink before closing my door.

My gaze returned to the phone still clutched possessively in my hand. I exhaled, not even aware that I'd been holding my breath. Rory couldn't read, well not much, so my response had to be short.

<Busy. Sorry.>

Thirty seconds later, I heard another ding.

<What are you wearing?>

'What am I wearing?' Where did that come from?

<Clothes. Why?>

I sat patiently waiting, surprised at how anxious I was for his response.

<Hello Kitty?>

Hello Kitty? Where the hell did that come from? And how did he know how to spell Hello Kitty? I reminded myself that he did know some words so 'hello' and 'kitty' wouldn't be surprising.

<Why do you think I'm wearing Hello Kitty?>

<Your pajamas>

My pajamas? Oh, God, that goofy-ass Hello Kitty pajama set Dana gave me for Christmas a few years ago. I'd completely forgotten I'd had it on when he came to my house the other night after standing me up and taking out that other bimbo.

<Why? Do you like Hello Kitty?>

<I like YOUR hello kitty>

Oh my God. This was a company phone, every call and email completely traceable and stored on the law firm's computer server. I searched around my office as if someone were standing over my shoulder, reading his overt sexual messages. The IT department would probably bust into my office at any minute.

<This is a work phone. This is a law firm. All messages are recorded and saved.>

I wasn't sure if all of that would fit into Google Translator, but I had to let him know there was no way he could send me stuff like that at work, even though his comment sent a thrill through my body.

A devilish grin stretched across my face at the revelation that he liked my kitty. I jumped when my phone buzzed, bringing me back from my thoughts. My face flushed when his picture appeared on my screen.

"You can't send stuff like that to my work phone, Rory," I said in a hushed tone as if I were being taped. Panic and fear ripped through my body at the thought of being videotaped. *Stay calm, Hindley. Breathe.*

"What? No hello...kitty?" His voice was raspy and deep and sexy as hell.

"Rory, this is a work cell phone too."

"So what? Is everything in your office bugged?"

"Pretty much."

"How's a guy supposed to talk dirty to his girl?"

'His girl?' Since when had I become 'His girl'?

"First of all, I'm not your girl. Second of all, you shouldn't be talking sexy to me. Not at work."

"You are my girl, my Drunk Girl. I think I established that when I put you to bed three sheets to the wind. And when I buried my face deep between your thighs."

Oh, god. My insides heated at the memory.

"If I can't talk dirty to you at work, then what's the point?"

I stifled a giggle, thinking of his erotic words.

"Are you going to answer me?" His gritty, seductive voice did things to me.

"What?"

"What are you wearing?" he asked again.

"Rory, I'm serious."

"Then have lunch with me so I can see you."

"I'm busy. I have a high maintenance client that I'm dealing with. He can be a real jerk."

"That sucks."

"Yes, it does."

"Maybe you should have lunch with him, to put him in his place."

"No lunch." Silence rang through the phone and I feared he'd hung up. "What about dinner?"

"I can't do dinner tonight. I'm going over to Bucky and Pena's house."

"Oh, that will be fun."

"You should come with me," he said.

"I wasn't invited."

"I'm inviting you."

"It's not your place to invite me. Besides, I'll probably be here late getting all your paperwork together for tomorrow. And I have tons of research I need to do."

"Maybe I could come by later and help you."

"Something tells me that you being here with me would not help me at all."

"It would help me."

I sat back in my chair with a sigh. "We need to talk."

"Ut oh. Am I in trouble?" There was amusement in his voice.

"We need rules."

"I don't like setting rules. I like breaking them."

"There are some we can't break, Rory. I'm serious."

"I know."

The defeat in his voice was unnerving.

"We both could lose a lot if this goes wrong," I said.

"I know, Hindley, I already told you, I get it."

I was surprised by the clipped, bitter tone in his voice. "Why are you mad at me?"

"I'm not mad at you," he said. "I'm…" I could tell he was trying to form his answer carefully. "I'm frustrated."

"Call me tonight after your dinner and we'll talk," I said.

"You told me I can't talk dirty to you on this phone. Give me your home phone number."

"Shit."

"What?"

"They cut off my home phone last week."

"Why? Couldn't pay the bills?" He laughed and I was surprised how much I craved the sound.

"I wasn't using it much and decided last week to cancel the service and use my work phone exclusively."

"So, you *do* use your work phone for some personal conversations?"

"I guess so, yes."

"I could come see you after dinner." His voice dipped lower, the vibration hitting me deep in my belly.

"I don't think that's a good idea."

"Why?"

There was more erotic promise in that one word than I'd ever heard in my life. My head spun with illicit images as I searched for a reason why he couldn't at least stop by my house after his dinner with the Kopras.

"You know why," I answered honestly.

"Yeah," he sighed.

I already hated disappointing him. "Look, let me get through our meeting tomorrow. Mr. Stedwick is expecting a lot out of me and I need to make sure I'm completely prepared. We can have dinner tomorrow night, okay?"

"I can't. I'm leaving tomorrow afternoon shortly after our meeting."

"Oh." I bit back the disappointment in my voice but knew I was failing miserably.

"Are you sad?"

"Yes," I answered before I could even stop myself.

"Maybe even disappointed?"

"Very." Shit. Again, my response was automatic, impulsive, with no thought, and no filter.

"So you *do* want to see me?"

I could picture his smirk in my mind. I needed to calm the hell down. "Of course I want to see you," I said quietly.

"I lied," he said.

"About what?"

"I'm not leaving until Wednesday morning."

"Are you serious?" Shit, had I just squealed?

"Well, I was supposed to leave on Tuesday evening, but I wanted to make sure you *did* want to see me. I'll change my ticket to Wednesday morning, if you want me to stay."

"Shit." I realized this was a company phone and I couldn't reveal any more.

"What?"

"Company phone."

"Yes or no?"

"I'm not sure what the question is."

"Should we meet Tuesday evening to discuss my contract and a marketing strategy since you're my agent too?" God, he was good.

"Yes," I said with no hesitation.

"I'll see you tomorrow morning, Miss Hagen."

"I'll see you then, Mr. Gregor."

The line went dead and a wave of relief washed over me, knowing I was no longer in danger. At least, not with the firm's telecommunications department. But the feeling quickly faded when a painful chill of disappointment wrapped around me as I realized I wouldn't see him for another twenty-four hours.

Memories of his mouth consuming me—my lips, my face, my neck, my entire body—had me hotter than a summer day in Texas. His skin on mine was like heaven to me. But should I do this? Could I do this?

I'd seen a lot of hell in my life, walked through hell many times. I needed a little heaven. I *deserved* a little heaven. And I had a feeling Rory Gregor did too.

CHAPTER 26

HINDLEY

I rubbed my eyes, focusing on the clock on the microwave. 10:14 p.m. Why did I feel disappointed? Because I still hadn't heard from Rory. God, I was pathetic. Or maybe it was the overwhelming inadequacies beginning to choke me again.

I'd been relentless in research on extreme sports over the last week. I hadn't studied this hard since law school, and yet I still felt completely incompetent. How in the hell had I convinced myself I'd be any good at being a sports agent?

I'd also spent a great deal of time researching adult illiteracy, the causes and the hundreds of ways to teach someone. I wanted to help Rory but the emptiness inside weighed me down as I questioned my own abilities to do almost anything now.

By his own admission, Rory had tried for years but still hadn't learned how to read. Why did I think I could do any better? I wasn't a teacher. Hell, I didn't even feel like a real lawyer sometimes. And where would that leave me if I couldn't help him learn to read? Where would that leave us?

I removed the cellophane wrapper from the popcorn package and shoved it inside the microwave, pressing the start button. I leaned on the counter as the package cooked, letting my thoughts wander.

Why had I told Rory not to come over tonight? Because Luis was right, I didn't need to end up in the unemployment line, holding my heart.

A buzzing sound caught my attention. I glanced around the kitchen. It couldn't be the microwave, I'd just started the popcorn. Shit, it was my phone. Where was the last time I'd had it?

My heart raced, giddy from the anticipation that maybe it was Rory. God, I was an idiot. I searched through the stack of papers on the kitchen counter like a mad person until I found my phone behind the toaster. How the hell had it gotten there? I stared at the screen, my eyes wide. Three missed texts from Rory. Shit.

9:42 p.m. *<Are you home?>*

9:50 p.m. *<Are you ignoring me?>*

10:17 p.m. *<Good night, DG. See you tomorrow.>*

Oh, crap. Should I text him back? Should I call? I didn't want him to think I was ignoring him. That would be rude. I knew I shouldn't but I wanted to hear his voice. I'll keep it to work stuff. *Yeah, right.*

Without trying to talk myself out of what I knew was wrong, I scrolled through my contact list and hit the photo of his beautiful face. I waited, impatiently, as it rang.

"This is Rory Gregor."

I bit back a laugh at his professional tone. "Good evening, Mr. Gregor. This is Hindley Hagen, your legal counsel. I hope I'm not calling you too late."

"Oh, no, Miss Hagen, I'm glad to hear from you. I definitely need counseling."

His voice sounded so erotic and sensual, I had a hard time focusing on why I'd called him.

"Well, I guess it's a good thing I called you then. Are you ready for tomorrow's meeting?"

"I think so. Are you?" he asked.

"I'm not sure."

"Why?"

"I've never done this before," I admitted.

"Done what? Phone sex?" He snorted.

"Rory!"

"Oops, sorry."

"No."

"No, what? No phone sex?" He chuckled.

"Rory."

"What? I'm just asking." He laughed louder.

"I've never been someone's agent. It's kind of scary."

"Why?"

"I want to do the best job I can for you."

"And you don't think you will?"

His question was so genuine it made my heart ache

"Not yet," I said.

"But?"

"But I'll try hard, for you." It was the truth.

"Then that's all I can ask for."

There was an uncomfortable silence between us and I realized that calling him had been a bad idea.

"Look, Hindley, I know there is nothing you can't accomplish that you put your mind to. You're that kind of person."

His words were so refreshing.

"I believe in you," he said. "That should be enough."

"It should be," I sighed.

"It will have to be. Trust me, you'll do fine."

The silence dragged on between us, but this time, I was thankful. It gave me time to process all he was saying, the confidence he was bestowing on me.

"Well, I better let you go," he said. "I've got a meeting in the morning with a hot chick and I want to look my very best."

"Rory."

"What? I need my beauty rest. I wasn't born this adorable, you know."

"No, I didn't know that."

"Good night," he stopped abruptly. "Miss Hagen."

"Good night, Mr. Gregor."

"I look forward to seeing you tomorrow. And trust me, you'll be fine. I would never have hired you if I thought any different."

"Thank you for your confidence." I smiled. "It means a lot to me." I blushed, finding it impossible to wipe off the silly-ass grin that had been plastered on my face the entire conversation.

"You're welcome. Sweet dreams, Hindley."

Before I could respond, the line went dead and my mind was once again filled with memories of Rory Gregor's mouth. That image would definitely bring sweet dreams.

"So, I think you'll find that we've drafted a solid contract for you, Rory," Mr. Stedwick said, his voice booming through the conference room.

I laughed to myself at the insinuation that he'd had anything to do with drafting Rory's attorney-agent contract. It had been my tireless work not his. It infuriated me that he was trying to take credit.

I hoped Rory's small scowl meant he knew the truth. He knew how hard I'd worked for him.

"Yes, I have no doubt you drafted a very fine contract, sir," Rory said, his eyes narrowed.

I ducked my head to hide my smile.

Suddenly the receptionist's voice rang through the conference room. "Ms. Hagen, I hate to interrupt you."

"We're in a meeting," Mr. Stedwick growled, cutting her off, his eyes narrowed.

"Yes, sir, I know," she said, her voice wavering, "and I'm so sorry. But Ms. Hagen has a delivery, and the company is insistent that she sign for it. Now."

Mr. Stedwick turned and glared at me. "What in God's name is this about, Hindley?"

His voice was laced with controlled fury. I felt like a disobedient child. I glanced up at Rory and saw something flash across his face.

Was it sympathy? Protection? No, this was something else, something that made my stomach flip.

"She'll be there in a moment," Mr. Stedwick bellowed. He banged the intercom button so hard, he nearly flipped the entire phone over.

He glared at me as if I were a peon, interfering with his meeting.

My body burned with anger. How dare he. First, he took credit for *my* hard work and now, he totally humiliated me in front of clients and colleagues after all the hours of work I'd put into this contract.

I scanned the room. "I'm sorry, gentlemen. If you'll excuse me, I'll be right back."

Rory took me by surprise when he stood. He cleared his throat, his lips twitching. "Take your time, Hindley. We'll be here."

What the hell was going on with him?

Suddenly the rest of the men stood as I moved to leave.

I flushed red and ducked my head as I bolted out of the conference room. I half ran to the reception area, thankful for the escape from Mr. Stedwick's douchery. What a dick. As I stalked toward the receptionist's desk, I wondered what on earth was waiting for me.

"This better be something good, Vanessa, because I basically had my ass handed to me in the conference room by Mr. Stedwick."

Her lips pressed in a fine line and her eyebrows rose as she nodded to a gentleman sitting in the waiting area.

"Oh, shit," I whispered. "Is that him?"

"Uh, yeah."

"He doesn't look like a delivery guy," I said to no one in particular. He was dressed in a dark dress suit and starched white shirt, void of any tie.

"That's what I thought," Vanessa said, "but he insisted he had a delivery for you and said it had to be delivered precisely at 9:47 a.m." I glanced down at my watch. It was 9:50 a.m.

"9:47 a.m.?" I asked.

"I know. Weird, right?" She shrugged.

"What is it?"

"Beats me? He's got a box."

"Do you know his name?"

She shook her head. "Nope."

I knew she'd be of no further help to me so I walked toward the delivery man. "Excuse me, sir, I'm Hindley Hagen. You have a package for me?"

"Yes." He stood. "Would you please sign here?" He pointed to a small clipboard.

There was only one sheet of paper. It was blank except for a long blank line with my name and the date printed below. Weird.

"What delivery service are you with?" I asked as I quickly scribbled my name. He looked down at my signature, satisfied with the result.

"Thank you," he responded, handing me the package then slipping away quietly without answering my question.

The package was roughly the size of a shirt box, only deeper. Every edge was sealed with clear tape, making it impossible to open without some kind of sharp object. What the hell?

"What is it?" Vanessa asked, rounding her desk to join me in the reception area.

"I have no idea."

"Well, open it," she encouraged.

My mind raced through a myriad of ideas of what could possibly be inside. I inspected the exterior but found no return address. Even my name and address gave nothing away.

"Thanks, Vanessa." I walked toward the double doors, heading for my office. There was no way I was going to open this in front of her. She was the biggest gossip in the law firm. I knew instinctively whatever was inside was meant for my eyes only.

"Ah, come on, Hindley," she begged, her words cutting off as the doors shut behind me.

When I was safely inside my office with the door closed, I grabbed a pair of scissors from my desk drawer and cut through the thick tape sealing the box. Once all the edges were freed, I removed the top, shocked to find the box entirely stuffed with tissue paper.

What the hell?

I pulled out each piece of paper one at a time, cautious of what lay underneath. I gasped in horror when I reached the contents.

The first item was a pair of Hello Kitty thong panties. I covered my mouth to hold back my laughter. "Oh my God," I whispered. "That asshole."

Rory had purposely had the box delivered during our meeting. He'd sat in that fucking conference room, with that smug-ass smile on his beautiful face. He'd watched me leave, knowing I'd have to return after opening this shit. I wanted to be upset but I couldn't muster the emotion.

I lifted the panties from the box, staring at the huge Hello Kitty face covering the crotch. Oh my God. There was a note attached to the package.

I love your hello kitty.

I was scared to dig any further in the Naughty Box, afraid of what I'd find. I drew in a deep breath and dug deeper.

Oh, my God.

I pulled out a box of Trojan Supra BareSkin Non-Latex Condoms. I dropped the box and squeezed my eyes shut, biting my lips to hold in a shriek. What the fuck? I opened my eyes and glanced down. The box said 150 condoms, Magnum XL. "Yeah, right." I laughed. There was another note attached to the box.

A good start, don't you think?

This man was insane.

Against my better judgment I reached back in and pulled out another smaller white box. The word 'iPhone' was engraved on the side. He bought me a phone. Another note was attached, no surprise there.

So you can talk dirty to me.

I plopped down in my chair in disbelief. I didn't know whether to be flattered or offended, excited or appalled. Honestly, I was all of them wrapped into one.

"Hindley, what's going on?" I jumped at the sound of Michael's voice.

"Oh, um, I'm sorry, Michael." I shoved the contents back in the box and dumped it in my bottom desk drawer. God, I hoped he hadn't seen all that stuff.

"Is everything all right?" he asked, studying me.

"Yes, it's fine."

"Can you get back to the meeting then? We're about to sign."

"Of course. I'm sorry." My heart raced with excitement, and fear, knowing I was about to come face-to-face with my not-so-secret admirer. I would have no choice but to sit, straight-faced, and watch in silence as he signed a contract, basically tying the two of us together for the next twelve months. All I could picture were those Hello Kitty panties, and what they'd feel like on.

"Are you sure you're all right?" he asked.

"Yes!" I blinked rapidly. I was lying. It was my tell but thankfully he didn't know.

I'd never been so freaked out, or aroused in my entire life. Just imagining what Rory and I would do with the contents of my Naughty Box had my mind racing. Unfortunately I only had a few seconds to compose myself.

We left my office and Michael opened the door to the conference room, holding it open for me. I kept my gaze glued to the floor, avoiding Rory's attention as I made my way back to my chair.

"Is everything all right, Miss Hagen?" Rory asked. Hopefully no one else heard the amusement in his voice.

I wanted to ignore him, have no contact with him whatsoever, but professional protocol wouldn't allow me. "Yes, I'm fine," I coughed, "thank you." I stared down at my fingers, praying everyone in the room was oblivious to the sexual tension between us. My insides burned with desire and a little anger for what he'd just done.

Even though I knew better, the masochist in me longed to see his face. My head remained down but I lifted my lashes, staring at the man who was slowly capturing my heart. His usually bright, crystal blue eyes were darker now. Was that desire? God, I hoped so.

He looked delicious, beautiful, his hair a tussled mess. His yellow button-down clung to his muscular body. All I could think of was ripping it off and licking that sexy tattoo.

God, what was wrong with me? He was about to be my client.

My breath caught when I watched one side of his delicious mouth curl into a wicked grin.

I breathed out a heavy sigh. This man was going to eat me alive. Oh, wait, he already had. I bit my lip to keep from smiling.

As if reading my thoughts, his grin grew wider as he winked. God, he was sexy.

Yeah, this was going to be a dangerous ride but one I wanted to take. I better buckle up.

CHAPTER 27

HINDLEY

"I CAN'T BELIEVE you did that, Rory!" I shouted into my new phone.

"What?"

"Sending me that box. And then delivering it to my work? Mr. Stedwick almost had my ass."

"Yeah, that guy's a dick."

I nodded, remembering his less than professional response to the interruption of our meeting.

"And then he tries to take credit for *your* work," he said. "The guy is a super douche bag in my book."

I smiled at Rory's defense of me. I'd never seen that side of Mr. Stedwick before and it worried me some.

"And then," I continued my tirade, "Michael almost caught me with the contents of your little Naughty Box in my office." My faced heated at the thought even now.

"What can I say? I'm crass."

"That's beyond crass, Rory Gregor. Do you know how much trouble I could have been in?"

"Do you know how much trouble you're going to be in?"

Oh, my damn. "None." I huffed out a sigh as I plopped down on my sofa.

"Why?"

"Because I'm not seeing you tonight."

"At all?"

"No, not after that stunt you pulled this morning."

"Well, as my attorney and agent, I'm requesting a meeting with you."

"Fine. You can call my office in the morning and we can schedule one tomorrow."

My doorbell suddenly rang. I stared at the entry. Who could be here?

"Hold on."

"Is someone at the door?" he asked. "Did you order something naughty? More panties?" He chuckled.

"Rory Gregor, please tell me you haven't had another box of sex toys and gadgets delivered to me."

"Why? Would you be happy or disappointed?"

Which would I be?

I chastised myself for even having the thought.

"I'll take your silence as a yes," he said.

"Whatever," I said. I reached for the door, pulling it open. My jaw fell open and I nearly dropped my new phone.

"You really should at least ask, 'Who's there' before you open your door, Hindley," Rory said. He was leaning against the wall of my porch, arms crossed over his broad chest as he stared at me with a deep scowl on his face.

He was dressed in the same light yellow, button down shirt from earlier today. God, he looked good in that shirt. *He'd look better out of it*, I thought. No arguments there.

He'd changed from his dress slacks into lightly faded jeans that had obviously seen better days. They clung to his well-formed body like a priceless work of art. It should be illegal to look this good when he wasn't even trying.

A bag of groceries hung in one hand and a bottle of sparkling water in the other. Instincts told me if he walked through my front door, I'd be letting him in too much more than just my home.

He tilted his head and raised a brow, smiling deviently. "I believe I have a meeting with you, Miss Hagen."

I swallowed hard. This guy was going to break me, I just knew it. I tucked my new phone into my pocket and attempted to put on my game face. "I told you to call my office, Mr. Gregor."

"Oh, I'm afraid this couldn't wait, Miss Hagen."

How could he make one simple sentence sound like a cry for the best sexual tryst known to womankind?

"What's so important that it couldn't wait until tomorrow, Mr. Gregor?"

"I have groceries here that could melt in this Texas heat if you don't let me in."

"I believe after your contract signing today, you'll have more than enough money at your disposal to buy additional groceries should those spoil while you wait outside."

He cocked a brow and tilted his head. Obviously I'd surprised him—and myself—with my sassy response.

"You'll have to come up with a much better reason than that if you want to meet with me tonight, Mr. Gregor."

"I want to cook for you," he said softly.

I bit back a gasp. No man had ever made me dinner. In fact, I couldn't remember a man making me anything, except mad.

"Then I want to feed you."

Oh, holy hell.

"Then," he moved closer, "I'm going to take you to bed and start making good use of the other two presents I sent you today."

I stood, mouth gaping, speechless.

He slipped a finger under my chin and closed my mouth. "May I come...in...Hindley?"

His prolonged enunciation of each word wasn't lost on me. My heart beat hard in my chest and my panties melted right off my body. It was a good thing he'd bought me new ones. Without saying a word, I stepped back and let the Big Bad Wolf into my home. Again.

~

"I thought you were going to feed me," I teased while cleaning up the last of our dinner dishes.

"I did. I made you dinner. That's feeding you, isn't it?"

I nodded, even though I was a bit disappointed on the inside.

"What, were you expecting something else?" he asked.

God, I loved his sexy voice. I shook my head, turning back to the dishes.

I jumped when his hands slipped around my waist and his chin rested on my shoulder. "I have another meal planned for you," he whispered in my ear. "But it's not in the kitchen. Trust me, Hindley. I will feed you. Tonight."

The heat of his breath on my neck turned my knees to jelly. No one had ever affected me on such a visceral level as Rory Gregor did.

"We shouldn't," I whispered, not fully believing myself.

His hands fell away and he stepped back.

I felt the loss of his touch deep in my soul.

"Whatever you say, Hindley."

Whatever I say? That's not what I wanted? What I wanted was him. In bed. But I didn't know how to be what he expected.

Guys wanted adventurous girls, confident girls, experienced girls. I was none of those. I was horrible at sex, had been told so by my last boyfriend. To be honest, I hadn't been surprised by his revelation. In fact, it was to be expected, given my history.

Drawing in a breath for confidence, I turned around, leaning against the counter. Rory stared at me, his gaze holding mine. His mesmerizing eyes sucked me in. He was so gorgeous. Desire burned in his eyes, changing them to smoky blue.

I couldn't do this. He was too much for a broken girl like me. I'd never be able to live up to his expectations. Suddenly all my assumed confidence was gone. I turned back to the sink, my breathing coming in loud pants like I'd just finished a race.

"What's wrong, Hindley?" Rory rushed to my side, pulling my hands from the water and drying them.

I couldn't answer, what could I say? I was trapped in a horror movie that constantly played in my mind. The ending was always the same. The man left unsatisfied and I lay in bed weeping until sunrise.

His huge hand cupped my cheeks and he raised my face to his. "Hey," he whispered. His warm breath tickled my skin.

I searched his eyes, looking for some semblance that he'd understand my situation. But I knew a man as experienced as Rory surely couldn't understand the depths of my distress.

"Talk to me," he said softly.

Hot tears stung the back of my eyes. I willed them away, swallowing hard and biting my lip. Why was I so fucking weak? My attempts were futile, as always. Slowly the tears spilled over my lashes and down my cheeks. Dammit!

"Hey, hey, what's going on?" Rory knelt down to stare into my eyes.

I squeezed my eyes closed. If I were going to tell him, I sure as hell wasn't going to see him. "I'm bad at sex." I punched out the words. "Awful some would say." I collapsed against the kitchen counter.

"You already told me." He half laughed as he released my face.

I slowly opened my eyes, surprised he was still here. "I know you're experienced," I said. "You're used to a certain kind of woman. That's not me. I'm not good in bed."

"Says who?"

"Says my last boyfriend."

"Who? Douche Bag from the wedding?"

"No." I shook my head. "I never slept with him."

"Well, thank fuck for that. Was it someone before him?"

I nodded, not offering more. He could never find out how fucked up I was. If he knew the whole story, not only would he leave my house, he'd probably fire me as his attorney.

Rory tossed the dish towel onto the counter and rubbed his

palms on his jeans. He crossed his arms across his broad chest and loomed over me, staring down at me. "Prove it," he said.

"Prove what?"

"That you're bad at sex. Prove it to me."

I stared at him like he was crazy, which he was. "What does that mean?"

"It means," he said, "I want to find out, first hand, just how bad you are."

I shook my head at his preposterous idea, unable to hold in my laughter.

"You see, Hindley," he stalked toward me, "I don't believe for a minute that you're bad at this." His hand waved between us. "You're too damn sexy to be bad in bed. And the way you screamed when I went down on you last weekend leads me to believe an entirely different story about you and your sexual skills."

He inched even closer. I drew in a deep breath, my chest almost touching his.

He smirked, leaning in, his lips caressing my ear. "Prove it."

Goose bumps spread across my body. I had no words.

"Will you do that, Hindley?" he asked. "For me?"

I swallowed the jar of cotton balls stuck in my mouth and slowly nodded.

He chuckled.

Oh, God, what had I just done?

"What would you do first?" he whispered in my ear.

I didn't understand his question. I leaned back to see his face. "What do you mean?" I asked.

"If you were going to have sex with me," he said, "what would you do first?"

I shook my head, still not understanding.

He took a long step back.

I was grateful for the space.

"If you told me you were a bad cook, I'd have you cook for me, so I could judge for myself."

Okay, that made sense, I guess.

He leaned against the refrigerator. "If you're as bad at sex as someone has obviously made you believe, I think I have the right to find out for myself. I have the right to make an informed decision, don't I?"

"But, I am bad, Rory." I turned to avoid his gaze. "Really bad."

He rushed toward me and took my arms in his hands. "Hindley," he smiled down at me, "it's been my experience that women are usually never bad at sex, it's the men who are. I suspect you've just been with the wrong man. But I'm willing to make sacrifices, go through the grueling task of having sex with you over and over again, to find out for myself."

His deep chuckle made my thighs clench and everything below my belly button tingle.

He pushed against me, his body crushing mine against the kitchen sink. "Now. For the last time." His voice was a whisper. "Show me what you would do to me before I bend you over this counter and show you myself that you're anything *but* bad at sex."

I gulped, audibly, like one of those cartoon characters and my body trembled at his command. I closed my eyes, rallying all the confidence I could muster. I tried to recall all the dirty magazines Dana had when we were in high school. I really should have paid closer attention to the pictures.

"Well?" He backed up but remained facing me. "I'm waiting."

I reached out and grabbed him around the waist, pulling him back toward me. "First," I said, "I'd kiss you." My hands skimmed up his chest and settled around his neck. I gently tugged on his shaggy hair and drew his head down to mine. Staring into his eyes, I pressed up onto my tiptoes and brushed my lips against his.

His eyes sparkled with mischievous pride, and a hint of desire that washed away all my insecurities.

Our kiss was light at first, like we were old lovers reacquainting ourselves. Within seconds, our embrace turned more impassioned as our lips and tongues fought for each other.

Before I could enjoy what was happening, Rory slid away from my grasp, leaving me standing breathless.

I freaked out, a full-on panic attack threatening. What had I done wrong?

I searched his eyes for understanding but they were closed, his lips tilted up in a small grin. His lids fluttered open, revealing eyes much darker now, like the blue in his denim jeans. "I'd say this old boyfriend must have you confused with someone else, Hindley," he said.

I couldn't hide my prideful grin.

"Anyone who can kiss like that *cannot* be bad in bed." He winked.

I hugged myself on the inside in silent jubilation.

"What would you do next?" he asked. The rich timbre of his voice had the insides of my legs quivering.

What would I do next? I mustered my most provocative voice, surprised at how sultry I sounded. "I'd undress you." Oh, God, what was I doing? This man was a predator, a dangerous lion, and I was poking him.

His eyebrows shot up and he grinned. "Nice," he said, raising both arms to the side in silent permission.

My hands travelled up his chest, my fingers tracing every detail of his lean, sculpted body. I cautiously undid the first button, exposing smooth skin beneath his collarbone. God, it looked delicious. Shifting onto the tips of my toes, I pressed a kiss in the hollow of his neck.

He groaned.

I smiled. Maybe I *was* good at this.

I slowly undid every button until his shirt fell open, revealing a well-defined chest. I slipped my hands down his abs, struck by how different our complexions were—mine fair and smooth, his dark and rough, reflective of our personalities, and our lives.

I slipped the shirt from his shoulders and slid my hands around his waist. I let my fingertips stroke his back, my fingernails lightly raking against his skin.

"Fuck," he growled.

I leaned back to study his face, afraid I'd done something wrong.

His jaw was clenched, the thick muscles of his neck strained as if he was holding back an attack.

"Are you okay?" I asked, pulling away.

He grabbed my wrists and held them against him. His eyes opened, the look so intense it ignited something in my belly. "Never better."

I smiled, happy that he was still enjoying my perusal.

My hands slid around to his chest again, my fingers tracing the tattoo as I leaned closer. God, I wanted to lick it. So I did.

Rory jumped and I pulled back. "Don't stop," he said, his voice strained.

I glanced up.

His eyes were closed, a look of contentment on his face.

I pressed on, tracing the outline of tattoo with my finger then followed the pattern with my tongue. I slowly moved down to the waistband of his jeans but stopped when the tattoo disappeared underneath.

"Looks like something's in your way," he said, his voice rough and teasing. I couldn't tell if he was in pleasure or in pain. "Go on."

Taking his cue, I slipped my index finger inside the waistband of his jeans.

He drew in a sharp breath. Again, I glanced up. His lips were pressed in a firm line.

"Okay?" I asked.

"More than okay," he said.

I bit back a smile, struggling to rein in my own desire. God, this was fun. Maybe I was good at this seduction thing. When I heard no protest, I pressed on, skimming my finger between the denim and his skin. I moved my hand toward his belt buckle, sinking down on my knees.

A low moan escaped his mouth but this time I didn't look up. I was beginning to understand his sounds.

I moved to the front of him, working his belt buckle open then sliding it from his pants. As with his shirt, I tossed it to the side and finally glanced a peek up at him.

He was staring down at me, his gaze so hungry and predatory I actually shivered.

His hunger made me brave. I cocked a brow and returned his stare, my own eyes growing more desirous.

One side of his mouth cocked up in a smirk. "See something you want?"

Keeping my eyes on him, I nodded and unbuttoned his jeans, easing down the zipper. My fingers brushed against his erection, held firm by his underwear.

"Fuck," he drew out the word.

I bit my lips to hold back a laugh. I couldn't believe I was affecting him so much. Sinking my thumbs into his waistband, I wiggled the jeans over his hips, careful to keep his boxer briefs in place.

He liked this game. I liked this game. And I was going to prolong it as long as I could.

"Off," I said quietly, tapping his shoes.

He toed off his shoes, shucking his socks as well and I tugged his jeans the rest of the way down.

He balanced on my shoulder, first one leg then the other as I slid his jeans completely off and again tossed them on the floor. I glanced up again, not surprised to see him studying me.

My gaze returned to his body. His erection pulsed in front of me, held in place by his boxer briefs. God, he was huge. I gulped. Again. Instead of feasting on him, I moved to the item I wanted. His tattoo.

I wrapped my hands around his muscular legs and brought my mouth to the edge of his tattoo. It disappeared behind the end of his underwear too.

"Stuck again," he said with a low chuckle.

I glanced up through my lashes, licking my lips as my fingers curled into the waistband of his boxer briefs. "Not for long."

He let out a low chuckle that turned into a moan.

Keeping my eyes on him, I dragged his underwear down, just below his hip bone to expose the remainder of the tattoo. God, that ink looked so sexy on him. It was the most beautiful tattoo I'd ever seen. He was the most beautiful man I'd ever seen.

My tongue darted out and I continued my delicious attack. I licked the skateboard as it trailed over his hip bone then down and around, skimming his back.

His body shuddered underneath my touch.

In that moment, for the first time in my life, I felt wanton, desirous...and sexy as hell. A new kind of hunger burned low in my belly. Not for food but for Rory Gregor. He made me feel... alive. I craved him.

I slid my fingers around to the front of his waistband, skimming across the soft hair under his belly button. His happy trail, I thought, smiling to myself. Slowly I pulled his underwear lower.

Rory's abdomen contracted and he squeezed my shoulder. "Hindley," he growled in what sounded like warning.

I ignored him, my desire for him too strong now. I gently pulled his underwear down until his erection sprung free in front of my face. Literally. God, I'd just thought it had been big. It was huge. And I was salivating.

I'd never looked at a penis this close up and in person. It was... beautiful? Was that even possible? It was for Rory Gregor.

Suddenly all my insecurities were back. I'd never had a man in my mouth. What if he didn't like it? What if I did it wrong?

"Hindley."

I froze, my heart beating out of my chest. I hadn't even started yet and already I must be doing something wrong. Slowly my eyes rolled up to meet his.

His were closed. The hand that had been on my shoulder now gripped the back of my neck. When had that happened?

"Please," he grunted, sounding as if he might be in pain.

Please? Was he begging me? Yes, he was. That one word, please, rolling off *his* tongue, gave me courage.

Extending my tongue, I gently licked the tip before leaning forward and sliding him fully into my mouth. The feeling of him on my tongue was exquisite, a mixture of hard man and soft sin. In that moment I knew I would never get enough of him.

"Oh, shit," he moaned.

His cries fueled me on, making me brave and bold. I wasn't exactly sure what I was doing, but he seemed to love it, so I had no intentions of stopping.

My head bobbed, each time taking more of him in my mouth. My tongue swirled around his shaft while I sucked him hard.

His hands dug deep into my hair, guiding my mouth, pulling me further against him. I struggled to take in his massive length, breathing through my nose. I wanted this to be perfect.

I relaxed my jaw and wrapped my hand around the base, taking in even more, slowly, inch by inch.

"Goddamn!" he yelled, clutching my hair to the point of pain but I didn't care. He obviously liked it. And so did I.

A dull ache burned between my legs and I felt myself grow damp. I wanted to touch myself, he felt so good. His intoxicating scent was driving me crazy. I had no idea it was possible for a woman to become so turned on by giving a blow job.

His hips began to thrust, pushing more of himself into my mouth. A few times I nearly gagged but I continued on. I wanted him to love it as much as I did.

His hold on my hair grew stronger, his hips moving faster. He was going crazy. And I was doing it.

The way I felt, the way I was making him feel—I couldn't believe it could be like this. Finally my hand slipped from the base and I wrapped my arms around to his ass, pulling him inside my mouth even further. I relaxed my throat, determined to take all of him.

"Hindley, I'm going to come," he called in warning.

I didn't care. I wanted him to come in my mouth.

"Hindley!" he shouted. "Oh, fuck, Hindley!" He yanked my hair and groaned, a deep, guttural sound.

He grew even bigger and I had to stretch wider. My jaw hurt, my throat was sore, but I was doing it and I wouldn't stop until he was completely undone.

With one final thrust, his dam burst and he released inside me. I swallowed quickly, trying not to gag.

His stomach heaved as he sucked in air. "Fuck," he said, slowly releasing his hold on my hair.

His body trembled from the aftershocks of his orgasm as I knelt in front of him. I kept him deep in my mouth, moving back and forth until he was done.

"Please, Hindley," he said, breathing hard. "You're killing me."

I pulled free, sitting back on my heels, staring up at his beautiful face. I fluttered my lashes, giving him my best shit eating grin. "That's what I would do," I said, wiping my mouth with the back of my hand.

"What?" he asked, scrubbing his hand down his face like he was intoxicated.

"You asked me what I would do first. To show you I'm not good at sex," I said.

"Holy fuck, Hindley." He shook his head and leaned back on the counter. "If that's your *not good at sex*, I sure as shit can't wait to see what you consider good."

I smiled. My first blow job. Obviously a success.

"Where the fuck did you learn how to suck a dick like that? Wait!" He held up his hand. "Never mind, don't tell me. I don't even want to think about you going down on other guys."

I laughed out loud. Little did he know.

"What?" he said.

"Nothing." Forget my inexperience. If Rory thought I'd done a good job that's all he needed to know. "So, you liked it?"

"Like it?" He laughed breathlessly. "Fuck, Hindley, like isn't the word. I've never felt anything like that in my life."

Oh, no. Did he not like it? "Really?"

He stepped into his boxer briefs, pulling them up his long legs. "Hindley. That was incredible. I don't know who this asshat of a boyfriend was who said you were bad in bed but he was a fucking moron."

I smiled.

"If you sucked his dick half as good as you did mine, then he must be dumb as dirt to say you're no good at sex. But..." He paused and I grew anxious again.

"What?" I said, holding my breath.

"Technically, you've only showed me that you can suck a dick like you're at a lollipop convention."

I giggled, covering my mouth.

"But you still haven't shown me that you're no good at *sex*, so..." He swept me up in his arms and carried me down the hall. He pushed open my bedroom door and carried me inside, tossing me on the mattress.

I flopped around like I was on a trampoline, giggling like a schoolgirl.

Rory crawled on top of me and gently stroked my hair from my face as he placed a light kiss on my lips.

Suddenly, my hello kitty was begging for attention.

"Why, counselor," he stared me up and down, "I believe you're overdressed for this meeting."

I glanced down at my body. I still had on my clothes from work, the outfit we'd signed our contract in. I looked up into his eyes.

His dark lashes swept up and down as he drank me in.

Keeping my gaze trained on him, I gently tugged on the bow on my satin blouse, letting the material fall open.

He lavished kisses on my cheek, my jaw, my throat, then down between my collarbones. God, it felt so good. He stopped at the first button of my shirt.

"Looks like someone's stuck." I smiled.

He stared at me, his face serious.

Even though he'd seen me naked before, something about this time felt different. I wasn't ashamed of my body this time. Feeling empowered from earlier, I lifted up and undid each button slowly.

His eyes burned with desire and need.

I untucked my blouse from my skirt and lay back on the comforter, opening the top wide, exposing my breasts and abdomen. My fingers trailed up my neck and into my hair, fanning out my thick tresses over the pillow.

"Oh, Miss Hagen," he said, smiling like a lion about to be served dinner. "Aren't you brave tonight."

I tilted my head and grinned. "Why, yes, Mr. Gregor, it appears that I am. With you."

He drew closer and my heart beat wildly in my chest. He was the reason. With this man, I *was* braver. And for that I would always be grateful.

CHAPTER 28

RORY

"Does that always happen?" Hindley asked. Her chin rested on my chest as her chocolate-colored eyes revealed an innocent seeking knowledge.

"Does what happen?" I twisted a piece of her gorgeous hair around my index finger. How in the world could anyone have told this amazing woman she was bad at anything, especially sex?

"An orgasm," she said. "You know, during sex."

"I should sincerely hope so. Why? Has that not been your experience, Miss Hagen?"

She buried her face into my chest.

"Hey," I whispered, pulling her hair.

She sat up, rubbing her head. "Ow. That hurt."

I leaned down and kissed her hairline. "I'm sorry."

"No, you're not."

Her eyes met mine and I was relieved to find them bright with amusement. I couldn't afford to lose her. Not after the mind-blowing sex we'd just had.

I'd been with a lot of women before but this was wholly different. As soon as I'd slipped inside Hindley, everything changed for me. Being intimate with her was strangely unique in a way that I couldn't even explain, let alone comprehend. Hindley felt like home to me. We fit. She molded to me perfectly in more ways than just sexually.

"You've never had an orgasm during sex?" I asked.

She shook her head.

I couldn't help but smile, knowing I'd brought her satisfaction in a way she'd never experienced. God, I was a dick.

"You're quite proud of yourself, aren't you, Mr. Gregor?" Her fingers caressed my chest, and in true male form, my dick twitched. It always did when she was near.

"Quite proud of myself." I grinned bigger.

"So, is it normal? Does it always happen?"

"Not always, but it's something I aspire to."

Her face turned a delish shade of pink. No way could she be embarrassed after sucking my dick like a vacuum cleaner earlier.

"I liked it," she said quietly. Hindley had a growing appetite for my sexual prowess and I couldn't remember a time when I'd felt more flattered.

"I swear, you're insatiable, Miss Hagen."

"What can I say, I'm addicted."

"Are you saying I'm a drug?"

She nodded.

I laughed at her words. I felt the same way about her. "Well, in that case, do you want another fix?"

She nodded again, rolling her lips inward and smiling.

I motioned to the three opened and discarded condom packages on the floor. "I guess buying the jumbo pack of condoms was a good idea?"

She reached up and caressed my neck with her lips, making her way up to my ear. "Um hum," she hummed.

Her words were my undoing. I grabbed her waist and flipped us until she was sitting on top of me.

She squealed. "Rory, what are you doing?"

"Well, Miss Hagan, I'm afraid you have thoroughly worn me out. This time you're working."

"What do you mean?"

Her innocent face transfixed me. I was captivated by every nuance. She was worldly yet innocent, beautiful yet guarded.

Her brown eyes were wild with desire. My gaze travelled down her body and I stared at her breasts. Her puckered nipples showed her readiness. Hell yeah.

Unable to stay away, I lifted my body up and devoured one nipple. She tasted like the sweetest nectar.

"Oh, God," she moaned, her fingers slipping into my hair.

I lifted her hips and shifted her back until my dick jutted between her beautifully landscaped mound. Reaching for the box, I grabbed another condom. These were different, much thinner, and part of me worried they may not be as strong. Remembering how good it felt to be buried inside of Hindley Hagen though, I let my fear pass.

"Here, doll." I held out the packet. She'd already said she was inexperienced but I hadn't found her lacking in any way. She was a natural vixen.

I smiled to myself knowing she wouldn't disappoint.

"What?" she asked. "Why are you looking at me like that?"

"You." I wrapped my hands around her neck, stroking her throat with my thumbs. Skimming my fingers across her collarbone, I trailed my hands lower, lightly tracing the curve of her breasts. God, they were perfect. She was perfect. "You. Are beautiful, Hindley."

She laughed nervously as if she didn't believe me.

"Hey." I grabbed her chin more forcefully than I'd intended.

She slammed her eyes shut.

Some asshole had done a real number on her.

"Hindley, look at me."

Slowly her lids fluttered open. I loved how she responded to my dominance.

I drew in a deep breath, wanting her to not only hear but feel my words. "Just because you don't believe you're beautiful doesn't mean it's not true." I gripped her hips, pulling her toward me.

"And I'm going to make you believe me, if it's the last thing on earth I do."

Her eyes widened and I wondered if I'd scared her. Slowly a small smile spread across her delectable lips.

"There's my Drunk Girl."

She laughed.

"Now, are you going to rub on that packet all night," I said, "or are you going to put it on me so I can bury myself deep inside you and make you scream my name in ecstasy?"

A small moan escaped her lips and I realized if I didn't get inside of her soon, I might explode.

I yanked the packet from her hand and rolled it on in record time. "Now, Hindley," I growled.

Bracing her hands on my chest, she lifted her hips and rose above me, her hair cascading around our faces like a veil. She looked like an angel, *my* angel.

Yeah, but she fucks like the devil.

As she eased down on my shaft, my head fell onto the pillow, my eyes rolling back in my head.

"Fuck," I groaned.

She quickly found her rhythm, her hips moving in tandem with mine. Every erotic fantasy I'd ever had since I was thirteen came to life as this beautiful, gorgeous, insanely sexy woman moved on top of me.

I opened my eyes, watching as her breasts bounced with every movement of her body. "Fuck, Hindley, you're amazing," I blew out. "God, you feel so fuckin' good."

"I do?"

I stared at her in disbelief. Did she still think she was bad at this?

Her eyes were closed, her lips slightly parted as she danced on my dick like a pogo stick. *Fuck.*

How could she seriously believe she wasn't good at sex? Oh, yeah, because some asshole had drilled it in her brain. Hindley

Hagen was fucking amazing. The sexiest thing I'd ever laid eyes on before.

I wrapped my hands around her hips, pushing up into her. My thumb worked its way down between her legs, giving her the pressure she craved.

"Oh, Rory, yes, right there, please."

She wanted me. "Please, what?"

"Please, don't stop."

"Never," I said. And I meant it. I could fuck this girl for years.

Her body coiled and tightened in preparation for her release.

"Not yet, baby," I said. "Wait for me."

"I can't," she panted.

"Slow, Hindley. Control it." She and I would be having sex for a long time to come. I needed her to learn how to take her time, draw this out.

Her eyes flew open and found mine. Holy shit. She was so hot and sexy, all mussed up and ready to shatter. She broke me in two. So much for control.

My fingers dug into her hips. "Now, baby. Let go. Give it to me!" I shouted. Heat spiraled down my spine, pooling in my balls as I thrust harder.

She exploded, pulsating around my cock, my name on her lips echoing inside her bedroom.

"Fuck," I moaned, my jaw clenched as I pumped into her twice more. I shouted a string of unintelligible curses and came inside her with the force of a rocket ship. Holy fuckin' shit.

Hindley collapsed onto my chest with a sigh, utterly spent and exhausted.

I wrapped my arms around her body, lovingly caressing her back. This shit was new to me. I didn't do this lovey dovey stuff, after care. But with Hindley I was doing a lot of stuff I'd never done before.

"Sleep, baby," I whispered into her hair.

She sighed contentedly against my chest as I stroked her back. My need to keep her safe was overwhelming.

For the first time in my life, my heart felt complete, like I had a purpose. I'd finally found someone whose happiness I would put above my own. I wasn't sure if that was good or bad, but for tonight, with this woman, it felt perfect.

CHAPTER 29

RORY

I GLANCED around the packed arena, nervous for some reason. Well, I knew the reason. I searched the crowd for a familiar face, my heart hammering in my chest when I couldn't find her.

Hindley's plane was scheduled to arrive in San Diego earlier this morning. She was supposed to head to today's event once she landed. It was close to start time and she still wasn't here.

I'd been registered for this event for several months but it wasn't until I'd discovered Hindley would be in attendance that I'd started *really* training for the competition. I'd begun a serious workout schedule and I was careful of what I ate for one of the first times ever. I wanted to win. Big time.

I was great skater, I knew that, but Hindley was my attorney, my agent, and I had to prove to her that I was worthy of all the hard work she'd been putting in for me. I wanted to make her proud of me.

"Hey, what's going on, man?" Jack's voice interrupted my thoughts.

"Oh, uh, nothing."

"Who were you looking for?" He glanced at where my gaze had been trained.

"Um, no one."

"So I guess you won't want to see this little lady?" Jack stepped aside.

Hindley stood directly behind him, beaming.

She was wearing the same red T-shirt with the River City logo she'd worn in San Antonio at the Pro Am. This time the shirt was knotted on the side, revealing a small patch of smooth skin around her abdomen.

I wasn't sure how I felt about others seeing any part of her, let alone an area I'd devoured with my tongue, teeth, and mouth multiple times. Shit, was this what jealousy felt like?

"Hey," she said softly.

"Hey." I stood dumbfounded like a blockhead. She was more gorgeous than ever.

"Like my shirt?" She twirled around in front of me, her hands stretched out like an airplane. "It has your signature. See?" She pointed over her shoulder.

The only thing I saw was her long blonde hair falling over her huge tits. My dick tightened in my shorts.

When I remained silent, her gaze met mine.

She looked like a fuckin' dessert, and I wanted to devour her.

She blushed, her gaze lowering but not before a small smile tipped her plump little lips. Yeah, she knew what she did to me.

"How was your flight?" Jack asked.

She glanced up, her eyes going from me to Jack. "It was good. Thank you."

I watched her intently. I'd never been so drawn to a woman in my life.

"Are you ready?" she asked me.

I couldn't force my mouth to work, my tongue was swollen, along with other parts of my body.

"Rory?" she said.

I shook my head to clear my illicit thoughts. "Oh, um, yeah, sorry."

"Are you ready for today?" she repeated.

It'd been over a week since her naked body had been underneath mine, rubbing against me. All I could think about was ripping that shirt off her and throwing her down right here in front of God and everyone, just to bury myself deep inside her.

God, I was such a dick.

"Uh, yeah," I said, "I think so. Hopefully, we'll see."

"Hopefully?" Jack stared at me like I was crazy. Which I definitely was. Hindley was making me crazy.

"Okay," she said, "well, I'm gonna go grab a seat." She lifted up on her tiptoes and wrapped her arms around my neck.

I slid an arm around her small waist and buried my head in her hair like a perv, inhaling. God, she smelled fucking amazing. I was pretty sure I wasn't supposed to be smelling my agent. Just before I pulled away, my lips brushed her ear. "I wish I was grabbing your seat," I whispered.

She shivered in my arms and pulled away, coughing repeatedly as she tugged down her shirt. "Well, um, okay. I'll see you soon." Without another word, she ducked her head and walked toward the grand stands.

I watched as she walked away. Her ass swayed from side to side, encased in a pair of skin-tight jeans that clung to her like Saran Wrap. Fuck me. How the hell was I supposed to skate with a hard-on?

Heads turned as skaters and spectators alike parted like the Red Sea, watching her walk away. My skin vibrated with anger as I clenched my hands. Where the hell was this jealousy coming from?

"Okay, so do you have your skating plan mapped out?" Jack asked.

I barely registered his words. "Yeah, I've got it," I said through clenched teeth.

"Rory!" He grabbed my shoulders.

"What?"

He shook me. "Focus."

"Okay, I'm with it. Sorry, man."

"Manny's going to be bringing his A-game today," Jack said.

"He's still pissed about last month's disqualification in Puerto Rico."

I laughed, remembering Manny Morales cussing out one of the foreign judges during the competition. He thought if he cursed in Spanish the judge wouldn't understand him. In his fury he'd forgotten he was actually in a Spanish-speaking country. The broadcasters had had a hell of a time covering up his expletives, and the governing board voted unanimously to disqualify him.

"Rory!" Jack yelled. "Focus. Please."

I held up my hands. "All right, sorry. You have to admit though, it was funny as shit. I mean, come on. Spanish, in Puerto Rico? Who doesn't know that?"

Jack's scowl faded, replaced with a hesitant grin. "Manny's dangerous today, Rory, so keep an eye on him. He'll crawl up that leader board and take over number one. Then you'll be saying *Adios*."

I laughed but Jack was right. Manny could be lethal when he was out for revenge.

"Okay," he continued, "you also need to watch out for Smitty. He's fresh off an injury and word is he's looking for a comeback as bad as you are."

Charlie Smith, aka Smitty, had dislocated his right shoulder in a fall earlier this year. Rather than rest it like the doctors and his manager had insisted, he'd decided to skate a week later and tore the shit out of major ligaments and tendons. His recovery had been slow and painful. I was pretty confident he still wouldn't be one hundred percent today.

"You've totally got Jake and Buzz, especially on your aerials."

Jack was right, I did have them on a lot of tricks. I didn't mean to brag but I was the best at a lot of things on the course. I worked hard to be. Now I was developing a new trick, one I'd informally called 'The Helly.' It was a seriously complicated trick and dangerous as hell, hence the name. It would be totally worth every point I'd get once I pulled it off though.

The trick required me to suspend myself in the air while

balancing and rotating on only one arm. I held the board, flush to my feet with the other hand, while making two complete revolutions on my free hand, my skateboard spinning like the rotors on a helicopter. The name of the trick came from the effect the skateboard gave, looking like a helicopter. I'd also called it 'The Helly' because I'd fallen so damn so many times, it hurt like hell the next day.

"Don't even think about trying it," Jack said as if reading my mind. "Not today, Rory."

I didn't need the reminder. There was no way I was doing The Helly today. It still wasn't perfect, and I didn't perform any trick I wasn't a master of. Plus, there was absolutely no way I was going to fall today, not in front of Hindley.

"You all right?" Jack put his hand on my shoulder, his brows furrowed.

"I'm fine, just going over my routine in my mind."

"Well, you know you need to watch Axel in your rearview mirror."

Axel Pretorius, aka Pretty Boy, was from Australia. He'd literally been a pain in my ass for the last five years. I'd first met the little prick at a Pro Am invitational similar to the one Leif and River City hosted. Back then, Axel was a snot-nosed amateur. I'd known from the very beginning he was a total dick. He had a shit attitude. He'd done nothing but prove me right ever since.

The pinnacle of our problems came last August. I'd started my comeback after falling from grace, and he loved to rub it in my face that I was no longer number one. He reminded me every chance he got of how fucked up I'd become and how far I'd fallen behind in the rankings. He claimed I was chasing his ass on my climb back to the top and assured me on a regular basis I would never catch him.

Guess again, little prick.

Last year I'd been standing in line on the deck, waiting for my turn when the dipshit took a side rail turn and completely clipped me at the ankles. My body buckled and I landed flat on my ass. He told the judges it was an accident, but everyone on the pro circuit knew he'd done it intentionally. That's the kind of shithead he was.

The judges had nearly disqualified him from the competition once they discovered my tailbone was actually bruised, but I wouldn't give him the satisfaction. I skated against him the next day in the finals and kicked his ass. I wished it had been literal, but I was willing to take beating him in a competition over kicking his scrawny ass for real. Since then, I worked hard to keep my composure every time I saw his dick face. I couldn't afford to fuck up, especially not today.

Right on cue, I heard his weasel-ass voice, with his grating Australian accent, ring in my ear.

"Nice agent, Gregor."

Just the thought of him looking at Hindley had my body on fire and my hands clenched.

"Do you mind, Axel?" Jack said. "Rory and I are discussing our game plan."

"Oh, no worries, mate. Don't let me stop you." He held up his hands in innocence. Jack and I knew he was anything but. "I think I'll go introduce myself to the little beauty." He turned to walk away.

"Don't you even dare think about it, asshole!" The words were out of my mouth before I could stop them.

"Whoa," he laughed, "sounds like someone's pretty attached to their agent." He glanced up in the grand stands as if looking for her. "From what I hear, she's a smart one too. So, tell me, Rory Gregor, what the hell is she doing with an idiot like you?"

Adrenaline and anger burned through my veins. Pretty Boy was just trying to get a rise out of me and I wasn't going to give him the satisfaction. Not today. I fought to steady my breathing, turning my attention back toward the course.

This competition was being held in a pool skate park, named for the hollow hole in the ground that resembled a drained pool. The course had varied depths along with bumps and humps on the bottom. The entire course was rimmed by a two-inch steel railing that skaters could ride for extra points.

I remembered in the last competition how Axel had fallen on his smart little ass when he tried to ride it for a fraction of a second too long. Much to everyone's surprise though, he'd recovered and impressed the judges enough on his next ride to land in first place. *Fucker.*

Mentally, I ran through the skating plan Jack and I had developed the prior evening. I walked through each trick, trying to ignore the little prick still standing next to me.

"Well, well, well, if it ain't Axel 'Pretty Boy' Pretorius as I live and breathe," came the voice of my good friend and fellow competitor, Buzz Dahlke.

Buzz and I were soul brothers, confidants on the skating circuit, and everyone knew it. You fucked with him, you fucked with me, and vice versa. When I'd taken a turn for the worse and my career nose-dived, it had been Buzz who'd stood by me, encouraging me to come back to the sport I loved. He despised Axel more than I did, and that was saying a lot. Unlike me, he had no problems voicing his contempt.

"What's up, dick face?" Axel said, nodding at Buzz.

"Ah, dick face," Buzz laughed, "how original, Pretty Boy. Remind me again why they call you that?"

Axel clenched his square jaw and stared Buzz up and down.

Pretty Boy was a nickname other skaters had given him years before. Axel thought it was an innocent play on his last name, Pretorius, but actually, we all called him that because of his constant need to primp before skating.

The weasel was supposedly a sports legend in Australia. No one in the world thought Axel Pretorius was better looking than Axel himself. If you didn't believe him, all you had to do was ask him and he'd be happy to tell you himself.

What really ate my shit though was the fact it was true. He was a good-looking guy, even though it killed me to admit it. Girls would shout out his name at competitions and ask for him to throw shit into the stands. It was annoying as fuck.

Most of the girls who followed the skating circuit had done the horizontal hump dance with him at least once or twice, if not more. He was notorious for sleeping around. There were rumors that there were at least four little Pretty Boy babies out there around the world, but he'd never claimed a one of them. Surprise.

What worried me the most about Axel getting close to Hindley wasn't his penchant to sleep with fans though. Hindley was smart, she'd never sleep with that idiot. What scared me more than anything were the recent rumors surfacing around the tour.

Apparently, not every girl Axel was bedding was a willing participant. In the past six months he'd had two girls accuse him of some type of assault, sexual and physical. No charges had been formally filed, but the governing board wasn't happy. Real or not, the threat was there and I wasn't going to take any chances when it came to Hindley's safety.

"What are you doing over here harassing the winner of this competition?" Buzz asked, shoulder checking Axel.

"Winner?" Axel laughed.

"Yeah. I said winner," Buzz repeated.

"Aren't you kind of putting yourself down already, Buzz," he said, "declaring that Rory's going to beat you?"

Unfortunately, what Axel said was true. Buzz was on his way down the leader board. I'd told him last year to retire and consider judging but he couldn't let go of the glory days. I hadn't mentioned it again, instead backing him no matter how I felt about his professional skills.

Axel went on. "Of course, my grandmother could beat you even on her worst day, and she's on a walker." Axel reared back and bellowed with laughter. No one else joined him.

"Yeah," Buzz said, "your grandma did beat me. Last night as a matter of fact. Great hand job by the way. Tell her thanks."

Axel's smile crumbled. "Don't talk about my grandmother," he growled through clenched teeth.

"Whatever, dick head," Buzz said. "As long as Rory wipes the pool with your dumbass, I don't mind coming in last place if it means I get to watch your fuckin' face pucker up tighter than your shit shooter from humiliation."

"Come on, guys." Jack stepped between them. "Let's take this out in the pool."

Axel was smaller than Buzz but no matter his size, he'd always stand up to anyone. I had to give the little shit credit, he had tons of self-esteem. Way more than me.

"With pleasure." Axel shoulder checked Buzz as he pushed through the mass of people gathered around the skaters' platform.

Buzz turned and hollered over his shoulder. "Tell your Granny she's got a sweet little mouth too. She can suck my dick again tonight if she wants. Tell her to bring that walker too. She's gonna need it after riding me all night long."

Axel flipped him off without even looking back as he disappeared into the crowds vying for his attention.

"Buzz, why do you insist on antagonizing him?" Jack asked, scowling.

"Calm down, Jack," he said, patting him on the shoulder. "It's all part of my master plan." Buzz glanced at me and winked.

"And what's your master plan, Buzz?" Jack asked, raising a brow. "Have him so pissed off and pumped up that he'll beat your ass?"

"Something like that." Buzz grinned, turning his attention to me. "Hey, who was the hottie wrapped around your neck earlier? Rumor has it she's your new agent. Wish my agent had an ass like that."

Even though Buzz and I were friends, it still infuriated me that he pictured Hindley in that way.

"Ease up, man," he said, squeezing my shoulder. "I was just kidding. You look like you ate a bowl of turd-flavored Cheerios."

God, what was wrong with me, pissing off one of my best friends? I had to get my shit together before someone found out about me and Hindley.

"I don't know," I said, "I just don't want anyone thinking of her like that." *Except me.* "She's smart and talented, as an attorney and agent I mean." *And hot as fuck between the sheets.* Yeah, no. Couldn't say that.

"Well, sorry, dude," Buzz said, "the chick is way too hot for any red-blooded man *not* to picture her ass naked in bed."

My eyes flared and I willed my fists to relax. Buzz was my friend, I reminded myself again, a good friend.

He leaned in closer. "Dude, are you fuckin' her?"

"What?" I shouted in mock surprise. Okay, it wasn't mock, I was worried as shit that he could tell, and even more petrified that he'd actually voiced his concern.

"I mean, it's okay," he said, smiling, "I'm not going to judge you. You know that."

My heart pounded in my chest and I had trouble catching my breath. I had to calm the fuck down.

"No, I'm not fuckin' her, man." Technically, it was true. I'd fucked a lot of women and I could say, without a doubt, what Hindley and I were doing was anything *but* fucking. Okay, maybe a little fucking, but there was a deeper connection with Hindley than just sex. God, I sounded like a pussy.

"Mind if I give it a try then?" Buzz smirked as he nudged my shoulder with his fist.

My jaw clenched so tight I thought I might break a tooth. I was pretty sure steam was pouring out of my ears like a cartoon character, I was so pissed.

"Dude, I'm just kidding." Buzz laughed. "Calm down."

I couldn't calm down. And that was the problem. "Look, man, she's good, amazing actually. She's doing an awesome job for me and I don't want to fuck this up."

"I get it, dude. You've been working hard. You deserve the best. And from what I can tell from her backside, she is the best." He bellowed with laughter.

Fucker. I willed my jaw to relax as he turned and walked away, his laughter echoing through the arena.

Feeling overly protective, I scanned the packed auditorium, searching for Hindley. This was a covered event, thankfully for her. I didn't want her to get burned again. Although rubbing lotion on her might be nice. I smiled at the memory.

"You sure you're ready?" Jack asked, slipping up next to me.

I pulled a piece of paper out of my back pocket and reviewed all the graphics, visualizing every trick. Since I can't read, I can't write down the actual names. "Yeah." I think so. But I couldn't kick the nagging jealousy threatening to destroy everything.

The announcers proclaimed the start of the event and called out each participant.

My mind raced and I still couldn't focus. I couldn't keep doing this with her. This jealousy I felt any time someone looked at Hindley was going to destroy me. I had to end things with her if I wanted to make the comeback I'd dreamed of.

I glanced up in the stands and saw her standing tall, waving at me. Her long blonde hair blew in the breeze and I remembered the taste her on my tongue. Fuck.

Who was I kidding? I was an addict and she was my drug. I'd need a serious intervention to give up this girl.

CHAPTER 30

RORY

THERE WAS a light knock on my hotel room door. I turned the knob and swung it open, not surprised to find Hindley standing outside, smiling up at me.

She wore a tight purple halter top that showcased her amazing tits. Her short-as-shit black mini skirt was cut higher than I was comfortable with for public display. She had an amazing body and my dick rose to the occasion.

"Oh my God, Rory," she said, bouncing on her toes, her perky breasts nearly popping out of her top. "You were amazing today."

It took everything inside me not to scoop her up in my arms and throw her onto my bed

She reached out for my waist but I pulled away, opening my hotel room door further to reveal Jack sitting on the couch.

"Oh," she whispered, pulling her hand back. "Sorry."

I shook my head, more in disgust of my own weak thoughts. If Jack weren't here, I'd have had her stripped down naked, her body spread eagle underneath me.

Hindley slipped by me, her body brushing against mine. God, she smelled fantastic, like heaven on earth. My mouth watered to have a taste.

She sat down beside Jack. "Rory did a great job this weekend, didn't he, Jack?"

Jack rolled his eyes. He was pissed at me, *way* pissed.

Yesterday during the semi-finals, Kara had called and informed him of my true feelings for Hindley. Thanks, Kara.

Jack had lectured me well into the night after the first round of competitions about how hard I'd worked to make a comeback. He sounded like Leif, a broken record stuck on the 'Stay Away from Hindley' anthem that even my *own* mind couldn't take off the fuckin' record player.

"I mean, come on, second place," she said with a huge smile. "That's awesome."

Second place wasn't jack shit to me and Jack knew it. Not for the kind of comeback I wanted.

"It's not first place," Jack grumbled, "and that's what we train for."

Yep, he was majorly pissed.

Normally, Jack wasn't into where I ranked but rather how I skated, or more importantly, how I *felt* about how I skated. Today I hadn't performed at my best. My second-place finish was proof of it. Jack was really more upset about *why* I hadn't skated to my potential. I was letting my feelings for Hindley get in the way and he knew it.

Last night his words had played over and over again in my head as I'd tried but failed to find solace in sleep. His reminders had been like a cold shower on my dick, forcing me to say no to Hindley last night when she'd come knocking on my hotel door after dinner. The sultry expression on her face told me she was ready for a replay of our time in her bedroom.

I'd fended off her advances, claiming that I needed to stay focused for the competition. So instead of spending the night rolling around in her bed, I'd ended up with my dick in an ice bucket, trying to ease the massive woody she'd given me with her mouthwatering good-bye kisses. God, that girl knew how to suck face.

She was disappointed, even a little hurt, I could tell. But fuck, so was I.

Hindley had no idea how hard it was to stay away from crack once you'd had a taste. I was turning into a crack whore for Hindley and that wasn't good. Anyone would tell you crack was wack, and that's why I had to let her go, for both our sakes.

Hindley's eyes darted from Jack's to mine then back. She tilted her head, pursing her lips as her brows furrowed. She obviously sensed the tension in the air. "Um, well," she said, standing, "I just came up say congrats. I've got a meeting downstairs in the lounge."

The fuck?

I flexed my hands, my eyes narrowed. "Dressed like that?" I said with all the bitterness of a jealous boyfriend. And *that* was exactly why I needed to let her go.

She remained silent as she walked toward the door, her long, lean legs flexing with every step in her high heels.

I blocked her way, scrubbing a hand through my hair. "Meeting with who?" I asked under my breath, biting back the bitterness. Even though my mind told me no, I wanted her, bad. I couldn't seem to let her go. The thought that she was leaving me to be with someone else had me seeing red.

"Matt Davis," she said.

"Who?"

"He's with Sonora Water. I met him during the finals today. Apparently, his company is quite taken with your comeback story."

I should have been excited that Hindley was working deals for me but I wasn't. All I heard was a dude's name. She was going to meet another man.

"I need to go," she said quietly.

I stepped aside, allowing her to pass, even though I wanted to yank her back and have my dirty way with her.

Her chocolate eyes narrowed as she studied me. A look of disappointment flashed across her face.

I was giving her mixed signals. She was doubting herself. I'd promised I wouldn't be that person, the one who hurt her again.

I walked her to the door and pulled it open.

On the threshold she turned to face me.

I caught a hint of her intoxicating perfume and thought I might pass out, she smelled so good. I was a starved man and she was the most delicious meal I'd ever seen. That was it. I was a weak moth-erfucker. I had no pride, I could admit it. I leaned in closer. "I'll see you later tonight?" I asked.

She glanced around my shoulder.

I followed her gaze.

Jack's face was still buried in his laptop, reviewing videos of my performances this weekend.

I turned back to face her.

She glanced up at me and bit her bottom lip. Fuck me, I wanted to take that lip and bite it too.

"Well?" I cocked a brow.

Slowly she nodded.

Oh, hell yeah. I slipped my hand underneath her hair, wrapping my fingers possessively around her neck.

She leaned into my touch, her chocolate eyes huge and full promise.

"There's my Drunk Girl," I whispered in her ear. Blood pooled in my midsection and I felt lightheaded.

Jack's voice broke through our moment. "You've got some work to do on your 720," he said, "but you landed it, so that was enough today, I guess."

"Later," Hindley whispered as she lifted up on her toes and brushed her lips against my cheek. I wanted a lot more but before I could respond, she slid through the door, closing it softly behind her. Damn she was good.

I walked back to the couch, wondering how I was going to sit by Jack with a massive hard-on. Falling down next to him, I mentally prepared for the ass whipping he was about to deliver. But all I could think about was Hindley. I'd never felt this way about a woman before.

I pictured her sitting in the lounge downstairs in her flimsy excuse for a skirt with some strange man, ogling her legs and tits. He was probably already fantasizing about being inside her like I did. Fuck. I was so screwed.

I wondered what this asshat looked like. He was probably some good looking, slicked back, well dressed, frat boy. Just Hindley's type. The dude was obviously smart. Hell, he was an executive for fuck's sake, and no doubt he could read and write. I was just some illiterate asshole who played on a skateboard and never finished high school.

Hindley and I were already doomed.

"Rory," Jack said, "did you hear me?"

"Oh, sorry, no. What?"

"Look at this footage here." He pointed to the screen.

An hour later, Jack thankfully called it quits. He packed up his laptop and headed for the door.

Meanwhile, my mind was still flooded with images of what Hindley and Mr. Executive fuck face were doing downstairs.

"Just one last thing, Rory."

I glanced up.

Jack stopped in front of my door, laptop tucked under his arm, his other hand resting on the doorknob. "You're worthy of her. Don't ever doubt that."

His comment surprised me. It seemed like Jack possessed the uncanny ability to read my thoughts like Kara.

"But being worthy comes with responsibilities," he added. "If you like Hindley, if she *is* different, then you have to treat her differently. I'm not saying you can't pursue her, I'm just saying you can't be reckless in your pursuit like you've been in the past."

I took in a deep breath, letting his words soak in. It wasn't anything I hadn't been telling myself since I'd slept with Hindley.

"She's good for you," he said, "good for your career. But if you can't treat her right then stop what you're doing. Right now."

"I want to treat her right, Jack. I just don't have much experience."

"You know you can't go public with this relationship, don't you? Not right now anyway."

I nodded. "I know. We both do."

"You're worthy of her, Rory. Stop trying to convince yourself differently. And stop comparing yourself to that executive downstairs."

I chuckled. Jack really did know me inside and out.

"Be careful with her, Rory. It's just a meeting. She's doing her job, for you. Don't go down to the lounge and go all Rory Gregor on her." He waved his hand in the air.

"What does that mean?"

"It means you'd probably be better off staying in your room the rest of the night. Let her do her job. That's what she does, she represents you. And that's what she's doing right now. Working."

I stared at Jack.

"That's *all* she's doing, Rory."

Jack was trying to quiet the voices in my head but I wasn't so sure he was doing a good job of it.

"I'll stay here," I said, "I promise."

He raised an eyebrow. "Really?"

"Okay," I sighed, "if I go downstairs, I promise to keep it professional."

He just stared.

"What?" I asked.

"Just be careful, Rory. Hindley's different. Way different. You're on your way back up. Don't hurt her and ruin both of your careers in the process." Without another word, he shut the door, leaving me alone with my self-loathing thoughts.

CHAPTER 31

RORY

THE ELEVATOR DOORS slid open and my palms broke out in a sheen of sweat. My pulse pounded in my head. This was wrong, I knew it in my bones, but for some dumb reason I'd convinced myself I was doing a good thing. I was traveling down to the lounge to make sure Hindley was safe. I just wanted to keep her from harm's way. It was a valid concern, considering how we'd first met.

Yeah, right.

I trudged across the lobby on my way to the lounge but before I could make it, someone caught my arm and pulled me aside.

"Hey," an unfamiliar female voice said next to me. "I saw you skate today. You were sooooo awesome."

I looked down at a petite chick in her early twenties, with short auburn hair, bright green hazel eyes, and tits the size of Mount Rushmore. I tried not to look, but seriously, they were almost as big as her head and out for public display. Like *really* out there.

"You totally should have won the competition," she said in that sexy purr that all chicks looking to score with an athlete use.

Back in the day, this was exactly the type of woman I would have taken to my hotel room and fucked all kinds of kinky ways. I'd bang her until she couldn't walk for a week. And by the look in her eyes, I could tell she'd come willingly, like most did.

But tonight I stared a little closer, examining her as a person. She was young, fragile, and alone. Just like Hindley the night we'd met. Why hadn't I ever noticed that in women before?

"Um, thanks," I said, wiggling my arm from her grip. "I appreciate that."

"You're just as hot up close as you are on the course."

I glanced over her shoulder, ignoring her comment as I scanned the entrance to the lounge. Where the hell was Hindley? Suddenly two hands pressed against my chest. Shit. I took a step back, breaking her hold and stared down at her.

She smiled, all toothy, her shiny lip gloss spread on thick as paint. "Would you sign my bra?" Before I could stop her, she raised her shirt over her head, revealing a hot pink bra.

What the fuck?

"Uh, no, sorry." I jerked her shirt back down.

She took advantage of my close proximity and sank her talons into my shoulders. Gripping me like a baby monkey to its mother, the chick pressed up on her toes to kiss me.

I jerked my head just in time and her lips met my cheek instead of my mouth. Thank God.

I reached behind my neck to remove her hands but she gripped me tighter, her arms like steel cables. Fuck, this chick was strong. I finally broke free from her hold but realized her lips were still firmly locked on my cheek and working dangerously close to my mouth.

Shit.

I grabbed her face to push her away when something caught my attention from the corner of my eye.

Hindley stood at the entrance of the bar, glaring at me, brown eyes blazing.

Fuck.

I hadn't wanted to get shitty with this girl but I knew if I didn't extricate myself from her, and fast, Hindley was going to kill me. I grasped the chick around the waist and physically lifted her up and off me.

She stared up at me with a glazed over look like we'd just fucked.

I coughed several times, shocked by the whole ordeal. Chicks were getting crazier every day. "Uh, thanks for your support," I said, ducking from her grasp as I all but ran toward Hindley.

The lobby was massive and filled with guests, which was unusual given the time of night. I weaved my way through the crowd but my gaze stayed trained on Hindley the entire time. She still didn't look happy, in fact she looked royally pissed, and who could blame her.

Before I could reach her, a tall, good looking man dressed in a suit stepped out of the lounge and stood next to her. I watched helpless as he slipped a hand around her waist.

What. The. Fuck!

My heart stopped and pain burned deep in my gut like I'd been sucker punched.

Hindley glanced up at the guy, her face softening with a huge smile. Fuck, she liked this guy. She finally stepped out of his hold but not before he squeezed her tight.

Something in my pea brain snapped. I couldn't clear a pathway to them fast enough.

"Here he is," she said, pointing toward me. Her smile was steady but not nearly what it had been up in my hotel room. "Rory Gregor, I'd like you to meet Matt Davis with Sonora Water." She swung her hand out toward fuck face.

Wait, Sonora Water? This was the guy she was meeting?

I'd heard of the company before but hadn't put the two together. Sonora made earth friendly drinks in special bottles that supposedly saved the planet. They claimed their water was filled with extra vitamins and electrolytes and other bullshit you didn't need. To me, it was all just a marketing ploy, a way for them to charge an ass ton of money for something that existed free all over the planet.

I hated him already.

"Matt, this is Rory." Hindley swept her hand toward me like she was Vanna White, presenting the next letter on Wheel of Fortune.

I stared at her, unable to speak. She was so fucking beautiful, my heart actually ached.

She smiled but I could tell it was fake, not like the one from my hotel room earlier. That little skateboard bunny from earlier had fucked stuff up for me.

She narrowed her eyes, nodding toward Dipshit. That was my new nickname for him. Dipshit.

As much as I didn't want to, I turned and surveyed the man standing beside her.

He was tall, as tall as me, clean cut, All-American, probably even played football in high school and fucked the head cheer-leader. *Dipshit.*

He had perfectly groomed dark hair that anyone could tell he spent way more time on than most girls he'd ever fucked. His shit-eating grin revealed gleaming white teeth that were straighter than most toothpaste commercials. All in all, he was a good-looking guy, if you were in to that shit, but I still hated him for touching my girl.

My girl?

Yep, that's what Hindley had become. Mine.

"It's nice to finally meet you, Rory," Dipshit said, extending his hand. God, he even sounded perfect, like a sexy DJ on the radio.

He was probably some Harvard MBA douche who graduated summa-cum-suck-my-dick. That was the kind of guy Hindley deserved though, not some high school dropout like me.

"Rory," Hindley called softly, breaking me from my one-on-one discussion about how much I already hated Dipshit.

"Uh, hey," I finally answered, "it's nice to meet you, Matt." I took his offered hand, giving him the best man-shake I could muster. He had a decent grip and strong hands. Fuck, he wasn't a pansy ass after all.

"I was just telling Hindley how much we at Sonora have enjoyed your comeback story," he said. "We believe it rings true to our own story of recycling, taking the best of the worst and making something new with it, something that sustains us."

Wait. What the fuck did he just say? Had he just insinuated that I was the worst?

I glanced at Hindley.

Her brown eyes narrowed in warning. I had to rein this shit in.

"Um, thanks, I guess." I shrugged, releasing his hand.

His now free hand slipped under Hindley's elbow.

My eyes narrowed as I stared at their connection. My nostrils flared and I flexed my forearms as I fought back the urge to knock the fucker out.

Hindley side-stepped from his reach and moved to stand next to me. Thank God. I blew out a sigh of relief. She glanced up at me, a genuine smile finally spreading across her face. "Matt said that Sonora may be interested in signing a deal with you for a national ad campaign they're launching soon. Isn't that amazing?"

The expression of sheer joy on her face was so beautiful I was stuck speechless. Literally. Again.

"Rory?" she said.

"Oh, yeah. That's great." Nice. Now I sounded like a buffoon in front of this guy, which I was.

"Especially if you're able to make it to the X Games this year," she said.

I remained speechless, studying Hindley's beautiful face. Of course this guy wanted to touch her. Anyone with half a brain would.

Hindley elbowed me. "Isn't that great news, Rory?"

"Oh, yes, sorry. That sounds great."

She smiled and I felt like I'd won something huge. "Their corporate office is in San Diego so I'm going to fly down on Monday morning and meet with their team to talk about the specifics."

"We could drive down," I said, smiling down at her. Yeah, taking a nice drive down the Pacific Coast Highway with Hindley sounded like the perfect way to spend a Sunday afternoon. "San Diego is only an hour and a half away from my house."

"Oh, you don't need to be at the meeting, Rory," Matt said with a cheesy, used car salesman smile. "I'm sure negotiations are much too tedious and boring for athletes, just a lot of big mumbo-jumbo documents. You need to focus on your skating right now." He gave me a joking jab on my upper arm.

I had to fight back the urge to punch him in the face.

"Actually," Hindley stepped between us, "Rory is very involved in all aspects of his career, contract negotiations being one of them."

Matt raised his brows and cocked his head as he studied me. "Wonderful. Then we'll see both of you on Monday. I'll email you the details, Hindley." He stepped in and kissed her cheek.

Kissed. Her. Cheek.

I tensed my legs, planting my feet to the floor so I didn't kick him in the nut sack.

"Until Monday, Rory." Dipshit stuck out his hand and stared at me with a smirk.

Yeah, until Monday, douche bag. That's how long I'd have Hindley in my bed, screaming out my name until she was hoarse. I smiled at the thought.

"Monday," I said, shaking his hand.

Matt stared at Hindley and gave her another dazzling smile. "Monday then. I look forward to it." He winked. The fucker actually winked at her. Before I could punch him in the head, he waltzed down the steps like Fred Astaire and headed toward the lobby.

Dipshit was not going to win this round. I wrapped my arm around Hindley's waist and raised my hand in the air. "Monday, Matt," I called out. "Can't wait."

He gazed back over his shoulder.

I waved at him like the douche bag I was.

He gave a slight nod but his smirk was gone. I'd knocked the fucker down at least a notch, maybe two.

That's right, she's mine, motherfucker. Even though no one's supposed to know it.

My lips curled up in a victorious smile. Rory—one. Dipshit Water Boy—zero.

Hindley elbowed me in the ribs, pushing me away. "What the hell was that, Rory? Dammit, I can't believe you just did that."

She was pissed, but I didn't care. A guy had to stake his claim early. *Stake his claim?* Yeah, I was an asshole.

She flew past me, down into the lobby.

"What?" I asked, following behind her.

"Why did you do that?"

"He wants you," I said like it was obvious. "And I wanted him to know that you're not available."

She glanced at me over her shoulder. "Well, you may have jeopardized this whole deal."

"I don't give a fuck about the deal, Hindley."

She stopped abruptly and whipped around to face me, her gorgeous blonde hair flying over her shoulders. Damn, she was hot, all mussed up and fuming.

"Well, you should care," she said through clenched teeth.

"I don't even like that fuckin' water."

She propped her hands on her small hips. "Who cares?"

"I care. I'm not going to endorse something I don't like."

She cocked her head and raised a brow. "What do you even know about Sonora?"

"I know a douche bag works in their marketing department and he's trying to get into my girl's panties."

"Seriously, Rory? That's your come back?" She blew out a breath and shook her head.

God, she looked adorable all pissy but I knew better than to say that now.

"And for the record, I'm not *your* girl," she said.

My ego took a direct hit and I lowered my head, my shoulders slumping. There went my testosterone high.

She grabbed my arm and yanked me into an alcove. "You know what I mean, Rory" she whispered.

I glanced up. "No, actually I don't."

"Look, you're the one who said no to me last night when I came to your hotel room," she said. "So I don't want to hear anything from you."

Okay, so she was just upset, not giving up. I could deal with that. "Maybe you should try again tonight." I waggled my brows.

"It's late. I can't be seen going into your room at this hour."

I glanced at the clock directly behind us. "It's just a little after midnight."

"Well, still," she huffed and crossed her arms over her chest. The movement pressed her breasts higher.

I smiled. Adorable.

"Stop smiling." She swatted at me as a small grin curled her lips.

I bit my lips to stifle a laugh. This wasn't as bad as I'd first thought.

"Do you really want to go to their offices with me on Monday?" she asked.

She was changing the subject. I welcomed the diversion.

"Sure. We can drive down to my house tomorrow, spend the night, then head down to San Diego early Monday morning."

She stood silent, her face giving nothing away.

Suddenly everything that had just happened earlier hit me like a rock in the face. I was fucking this up, big time. My grade-A douche maneuvers may cost me this girl.

I drew in a deep breath and heaved a sigh, scraping a hand through my hair. "Look, Hindley, I couldn't give a rat's ass about the meeting on Monday. I just want to spend more time with you, just the two of us, however I can." I gave her my best panty-dropping smile.

She balled up her fist and punched me in the chest.

"Shit, Hindley, that hurt." I rubbed the spot she'd hit. Damn, she was strong.

"Good." She turned and headed toward the bank of elevators.

"So?" I asked quietly, nudging her shoulder as we waited.

"So what?"

"Are you stopping by?"

"No," she said, jutting out her chin.

"Why?"

"It's late, Rory. We can't be seen like that. It's important to me."

Shit, had I gotten this all wrong? Maybe this wasn't about keeping our relationship a secret but about her not wanting to be with me at all.

She poked my arm. "Stop."

I glanced down at her. "Stop what?"

"He holds no appeal to me, Rory. I don't know why you're so pissed."

"Who?" The elevator doors opened and I stepped back, allowing her to enter first.

She rolled her eyes at me. "Who?" She laughed. "Matt Davis. Or whatever derogatory name you've given him."

"It was Dipshit. I've actually named him Dipshit."

She snorted.

"Only me?" I asked with real sincerity. I was a man who need reassurance.

"Only you." She reached up and rubbed my cheek, brushing my bottom lip with her thumb as the doors slid closed.

I pressed my hands on her hips, smirking as I slid them lower toward her ass.

Her brown eyes flared, her lids lowering as she stared at my mouth.

Shit, we might start this make-out session right here in the fucking elevator. Which was fine by me. I pressed her into the wall.

Just before the elevator closed all the way, a hand slipped through the doors, stopping them.

"Hold the elevator, please."

My stomach clenched when I recognized the familiar voice.

Axel 'Pretty Boy' Pretorius.

His skinny-ass body slipped through the doors just as they were about to close.

Great. Could my night get any better?

"Thanks, man." He looked up at me like I'd saved his life. "Oh, hey, Rory, didn't know it was you."

Fucking liar.

"Oh, hello." He turned to Hindley. "You must be Rory's new agent. I'm Axel Pretorius." He extended his hand as his beady eyes drank her in from head to toe in a predatory gaze.

I was going to kill this fucker too.

"It's nice to meet you, Axel. I'm Hindley Hagen." She grasped his hand, her tone friendly but professional. Very different from the deep, sultry voice she used when she was in bed with me.

"She's also my attorney. And my agent," I added.

"Oh, that's impressive, Ms. Hagen."

"Please, call me Hindley." She smiled. God, she was gorgeous when she smiled.

"Oh, Certainly, Hindley," he said, grinning like a jackass. "Thank you."

"I love your accent," she said.

Ah, fuck me. Why was she complimenting Pretty Boy? That was the worst thing to do. He had an ego the size of the Grand Canyon and she was just feeding it.

"Where are you from?" she asked.

"I'm from Australia. Brisbane to be exact."

"Oh, cool."

Cool? What the fuck was that about? Was she actually interested in this prick?

"You know, I've always wanted to go to Australia," she said.

Oh my God, my night was going from bad to totally fucked up in a nanosecond.

Pretty Boy scooted closer. "You know my agent's contract is up in a few months. I may be in need of a new one." He stepped even closer. "Do you have any cards?"

No way, no fucking way. I stepped between them. This was not happening.

"I'm sorry, I don't have any on me," she said.

"That's all right. I'll add you to my phone right now," Pretty Boy said.

Was there a step lower than "*totally fucked up*" for this night to reach?

"What's your number?" he asked.

I stood like a cement statue, my heart hammering in my chest as she rattled off her number. There wasn't a goddamn thing I could do without revealing that our relationship was more than it appeared.

Bing.

Thankfully, the elevator doors opened onto our floor.

"Oh, you're on the sixth floor too?" Pretty Boy asked, as if he gave a shit. "After you." He stood outside the elevator, holding the doors for Hindley like he was the most chivalrous man on earth.

I made my way past the door and stared down at him, silently marking my territory. Much to my surprise, the little fucker actually smirked.

It took everything inside me not to punch him straight in the face and scoop up Hindley like a caveman.

"Nice to meet you, Hindley," Axel hollered behind us.

Hindley gazed over her shoulder, smiling, a genuine expression. Fuck. "You too, Axel. Call me if you need anything."

Yeah, that wasn't happening.

"Oh, I will!" he yelled back.

I knew I should keep my cool. I knew I shouldn't worry about this little prick. I knew, I knew, I knew, but I still couldn't help myself. I had to put this little fucker in his place.

I glanced back at him. "She'll be pretty tied up with me for a while though!" I yelled, giving him a single wave and an all-knowing nod.

Oh, shit, what had I just done?

I glanced down at Hindley from the corner of my eye and tensed.

She didn't look pissed. She looked hurt. Betrayed. Scared.

Shit. "I'm sorry," I whispered.

She stopped in front of her door. "Good night, Rory." She stuck her room key in the reader and pushed the door open. Slowly she turned to face me, squaring her shoulders, her eyes narrowed.

Oh, fuck.

"You might want to wipe off that tacky ass lip gloss from your face before you go to bed," she said.

"Hindley, wait." I moved closer.

She held out her hand. "No, Rory. Just...no." She shook her head. "I can't do this." Before I could plead my case, she closed the door in my face.

I can't do this?

What did she mean? Not tonight? Or worse yet, not at all?

I leaned against the wall, rubbing my face. "Fuck." What the hell had I just done? Something deep in my gut said I'd lost her. And not just for the night. She may be gone forever.

~

Thank you for reading
Extreme Risk
Hindley and Rory's story continues in

Extreme Devotion
X-Treme Love Series, Book 2

For the first time in her life, Hindley Hagen has found unconditional love. As attorney and sports agent for pro athlete, Rory Gregor, she's worked hard to help rebuild his reputation. This time, he's won more than just a gold medal, he's captured her heart.

Now she's trapped, caught in the snare of a man playing a deadly game. She must choose - protect the one man who's made her come alive or risk losing everything she's worked hard for, including him. Hindley must learn, in love and life, there is no such thing as a safe secret.

Trust isn't something that comes naturally to Rory Gregor. Even his achievements as a multi-gold medalist in extreme sports can't wash away the insecurities from a childhood filled with abuse. But Hindley's devotion to him personally and professionally has given him hope. Will his self-doubt drive her away?

As their need to protect one another grows to escalating heights with deadly consequences, will Hindley and Rory finally find the future together they deserve? Or will they discover the one thing that could destroy them both is each other?

Available now
Click here to purchase

Or...
**Purchase the bundle pack
X-Treme Love Series, Books 1-4
and save!**

You'll receive Hindley and Rory's complete story in:
Book 1: *Extreme Risk*
Book 2: *Extreme Devotion*
PLUS, you'll also receive Dana and Peter's story in:
Book 3: *Extreme Sacrifice*
Book 4: *Extreme Trust*

<u>Click here to buy now</u>

WANT TO RECEIVE A FREE EBOOK?

Join my email list and I'll send you *Extreme Beginning*, the X-Treme Love Prequel for free. It's the story of Caroline Hagen and Paul Barton. Just visit my website below and join today.

I also give away free things all the time, including ebooks and signed paperbacks (my own and from best-selling authors) and more.

You'll also receive exclusive sneak peeks and teasers of upcoming books in my series.

Join now and receive your free ebook today!

www.kaymanis.com

IF YOU ENJOYED THIS BOOK

Please:

    1. Write a review. It's so important to my work.

    2. Tell your family and friends about my books.

    3. Visit my website and sign up for my newsletter. You can also send me an email. I love to hear from my readers.

www.kaymanis.com

    4. Follow me on social media.

Facebook: www.facebook.com/kaymanisauthor2

Twitter: www.twitter.com/kaymanis

Instagram: www.instagram.com/kaymanis

JOIN MY PRIVATE FACEBOOK GROUP

THE MANIS MOB SQUAD

We support and enable those diagnosed with **MOB Disease (Mania of Books)** - a rare and debilitating disease that causes sufferers to become unable and/or unwilling to stop reading and obsessing over all things book related.

Are you a book-aholic? Do you have a One-Click addiction? Then come join our support group. We're all about fun in here, no judgment.

ALSO AVAILABLE BY KAY MANIS

ACKNOWLEDGMENTS

I found out when you write a book, there are *a lot* of people to thank along the way. So here goes...

Kimberly, my daughter (a girl who's more like me than she'll ever admit) — You were the first person to believe in my abilities as a writer. My intense, late night therapy sessions with you really are the reason I'm still writing. I can't thank you enough for making me believe in myself. I love you, shoogie and wish you much success in your own life. I hope I can be there for you as much and as often as you have for me.

Tony, my husband — You've been my best friend since we met, and one of my biggest supporters throughout this process. Your belief in me boosted my confidence and made me take this crazy-ass journey into the unknown world called writing. Your support has allowed me the freedom to pursue a dream I never even knew existed. I love you.

Melody, my bestie — I gave you my first novel in 2012 and you read it with love and care, knowing your critique might very well end our friendship, and my career as a writer. Ha ha! I can honestly say this with no doubt; if it weren't for your belief that I could do this, and your words of encouragement to continue, I never would have written another word. And that is the truth. I wuv you!

Christina, my crazy niece — You offered to do a read through on *Extreme Risk* and never put it down. Thank you for believing in me and helping me grow a thicker skin.

Julie Deaton — My proofer extraordinaire.

Julie, Stacy, Christina, Jessica, Elisabeth and Jane, my Beautiful Beta Bitches — You girls helped me find the voice within me that I never knew existed. Thank you for giving up your spare time to help me make my series the best it could be.

～

There is nothing more powerful than living your dream. I hope each of you have people in your own life that give you the courage not only to dream big, but to go for those dreams. If you ever need a kind word, don't ever hesitate to email me. I'd be honored to be your voice of encouragement. Email me at: kay@kaymanis.com

A NOTE FROM THE AUTHOR

People ask me all the time, "Where in the world did you come up with the idea to write a story about a skateboarder?" No I'm not a skater or extreme sport participant.

The idea came from Rob Dyrdek, the host of MTV's hit show, *Ridiculousness*. It's a hysterical show similar to America's Funniest Videos, except Rob's show has much more painful clips of people doing insane-o things. Oh yeah, and Rob is much funnier.

I saw Rob one day on the show and thought to myself, "He's so successful and talented, and so ghetto." (Hey, don't get me wrong, I grew up in the ghetto, I speak ghetto, I love ghetto.) But I wondered if, despite his success, Rob ever dealt with issues of low self-esteem and self-deprecating thoughts. And if he did, how would he react when he met a girl that he thought was out of his league. Viola! That's where Rory Gregor and *Extreme Risk* were born. Rob not only gave me inspiration for one book, he sparked an entire book series based on extreme sports.

My daughter thinks I fashioned Rory after Rob and maybe I did. It wasn't intentional. She thinks I have a crush on Rob, which I probably do but I'll never admit to her. Rob's cute, he's talented, he's funny as hell...so sue me. The idea from the story wasn't Rob himself, it was the character who I saw Rob becoming in my mind. I saw Rory. That probably makes no sense but hey, that's me.

My goal after finishing *Extreme Risk* and *Extreme Devotion* is to have Rob personally endorse my books. I mean, how cool would that be. So if you liked the book and the series, send Rob a message on Facebook, Instagram, Twitter or his website and tell him to read my damn books.

Thanks so much for coming along on this wonderful ride with me as I embark on my new journey. I hope to keep you interested, intrigued, engaged and entertained. If I have, let me know.

– *Kay*

ABOUT THE AUTHOR

Kay Manis is a funny chick who's sprinkled with a little crazy on top. Okay, let's be honest. . . there's ALOTTA crazy up there.

She writes books filled with passion, promise and purpose (with laughter and a few tears, but always an HEA).

She is a native Texan and lives with her family in Florida. When not reading or writing, you'll find Kay eating out with friends or napping with her favorite pillow (stolen from an Inn in Vermont - true story).

Please feel free to contact her at: **www.kaymanis.com**

f facebook.com/kaymanisauthor2
X x.com/kaymanis
⊙ instagram.com/kaymanis